REBELS' SEED

F. M. Busby

BANTAM BOOKS
TORONTO • NEW YORK • LONDON • SYDNEY • AUCKLAND

For Karen J-C,
who knows why

REBELS' SEED
A Bantam Spectra Book / August 1986

ISBN 0-553-26115-0

Published simultaneously in the United States and Canada

Bantam Books are published by Bantam Books, Inc. Its trade-
mark, consisting of the words "Bantam Books" and the por-
trayal of a rooster, is Registered in U.S. Patent and Trademark
Office and in other countries. Marca Registrada. Bantam
Books, Inc., 666 Fifth Avenue. New York, New York 10103.

PRINTED IN THE UNITED STATES OF AMERICA

O   0 9 8 7 6 5 4 3 2 1

REBELS'
SEED

I

From the personal journal of Captain Katmai Delarov, commanding the starship March Hare, *having arrived from Earth to the Shrakken outpost world Shaarbant. 4/18/2116.*

So we got here a few days ago, close onto 120 lights in only three ship's-months with the second-generation Hoyfarul FTL Drive, and it seems that the big war against the new alien species, the Tsa, is over. Or rather, didn't get fully started. I've talked with Bran Tregare Moray (once known as "Tregare the pirate") and his wife Rissa Kerguelen. Both of them members of the Board of Trustees, no less, that governs Earth! Because they led the attack that destroyed the slave-owning government of UET, the United Energy and Transport conglomerate. It's all in the history texts the kids are taught today: how Tregare took one of UET's armed starships and Escaped to the Hidden Worlds, put together a fleet of ships, and brought them home "to tear UET out by the roots like a rotten tooth."

(I guess I remember that quote because I *like* it. I was fourteen, winding up my first year in UET's Space Academy, "the Slaughterhouse," when Tregare took over and civilized that damned place! In a very real sense the man saved my life; I couldn't possibly have survived the forced fights, to the death, that cadets had to undergo after the "snotty" year.)

Coming now to recent events here on Shaarbant, first some data on the two races of aliens, Shrakken and Tsa. The Shrakken, more than a century ago, landed a ship on Earth. Its crew was killed by UET's Committee Police; then UET copied its Drive and began to colonize other worlds. But a number of UET ships mutinied; unknown to UET, they established the colonies called Hidden Worlds.

Even before UET was overthrown, Rissa and Tregare

1

made peace with the Shrakken. And later the Shrakken were attacked, from farther down the Galactic arm, by the Tsa. A different kind of attack, for Tsa strike the *mind*, causing pain, madness, even death. And Earth owed the Shrakken two great debts: star Drive itself, and UET's murderous treachery in the stealing of it. (Note to myself: if I hope to sell this account, back home, I need to put in more background detail. *Research* all these things. Describe tall, toe-walking Shrakken, partly exoskeletal, ochre-colored, with the pair of stubby tendrils above each triangular eye. Also squat, weighty Tsa: the dark brown skin, movable snout hiding the mouth below, etc. Get more pictures!)

The mission, to aid the Shrakken, was too important to be left to underlings. No less than three members of Earth's Board of Trustees rode *Inconnu Deux* here to Shaarbant, where the Shrakken maintain two settlements (this one, Sassden, is the lesser). Rissa Kerguelen chairs that Board. Bran Tregare's authority exceeds that of any admiral. Rissa's late brother, Ivan Marchant, also held a Board seat. Yet for this task Tregare was a mere ship's captain, Rissa his First Hat, and Marchant their gunnery officer. (Note to me: that's *good!*)

The *Deux* with its first-generation Hoyfarul Drive brought them here in approx one year of ship time, perhaps two-point-five years by Earth's clocks. (Note: on the *Hare* we experienced three months of travel while possibly six passed on Earth.)

I don't have all the story straight yet, but seven Tsa ships were near this planet. As a result of Tsa mind-attacks, Tregare and Rissa, along with two Shrakken and three other humans including their nine-year-old daughter Liesel Selene (usually called Lisele) were marooned on a crashed scoutship in the middle of swamp country, and eventually *walked* their way back here. It took them something like four or five years; personally I shudder to think of such an ordeal.

Meanwhile, although *Inconnu Deux* is of course faster-than-light and the Tsa ships weren't, the *Deux* was caught groundside. Ivan Marchant got the ship away, destroying two Tsa ships in the process, but the Tsa attack did something to his visual centers; the man was blinded. Also his Hoyfarul Drive failed; the ship was left, light-years from Shaarbant, with only STL capabilities. And there simply wasn't enough food aboard, for that mode of travel. So most of the crew rode back to Shaarbant in the ship's freeze chambers.

What happened then isn't wholly clear to me. The girl Lisele somehow attained rapport with the Tsa commander, Elzh, and set up the basis for a possible truce. But only hours before that development, Ivan Marchant, in *Inconnu Deux*, reached this planet. And when Tsa ships rose to meet the *Deux*, Marchant with a crew of two women bailed out in a scoutship. Not much later, with his blindness apparently in remission though I'm not sure how, he rammed that scout into a Tsa ship, destroying both craft. "He did it to save the *Deux*," Lisele says. "He thought he had to; he didn't know, you see, that the Tsa *can't* lie."

I like that kid; she reminds me of myself at her age. Except that I'm a little nervy, considering the load of *responsibility* for anyone with such important connections, I'm glad she's going to be riding back to Earth with us.

II

"I still don't see why I have to go." Keeping her voice down, because showing anger at her parents was no way to win any kind of argument, still Lisele Selene Moray couldn't restrain a certain glowering.

Everything had been set up fine. With peace agreed, Elzh of the Tsa had waited while his two remaining ships were converted for FTL capability, then sent one ship after the two that had gone ahead, to turn them from the grim task of attacking other "Mindbeast" worlds. Lisele wasn't sure whether Elzh was still male; the Tsa had three sexes and rotated between them. But Elzh hadn't said anything about change, so Lisele still thought of the alien as "he."

Elzh planned to take the last Tsa ship to the home world of that species, to confront its governing body, the Tsa-Drin— and, if necessary, *force* that group to reconsider its Draconian policy against "Mindbeasts." The humans would follow in *Inconnu Deux*, lagging enough to give Elzh a chance to announce their peaceful intent, but sufficiently close behind if the Tsa-Drin turned nasty and Elzh needed any help.

Lisele looked to Rissa, then to Bran Tregare. "We had everything all worked out. I was looking forward to it. And now this *March Hare* ship comes, and all of a sudden—nobody asking *me*—you have me booked to ride it back to Earth. *Why?*"

Rissa Kerguelen shook her head. Her dark hair, now regrown to fall well past her shoulders, swirled with the motion. "We have discussed these matters, but it seems you have not listened. Last week we celebrated your fifteenth birthday; remember?"

Lisele nodded. "Sure. Great party, and I thanked you at the time." It *had* been nice: first the all-human part, then a time when Stonzai and a few other Shrakken joined the group. And finally the aircar ride over to Elzh's ship, taking along only humans who could control their emotions and deal safely with Tsa. So that Lisele could take pieces of birthday cake to Cveet, the young Tsa who had first communicated with Lisele without pain, and to Elzh and Tserln and Idsath, Cveet's parents. "But what does that have to do with it?"

Bran Tregare cleared his throat. To Lisele's eyes, the long trek—almost a quarter of the way around Shaarbant—hadn't aged her father much. The dark, curly hair above his high forehead showed only hints of grey; long-term exposure to weather had reddened his normally sallow complexion. Possibly, she thought, all that exercise had done him good!

Now he said, "Look, princess. Fifteen last week means less than a year 'til you hit legal age. Eligible to be nominated to the Board."

"Me? But that's silly. I don't *know* enough."

"Which is precisely the point," said Rissa. "So now would you please pay attention to what your father is saying?"

As he spoke, Tregare's frown showed concentration, not anger. "Don't fool yourself, Lisele. *March Hare* brought word that your great-aunt Erika died. Which I was sorry to hear—I came to like that old tiger—but she lived to about ninety-two, bio, which beats par a lot." Lisele's interruption didn't make it; Tregare continued, "My own mother, your grandmother Liesel Hulzein, has to be past eighty by now—maybe eighty-five, by the time you could get home. And your uncle Ivan's gone."

"I still don't understand. What—?"

Rissa spoke. "On Earth's Board of Trustees, our family provides stability, and our representation is badly depleted. *Of course* you will be elected as soon as you are eligible."

"But I—"

"And for the past seven years, almost, you have been separated from any kind of formal education. This lack must be remedied."

"Why?" Lisele heard her voice pitched higher than she'd intended. "Why formal, I mean? I studied on the *Deux*, coming here, and on the scout when we were stuck in the swamp. I have every bit of math a ship's officer needs, and I know all the history that really applies—up to when we left Earth, anyway." Rissa tried to speak, but Lisele actually glared at her mother. "Political science, maybe? But you've said, yourself, these days we're making that up as we go along!"

She turned her gaze to her father. "I don't want to sit at a desk. You said, someday I'd have a ship to command; *that's* what I want. And going with you, following Elzh, is how I can learn what I need. So—"

Tregare shook his head. "You can do both, princess. But Rissa thinks, and I agree, that you've been out of the mainstream too long. Stuck here in the boondocks with just a few of us, not learning how to deal with people you *don't* know. We—"

Interrupting wasn't polite, but the young woman couldn't help doing it. "How to deal with people I don't know? Like the Tsa, for instance? Who got the truce for us, anyway?"

Tregare's stern expression broke; laughter erupted. "Good point; you shot me down. But—"

"But that achievement," said Rissa Kerguelen, "is not the same as learning the ins and outs of relationships with humans who know, by experience that becomes almost instinct, how to get along with each other and to *persuade* others. The term, I believe, is 'socialization.' And you, Lisele, simply are not socialized to your age-level, with regards to life as it is lived groundside, on Earth." She shrugged. "None of this is any fault of your own. But the lack needs correcting. So you will, aboard *March Hare*, return to Earth."

"And now," Tregare put in, "what say we bring you up to date on what else is going on? The personnel-switching, and all. So's you know who you'll be riding with, and why."

* * *

Lisele already knew the why of it all. The Tsa were telepaths who could control their sending but had no control over what they received. Whereas humans and Shrakken *sent*, without knowledge or intention. When the sending carried painful emotion, reception *hurt* the Tsa, who by reflex struck back with pain. Damage to both sides was great, and constituted the basis for the original Tsa-Shrakken conflict.

Some humans, Lisele for one, could control their sendings by means of alpha-wave techniques. Others didn't have that ability, and could not meet safely with Tsa. Tregare had originally made do with tranquilizers, light hypnosis, and "key words" he could subvocalize to head off dangerous sendings; now he'd worked with Lisele's biofeedback machine until he could skip the tranks.

With the Shrakken, none of those techniques worked. The species didn't have alpha waves; their brain functions were divided or assigned, by their unique biology, so differently that the humans could find no points of reference. For the time being, Tsa and Shrakken could not meet; all communication would have to go through human intermediaries.

Still, some humans weren't suitable and never would be; due to one reason or another they couldn't manage the necessary degree of control. And of the twenty adult human survivors aboard *Inconnu Deux*, eight were in that category.

"Since we're going to a Tsa world," said Tregare, "putting forty percent of our crew in freeze would leave us pretty much shorthanded when we got there. So we tested everybody on *March Hare*, too, and are taking on seven of their people. Here's the rundown. . . ."

From the *Deux*, five of the crew were being transferred. Second Hat Anders Kobolak could never deal with Tsa because he couldn't forget that his sister Dacia had died with Ivan Marchant; his wife Alina Rostadt would go with him. Jenise Rorvik, her smashed wrist now regaining function after surgery, had come through the cross-continental trek in better spirits than when it began, but her horror of the Tsa yielded to no restorative attempts. The blond woman's mate, Chief Engineer Hagen Trent, was staying with the *Deux*; maybe they'd be reunited on Earth someday, or maybe not.

Melaine Holmbach, a Drive Tech, hadn't suffered much in the way of Tsa attacks, but couldn't control her reactions to the species. And—

"But why are you sending Arlen?" Lisele asked. "The Tsa don't bother him one bit; he was in freeze when Uncle Ivan took the *Deux* up and fought them."

Tregare sighed. "The *Hare* needs Arlen as Third Hat. That's the only trade I could make, to get a Gunnery Officer along with a replacement for Anders. Thing was, you see: they didn't need any changes, and we did."

"Also," Rissa said, "Captain Delarov brought word from Derek and Felcie. A request that if at all possible, they would like their son to return at the first opportunity."

Lisele pondered the matter. Was somebody sick, back home? Her feelings toward Arlen Limmer were mixed. Both born on the fortress world Stronghold, after Bran Tregare wrested it from UET, the two children were originally almost the same age, and the dearest of friends. But Lisele went to Earth with Tregare's fleet, riding so close to c that only six shipboard months passed while planets' clocks registered ten years. While Derek Limmer and his wife Felcie Parager brought their children home later, in a Hoyfarul FTL ship that avoided time-dilation almost entirely. So that when Arlen and Lisele next met, her bio and chrono ages were nearly a decade apart, and his weren't.

The whole thing had embarrassed her: she'd had a crush on Arlen, but here he was almost grownup and she was still a little kid. Later, when he'd spent years in freeze on the *Deux* while Lisele shared the perils of Shaarbant with her parents and others, covering several thousand kilometers on foot, they met again. Now Lisele was fifteen and Arlen a bit short of nineteen, bio-ages. But because of what she'd lived through and he hadn't, now she felt that *he* was the kid.

Certainly, going by looks, no one would judge him to be much the elder: he stood less than a decimeter taller than her own seventeen; her figure might be slim, but hardly immature; and with her dark, waving hair trimmed neatly to chin-length she knew she gave an adult impression.

Now she said, "What do you mean, you had to trade? You're the admiral, and on the Board of Trustees. You could—"

Headshake. Tregare said, "Rank or no rank, if I want loyalty I have to deal fairly. Think about it."

Feeling stupid, she said, "Sure. You're right. It just

seemed—" Time to change the subject. "One good thing. I think I'm going to like Captain Delarov."

III

When Lisele had ridden Tregare's original *Inconnu* from Stronghold to Earth, she was too young to appreciate its vastness. STL ships of that time carried crews of at least a hundred; the armed ones each bore two scoutships. The levels of *Inconnu's* decks, from cargo holds through crew's quarters and galley and Control room to the projector turrets topside, were beyond Lisele's childish imaginings. Oh, later she'd explored that ship, and learned its capabilities and limitations. Now she appreciated how the *Deux* could go from zerch to lightspeed or vice versa in about a week; the older ships had needed a month.

FTL ships of the *Deux's* class had the same-sized hulls, but the Hoyfarul FTL Drive was so bulky that they held quarters for only thirty. Crews were less than that figure, about two dozen; the surplus gave cushion for a few to ride as supercargo.

Before the Battle for Earth, Tregare's fleet against Ozzie Newhausen's UET ships, Rissa and Tregare had sent Lisele off in a specially-crewed scoutship. The scouts bedded a maximum of twelve; their accel capabilities were roughly half those of full-sized ships—their max range, light-to-zerch, about one-fifth of a light year. A scout's supplies were planned to keep twelve people alive for six months: as Tregare said, "If you run out of fuel, food won't help—and the other way 'round, too." But Lisele reached Earth safely.

Now, boarding *March Hare* with all goodbyes said, Lisele had some comparisons to make. *Hare* bulked smaller than *Deux* by about a third. Quarters fit that ratio: a normal crew of sixteen, with space for twenty overall. The new Drives were the same size as the *Deux's*, but improved; with less mass to push, *Hare* could mount twice the older ship's accel.

It carried one scoutship only, and this too was a new model: smaller, sleeping only six. But roughly, Lisele learned, with the same range and acceleration; the six-month limit still held. Barring a totally-unforeseen breakthrough, FTL drive would never be reduced to scoutship size.

"Well," said Katmai Delarov, sitting across the table from Lisele in captain's digs, "is there anything more I can tell you at this time?"

Nursing the last of her dessert, Lisele regretted that there wasn't more of it. Dining with the captain, a day out from Shaarbant and just the two of them talking, had been both pleasant and informative. "No," she said, "I think you've given me as much as I can take in one bite."

Delarov smiled, showing white, slightly uneven teeth. Lisele found the woman's face interesting: broad, with strong cheekbones and a sturdy chin. Eyes tilted, almost to an Asiatic slant. Her black hair was cut in a heavy bang, level from across the front where it almost reached her eyebrows, to just behind the ears; the back part, waved to fluff out massively, fell below her shoulders. Her earlobes hid behind two discs of jade.

The captain stood. Her body, too, was broad for its height: not fat, but definitely sturdy. Stocky-looking or not, Katmai Delarov moved like an athlete. Going to the sideboard, bringing out a bottle and starting to apply a corkscrew, she said, "Do you take wine? I should have asked earlier, but I prefer mine after a meal, when I'm more apt to pay it proper attention." Brows raised, now hidden under the black fringe of hair, she waited.

Lisele nodded. "Yes. One glass, maybe two; no more." She smiled, and at the woman's look of inquiry, said "I was remembering. On the *Deux*, going to Shaarbant. Our first gunnery-simulation tournament. I placed better than anyone expected, and after dinner someone filled my glass with wine. I'd had tiny amounts, at meals, with Rissa and Tregare, but I was barely nine years old. I looked over to Tregare, and he held two fingers about *this* far apart, and smiled. So that's all the wine I drank. And still felt a little funny, later, going downship."

Full-throated, Delarov laughed; then she finished uncorking the bottle, and poured. "Well, if you've dealt with the stuff for six years, I assume you can handle your own rationing."

Lisele caught herself frowning; the captain said, "You have to understand, Ms. Moray: all anyone told me was who you are, and how old, and that you'd be riding aboard as a Nav/Comm trainee. Nobody said whether I was to mother-hen you, or how much. What I mean is, I know how important you are, and your whole family, too. What I *don't* want to do, is screw up. You understand?"

Feeling a bit deflated, Lisele said, "So that's why our intimate little supper? Which I've enjoyed a lot, and thanks."

"No; that's not why. It's why I ask some questions, yes. But you're here because I like you, and want to know you better."

Disarmed now, Lisele shrugged. "All right; I feel the same way. I'd like to know more about you, too." She grinned. "Your turn. Okay?"

"Why not? Fire away."

"Well," as Lisele felt herself make a slight scowl, "I can't place your background. Ancestry, I mean. Would it be partly Asian, maybe?"

Delarov grinned. "If you go back far enough." She sipped at the pale wine. "I'm Aleut, if you know what that means. Aleut with a little Russian mixed in, three or four centuries back. My several-greats-grandparents lived on Amchitka Island, between the Pacific Ocean and Bering Sea, and were evacuated to the Alaskan mainland during the second World War." Grimacing, she shrugged. "For a number of decades the Aleuts had a bad time of it: poverty, and no skills that were usable in a changing economy. Ready for that second glass?"

"Make it just half, please."

"All right. Well, enough lecture. My grandfather worked his way through the university at Fairbanks, became an attorney, and pulled his whole branch of the family out of hut-style living. So my parents, and then my brother and I, got off to good starts."

Lisele nodded. "So then you went through the Slaughter-house."

"Not exactly. I'm only twenty-seven, bio; I was in my snotty year when Tregare smashed UET. Afterward the Space Academy was still tough, but fair. No more of the savage random cruelty that kept us all so scared." She smiled. "I can't match scars with the oldtimers, and that's fine with me."

"I certainly believe you!" After another minor question or two, Lisele couldn't think of anything more to say or ask. So she drained the last drops of her wine, thanked the captain again, and excused herself.

As an officer-trainee in communications, navigation, and the fine art of piloting a ship, unofficially Lisele held the equivalent of a Chief's rating and was quartered accordingly.

As she headed downship toward her smallish but adequate cabin, behind her came a hail. "Lisele? Wait a minute."

She turned to see Arlen Limmer making fast work of his own descent, three steps at a time with only an occasional grab at the handrail to keep balance. Dark like scarfaced Derek, his father, but with his own face unmarred, the young man was handsome enough, she supposed. And he had a good disposition, really. What bothered her—well, it was hard to pin down. Maybe that whatever he wanted, he wanted right now. Unlike Lisele, he'd never had to learn to wait.

For him to catch up to her now, she was the one who waited. As smiling, with hair tousled and face sweating, he approached. "Hey; glad I caught you. I'm just off watch. Soon as I shower and change, I'm headed back upship, to the galley. Join me?"

"I've eaten." But as she saw disappointment begin to cloud his expression, she said, "Sure, though; I could use another cup of coffee, and we can talk while you eat."

"Fine. I'll stop by your digs; all right?"

She nodded; as he turned away to his Third Hat's cabin, he waved a hand.

Lisele went to her own deck, one level below. Inside her quarters, her home until *Hare* reached Earth, she paused. No need to bathe again so soon, but she might as well change clothes. To dine with Captain Delarov she'd worn her best outfit: not quite a uniform but fancier than the standard working jumpsuit. And although the galley was kept as clean as such places could be, why chance getting spots? So she undressed and hung the clothing up neatly, then picked up the jumpsuit she'd been wearing before.

Absently she scratched an itch at the outside of her right thigh. The redness was gone, and nearly all the swelling, from the contraceptive implant. Rissa, the last night before *March Hare* lifted, had shown her how to work the ampoule and pop the tiny capsule into muscle tissue. "Lisele, I know that you are not planning to get romantic with Arlen," her mother said. "Not in the immediate future, at least. Still it cannot be harmful for you to know that in any case you are protected. After your next menses you may assume that the implant has taken effect."

When Rissa also gave her the packet, still containing two more ampoules, Lisele protested. "But these are two-year implants. Why would I need extras now?"

Rissa shrugged. "The things come three in a box. And this prescription is designed for your general age group, not mine." So Lisele accepted the small container.

Now she thought, *I don't really need any of them, yet. But as Tregare would say, it can't hardly hurt a damn thing!*

Arlen must have showered fast; before Lisele expected it, his rap came at the door. She met him there, and they climbed upship to the galley, rapidly enough to arrive slightly short of breath. As he took a tray and went through the food lineup, Lisele bypassed that part and carried a small pot of coffee to a vacant corner table.

As Arlen, his tray laden, joined her, she saw Anders Kobolak come in with his wife, Alina Rostadt. Anders, she thought, was looking better these days; his thin face, under dark hair, was never exactly jolly in expression, but the sulky look he'd worn so long, for months after the death of his sister, was gone now. She waved to the couple; by nodding, they accepted her invitation.

Arlen frowned. "I thought *we* could talk."

"We can."

"Not about anything personal."

She scowled at him. "After, then. All right?"

"I guess so." He poured coffee for both of them, as Anders and Alina came to sit.

Lisele gave greetings. "How's everything going, so far?" At one time, she knew, in a dangerous situation Alina Rostadt had been trained and disguised to pretend to be Lisele's mother, while Rissa Kerguelen herself carried another *persona*. The trick had worked—but now, Lisele thought, it couldn't. Not while Alina carried at least ten kilos over Rissa's highest weight. Oh, well; Rostadt simply wasn't the athletic type.

Kobolak answered. "We're settling in; no problems. I'd hoped to get First Hat on here, but Ms. Lu-teng has seniority on me and moved up from Second. That's all right; I'm Gunnery Officer as well, which gives me bonus pay. For six months, I can wait the other promotion."

"Six?" Puzzled, Lisele thought back. "*Hare* went from Earth to Shaarbant in three."

Kobolak had a mouthful of food, so Alina answered. "There's a side-excursion, going back. You hadn't heard?"

Lisele hadn't; his food swallowed, Anders explained. "It's a gravitational anomaly of some kind. Coming to Shaarbant, with the *Hare* well above c, the inertial detectors went fruitcake. So on our way back to Earth, Captain Delarov has clearance to take a side-jog, cut the Hoyfarul Drive and drop to STL, have a closer look. Maybe something's there, or maybe it was just an instrument glitch; either way, we'll find out."

"I wonder what it could be," said Arlen. For the rest of the meal, Lisele nursing her coffee to make it last, everyone speculated. The end result was, no one had any clues at all.

When the other two left, Lisele said, "Now we can talk."

Arlen looked over to the next table, where several ratings were telling jokes, having a high old time. "Not here."

Lisele knew what he wanted: her quarters or his. She sighed. Clearly, perhaps even inevitably, she felt that Arlen Limmer would someday be her first (and perhaps only) lover. Because they'd been close friends from infancy, and toward no one else of her own age did she feel such fondness.

But not yet. For one thing, until her menses which weren't due for a few more days, she'd be vulnerable to an unwanted conception. And for another, she didn't feel ready. Yet Arlen kept pushing at her; it was one of his more irritating qualities.

So she said, "Turret Four. I need some gunnery practice, anyway, and Four's set up for simulation runs."

She had to hand it to Arlen; at least he tried to look pleased at her choice. He wasn't, though. He couldn't be, because the turrets weren't all that private.

Scaled down in size, *March Hare* mounted only four peripheral turrets, not six. The peripherals had traverse capability, while the central, more powerful projector aimed always straight ahead, along the ship's major axis. Spaced between the outer turrets were torpedo bays, but Lisele hadn't asked what kinds of warheads those missiles carried. Now she seated herself in the gunner's chair; it was adjusted comfortably for her height and lengths of limb, so she put the option switch to Simulate and applied power.

In the monitor seat, Arlen fidgeted as Lisele checked the panel's indicators. A projector consisted of two UV lasers, designed to heterodyne at peak energy in the infrared range, and to converge where the beams met their target. In practice, though, the fine tuning required human control. The ship's computer chose a gunner's targets and would only

"give you a shot" if heterodyne and convergence were tuned
properly.

The indicators and their controls were these: on the
panel's small central screen, a circle glowed. If it tilted to
become an ellipse, heterodyne was off; "pushing" at it,
laterally with the righthand control lever, would straighten it
up. At each side of the screen was a range light; when
convergence was correct, both lights were out. If one lit,
pushing the lefthand lever toward it would correct matters.
There was also an override pedal, not especially useful in
Simulation; in real combat, if the situation became desperate,
that pedal doubled the combined convergence-heterodyne
tolerance, to allow chancier shots.

Which all sounded simple enough. The trouble was that
when ships fought, things happened very fast indeed; control-
ling both variables at the same time took good reflexes and
plenty of practice. Lisele had the former, but for a long time
now, not the latter. So, unfocusing her eyes slightly, in order
to see the screen and range lights simultaneously, she punched
for the first Sim in the turret's program. "Call my scores, will
you, Arlen?"

"Well, sure—but when do we *talk*?"

She thought for a moment, then grinned. "After I take a
half-dozen sim runs or so, and before you do."

The run began; the range lights told her of an enemy
ship coming in fast, but decelerating on a skew pass. By the
time she had that part solved, heterodyne was drifting; for
seconds she couldn't coordinate, and when she did, the
computer abruptly switched targets, Out of practice, she
fumbled for a time, but by the end of the run she felt she had
the feel of it again.

Her next five exercises proved her to be correct.

Reading off the scores—percentage of time effectively on
target as compared to what was possible—Arlen nodded. "It
comes back fast, doesn't it? For you, anyway."

"Want to try six for yourself, now? Put a bet on it?"

"Not just yet." He reached across to clasp her hand.
"Lisele, you know how I feel about you. Why don't you want
me to say it?"

"If I know, why do you have to?"

"Because you never give me an answer. Why not?"

Feeling pressured, she wanted to jerk her hand free of

his. Instead, she disengaged it gently. "You ever think, maybe I'm just not *ready*?"

"You're fifteen. Less than a year from full adult status."

"But not there yet."

"Fourteen's marriageable age, with parents' consent."

"Except, my parents aren't here."

"What if I told you I'd asked them, and they said yes?"

Unable to suppress her reaction, Lisele laughed. "And Rissa simply forgot to tell me? Oh, *Arlen!*"

He had the grace to show a sheepish grin. "All right, I didn't. But I'll bet that if I had, they'd have said it's up to you. Wouldn't they?"

To be fair, Lisele had to admit he was probably right. So she hedged. "Still, though, you didn't ask. Never mind; what I do is up to me, anyway. Marriage aside, that is."

"Sure," he said. "I knew you'd see it. Lisele, we could just be lovers for a while, and get married when you're sixteen."

How had she let him pin her down to specifics so quickly? Physically she didn't shake her head, but her thoughts included that action. Now what to say?

Well, why not the truth? "Arlen. I know you and I like you; maybe I even love you. I did when we were little, and it probably hasn't all worn off." He tried to speak, but with a finger to his lips she shushed him. "No, listen. Someday I'll have a lover or a husband, and unless you get tired of waiting around and run off with somebody else, you'll probably be him." She took a deep breath, and sighed. "But not right *now*."

"Can I ask why?"

"Sure. Ask all you want. But it's none of your business." Tell him it wouldn't be safe for her, until after her period? Fat chance! Not that she usually had qualms about discussing physical processes, but in this particular case it was simply too peace-wasting *personal*.

So she said, "You want to take some sim runs now?"

He shrugged. "I guess so." Then, "You said, how about putting a bet on it. All right. If I win, will you answer my question? About what's wrong with right now?"

"And if *I* win?" He said nothing; suddenly Lisele snapped her fingers. "I know. If I win, the subject is closed until I bring it up, all by myself. You agree?"

The way Arlen frowned, she knew he was looking for

loopholes. Whether he found any or not, finally he nodded. "All right; you're on."

Arlen came close to winning that bet, but on his final run he pushed too hard, and lost by less than ten points overall. Lisele felt friendly enough to share a warm hug and a quick kiss; then they went downship to their separate quarters. What with the stress of simulated gunnery runs, not to mention the impact of more personal emotions, now she *did* need a shower.

IV

Over the next few days Lisele got into the swing of her training routine. Once the *Hare* passed light, none but the inertial instruments would register, so while she could, she concentrated on navigational studies and pilot's skills. She was sitting watch, working with the computer at an auxiliary position, when the ship broke c.

So she cut the screen's now-irrelevant navigational display. The only piloting chores at supercee would be changes of course and accel; since none of those were planned for a time, she switched her monitor position to communications mode. Ranging above light, though, even the comm-panel could run nothing but computer simulations.

Stretching, sitting back, Lisele turned to Jenise Rorvik, who had the official comm. "Well, you're on vacation now, again. Any good ideas, to pass the time?"

Shaking her head, the blond woman smiled. She was about twenty-five, bio, but the years on Shaarbant had aged her: the trek that seemed would never end, the pain of her crippled wrist. She had changed, from the spiritless creature who at first wanted simply to lie down and die; she had, now, a kind of strength.

But she'd paid for it; she looked ten years older. On the *Deux*, before reaching Shaarbant, Arlen Limmer had for a time given her a certain amount of romantic attention. Somehow Lisele doubted that Arlen, only a few months aged since then, would be interested in the Jenise of today.

The woman's headshake didn't help conversation much. Lisele thought, and said, "Do you have any plans, especially, for when we reach Earth?"

Another headshake, but then, "I'm not going out again." The once-delicate pale complexion, now lined and roughened, showed sudden color. "I know Hagen can't get back for a few years, groundside time. But when he does, I intend to be there." She put a hand to her abdomen. "His child and I, both."

The pregnancy had to be on purpose, probably decided after the long journey had ended at Sassden but before *March Hare*'s arrival. Lisele reached across and squeezed Rorvik's hand. "That's great. And maybe the *Deux* won't take so long, backing Elzh's play with the Tsa-Drin, as everybody expects."

"I hope you're right." They talked about Jenise's plans a little longer; then Lisele's watch-shift ended. She was working a rotating "split-trick"; Rorvik still had four hours to go. But Lisele hadn't eaten before watch, and was hungry.

Going into the galley, getting a tray and filling it, she looked to see who was there that she'd like to talk with. Nobody present, that she really knew. One table with four people she hadn't really met. Melaine Holmbach, a Drive-tech from the *Deux*, sitting alone; Lisele didn't know why the woman was so solitary, and at the moment was in no mood to find out. But at the nearest table were *Hare*'s First Hat, Chief Engineer, and Comm Chief. Looked like a good mix, so that's where Lisele went.

"May I join you?"

Mei Lu-teng, the First Hat, looked up and nodded. The woman, Lisele knew, was descended from Tibetan refugees. She sat tall and lean, gazing from dark slits of eyes above massive cheekbones, gaunt cheeks, and a long, prominent jaw. One hand brushed at a wisp of black hair escaping from the swirl atop her crown, as she said, "Yes. Please sit down. Do you know my fellow-officers?"

Lisele set down her tray and seated herself. "Just barely. We've met, but that's about all."

So she was reintroduced to sandy-haired Chief Engineer Darwin Pope, a tall skinny man looking sunburned even though he probably wasn't; his oversized Adam's-apple moved as he said, in a quiet but rasping voice, "Stick around; we'll get acquainted."

"I'm sure." Well, he had a nice handshake.

Comm Chief Eduin Brower hadn't impressed Lisele the first time and still didn't. It wasn't merely that the man was short and fat and generally untidy, with cigar ashes all down the front of his none-too-clean jumpsuit. He talked like a slob, too—out of the side of his mouth, around the cigar, slurring his words. And the cigars themselves: Tregare smoked one now and then, but his smelled nice. She knew how he'd describe these of Brower's: like somebody frying a chicken with the feathers on!

But when he mumbled "Hi'ya, sis," she took his lax, moist handshake and smiled. *It can't hurt to act friendly.*

"Hi'ya, Chief."

The conversation, desultory and concerning ship's problems she knew nothing about, went over her head. So she thought on what she know of the *Hare's* personnel complement. All right; the captain and three Hats, to run Control. Drive Chief and three subordinates. But both Comm and Engineering were three-person contingents; the Chiefs also had to stand regular watches. Fourteen people, then, all told. Plus herself as a sort of cadet, maybe to fill in if somebody got sick, or something.

She guessed it would probably work; shipside, things usually did, if the people were right for their jobs.

And were they? It might pay to listen, and find out.

First Hat Lu-teng was speaking. "Darwin, before we cut Hoyfarul drive I want an extra tuning. Out of sked, I know—but with an anomaly to explore, and the breakout due to happen on a new officer's watch, I'd feel safer."

Pope shrugged. "Sure, Mei. I'm not overworked."

"And you, Eduin." She turned to the cigar-smoker. "An extra check on all comm-channel gear, before dropping to subcee?"

"You want it, you got it."

The woman nodded. "Thank you, both." She stood. "Excuse me, please?"

The woman left. Lisele, now finished eating, felt she should be trying to learn more about the ship, but couldn't think of questions to ask. She looked up, to find Darwin Pope's gaze on her. He said, "You're thinking, perhaps, that it's the captain's place, not the First Hat's, to assign extra maintenance?"

She hadn't thought about it at all; now she did. "No. It's any officer's job to see to such things. Long as she logs the request, and I expect she will. If you'd objected, now—which you didn't—then it'd be a matter for the captain."

Brower chuckled. "Thought you'd catch her up, huh, Dar? Hey, this is *Tregare's* kid you're out to spoof." To Lisele, then, "How the hell far *did* you walk, around that mudball? And how'd you bust through to talk peaceful with them Tsa, which nobody else ever done?"

So instead of asking questions, Lisele found herself answering them. In the process, she began to change her opinion of Eduin Brower. His speech and person were sloppy, but his thinking wasn't.

Driven by the coherent, ellipsoidal field of the drive named for Pennet Hoyfarul, *March Hare* began to pile up Big Vee. The velocity-derived mass, that had limited the earlier acoherent drives to STL speeds, manifested itself in parallel, matterless universes where such things as velocity and acceleration had no meaning. As Tregare once said, "Einstein wasn't wrong, you understand. He just didn't have all the facts."

A bit short of three weeks out from Shaarbant, on the day when the onset of Lisele's slightly-overdue menses had her feeling tense and a little uncomfortable, she came on-watch to find Anders Kobolak talking with Captain Delarov. "It was right along in here, that you got the peculiar indications?"

"Close to it," the woman answered. "Of course we're on a different route now; the angle of approach is changed. But I think we should cut the Hoyfarul Drive and drop to STL, some time around the end of your watch."

"How about an hour before? Fifteen hundred. That way we won't have a watch change until we're stabilized."

"Sounds fine." She looked at her wrist chrono. "A little less than three hours. I'll be back here then, to observe." Kobolak nodded, and with a brief smile to Lisele, Captain Delarov left Control.

Lisele greeted Anders, and Alina Rostadt who had the comm panel, then sat down to her aux position and opened the circuit to Tinhead. On this ship they didn't call the computer that, but Tregare always had.

For the next two hours she ran navigation sims, including several of Tregare's favorites.

As a trainee without real watch duties, at break time Lisele had the option of going down to the galley. Of course she observed the formality of asking Kobolak's permission. "Sure." He shook the coffee pot; it sounded nearly empty. "Bring back a refill, would you please?"

"Freshest I can find." She took the utensil and went downship; in the galley she turned it in, got a fresh cup for herself and picked up a slice of toast to go with it, then looked around the place. No one she knew was there, except Melaine Holmbach, the Drive Tech from *Inconnu Deux*, sitting alone as usual. Well, maybe it was time Lisele found out what was eating on that one, so she went over to the table.

"Hi. Could you use some company?"

Holmbach looked up, and for long seconds Lisele thought she wasn't going to get any response at all, but then the woman said, "Do sit down. Excuse me; I was thinking."

"What about, if it's any of my business?"

A tentative smile lit the pale, round face. Melaine pushed back curly brown hair that hadn't been combed recently. "Your business? Maybe; I'm not sure. Ivan Marchant was your uncle; he's the one I was thinking about."

"Yes, of course. You were on the *Deux* when he brought it back to Shaarbant, stuck with STL and chewing time."

"And blind," said Holmbach. "Blind—helpless, some thought—and yet he *ran* that ship. And in the end, saved it. For Bran Tregare, as he'd promised to do."

Tears welled in the woman's eyes. Not only for that reason, Lisele gave no voice to her disagreement with Holmbach's view. Uncle Ivan had *thought* he was saving Tregare's ship, so why pick nits? She said, "He was important to you? But I thought—"

"Oh, Dacia Kobolak was his woman. The Second Hat's sister. But there was a time, he seemed so forlorn and discouraged—" The smile again, now full of tenderness. "So I sneaked in when he was asleep, woke him without saying who I was, and we made love."

The smile twisted. "But afterward it went wrong. When he learned he'd been fooled, it made him angry. He did forgive me later, and we had each other once again. But no more, he said." Holmbach shrugged. "So I took up Rance Peleter's offer. You remember him? Second Engineer, a black man, soft-spoken? Shorter than me, but I didn't mind that; a strong gentle man can be any height he pleases!"

Partly, Lisele began to see Holmbach's problem. "But he's not here now."

The tears spilled down. "No. Ivan, Rance, neither one. I think I nearly worshiped your uncle; when he died I felt it killed half of me. But Rance was so good a man, I could manage."

"Why, then—?"

"The Tsa, is why. If the *Deux* had gone back to Earth I'd still be on it. But they had to go off to a Tsa world. I'm one of those who can't be within mind-range of those aliens. Rance can, and Tregare needed him. So I'm alone now."

There were other questions Lisele could have asked: four Tsa-phobic persons had stayed with *Deux*, so why—? But she decided not to raise that issue; all she did was reach and pat Melaine's hand. "Never mind; we'll be on Earth soon. No Tsa there—but lots and lots of people."

Leaving things at that, she went to get a coffee pot filled from a freshly-brewed urn, and climbed upship to Control.

Waiting, as the time for subcee breakout neared, Lisele wondered why she couldn't shake her mind free of Holmbach's trouble. Objectively she could see the woman's problems, but couldn't identify with them. Why?

Eventually the answer came. Melaine Holmbach needed someone else—specifically, a man—to be *real*. Taking a good look at her own feelings, Lisele decided what the difference was: she felt complete, all by herself.

Hmmm—maybe not entirely. All her life she'd had the support of Rissa and Tregare; her parents were the pillars of her stance with the universe. All through the years-long trek on Shaarbant she'd pushed herself, not to let them down. But they'd never let her down, either; always, in the worst times, they were *there*. Well, except when Elzh the Tsa found her on a hillside and took her to his alien ship. But then, she'd had to focus so hard on her own deadly peril that only later

did she realize she was operating solo, no help at hand.
Well, it had worked, hadn't it?

Even now, light-years from her parents, she didn't *feel*
alone or deserted. And why not? Well, maybe because the
separation was both deliberate and temporary; she'd be on
Earth for some time, probably, before Rissa and Tregare got
back from the Tsa-Drin world, but on Earth she had friends
and family. So she wouldn't feel alone, not really.

And for now? She smiled; what's wrong with a vacation?

Captain Delarov's entrance into Control broke Lisele's
reverie. A quick glance at her panel's chrono showed that
scheduled breakout time was only minutes away. Taking a
seat beside Anders Kobolak, the captain said, "Everything's
checked out, I assume?"

"Right, captain. The Chief Engineer's handling this part
himself."

"Good. Anything else?"

"One item, I guess. You haven't said whether you want
to do Turnover immediately, or coast for a while first, observ-
ing through the forward viewers."

Delarov nodded. "Good question; I hadn't considered it.
Yes, let's do coast, before turning and applying decel. We
might see something useful."

For Lisele, the last minutes of waiting went very slowly.
Finally the chrono came up to mark. With a nod toward
Katmai Delarov, Anders opened the intercom to the Drive
room. "You there, Chief? And ready?"

"Ready, Second Hat," came Pope's voice.

"Then cut FTL—*now*."

She'd been through breakout once before, when the
Deux was nearing Shaarbant, but still the sense of plunging
lurch, the grinding shudder that made no sound but hurt the
ears anyway, caught Lisele unprepared. Her stomach jumped,
not with nausea but just trying to get back where it belonged.
When she got her eyes unsquinched and her ears listening,
what she saw and heard was big trouble.

"That ship!" Katmai Delarov's voice came hoarse. "What
is it? What's its course? Intercept?"

Automatically, while no one answered, Lisele checked
her screen. Not intercept, but a skew meeting: two ships
passing at an angle in different planes. Before she could
say so, which probably wasn't her place anyway, Anders

Kobolak told the same thing. But said, "*Whose* ship?"
And that answer, Lisele did know. "The Tsa."

V

Lisele cranked her screen to highest-mag. The other ship's
markings meant nothing to her, except that she hadn't seen the
pattern before. She said, "All I can tell is, it's not Elzh's ship."

To Kobolak, the captain said, "How close will it come?
Within their mind-attack range?"

Pale, tense and almost shaking, the Second Hat said,
"On present course, I'm not sure. But it could turn, and—"

Why were they just *talking*? Lisele cut in: "Captain
Delarov! You have to get all the Tsa-phobics in freeze. Right
away. So that if there's contact—"

Anders stood. "Yes, she's right. If the Tsa caught *my*
feelings—I tried the control methods, but couldn't make
them work—it'd be like a lightning rod to this ship. And
same with Alina, here. Captain: request relief from watch?"

Delarov's puzzled frown smoothed out. "Certainly. It's
simply that this happened so *fast*. You're both relieved."
Sliding into Kobolak's pilot-navigator position she turned to
Lisele and said, "You'll have the comm now, Moray."

As Lisele moved to take Alina's place, Delarov punched
up the intercom and called the galley. "First Hat? Are you
there?" A male voice answered in the negative; Delarov
muttered, "In quarters, then," tried that option, and got a
response. "Mei, drop everything and heat your feet to the
accel tanks; start setting them up for freeze." She paused.
"Let me see: eight, we'll need. Off the *Deux* there's Kobolak,
Rostadt, Rorvik, and Holmbach. Of our own, Molyneaux,
Fredericks, Hassan, and Gray."

Lisele didn't get the words of Lu-teng's answer, but the
tone of protest came clearly enough. Delarov shook her head.
"I *know* it scalps us in Drive and Engineering. Can't be
helped. There's a Tsa ship on the forward screens; if it comes
within danger range we mustn't have any conscious minds
aboard, that can't hold calm at all costs."

Then came sounds of assent. Katmai Delarov ended the call and switched to all-ship broadcast mode. "Now hear this, and move fast." Quickly she gave the orders, getting acknowledgment from each person and making sure no watch station would be left totally unattended.

She turned to Lisele. "I think that does it. You agree?"

Nodding assent, Lisele thought: after that first few seconds, getting oriented to the unexpected, Katmai Delarov took hold and really *moved* things.

At normal end of that watch-period, nothing had changed much. Lu-teng had the eight into freeze but was still checking adjustments on the tanks, so Arlen Limmer reported out of turn, to take the First Hat's watch. Delarov moved to give him the major Control panel, and took a nearby aux position. After Arlen had checked the log and his screens, and acknowledged that he was taking over the watch in good order, Delarov said, "Very well. Now, Moray, give me all-ship again."

So Lisele flipped the intercom switches, and the captain spoke. "Delarov here. All-ship circuit. Status report. First, we made breakout about where we intended, a little over ninety billion kilos from where we expect the anomaly to be, which would give us leeway to decel down to zerch if we wanted to. We haven't had time to check any of that, or even look for the thing, because of detecting the Tsa ship."

She ran fingers up through her hair, splaying the heavy bangs into disarray. "That ship hasn't changed course; approaching us it's crossing from starboard to port. The angle between courses is not quite a radian. But its path lies a bit above us, so to speak—toward galactic-north from galactic ecliptic; it may not come close enough to be a danger."

From the intercom, Mei Lu-teng's voice came. "Are you saying I've done all this work for nothing?"

Lisele knew she should keep her mouth shut, but still she couldn't help saying, "If you'd ever seen what happens to Tsa-phobics in mind-attack range, you wouldn't say that!" Then she looked at Captain Delarov. "I'm sorry, I—"

"No. I've heard about the problem, but you've experienced it. So you said it better."

When no answer came, the captain went on to other matters. "You all know our personnel complement is sadly depleted. To be exact, we now have seven people up and awake. Seven, no more."

She spelled it out. Herself, Lu-teng, and Arlen Limmer to handle Control, all the pilot-navigator work. Chief Engineer Darwin Pope with no subordinates awake, at all. Drive Chief deWayne Houk, and Comm Chief Eduin Brower, in the same predicament. No gunnery officer. "What we have," she said, "is nowhere nearly enough people to keep this ship running."

Her smile, then, startled Lisele. "So what we'll have to do, my friends—assuming we survive our near passage with the Tsa ship—is figure out how to make it work, anyway."

The Tsa did not break course. Aboard *Hare*, all seven persons awake were under orders to work at calm-maintaining methods, not to allow *anything* to break alpha-wave concentration so that fear or anxiety or anger might reach the Tsa.

And it worked. Closer and closer in the forward screens, though well "above" *Hare*'s path, the Tsa ship came. Then it moved offscreen, was picked up by the side monitors, and finally receded past any possible danger point.

Once, half into sleep between two long watches, Lisele thought she felt the feathers-and-chimes feeling of a Tsa probe: the friendly kind, seeking to communicate. But when she came fully awake, it was gone. She called captain's digs and reported. But either way, there was nothing to do about it.

Before her next watch, Lisele got a little sleep. Not as much as she needed, but enough to make do with.

"So," said Katmai Delarov, "let's get on with it." Eduin Brower, working comm, had spotted the anomaly they intended to explore. It wasn't exactly at the expected location, but near enough. From *Hare*'s position, less than one-percent of a light-year distant, the normal monitors showed only a dust cloud that spewed great jets of gases, charged particles, and radiation.

Meanwhile the inertial indicators reported that the thing's gravity field varied, sometimes fluctuating off the meters' scales. What this did to navigational data kept the Control crew on its toes, estimating and trying to correct. It would have been nice to have more help, but no one could be

spared for the laborious task of getting the rest of the crew up
out of freeze.

For one thing, first there was Turnover: swinging *Hare*
end-for-end to point the drive-nodes forward and apply deceleration. With only Darwin Pope and Drive Chief deWayne
Houk left, of six people qualified to work in Drive, the
two men were working twelve-hour watches and sleeping on
improvised bunks: Houk in the aisle beside the log desk,
and Pope behind the exciter racks. Nonetheless, between
them coordinating three control consoles, the two men swung
ship smoothly and brought the Drive solidly up to redline-
max thrust without pause or misfire.

What nobody liked, though, was the way the anomaly's
variations screwed up the approach schedule. Only a light-
day out, with the screen and other instruments showing vast
and frightening phenomena in the space ahead, Lisele reported
for watch duty. Short on sleep, her hair a tousled mess and
skin itching for an overdue shower, she tried to remember
what her job was, on this particular shift. Comm, probably,
because Eduin Brower, seeing her, was leaving that position.
Brower was another who had made impromptu sleeping
arrangements; his pile of bedding lay over to one side of
Control, behind the aux positions. When he ran out of energy
and Lisele couldn't be there to relieve him, he set audible
alarms on his circuits and sacked out anyway.

Now he waved her a grumpy hello and shuffled his way
out of Control. Probably to go fix himself something to eat.
Oh, damn! A little more awake, Lisele would have thought to
visit the galley and bring up some kind of snacks. Well, she
hadn't.

Arlen Limmer was sitting Nav. Lisele said, "Any better
figures now?"

Scowling, Arlen shook his head. "We're not getting the
decel we ought. It's that damned variable gravity. And going
in tailfirst, we're having trouble getting any lateral course
change away from the nasty bugger."

Lisele knew what he meant. "Tregare used to say about
that. When you go in bassackwards, it makes your steering
tough."

His face showing fatigue, young Limmer glared at her.
"Oh, that's fine! Words of wisdom. So tell me, then: what did
he *do* about it?"

Her mind blanked. "I guess I don't know, Arlen. Except, maybe—well, he could have swung ship and steered straight-forward again."

"When we're already going too fast?"

"It could be a thought," said Katmai Delarov.

Lisele hadn't heard her come in, and now turned to give greeting. Then, "Are we in real trouble?"

"I can't know; I have no data on anything like this. I've been trying to think what this thing could be."

"Any ideas, skipper?" said Arlen.

Delarov waved him free of watch duty, sat to check his log and then okayed it, before she answered. "Some theoretical ones. No, not even theory; call it speculation. In the latest text Pennet Hoyfarul published before we left Earth."

Lisele cleared her throat. "Not easy reading, then."

Tired or not, the captain smiled well. "Is he ever?"

Arlen broke in. "What does the book say?"

Delarov's face wrinkled with scowl lines. "Do you know what 'anisotropic' means?"

Arlen didn't answer, so Lisele did. "When the properties of something aren't the same in all directions. Like a magnet; it's polarized from one end to the other, but not sideways. Right?"

"Right." The captain nodded. "And Hoyfarul hypothe-sizes, which is at least one jump better than speculating, that perhaps even very dense forms of matter/energy can be anisotropic."

"You mean neutron stars?" Lisele said. "Black holes?"

Delarov's hand waved the question aside. "Those are just labels. Guesses about various stages of things nobody's ever seen, close up. Or come back to tell about, at least. But yes—that's roughly the class of phenomenon the doctor had in mind."

"But supposing it's *not* the same in all directions?" Arlen said it. "How does that explain anything?"

Lisele knew the answer, but shut up to let the captain say, "Well, think back to the magnet your colleague mentioned. If you spin that around one of its short axes, the magnetic poles whizzing along at the ends of the rotation, at any outside point you're going to notice a big variation in magnet-ic attraction."

"Oh, sure," said Arlen . "That's how we get AC current."

He frowned. "You mean, a neutron star could be long and skinny, spinning like this magnet Lisele mentioned?"

Delarov sighed. "I haven't the faintest idea. Read Hoyfarul, if you can penetrate his math; I can't."

Carefully, Lisele said, "Anisotropic doesn't have to be size or shape. Arlen, you want to read that book along with me, if the captain would lend it?"

Arlen nodded, and Delarov agreed. But as it happened, the anomaly never gave them time to do any such reading.

When the crunch hit, *Hare* was too close, going too fast, and pointing too near the anomaly. Delarov relieved Arlen Limmer at the Nav seat and ran the Drive's decel up past redline to absolute max. And still it wasn't working; the deadly thing out there, whatever it was, still pulled the ship closer and closer. The screens sputtered with ionization; if it weren't for the Drive field's shielding effect, Lisele knew, they'd all be fried by now, from sheer radiation density.

She punched into Tinhead and plotted the ship's trajectory. No good; it ended inside the anomaly. *We're all dead.*

"I'm afraid you're right," said Katmai Delarov. "But what is there to do about it?"

Lisele hadn't realized she'd spoken aloud. She had, though—so now she had to back her words. Her mind searched wildly; a thought came. "What Tregare would. The power sling!"

It took some explaining: if you can't pull away, you dive *at* the damn thing, a little off to the side, accel all the way, and use its own grav to build enough Vee to sling you free and away. Many's the time Bran Tregare in his pirate days had used the move, not to escape a natural force but to evade UET pursuers. Once around a star or giant planet, he cut Drive and coasted, letting UET whistle for his spoor and head for all the wrong places. Or sometimes he cut Drive and did a dead sling. But even discounting the hell of radiation out there, in a gravity well as steep as this one, that option wouldn't work.

Interrupting a lot at first, then listening more carefully, finally Katmai Delarov nodded. "Yes, I see it. But child, I've never *done* any such thing. I don't know the parameters."

"I do." Calm and assured on the outside, she hoped, all ice inside but refusing to shiver, Lisele stood. "I've run

Tregare's logs a lot, on computer sim. The figures are different; he never tackled this kind of gravs. But the equations are the same; it should work."

So Captain Delarov vacated the pilot-navigator seat, and let Liesel Selene Moray sit down. "I hope you're right."

The words sounded cold, but Delarov's hand brushing across the top of Lisele's head didn't feel that way.

Lisele cranked up, at the periphery of her main visual screen, all the figures she might need. For starters: distance, velocity, decel. Angle, of course, from center of the anomaly.

Now what? Oh, sure: third-derivative, the rate of *change* of accel or decel. And curvature of the ship's course, which was reciprocal to the radius from the anomaly's center, and then the rates of change analogous to Vee and accel. Third derivative on this, too? She shook her head. If she needed to know that, they might just as well all go out the airlock.

So she took her readings and called the Drive room. "Pope? Houk? Moray here. On captain's authority, get ready for Turnover. To swing ship and accelerate ahead. Acknowledge?"

"Are you crazy?" Both voices shouted from downship—and there was more, until Captain Delarov confirmed the order. Then, after time for a hasty attempt at battening down for Turnover, the Drive cut. For moments that seemed interminable, everyone sagged against seat harnesses in zero G. With the Drive field's protection gone and only the weak transverse nodes swinging ship as fast as she could manage it, Lisele tried not to think of the radiation they were taking. Then the Drive, sputtering momentarily before taking solid hold, pushed again.

And in the forward screen, closer to center than Lisele would have liked, glowed the malevolent thing that drew *March Hare* ever closer.

VI

Checking the numbers on that screen, Lisele didn't like them much. She had accel at redline max and it wasn't going to be enough. She punched estimates into Tinhead and got an answer that didn't stay constant. Well, of course: as the gravitational force varied, so did the need for acceleration. She couldn't follow those changes herself; she'd always be one jump behind. So she set up the requirements and punched for vector solutions.

Then she sat back and watched. The captain reached and nudged her. "Why aren't you doing anything? Are we getting enough velocity yet?"

"Velocity, by itself, isn't the point. I'm having Tinhead regulate the Drive, balancing V-squared-over-R against whatever the gravity well is doing. And—" She waved off further conversation, because there was a flaw in her setup: it wasn't heading *March Hare* at an angle that would pass the anomaly, at closest approach, by any chance of a safe distance.

"Oh, peace *take* the thing!" She only muttered it, but saw Katmai Delarov frown with anxiety. So as she made new adjustments to her program, Lisele explained. "I have to throw more side vector, tilt the ship at an angle to our course. And that means that for building Vee, we don't get the full effect of our Drive force."

"Yes, of course." Delarov nodded. "Only the normal accel value times the cosine of your tilt angle."

Well, just because the captain hadn't done sling turns, didn't mean she was ignorant! Lisele swung *March Hare* half a radian, cosine nearly point-eight-eight. And the tilt wasn't enough; Tinhead said so, in numbers Lisele couldn't refute.

A full radian, then, and after looking at the screen, she knew this was the angle she'd have to go with. Only fifty-four percent of Drive power pushing on-line, not enough to build the necessary Vee. And also giving, at that angle, a minimum of safety clearance when they passed the anomaly.

Not enough, either way. But Lisele had one more move left. She turned to Delarov. "We'll have to go to max accel. Full max, not safety redline. I know it's not safe. But if the Drive holds, we *might* get away from this peace-waster!"

Except for Darwin Pope and deWayne Houk, down in the Drive room, all unfrozen personnel were gathered in Control, seated peripherally to the positions occupied by the captain and Lisele. Eduin Brower sat at Comm as though, in this situation, he could perform any function there. Mei

Lu-teng and Arlen Limmer had taken aux-position seats;
sidelong vision showed Lisele that the two, white-knuckled,
were holding hands. Not for romance, she figured, but
merely to share human comfort.

As the grav-field varied, *March Hare* bucked and
shuddered. On the screen, both forward view and numbers
showed the ship edging slowly away from collision course,
and building Vee toward the figure that might mean safety.

Lisele felt an ache in her hand. Looking, she found she
had her fingers crossed so tightly that she was cutting off
their circulation.

As the hellhole loomed, closer and greater, Lisele couldn't
make herself believe. This had to be a nightmare; how could
it be real? The screen, its inputs overloaded, now showed
the anomaly only as a black wavering circle, haloed with the
ravening jets of its emissions. Inside the ship, even protected
by the shielding of its own Drive field, came occasional pale
blue sparkings of ionization. Enough radiation to be lethal?
Lisele shook her head. Right now she had enough to worry
about; that one would have to wait its turn.

Periastron neared; in Control, ionization built to a blue
crackling haze, so that Lisele could barely read the screen.
She didn't need it, though, to feel Drive shudder and hesi-
tate, before the blazing horror slid off her forward screen,
moved across the side monitors, and then in the rear pickup
began to shrink.

An hour later, everyone still sitting and watching, the
screen image again showed the anomaly as they had first seen
it: a flaming ball, throwing gouts of more flame. One could
touch metal, now, without drawing sparks. But somehow,
ever since Lisele had run the Drive up to full max, no one
had said a word.

She'd cut the tilt angle gradually, as the need for side
thrust lessened. Now the ship was heading straight away, no
tilt necessary. It was time, then, for Lisele to recheck Tinhead's
parameters and see when she could safely cut Drive activity
below all-out max.

But just as the numbers began to arrange themselves on
her screen, a great *clang* ran through the entire ship. And as
Lisele shook her head, trying to regain her senses after that
jolt, she realized that *Hare* was in free fall.

"Well, *now* you've done it!" The hoarse shout came from

Eduin Brower. "Smartass know-it-all kid, don't know when to ease off, you blew the damn *Drive!*"

Lisele didn't want to get up, because if she did, everybody could see she was shaking. And she hadn't actually moved around much in zero-gee since she was nine years old, when the *Deux* did Turnover on the way to Shaarbant. But if she didn't go soon she was going to pee in her pants.

So she unbuckled and pushed free. Not far, and hanging onto things, in case the Drive came back on. It didn't, though, and she dared a floating leap from the last available handhold to the door of the small latrine just off Control.

Inside, she realized it wasn't going to be all that easy. Turnover never lasted very long, so the fixture wasn't built for zero-gee elimination. Like all the others, shipside, it had no free water in it except when in use; that was so nobody had to check all those things before Turnover.

But now what? All right, no problem. She held a big wad of tissues to herself, soaked it, and disposed of it. Then another. The third one was just to get good and dry.

Heading back into Control she saw the captain talking on intercom; closer, then, she heard, too. And scrambled to get her seat buckle latched, just as Darwin Pope's voice said, "Mark ten and counting; I hope everybody's strapped in."

On the count, Drive hum and accel resumed. "Congratulations, Chief," the captain said. "That's a load off everybody's mind."

"Not so much as you might think." A different voice; that would be deWayne Houk, the Drive Chief. Lisele knew him by sight, but that was about all. Now he said, "We have Drive, yes. But not all of it. The Hoyfarul circuits won't come up."

Looking calm enough, Delarov said, "Go on, Chief."

The intercom muffled voice overtones. Lisele couldn't gauge the man's stress, as he said, "What we have working is STL, only. And the Nielson Cube, it barely supports *that.*"

Having done all they could, the two men came up from Control; it was time for parley. Katmai Delarov asked all the questions Lisele had in mind, and a few more. The answers didn't change, though. *March Hare* was stuck with slower-than-light Drive, and the ship's supplies weren't geared for that rate of travel.

Blinking once, Delarov asked, "Moray? What's our course? I know there was no opportunity to choose one."

Embarrassed for not having checked the matter earlier, Lisele did so now, and read off the coordinates. "From a course toward Earth, we're about a right-angle off. Heading into unknown space. At least, Tinhead's log has no data in that direction."

The captain frowned. "Tinhead? You said that before." So Lisele explained that it was Tregare's term for any ship's computer.

"All right; it's as good a name as any." Now Delarov's gaze surveyed the group. "What's our next priority? Any ideas?"

Lisele thought. In a similar situation, with too little food to get *Inconnu Deux* back to Shaarbant with very many people alive, Ivan Marchant had put nearly everybody into freeze. All but the few needed to maintain the ship, and stretching that a little.

As she began to make that suggestion, Mei Lu-teng overrode her. "The very first item on our agenda: do you have any idea how much radiation we all took, back there?"

Lisele didn't, so she waited, until the First Hat said, "We need anti-radiation drugs; we need them immediately. I know they'll make us sicker than anyone's going to like, but—"

"But it beats hell out of dying," Lisele put in. Strangely, she heard herself saying it in Tregare's voice, not her own.

"Quite true," said Lu-teng. "I'll go fetch the stuff, and we can get it over with."

"Just a minute, First." Eduin Brower said it. "What about the ones in freeze? They get the same dosage? We need to wake everybody up and shoot the dope in, right now?"

Lu-teng looked puzzled; then she said, "No. Their life processes are vastly slowed. They took nearly the same damage, yes—but their medication can wait until they're revivified."

*　　*　　*

She exited from Control; the rest were left sitting, looking at each other and saying very little. Someone made a throat-clearing sound; looking toward it, Lisele saw that deWayne Houk had something to say.

She'd seen Houk only a few times, spoken hardly at all; her impressions of the man were not favorable. Medium-tall, narrow in build and face, posture slightly hunched, he presented an image she didn't care for. His pale hair, clipped almost to stubble, barely showed against white scalp.

His voice, though, drew attention; it had resonance she wouldn't have expected from such a skimpy thorax. Now he said, "You've not yet heard, from Darwin Pope, all the Drive problems. I don't have the tech background he has, to give it full. What I do know—" Houk paused, mouth twisted as though trying to invent words he hadn't known. "The Nielson. Accel or decel, maybe half of redline max it's good for, just about."

He shook his head. "But land? Get down safe, groundside? Not to think about."

Questioned, Chief Engineer Pope wouldn't contradict his Drive Chief. "Tuning might help; I don't know yet. But if deWayne says we can't land, I have to trust his judgment."

Then Mei Lu-teng brought the radiation med-kit; what with pills and needles, glumly the seven people ingested their loads of future discomfort. Still, though, Lisele knew that Tregare had it right: no matter how bad it might be, this stuff beat hell out of dying.

An hour later, Arlen and Lisele sat in control with Captain Delarov; the other four had left for duty-watch or sleep. Mostly the latter, since just now there wasn't much need for any kind of alert surveillance. Pope and Houk would be down in Drive, either working on the tuning job or sleeping with all alarms set. Brower, after looking at the forward screen and growling to Lisele, "Check your upper left quadrant; seems might be something there," had dossed down in his usual corner.

So with nobody talking, and nothing else to do, Lisele checked the area Brower had suggested. And found something.

"Captain?" Delarov looked up. "I think the Comm Chief was right. Up there—" She pointed. "—the screen shows at least one star we might be able to reach. Limping, the way we'll have to, I estimate four months. Six at the outside."

"Six months? The lot of us? Eating what?"

"*Not* the lot of us." Delarov didn't look as if she wanted to listen to any long stories, so Lisele skipped the part about her uncle Ivan. "The way it is, how many do we need awake? There's Control here, and there's Drive. Down there, already they've been doing it with the men sleeping alongside, and alarms on. Maybe you need two there, maybe only one. I know it's not the best way things should be done—"

"But perhaps it's the best we can do." The stretch of Katmai Delarov's lips across her teeth couldn't be called a smile. "All right, Moray; I get your point and I accept it." Now she shrugged. "So tell me. Who else do we freeze, now?"

That part, Lisele hadn't thought about. Now, she did. "Captain, those are your decisions to make, not mine. But you did ask, so—" And thought some more. "In case something else happens from outside, Control needs at least two people. Drive, maybe only one, now—so long as somebody's up who can revive others if they're needed."

"I could do that. And regardless of anything else, Moray, I will stay out of freeze and maintain command of this ship."

"Well, sure, captain."

"Then what are your other recommendations?"

Sidelong, Lisele looked at Arlen. He'd want to stay up—but did the ship *need* him? Or her, for that matter. Not sure of her own judgment, she said, "Along with you, to do Control, you could have the First Hat, or Arlen here, or even me. Comm Chief Brower, for that matter." She paused. "Down in Drive, I like Darwin Pope and don't like deWayne Houk. But you know them both, better than I do. So on that one I'd like to pass."

Delarov said, "In this mess I think Houk's my best choice. Now then—any suggestions from you, Limmer?" Looking baffled, Arlen shook his head. "Then first thing tomorrow, when Mei's awake to do the honors, you're for freeze."

Arlen didn't answer, so Lisele said, "That leaves, besides Houk down in Drive, just you and the First Hat, and Brower and me. How many more need to go? That is, how many can our supplies support for very long?"

Delarov's stare, continuing, made Lisele uncomfortable. Finally the woman said, "I'm torn. If we include the scoutship's stores, I could leave at least five of us awake until we reach that star. But what if—oh, it's the right color, but what if we get there and it's no good to us?" She shook her head. "And since we can't land, we're going to need that scout. We may even need it in fully-supplied condition." He hands clenched together. "So I'm going for the bare minimum; two up here and one in Drive. Chancy, but in clear space it's a reasonable chance." Abruptly, then, she said, "Moray—tomorrow you and Brower join Pope and Limmer, at the tanks."

Sitting up, spilling blankets off him, Eduin Brower banged his fist on the deck. "Are you crazy, skipper? You—"

"I'm sorry, Eduin." The way Delarov said it, Lisele wondered what might be between those two. "But you know as well as I do that Mei or I could handle any communications need that might arise. Especially since you've just checked all the circuitry."

Standing now, Brower roared, "It ain't *me* I'm talking about, you spear-fishing squaw! It's the kid. All right, so you and Lu-teng have the experience, all that damn training. But the kid's a *pilot*, dammit!"

"But I thought—" For a moment, Lisele was too surprised for speech. "When the Drive blew, you said—"

His hand swiped at her words. "Aah, that was just me, scared spitless and shooting off my face. Didn't mean nothing by it. And ain't nobody else on here could've pulled us out of that death trap,. at all."

Delarov stared. "Eduin, you squaw-chasing old renegade, you do have a point. I think I'll go along with it." And before Lisele could speak, "Don't argue, Moray. Brower and Lu-teng go to freeze. You stay up, and work."

Well, that's what she'd wanted but hadn't dared hope for. Trying to keep her breathing compatible with the alpha-wave state, Lisele nodded. "Whatever you say, skipper."

The others left, but one thing nagged at Lisele. The way a sling turn works . . .

She checked it out. Tearing free from the incalculable mass of the anomaly, on a course at right angles from Earth, *March Hare* had gained so much distance and velocity that no turn toward human space could bring the ship anywhere near that gravitational vortex.

Well, she'd thought as much, but it never hurts to be sure. Satisfied, she logged the data.

VII

Briefly, early in the next ship's-day, the remaining seven persons met in Control. All screens indicated relatively clear space; of the stellar objects visible, only two were within *March Hare*'s current range. At forty-five percent of redline max accel, the Drive mumbled steadily.

"We have a better fix on Goal Star now," said the captain. "Mei pegs it at a little over five months away, ship's time. So that's how long it will be for the three of us, until we see four of you again. Eduin, Darwin, Mei, young Limmer— you won't experience that time, of course. But we'll be missing you—as well as the others, already in freeze." She blinked twice: tears, Lisele wondered? "Well, let's say our temporary goodbyes, and then Mei will tuck you all in nicely."

"Who tucks *her* in?" Arlen's lower lip protruded, Lisele decided, in a definite pout. "And who wakes us up?"

Lu-teng smiled. "I'll put myself away, of course. Necessarily, the units are designed to make that possible. And I suppose Captain Delarov will rouse us. That part's much easier, though it takes longer. But anybody who can read the instructions can do revivals safely."

The goodbyes, then. Arlen looked so forlorn that Lisele put more into her kiss than she really felt. For a moment she thought he was going to make some kind of embarrassing, last-minute request, but he didn't.

The captain's embrace with Eduin Brower didn't surprise Lisele as much as it would have a day earlier; she herself received a rib-creaking hug from the man and returned it with equal zest. Releasing her, he grinned. "Don't let this tub fall into anything, youngster." She assured him she wouldn't.

Stiffly, trying to hide his obvious resentment but not quite succeeding, Darwin Pope shook hands all around and spoke polite words. Showing definite concern and not gloating at all, deWayne Houk said, "It ought to be you up, Dar, not me. But the captain decided."

"I know." Turning to Katmai Delarov, Pope shook her hand also. "I'm sure you had good reasons, and of course they are your own business. But it bothers me, not to know in what way I failed to measure up."

She put both hands to his one, and squeezed. "No such thing, Darwin. It's only that—" She shook her head. "A hunch, I guess. I've never faulted your work, your skills or knowledge. But I have the feeling that Chief Houk is a better improvisor, and in a fix like this, ad-libbing might be exactly what we need."

His scowl, now, showed only puzzlement. Then it cleared. "Yes, I see. I *do* tend to go by the book, don't I?"

Mei Lu-teng gave Lisele a handshake, then a light embrace. "I don't have to ask why you're needed more than I am. *My* father never played tag with UET ships and left records of his maneuvers in a computer log, for me to study. That unbelievable gravity pit—I'd never have gotten us free of it."

Speaking honestly, Lisele said, "It took some luck, too."

Lu-teng chuckled. "Yes. Luck that we had you aboard."

It all seemed to be mostly over with, and Lisele hoped so, because her breakfast wasn't sitting too well and she felt a bit feverish. Probably the radiation drugs getting their licks in, so she could expect to feel a lot worse soon, and not really good again for at least forty-eight hours. Anyway, the First Hat and Captain Delarov had a rather tearful farewell; then the four left for freeze and deWayne Houk went down to the Drive room.

From that location he reported that within its present limitations, the Nielson Cube was performing steadily.

Delarov acknowledged. Then, to Lisele she said, "Moray? I think we'd better take a leaf out of Eduin's book and do most of our sleeping here in Control. Save a lot of time running upship and down, two levels at a crack."

"Two? My quarters are down four."

"No; as Acting First Hat, move your things to the officers' deck. Any cabin you prefer." Which meant she had the choice of Mei Lu-teng's digs, or Anders Kobolak's, or Arlen Limmer's. None of the alternatives pleased her. But it made no sense to have her duffel two levels farther down than need be, so she said, 'I'll move into Arlen's place. It won't be quite as much like intruding; we've been friends since forever."

"Friends? Is that all? I'd thought—"

It was none of Delarov's business, of course, but Lisele said, "He's ready for more; that's true. I'm not, yet."

The captain smiled. "I see. And I suppose you're wondering about Eduin and myself."

"Not since yesterday, I'm not. Except—"

Now Delarov gave a soft laugh. "I know. He's older by a lot, he's messy, and he enjoys being taken for a slob. But if you ever find as tender a man, Moray, hang onto him."

Lisele thought she understood. But now her breakfast was behaving even worse than it had earlier. So before she could spoil things by throwing up all over her pilot's console, she said, "I'll remember the advice; thanks," and bolted for the latrine cubby.

The next two days, whether she lay trying to sleep or forced herself through a semblance of standing watch, were the most agonizing Lisele had ever experienced. Slogging across the swamps on Shaarbant, with everyone on the verge of heat stroke—compared to this, Shaarbant had been a picnic. She ached all over: head and body, bones and muscles and organs, all throbbing to create agony. When, on top of everything else, her gut convulsed in nausea, she came close to passing out.

So when she woke in her new quarters for the second time, painfully dehydrated but with nausea and fever gone, and could sit up without dizziness, she figured the worst was over.

She pushed her hair back from her eyes, and the action felt odd. Looking, she saw that quite a lot of hair had come free in her hand, and then that considerably more lay tangled on the pillow. Her moment of panic passed quickly, because she knew what had happened.

If radiation dosage were heavy enough, this was one effect the drugs couldn't counter. Her general feeling of health assured her that the really bad stuff had been counteracted. So first she drank nearly a liter of reconstituted fruit juice, to quench the fires in her stomach. Then with a brush she cleared the remaining loosened hair from head and person, and dumped the lot into a wastebasket. After that, she had a shower.

* * *

Looking in the mirror as she dried herself, Lisele wasn't too happy with what she saw. She'd worn bare scalp before— well, close-clipped enough to feel like sandpaper—when that was the only way to cope with the itchy, sticky mud of Shaarbant's swamps. This time, with roots and all discarded, not even a shadow indicated the boundary between face and scalp; totally smooth, her skin was. Irritated, though; taking her time about it she rubbed herself with lotion, and welcomed the soothing effect.

At the mirror again, she decided the lack of eyebrows was the worst part. Until now she hadn't realized how important they were in defining expression; her face had a *blank* look to it. Hmmm; no problem there. With cosmetic pencil she drew in brows as near her natural look as she could manage. Yes, *much* better.

Anyway, from all accounts the condition wasn't permanent, though she had no idea how long it might last.

Well, Houk and the captain would be in the same boat. And by the time the others came out of freeze she should be looking reasonably ordinary. Come to think of it, at that time they'd likely go through the same ordeal. Her chuckle died quickly; the misery she'd endured wasn't funny at all.

She dressed. Time to go topside and see what the captain was doing. Entering Control she found Katmai Delarov in the pilot's seat, wearing no more hair than a hardboiled egg, and said, "Morning, skipper. I see the radiation hit us about the same."

Looking around, Delarov said, "Seems so. Not permanent, though, I understand. Funny how we all put so much importance on that non-essential protein fiber; women, anyway." She cleared her throat. "Do you happen to know how long—?"

"Not me. Before we get anywhere near Goal Star, though, I'd think." Delarov hadn't faked any eyebrows yet. Lisele decided to suggest the idea—but later, not just now!

"Yes. Well, being recovered from that ghastly bout of radiation sickness, I count this a small price. Now sit down, and see what you think about this most recent parcel of data."

As Lisele moved to comply, something caught her notice. Delarov's jade disc earrings had been replaced. Now the woman, in her left lobe, wore three small gems that formed an equilateral triangle, point down: ruby-red forward, emerald-green aft, and below, the sparkling brilliant blue-white of diamond.

Lisele's staring must have been obvious; the captain touched that lobe and said, "A few extra ornaments, in compensation." She turned her head, revealing that on her other ear the pattern was reversed, the triangle pointing up with a diamond at the top, green at front and red behind. "Do you like it?"

"Sure. Seems like an awful lot of piercing, but the way it all looks, I expect it's worth it." Lisele's own earlobes were still intact; she was in no hurry to change that status. But it was interesting to see the configuration Delarov had chosen. Well, enough talk of appearances: Lisele took her seat, saying, "New data, you mentioned? Okay, let me look, now."

The main thing was that Tinhead thought Goal Star had at least one huge, non-habitable planet. What else the computer's guess might mean, neither Delarov nor Lisele could predict. Over the next few days they took more observations and readouts, but at such a distance, decreasing but still vast, Goal Star wasn't telling anybody very much. Mei Lu-teng's estimate still stood as anyone's best guess: another twenty weeks, now, until that stellar system could be reached.

From here, only the star itself was visible. Odds were that it had more planets than just the big one hypothesized by Tinhead, but odds didn't always pay off.

And with a weak Drive, the decel for that rendezvous was going to take some careful figuring and a lot of luck.

One thing that annoyed Lisele was that deWayne Houk still had his pale, scarcely-noticeable hair. Hindsight showed that during the ship's worst radiation exposure, the man's duty station had been shielded by the bulk of the Drive itself. So he'd had a great deal less sickness and no depilation at all.

And to top it off, she thought, instead of keeping his hair stubble-short he was now letting it grow. *Just to show us he can do it and we can't!*

She knew her unvoiced complaint was irrational: maybe he just didn't have time, or someone else usually did his barbering for him. But the fact was, she didn't like the man anyway, so nearly everything he did got on her nerves.

Delarov had been right about Houk's ability to impro-

vise. Within days he'd programmed circuits to allow him to
do most of his monitoring and adjustment functions from
Control. So that Lisele had more of his company than she
really wanted, which would have been practically none.

When all three were present he was polite enough. But
once the ship's affairs settled into reasonable order, the
captain had rescinded the business of sleeping near their
watch-posts; now she went to her own digs, and Lisele to
hers. And when Lisele and the Drive Chief were alone in
Control, Houk's talk became more and more insinuating.

"It must get lonesome, a young woman like you, with
your handsome fella down there in a tank, cold as a ship's
outside. Really lonesome, I guess."

Unwilling to look into his probing stare, she said, "Not
especially." The screens showed no need for possible action
on her part, and the galley terminal was set on permanent
monitor, anyway. So she said, "Excuse me. Galley break,"
and left.

The only way three people could run the ship and keep
fed, without a mess piling up, was by taking turns on joint
meals: both preparation and cleanup. And handling individual snacks the same say. *Never leave the galley any way but
neat.* In this matter, Lisele had to admit, Houk did pull his
own weight.

Now she fixed herself a lunch from the frozen stores,
made enough coffee that she could take some up to Houk,
and sat. Eating, and enjoying relief from the man's company.

Eventually, with reluctance, she took the coffee pot
upship to Control. Setting it down where Houk could pour
for himself, or not. He said, "Thanks, Moray. Now what I was
saying—"

She might have known he wouldn't let it drop. "I thought
we settled that. I'm not lonesome."

His eyebrows—a scraggly pair, but maybe better than
pencil marks—rose, then came down again. "Ah—*I* see. Well,
I suppose that's fine, for women who take to each other in
such fashion."

At first she didn't catch his meaning. When she did, she
had to laugh. Because obviously he thought he was insulting
her, her and the captain both. Lisele didn't know about the
captain's tastes, one way or the other. And didn't care; they
were none of her business. For herself, she could have strong

feelings toward a man or woman, either one. With women, there was nothing physical about those feelings. Had there been, she supposed she'd accept the fact as just one more aspect of herself.

Now, though. If Houk could ad-lib, so could she. "In such fashion? Your guess is wrong. If you don't believe me, try that last remark on the skipper. And to set things perfectly straight, Chief Houk, I don't take to *you* in any fashion at all."

"Hey, now, you don't have to get unpleasant about it."

Maybe a little easier, yes. So, "All I meant was, propositioning me would be a waste of your time." She felt she should add, "Nothing personal," but that would be a lie so she didn't. As Tregare said, save lying for when you need it.

The intercom sounded. "Captain here, Moray. I'll be up to relieve you on sked."

"Right enough. There's coffee." Delarov signed off. Lisele turned to deWayne Houk. "If you want to ask your skipper the same questions you asked me, I'll go below, out of your way." Seeing how he avoided looking straight at her, Lisele knew she had him on the run. So she added, "Or you might want to visit your own duty station. You've been away from there so much, lately, maybe the place could use some dusting."

"Yes, of course. Good suggestion." As Houk stood, his look said that if he hadn't been her enemy before, he was now.

But it also told her that at least she had that enemy's respect. Whether the changes would work for or against her, she'd have to wait and see.

Over the next few days Houk did keep his distance; during Lisele's watches he came up to Control only rarely. His stays were brief, and his talk restricted to the line of business. How he behaved when the captain was on duty, Lisele had no idea and didn't feel like asking. If Delarov had any grounds for complaint she didn't mention them.

Nearly three weeks after Lisele had her joust with the Drive Chief, he entered Control just as she was relieving the skipper at watch. The man looked worried. "Efficiency's dropping, captain. Nielson Cube, I mean. After the *accident* to the Drive—" He gave Lisele a disapproving look. "—we

could manage forty-five percent of redline max force, accel or
decel. It's down to forty-three now, and still losing."

Katmai Delarov said, "What's your extrapolation, Chief?
Is the rate of loss increasing? If so, how fast?"

Houk shook his head. "That kind of math? Not my strong
point; for that you'd need Darwin Pope." Sulkily he added,
"Maybe you should put me down and get him up. As things
are, I might as well be froze as the way I am!"

Now his look at Lisele was a positive glare. *Why?* she
wondered. If he was peeved about having no bedmate, why
not at Delarov also? Then she realized: he hadn't dared to
approach the skipper, so all his resentment was focused on
herself, for not acceding.

None of that was important now. Thinking fast, Lisele
said, "You may have a good thought there, Chief." And before
Delarov could protest, "You'd want to rouse the First Hat.
Better that she go through the sickness now, out here where
we don't need her to work, than when we get to Goal Star.
After she's past it she can wake Pope—give him and the
Chief, here, some time to talk things over. And then see that
Houk goes into freeze safely, before she puts herself back in."

Houk's look lost its rancor. "Captain, in a way I hate to
have to say this. But I think she's right."

VIII

Mei Lu-teng, before the inevitable bout of illness hit,
constantly asked questions to bring herself up to date. She
agreed with the others' planning, and was apologetic when
pain and nausea forced her out of active participation.

Two days later, looking even more gaunt than usual, the
First Hat returned to duty. To Lu-teng, loss of hair was a
special affront; hers had been more than waist length, and its
absence bared a skull not smoothly rounded like Lisele's or
Delarov's, but sloping to a central ridge—and behind that,
dropping off at an abrupt angle. Lisele was reminded of
pictures she'd seen, of the Easter Island statues.

For what the woman may have felt, there was no remedy. But while Lu-teng was up and awake, Lisele quietly took care of the extra share of galley chores.

The First Hat wouldn't have had time for them, anyway. Conferring first with the captain and Lisele and Drive Chief Houk, then with the revived Chief Engineer until his own stretch of illness, Mei Lu-teng was much too busy to bother with cooking or the cleansing of utensils.

Darwin Pope constituted a different case. Once he was recovered, and had time for confab with Houk before the latter went to freeze, Lisele explained the need for cooperation on galley matters. Not seeming to pay much heed, he nodded. "Oh, certainly. I'll take my turn and keep things shipshape." And henceforth, he did.

If his altered appearance bothered him, he gave no sign. So far as Lisele could see, he hardly noticed. And possibly for that reason, the man didn't *seem* changed.

Which wasn't to say that Darwin Pope was any great bundle of cheer. He was pleasant enough, but after talking with Houk and checking the Drive Chief's figures, then making a few computer runs of his own, he didn't pretend that the news was good.

He and Delarov and Lisele, just the three of them out of freeze now, sat in Control. "Here's what it looks like. We've been losing thrust, and will continue to do so. We can't maintain the decel we'd hoped to manage."

"And what does that indicate?" asked Katmai Delarov. "When we arrive at Goal Star."

"Well, obviously," the man said, "we'll be traveling much faster than we should be."

Leaning forward, Lisele said, "You mean we can't stop?"

For a moment, Darwin Pope frowned. Without eyebrows, the expression lacked force. "If habitable-sized worlds exist in that system, and I'm getting computer indications that one or more might be there, we couldn't achieve orbit around one. Insufficient mass, you see, to slow us properly."

As though she were asking if any coffee was left, Delarov said, "We're dead, then, no matter what we do?"

While Pope was considering his answer, Lisele's mind raced. What did she know, that could help? Sling turns didn't lose velocity, they built it. But still—all right! "Just a minute. It's a long chance, but *listen*. We know our course, roughly, and which way we'd need to turn, to go toward Earth and the colonies. The shipping routes, and all."

Delarov shook her head. "You know we'd run out of food—long before we could crawl, relatively speaking, to those parts of space. Food, fuel, maybe even recyclable air. So why condemn ourselves to slow starvation?"

"You don't understand yet. If decel isn't going to do us any good, and Mr. Pope says it won't, let's do Turnover and go accel. Take a power sling around Goal Star, to head toward humanspace." Everybody wanted to interrupt, but she didn't let that happen. "We *all* go into freeze, and leave Tinhead with a timed command to turn off every bit of power drain we don't really need. Which would be—" On her fingers, she checked the needs. "The freeze chambers. Tinhead itself. And a radiating beacon, telling who we are and what our problem is. So that human ships could detect us, and make the intercept."

Nobody looked enthusiastic. She said, "I *know* it might be a hundred years, even more; I don't like that any more than you do. But it beats just coasting past Goal Star and starving to death." Well, she'd said it the best she could. . . .

"Actually," said Katmai Delarov, "I've heard worse ideas."

Darwin Pope shook his head. "In Goal Star's system we can't achieve orbit with an Earthsized planet. But around the huge one we've detected, or the star itself, we very well could."

Unconvinced, Lisele said, "Say we do that, and then there *isn't* anything habitable? We'd be stuck; right?"

The man nodded. "That's true, of course. But on the other hand, why don't we wait until we see at closer range what the system has to offer, and *then* make our decisions?"

"And for the time being," the captain said, "ease back on decel, as much as we can and still be able to snag orbit on the star or its big planet. To conserve our Drive capability."

Lisele couldn't argue with that logic, so she didn't.

Time passed. Unlike deWayne Houk, Darwin Pope was easy to get along with; he and Delarov and Lisele settled into an easy routine that still kept good check on things they needed to know. Goal Star neared, and Tinhead confirmed its earlier guess that the system harbored Earthsized worlds. Two, as it happened, but only one of those orbited in the zone that allowed water to be liquid. The ship's light-amplifying

circuits showed atmosphere around that planet. But whether
it was enough and not too much, or breathable, Tinhead
could not yet determine.

"If we can get ourselves there," Delarov said, "it's
possible that we might have a chance."

Privately, Lisele thought she'd rather ride *March Hare*
in freeze, into Earthspace, and take her chances on rescue.

For the first month after her hair fell out, Lisele knew it
was too soon for a comeback and didn't expect one. As the
second month passed and nothing showed, she began to
worry: maybe this thing was permanent, after all. Discouraged, she stopped checking in the mirror when she got up
from sleep.

But one "morning," while brushing her teeth before that
mirror, on her reflected scalp she saw faint darkness. Looking
closer she found a few hair tips showing, sparse and scattered.
Then she noticed more dark dots, and realized these were
new growth that was close to surfacing but hadn't quite made
it yet. Still awfully scanty—but now she remembered that
follicles had their individual cycles, and certainly wouldn't all
have been at the same stage when the radiation hit.

So it would take some waiting. But eventually she would
look more like herself again.

Well ahead of her time to relieve the skipper on watch,
Lisele went up to Control, to see if Delarov was showing any
similar progress.

She was, and a little better. But the funny part: until
Lisele told her, the captain hadn't even noticed!

By a certain amount of fine-tuning, plus disconnecting
the power drain of the inoperative Hoyfarul FTL circuits,
Darwin Pope stabilized *March Hare*'s Drive. "Houk should
have thought of that," he grumbled, "but his oversight hasn't
cost us anything of more than marginal importance. We're
leveled off at roughly forty-two percent of redline capability,
and quicker action might have got us forty-seven. Which still
wouldn't have slowed us sufficiently to orbit an Earth-class
world, at Goal Star."

Parts of his explanation went over Lisele's head, so she
asked questions. All right; the FTL gear itself was undamaged,
but the deteriorated Nielson Cube couldn't muster enough
power to fire it up.

Lisele felt herself scowling in concentration, and forced those muscles to relax. "Is the Cube down for keeps?" Because she knew, vaguely, that at least once Tregare had traded a sick Cube for a rebuilt one.

"As far as we're concerned, yes. Groundside I could fix it, but we can't get there. Even aboard it might be done, *if* we had a replacement power supply to keep the ship running. But we don't."

Well, that was a stopper—or *was* it? "Hey—just a minute! What if—why don't we—how about the *scout's* Cube? I know it's smaller, but shutting down all the drain we don't really need—"

Pope looked first startled and then interested, but after moments he shook his head. "I like your thinking, Moray, but the idea isn't physically possible."

She wouldn't quit without an explanation, so he gave one. "If it were a simple matter of changing to a new Cube, a job of only a few hours, we wouldn't even need to go to scout's power. The ship's accumulators could handle our minimum emergency load. But troubleshooting and repairs, in place..." He shook his head. "No telling how long that might take. Weeks? Months? We could run out of power totally."

And no, the scout's Cube couldn't be installed in *Hare*, because of the differing sizes: "I'm a fair machinist, but all those adapters? Again, the situation simply doesn't give us enough time."

Glaring, although Pope certainly wasn't to blame for her frustration, Lisele stood. "Galley break time. Sit in for me?" At his nod, she added, "Anything you'd like me to bring up for you?"

He smiled. "At this point, and the hell with regs for the moment, I could use a beer. If you can locate a cold one."

She could, and did. Then she asked questions about putting ships into orbit. Except for the math part, such maneuvers didn't seem to be Darwin Pope's specialty. So she'd have to ask the skipper.

As *March Hare* came closer to Goal Star, Tinhead gave more and better information. The system contained two gas giants, but the smaller was far to port of the ship's course, and maybe not massive enough for its needs. Whereas Jumbo, the one first spotted, was only slightly to starboard and now well on the far side of its primary. "So we can pass the star if we like," said Katmai Delarov, "and have a chance for some kind of look at the inner planets, before deciding whether to orbit Jumbo or not."

Accordingly, there were two opportunities that could be taken, to stop in this system, before Lisele's own suggestion might be considered.

She made a mental shrug. Because now that she thought about it, Lisele wasn't all that enthusiastic about riding freeze for a long time, and no guarantees. Maybe waking up to a future in which she knew no one but her shipmates?

So, reconsidering, she said, "That's good. The more choices we have, the better."

Running deceleration as hard as the Cube would give it without alarm-noted protests, *March Hare* slowed into Goal Star's reach of space. On this side of the system no large planets appeared; Jumbo and Junior now rode the far quadrants.

So for a time, noting only cosmic debris of little importance, Lisele and her captain waited. Until closer approach might tell them something about the two inner, smaller, detected planets.

One was too far out to be habitable; well, Tinhead had already indicated as much. The other, though: Sitdown, they'd called it, possibly hoping the naming would influence its characteristics. But as yet, even hi-mag didn't show enough detail to call it livable or not. Another day or two might tell. Leaving watch-duty, Lisele wished the waiting could be over.

Waking up, she felt good. She showered, then checked the mirror to see how she looked. Not too bad; some of her hair was nearing a centimeter in length while other parts were barely poking through, but in another month the differences wouldn't show, to speak of. And meanwhile only she and the captain and Darwin Pope, who was only beginning to sprout at all, were around to notice. So, good enough. When the rest of the crew was roused, the three now awake would, by comparison, look perfect!

She reported to Control, hoping for new data. There wasn't much. Nearest approach to the possibly-habitable world Sitdown was nearly a standard day away. And that would be a mere fly-by, anyway. Jumbo, where *March Hare* might grab orbit, was some days farther.

Lisele sighed. Tregare had told her how military life was: all "Hurry up and wait!" And though this situation wasn't exactly military, she began to see what her father had meant.

Cranking up hi-mag she looked at Sitdown again, and spotted new detail. Definitely not a Venus-type world, cooking under miles of CO_2. For now, clearer as the moments passed, Lisele saw swirls of color! Cloud masses, as on Earth? Surface features, even? She couldn't be sure. But she checked to be sure the monitor was still taping this view.

And consulted Tinhead again. Yes, the nearest approach still checked at slightly under a third of a million kilos—about the distance from Earth to Luna. At that point they should get a pretty good idea of conditions on Sitdown; from here, though, the temperature readings weren't steady enough to tell much.

The next day, as *March Hare* closed on Sitdown, all three persons sat in Control. Running the past few days' tapes at fast speed, compressing hours to minutes, Delarov said, "You can see the overall rotation, this way. Some of my figures aren't too accurate yet, because we don't have enough of an observational baseline. But if you're interested . . ."

Lisele was, and Pope also, so the captain went on, "Axial tilt looks to be slightly more than a radian."

Pope nodded. "Interesting. In other words, by definition the planet has no such things as Temperate Zones."

Puzzled, Lisele said, "Why not?" Instead of answering, he asked her to define the term. All right: the tropic zone was the belt where sometimes the sun could shine straight down; the frigid zones were where there could be one or more full days of light or darkness. "And Temperate's everything in between."

Except for combat and navigational sims, the *Hare*'s Tinhead wasn't much for screen graphics. But with a little mild-voiced cursing, Pope punched up a line drawing: a circle representing a planet, with lines showing its axis, equator, and its light and dark sides. Then, slowly, he tilted axis and equator. "So you see, when tilt reaches pi-over-four radians— half a right angle—tropics and frigid zones meet; the temperate zone disappears."

"And when it's more, like this world?"

"Then the extremes overlap, giving two belts that in

Earth terms can be tropic *or* frigid, with temperate periods in between." He waved off further questions. "No, I haven't calculated the ratio of these stages for this planet. If you like, I'll save this program and you can check it for yourself."

Lisele nodded, and Delarov, looking bemused, continued. "Goal Star's mass and luminosity are less than Sol's but Sitdown's orbit is smaller than Earth's, so maybe those things will even out. I rough-guess a year of three hundred Earth days, but Sitdown's own day is something like thirty hours. I—"

Lisele's comm-panel beeped, and showed a blinking light. She looked, unbelieving. On one of the aud-vid channels, used for offship communication, a signal was showing.

IX

Screen and speakers, when she brought them on line, gave only rapidly shifting patterns of varying pulses. She twiddled sync frequencies; no luck. While Delarov and Pope watched but said nothing, Lisele put Tinhead to sampling input.

No results there, either, so it wasn't computer code. She squinted at the screen: the stuff was too slow for video signal. So what *was* it?

"Try digitalized voice. Ships don't use it much now, but they did for a time."

Until the captain spoke, Lisele hadn't realized she was making her guesses out loud. "Oh, sure," and now, cutting the screen, she set Tinhead to identifying—decoding—the possible modulation pattern. Whoops and squawks came from the speaker—then, click-ridden and barely intelligible, a voice.

"—months now, ship's time, and damn all, we're stuck! The Drive—" A burst of static hash. "—to fix it with. Bad landing; green pilot, with all the good ones dead."

Sometimes the words came clearly, then voice quality would drop and meaning vanish. "Black, dirty mutiny! . . . left Earth in New Year Ten, thirteenth ship out from Earth . . . to carry UET's emblem . . . did a lot of joking about our number, some better-natured than others . . . two fine planets, coordinates in our log and we'll share finders' bonus with any ship that—"

"That's a tape," Lisele said. "Can't be live voice."

"It's neither," said Delarov. "New Year *Ten*, he said. That's at least a century ago. Even allowing for t/t_0 during the ship's time it took them to get here, that recording can't be less than fifty years old." The captain shook her head. "It's a disk; tapes don't hold up that long. And even so, it's badly deteriorated. Perhaps with computer enhancement . . ."

The voice quality improved. "—farther out than anyone before, yes. Everybody saw the orders before we signed, though, and nobody asked for transfers. After the second new world we found . . . the lower ratings complaining . . . the unrateds, they *always* bitch, so why should we—"

Pope began to say something, but again the voice came up. "—the officers, and us Chief Ratings; we didn't worry. I was in Comm . . . turned out, Navigation was where we needed—"

Partly it made sense, but not enough. "—mutiny, details are in the log. Crew, over a hundred, only forty-three lived to reach—"

The signal's energy was dropping; Lisele boosted her input level. "This *hellhole!* Animals here are poison . . . two unrateds dead that way. If the meat tank had failed—"

"Incompatible amino acids, possibly," said Darwin Pope. "Or poisonous trace elements in deadly quantities. Bad luck; most colony worlds have had better."

"—except for the purple ones. But even the harmless plants are only good for calories and no . . . better than nothing . . . climate's fierce . . . way the poles tilt; I'm not sure . . . see when you get here."

A pause came; the channel spouted noise without message. Then, with an abrupt surge, the voice came in. "To any ship passing . . . signal range. Acting Captain Orval Sprague, speaking for the *General Patton* . . . down on the only habitable planet, if you call it that . . . best guess is groundside date New Year Sixty. We've been here about six months, ship's time, and damn all, we're stuck! The Drive's down, and no spare nodes—or enough extra facet plugs to fix the ones we have. We—"

Lisele punched for Stop. "It's repeating now."

Katmai Delarov nodded. "Yes. But let's record the message several more times, run all versions through the computer in parallel, for congruence, and see if it has more to tell us."

"Sure." *Now why didn't I think of that?*

What Lisele did think of, though, was to lay down a directional scan, and pinpoint on Sitdown's surface the source of the signal. Then, needing to tie it down so she could find it again, she put radar to looking for contour landmarks.

She got lucky. To the west, as defined by the planet's rotation, lay a deep canyon that when viewed as running north-south, had a slight easterly slant. And not too distant from the signal's origin, roughly at east-northeast and all by itself in relatively flat terrain, stood the biggest mountain within scanning range. Twice as high, at least, as Earth's Everest.

So when Captain Delarov asked some inevitable questions, Lisele enjoyed coming up with good answers.

Delarov nodded. "Good; we can find it when we need it. The question is, do we try to speak that ship now, let them know we're here? Or wait and make our visit unannounced?"

"Visit? How?" Lisele's startled query showed her surprise.

"Of course, visit. In the scout, I'd think. After we've made orbit around Jumbo."

"But what good—?"

"You heard the man. That ship still has power. And—"

"Did have," said Darwin Pope. "Present condition, we can't know. I've been figuring out how long it's been there. Do either of you know what New Year it is now?"

Lisele thought. In the year 2005, when United Energy and Transport took roughshod control of North America, it began its own chronology with New Year One. "Depends. What *real* year is it now, groundside time?"

"Twenty-one-seventeen, I believe. Right, captain?"

"If our t/t_0 calculations are, for our new Drive."

"New Year a hundred and twelve, then," Lisele said. "So if that man had his own numbers straight, the ship's been down for fifty-two years. But—" Another thought struck. "We know it has *some* power; the beacon's working. And for them to be still alive, so's their meat tank. Whatever that is."

Pope shook his head. "But are they alive? We don't

know." Then he had to explain the meat tank: growth of
animal tissue in a bath of synthetic nutrients, with highly
efficient recycling. "First done nearly two centuries ago,
using a bit of a chicken's heart. The earlier ships used that
process, before they began transporting meat animals in
frozen-zygote form."

Obviously impatient, the captain finally got a word in.
"The point is, I see a way to get us out of this mess, and
maybe that ship's survivors, too. If any."

"Them?" In Lisele's mind, alarms rang. "They're Uties,
you know. You heard what Sprague said. We'd have to—" But
rather then belabor the obvious, she said, "What's your
plan?"

"Plans, is more like it." Katmai Delarov grinned. "If the
marooned crew hasn't survived, we take the ship's Cube out
to *March Hare*. Wrapped for thermal insulation and riding
outside the scout, it won't warm up appreciably. With luck,
its remaining charge plus what we can feed it from our own,
possibly even the scoutship's, will be enough to activate our
FTL Drive."

"Or," said Lisele, "what the Chief told me, earlier. Use
the *Patton*'s cube to keep *Hare* alive while he fixes ours. Still,
though—supposing there *are* survivors?"

"Then we dicker. For their Cube, we offer to take as
many directly to Earth, either in freeze or jampacked to the
limit, as we can manage." Before Lisele could voice her next
objection, Delarov answered it. "We'd have to land our ship
here, anyway. So we'd leave the scout to power all their
essentials, and promise rescue to the left-behinds. On an
FTL schedule."

"And what," said Darwin Pope, "if they don't trust us,
and won't cooperate?"

The captain shrugged. "To that one, I don't have an
answer."

Lisele said, "There's one other way. It means going
home at STL, but it could work." With the others waiting,
she tried to think her idea together quickly. "The Drive
nodes. Theirs are shot; ours aren't. And that's one thing that
hasn't changed—circuits or fittings, any of it—since the first
ship UET stole from the Shrakken. I know, because until
Hagen Trent got one of *Inconnu Deux*'s back to top perfor-
mance, Tregare was talking about putting a Shrakken unit in."
She added, realizing that the information wasn't important

here, "The Tsa use a different physical design; same functions, though."

Delarov frowned. "All this assumes the grounded ship's Cube has enough charge to make its Drive function. What if—"

Darwin Pope beat Lisele to that answer. "Charge can be transferred. From *Hare* to the scout to the *Patton*, as many round trips as necessary." He turned to Lisele. "But what if the colony has grown—beyond the numbers that ship can transport? Even including freeze?"

Briefly she was stumped. Then, "It can't have, not that much. How many people can this meat tank thing support? And then there's what the captain said, before: leave our scout, with its Cube charged up all the way, to power their needs."

Delarov waved a hand. "Enough. I'm drowning in alternatives. Let me think them over, and perhaps by the time we reach orbit, they'll make sense to me. But for now, I can do without *any* further suggestions."

The captain's luck, apparently, was out. A channel-buzzer bleeped, and when Lisele automatically turned it on, a voice spoke. Live, this one; distorted a little, but not with the clicks or hash of deterioration.

"Hello the ship up there. Somebody finally paid attention to the detectors, and called me. Cray Malden, in command of the *General Patton*. No picture, and I can't find your beacon if you have one, but I have your course and position."

All three sat, saying nothing, as the man continued. "Well, come in please, damn you! Talk, at least. You can't just go on by and leave us here!"

Delarov reached for the Talk switch, but Lisele's hand was there first. "No. Let *me*?"

Looking mildly irritated, the captain said, "Whatever for?"

"Because they're still UET down there." That wasn't good enough, so Lisele added, "Do either of you play poker?" Two headshakes. "Well, I do. I've played in games with my father, Bran Tregare. And sometimes I even win."

The captain looked puzzled, but Darwin Pope said, "I think I see what she means. This is a job for someone who doesn't necessarily tell everything she knows."

With a grateful look to the Chief Engineer, quickly
Lisele explained. "They mustn't know we're not UET. Peace
be thanked, they can't read our beacon." Belatedly, just in
case, she shut down that circuit. "*March Hare* isn't a UET
ship's name, so we'll be—oh, anything built later than when
they left Earth. I know—the *Tamurlaine*, the ship Tregare
took and renamed *Inconnu*.

"Let's see—I can be who I am, because Tregare came
along after their time, too, and it'll make it simpler when we
return here. I'm a Third rating, in Comm and Nav."

Something else, though. Oh, yes. "They can't know
about FTL, the Hoyfarul Drive. So until we make sure the
telling would help *our* edge, let's keep that just to ourselves."

Deciding she had most of it straight now, Lisele opened
transmission to groundside. After identifying the ship and
herself, she felt comfortable enough with the time-delays
between responses to get down to the grits.

"Yes, the *Tamurlaine*." Rapidly thinking in Long View
terms, she picked a number. "Left Earth in New Year Ninety-
one. Stops enroute were Far Corner and Franklin's Jump."
Seeing disapproval on the captain's face, Lisele briefly cut the
Talk switch and said, "I don't have time to figure a route that
works. But *they* won't know the difference!"

Transmitting again, she said, "Captain Delarov's not
available just now." Oh, peace! Her first real mistake—for
UET had never allowed command to women. So she said,
frowning toward the others to ensure their attention, "He's
sleeping now. He hasn't been feeling too well. But he's
improving; I'm sure he'll be all right in another day or two."
Delarov nodded, so Lisele knew she'd got the point, and
went on, "Our present mission has Security aspects, so you'll
understand why I can't discuss it. But," overriding groundside's
attempts to interrupt, "I can say that it involves the gas giant,
ahead on our present course."

She hadn't paid much heed to Cray Malden's queries and
comments; maybe it was time to give him a little jelly for his
bread. He was saying, "—coming here, aren't you? We're
short of so many things, or out of them entirely. Medical
supplies, for instance. How soon—?"

Katmai Delarov shook her head, so Lisele answered,
"That information isn't available yet. It will be the captain's
decision, of course." And the captain's look told Lisele that it

was time to quit chattering and get some data on her own account. So she said, "According to standard procedure, we're ready to receive and record your status report. Go ahead, please."

"I'm afraid I don't have one," said the voice from groundside. "Not in official form, anyway."

Delarov leaned forward. "Comm officer here. Then just tell it; I'll boil it down shipshape for the captain." Smiling, she sat back again, and Lisele thought, *maybe she hasn't played poker, but I bet she could learn in a hurry!*

"You've read our beacon message, I guess," said Malden. "That disk was recorded about fifty-two Earth years ago; call it sixty-three of ours, here. I suppose we should have kept it updated, but there didn't seem to be much point."

Lisele spoke next. "That was then. How are things *now*?"

The man's voice held a decidedly unpleasant whine. "But it all ties in, you see. We got here, best we could, with forty-three of us alive. Twelve men, thirty-one women: on account of, men got killed more, putting down that dirty mutiny. Names and ranks, dead and living, you can take off a log readout when you get here." For long seconds the channel carried only the hiss of stray electrons; then Malden said, "Down here we lost some at first, gained none back until the women's contraceptive implants began to wear off. Before that, you might say it was fun but no profit. We—" Whatever he'd intended to say, he didn't finish it.

"*Present* status, we're asking now." Delarov again.

Signal delay, as *March Hare* receded from the planet, was increasing. "Population, yes. Two hundred and fifty, at a rough estimate. With infant mortality, and the submissuals coming up soon, it's hard to project a firm total for very long in advance." A pause, and then, "Call it two-fifty. Or come back and count us yourself, why don't you?"

Delarov gestured; in response, Lisele cut the Talk switch. "Submissuals?" the captain said. "What could those be?"

Darwin Pope shrugged. "I don't think this is the time to ask questions."

Digesting what they'd heard from groundside, neither Delarov nor Lisele found a comment, before Malden said, "If that's all you need, I'll power down. Leave the beacon on for you, so you can find us. If your captain wants to." The whining again.

Lisele thought of one more thing. "Captain Malden? Talking about the time of landing here, you keep saying 'we'. Do you mean you were—?"

Delay didn't soften the man's chuckle. "That's right. Of all us down here, I'm the only one alive, from when the *Patton* landed. And I've kept the Regs alive, too!"

Abruptly, his signal vanished. Lisele cut the channel. Turning to the others, she said, "That's our basic, born-and-bred Utie, in charge down there. And peace only knows what he's made the rest of them into!"

X

Leaving the planet behind, *March Hare* continued its sedate deceleration toward rendezvous with Jumbo. Darwin Pope had taken his turn in the galley, preparing a meal and bringing it up to Control. Now he and Captain Delarov and Lisele ate together, no one talking much.

Over coffee, Delarov spoke up. "Lisele? You did very well, I thought, in dealing with groundside. Yet I'm puzzled. Why did you feel it necessary to take over the communication, without prior discussion?"

Because there wasn't *time;* the skipper should know that much. No point, though, in arguing. Instead, "One thing, captain. Lisele is for when we're being unofficial. When I'm getting chewed out, the name is Moray. Liesel Selene Moray. It's on the ship's roster."

With a nod, Delarov said, "I see. But you're not getting chewed out, Moray. I'm asking for information I need to know. Why did you feel that I couldn't deal with the *Patton*?"

"Because—" Oh, *how* to explain it? "Because you said, yourself, Tregare civilized the Slaughterhouse before you'd finished your first year there. You never had to—"

She wasn't saying it right. "I grew up with Rissa and Tregare; they'd fought UET all their lives and they *think* that way. Sure, when all the big part happened I was too young to know. But all my life I guess it's sunk in, at some level."

Shaking her head, she tried to explain the rest of it.

"Because when that peace-crapping Utie came on the horn and started talking, it seemed to come naturally, how to deal with him." She paused. "Maybe I was wrong; if I was, I'm sorry. But I thought you might not know, so I had to try."

Delarov's silence lasted for a time. Then she said, "I see. Perhaps not all of it, but that your motives were good. Very well. You're overdue for sleep. Why don't you go get some?"

Done eating now, Lisele said, "Sure, captain," and left.

Sixty-five hours later, *March Hare* was nearing Jumbo and was slowed enough to have a good choice of orbits. The main thing was to park well clear of the huge planet's radiation belts—because coasting with the Drive off, the ship would have no protection. Not necessarily outside all the belts; between them would do just as well.

Coming out from Earth, Lisele had seen gas giants at fairly close range: Jupiter and one of its neighbors—she couldn't remember which one, now. According to Tinhead, Jumbo had some size on Big Jupe, but it looked much the same: oblate, ruddy-banded, with obvious surface storms. Watching the planet grown vast in the forward screens, Lisele felt the fascination of the spectacle it made, but right now, other things were more important.

"Our orbit needs to tilt," Delarov said, "toward Sitdown. Or toward Goal Star if you like; from out here it's the same thing. So that when we're behind Jumbo with respect to Sitdown, we'll be clear of the ecliptic, not blocked from communication with the scoutship. I'd hoped to synchronize with Sitdown's day or a multiple of it, but those slots are either loaded with debris or too near the hotbelts."

Yes; Sitdown's own rotation would limit talk-time more than anyone liked; they didn't need extra blockage from Jumbo. Lisele considered the other parameter: time delay. At roughly a billion kilos, one-way transmission time was almost an hour. Even using tape, sending everything by the fast-burst method so that transmission time was negligible . . . Well, let's see now. Sitdown's basic day was roughly thirty hours; half of that was fifteen, but of course you couldn't expect to punch offworld signals through—or receive them—at angles too close to the horizon.

How close? She wasn't certain, and Delarov looked too busy to be bothered with non-urgent questions. So Lisele's best guess was that during one of Sitdown's thirty-hour days,

communication between ship and scout could be no more
than six two-way exchanges. Maybe seven, with precise scheduling and good luck—but she wouldn't bet any real money on
that seventh.

Delarov was guiding *Hare* in toward orbit. Lisele was
the hot pilot when it came to emergency tactics she'd picked
up from Tregare's recorded logs, things that Delarov had had
no reason or opportunity to learn. But in this delicate matter
of balancing velocity against gravity to achieve an "at rest"
state, she had theoretical background but no practice at all.

So she sat, watching and making mental notes, while
Katmai Delarov curved *March Hare*'s path in, toward and
then around their chosen primary. She got her orbital tilt by
approaching on a path slightly below the ecliptic, then making a slight upward course change. And how the woman
chose the exact moment to initiate that change, Lisele hadn't
the faintest idea!

But not much later, the captain hit the intercom switch
and called down to Darwin Pope in the Drive room. "On
count, cut Drive. Five, four, three, two, one—CUT!"

As the great engine's hum dropped to almost-subliminal
levels, gravity dwindled, also. Somehow, even knowing beforehand that being in orbit would be like a constant state of
weightless Turnover, Lisele was caught by surprise.

She adjusted quickly enough; zero-gee had never affect-
ed her adversely. But she wondered how it might be for the
crew members, wakened to go through radiation sickness
with no gravs! *If we'd been thinking, we could have got them
through all that, one or two at a time, before we got here.*

Darwin Pope, when he came upship to Control, voiced
similar concerns. "Which of the crew do you plan to rouse,
captain? To return to that planet, I mean. And how large a
group, in any one batch, can we nurse through the sickness?"

Delarov scratched her head. "Besides the three of us,
Mei and Houk have been through the ordeal. That leaves ten
to go. I haven't made up my mind yet, who goes on the scout
and who doesn't, but one thing I have decided." And when
nobody asked, she said, "While I'm making those choices,
we'll see *everyone* through the sickness and out of it. So that
later, when we might not have time for such measures, we
won't need it."

*   *   *

Next ship's day the captain still wasn't certain who should ride the scout back to Sitdown. "I'm thinking about it," she told Lisele. "If you have any advice, I'd like to hear it."

What Katmai Delarov did know, was who would *not* leave *March Hare* to reconnoiter the situation with UET's leftovers. "So they're the first we'll rouse. Get them up, get them well, put them back in freeze. Then we can consider the rest of the lot."

So Lisele found herself, along with Pope and Delarov, tending overlapping relays of radiation victims: on the average, five days each, with only two days in the middle being bad enough to need a great deal of care. There'd be two people not yet really sick, two in bad shape, and two mostly recovered.

"For the duration" the skipper put on point-two gee. It widened the ship's orbit, but not excessively.

Lisele had never really come to know Theotis Fredericks or Eldros Hassan; she didn't now, either. She took her turns nursing them through the nausea and convulsions; then they were gone again. Up and sick and well and down: right you are, skipper.

And the same routine with Jenise Rorvik and Melaine Holmbach from *Inconnu Deux*. These women Lisele did know, especially Jenise who had shared the long trek around Shaarbant. But Delarov scheduled them back into freeze, so that was that.

At one point, argument arose. Delarov wanted Anders Kobolak to pilot the scoutship, but his wife Alina Rostadt was scheduled to return to freeze. Lisele shook her head. "It won't work, captain. You don't know Anders. He took a bad hit, when his sister died with my uncle Ivan. A while there, we weren't sure he'd pull out of it. No—either Alina's with him, or he's no good to you."

Slowly, the captain nodded. "You know these people. I suppose I must take your word about them."

Lisele nearly said, "You'd better!" But didn't. The upshot was that Anders and Alina were left as last to be revived. Decisions about them could be made when the time came.

Before, though, next up were Alys Molyneux and Naomi Gray, both Engineering aides to Darwin Pope. Molyneux,

blond and robust, got through the illness better than most—
but took the incident baldness as a personal insult, and
sulked accordingly. The other woman—thin, only in her
mid-thirties but looking older—came near to dying before
her fever could be controlled, but never complained.

Then it was the turn of Arlen Limmer and of Comm
Chief Eduin Brower. Lisele didn't expect the bulky Chief to
give trouble, and he didn't. Arlen, she had worried about; he
was nice, and she liked him, but his weak point was that he'd
never had to *endure* much of anything. So how would he
handle this?

Through the worst of it, better than Lisele had expected.
Then, though, recovering but suddenly bald, stubbornly he
wore a cap. When Lisele saw it on him, she said, "Arlen, you
don't need that thing."

Grumpy voice: "I'll wear it if I want to."

She couldn't help but laugh. "Of course you can. But you
don't look any worse than the rest of us, at that stage. So why
bother?"

For the first time he took a careful look at the irregular, tufted outline her hair showed. *Messy*, she thought,
was the operative word. Arlen said, "Yours all came out,
too?"

"Along with everybody else's, on this ship."

"Oh, *well*, then." From the bed, Arlen flung his cap at
the nearest wall. "That way, it's all right."

So she gave him a friendly kiss, and left feeling good
about the young man. Until it came to her mind, that it
would be nicer if Arlen didn't need a unanimous vote, to
know how he *felt*!

Last roused, Anders and Alina suffered through to recov-
ery. Then, in the temporary situation with nine persons up
and doing, Delarov called council.

"We don't yet know," she said, "whether we can deal
with the colony on Sitdown." Having explained that situation
earlier, she didn't repeat herself. "To find out, the scout has
to go there. My feeling is, it should carry its maximum
personnel complement." She turned to Lisele. "I believe
you've calculated the scout's travel time, from here to Sitdown?"

"Yes. With normal redline accel and decel, a little over
seventy-three hours."

Delarov nodded. "That agrees with my own estimate. So for such a short time, it's feasible to run a bit crowded. Eight people, say, won't tax six bunks too much." She paused, then said, "The question is, who goes?"

"And who stays?" said Anders Kobolak. "Awake, I mean."

Delarov smiled. "Awake? Myself, only. To conserve supplies. No emergency can arise, here, quickly enough that I couldn't rouse others, if need be."

Impatient now, Lisele said, "All right; who *does* go?"

Fingers twisting a tuft of hair that had outgrown the rest, Delarov said, "You, for one, if you agree. Because of your background, your assimilated knowledge of UET." Lisele nodded. "The Kobolaks, likewise." Anders signed assent. "Arlen Limmer and deWayne Houk." Lisele had misgivings about Houk, but—

From the look of Arlen, he was not only willing but eager. "Eduin Brower." The man looked both pleased and dismayed. "Plus Alys Molyneux and Naomi Gray, because I think Chief Houk is going to need some engineering assistance."

The captain paused. "Do I hear any objections? From the persons named, or otherwise?" No one spoke. "Then I think we have our landing crew set. So at this point, I'm afraid everyone else goes into freeze. Because it's vital that we conserve supplies."

Well, Lisele thought, one thing was certain. Poker player or not, Katmai Delarov knew how to conduct an operation.

As soon as deWayne Houk was revived and briefed, Delarov called council. "This is going to be a seminar, or orientation session, on keeping your stories straight when you get to Sitdown. Here are some of the parameters."

Since the *Patton*'s last contact with history was its departure from Earth in New Year Ten, Sitdown's Uties would know nothing of Escaped Ships or the Hidden Worlds they'd colonized. And certainly not that UET no longer ruled. The *Tamurlaine*'s personnel would be expected to know at least some of the names on UET's current Presiding Committee: Lisele had heard of Gairn Forbisher, that Committee's last Chairman, and Maita Pangreen, daughter of a previous one. "Aarem Zavole," said Eduin Brower. "And Hrodicken; I forget her first name. She was second gun, under Forbisher."

So far, so good. Now, UET terminology. "Kobolak," the captain said, "you'll be the *Tamurlaine*'s First Officer, not

First Hat. And don't forget the 'the,' which they use and we don't. They have my last name, as captain, but not my first. Since UET never gave command to women, you will keep in mind that your captain's name is *Karl* Delarov. But of course Karl will never speak over the comm-link; I will. Under my own name, to keep things simple; they can assume the captain and I are married. Also—"

"Just a minute!" Lisele had remembered something. "The tattoo."

"What?" Delarov looked puzzled.

Eduin Brower said, "She's right. UET officers had their insignia of rank tattooed on their left cheeks. Unless we have somebody who can do the job, and remembers those designs well enough to fake it, Kobolak won't pass for any First Officer." He looked over to Lisele. "That what you meant, youngster?"

She nodded. Then another idea came. "Why not a Third Officer, instead of First? And—and promoted from a Chief rating, not too long ago? In space, when our original Third— oh, what *did* happen to him?"

Anders Kobolak grinned. "He went outship to replace a broken antenna. And then—" He spread his hands. "Who knows? Up in Control they heard him yelling as he drifted away, but he didn't say what happened." With a mock frown, he spoke in very self-righteous tones. "Carelessness has a thousand ways of killing."

Delarov nodded. "It's good; I like it. Solves the tattoo problem, anyway." Her brows raised. "What was his name? Surely we should know that, in case someone asks."

It was becoming a game now, Lisele thought, and the way everyone was getting into it, as good as dress rehearsal for a play. For no reason she could identify, she said, "Ivan Marchant." Then, "Well, he's dead, and if just using his name can help us, he'd like that."

"Good enough reason," said Delarov. "Now, then—" So she went over some additional matters. These Uties knew only STL ships with hundred-person crews, so that's what the *Tamurlaine* had to be. Control and Engineering each had one officer in charge with a First, Second, and Third working watches, so names had to be put to these positions. "Just in case," the captain said. "What we can't afford is contradictions."

"Too true," said Brower. He was punching all the agreed

fictions into Tinhead; later, everyone would have readouts to study.

They went through three more major items. First, the state of things on Earth at the *Tamurlaine*'s departure date: Houk, Brower and Gray provided most of that information. Then the ship's route and stopovers: suddenly Far Corner and Franklin's Jump acquired new coordinates that *would* fit the timing.

And finally the ranks and titles of the entire scout-riding group. Molyneux and Gray were Second and Third Engineer, respectively. Houk, not Drive Chief but Drive Tech, First. Brower and Rostadt both to be rated Comm-techs. Kobolak the new Third Officer, as previously agreed. Arlen agreed to be a Second rating in navigation.

To fit the circumstances, Lisele's recorded bio-age was upped from fifteen to eighteen. Her status became that of a recent cadet, now holding a Third rating, and her trainee specialties were Comm and Nav. "Gunnery, too," she said.

Waiting while the most recent revivees came back to nearly full vigor, the group had two more such meetings. Little new ground was broken, but some earlier constructs underwent refinement. And then came time, with everything aboard the scoutship fine-combed to show no contradictions, that *March Hare* had its best velocity vector for the scout's launching.

So with Anders Kobolak in First Pilot's seat, the small craft exited to space. *Sitdown, here we come!*

XI

From the way Anders flicked the scout out of its berthing bay, then briefly overcontrolled as he set his course, Lisele knew this smaller model was more agile than the ones he and she were used to. And that the difference had surprised him. "A little twitchy, is it?" she said.

He grinned at her. "You'll find out, when it's your turn. I'm assigning you the next watch, and then Arlen."

She shrugged. "Just riding herd on it, in mid-course, won't show me much."

"Turnover will, though. And it comes during your second tour of duty." Now the man looked positively smug. "You might want to practice some simulated landings, too."

"Me?" What was going on, here?

"Who else? I haven't landed a scoutship since before the *Deux* left Earth; I don't think Arlen ever has. But for two-three months, back on Shaarbant, you had Tregare's remaining scout on a regular milk run between Sassden and Shtegel."

Well, that much was true; Lisele nodded. "I'll practice."

"So will Arlen and I, of course. Just in case. But you're my first choice."

She nodded. "Don't worry; I'll do it."

She left to have a snack; this mission had her stomach too jumpy for full meals. The scout contained no galley as such: there was a cubby for food preparation, and one small table. Alina Rostadt sat there now, with an emptied plate and a full cup. "Join you?" Rostadt nodded, so Lisele also sat.

Between bites, she said, "Could you do me a favor?"

"I imagine so. What is it?"

Feeling an odd embarrassment, Lisele pulled at one of the longer tufts of her irregular growth of hair. "This is how it comes back in; yours'll be the same way. Could you cut it back to look more even, all over, and maybe trim the edges neater, sides and back?"

Alina smiled. "Surely. When I need it, you can do the same for me." So a few minutes later, the dinette became a barber shop; at the end of the process Lisele wore a reasonably smooth cap of short hair—about two centimeters—and the edges were indeed neatened. Looking at the hand-held mirror, she realized what she saw. Quite by accident, she would arrive on Sitdown with a standard UET cadet haircut.

There'd been some discussion of the "appearance problem." Consensus was that partial truth would make the best story: the *Tamurlaine* had narrowly escaped the radiating gravitational anomaly, and of the scout's crew of eight, only deWayne Houk and Lisele had been shielded, fortuitously, from the effects. How many more of the fictitious hundred had also been lucky? "Well, how about twenty, give or take a couple?" said Eduin Brower. So, if asked, that was the way the question would be answered.

For the trip's duration, Captain Delarov specified a communications sked: four-hour intervals. At the first of these, all the scout's crew were awake and present. There weren't enough seats to go around, so deWayne Houk stood leaning over Lisele's position while Alys Molyneux sat on the deck beside Anders Kobolak's. Houk had his hand on Lisele's arm, but the move might not be on purpose, so she didn't say anything except "Excuse me." And moved her arm free of his touch.

". . . roused Mei again," the captain was saying. "Both because she's our best at committing persons to freeze, and in order to bring her up to date on our current situation. But now she's putting Darwin down once more, and then herself. So as you know, from now on I'll be your only contact."

She paused. "I'll keep our channels open at all times, of course. And set to record if I'm asleep, or absent for other reasons. In particular I want you to forward, for recording, *all* communications you receive from Sitdown as you approach that planet." Another pause. "No such contact yet, I take it?"

Anders Kobolak affirmed the captain's guess; Arlen Limmer added, "We're in no hurry to talk to those Uties. When we get there, that's time enough."

Before Delarov could answer, Eduin Brower spoke. "You got you a point, Limmer. But not what you think. Uties don't call each other that, so we don't either. You get it?"

"I think *I* do," said Naomi Gray. "When the *Patton* left Earth, that term probably didn't exist. It's a dissident invention, and just by our tone of voice we can't even say it without sneering. I agree with Chief Brower; we have to wipe the word from our vocabularies."

It was the most talk Lisele had heard from this quiet woman, and it impressed her. She said, "I vote the same way."

She could visualize Delarov's nod, before the captain said, "Another discrepancy caught. I wonder how many more there'll be, that we may overlook." Her sigh was audible; then she said, "If there's nothing else, for now, this is Delarov, signing out."

Lisele's first watch brought no problems. She did run sims, on maneuvers as well as landings, and began to get the measure of this new spacecraft. When Arlen Limmer relieved her, she was hungry again.

At the cooking cubby she found Eduin Brower cursing in a monotone. "Damn; I can't get the timing right!"

Lisele saw the mess he'd taken from frozen to charred. "Here; let me do one for you." When she'd prepared two packets, they ate without talking much. While she dawdled over coffee, Brower left.

"Well. Hello, Moray." She looked up, as deWayne Houk came to sit alongside her. "It's been time, hasn't it? Time to think more, might be."

As he sipped coffee, she said, "Think? About what?"

"Us, could be. Your young fella, bald he doesn't look so much; I'm right?" He ran a hand over his own hair. "Your own self, and me, we look better."

Houk's colorless mop, now hanging raggedly over ears and nape, didn't strike Lisele as more than marginally presentable. She said, "If you want to pass for a UET Drive-tech you'd better get someone to cut that for you. It's getting scraggly."

"Well, sure. I'd like *you* to do for me." The man put his palm to her cheek, fingers curled behind her ear and stroking the skin there. "Yes, I like that."

"I wasn't volunteering." Now as he turned to face her his right hand clasped the top of her left shoulder, near the neck, with fingers kneading.

Peace take the man! Always before when he'd touched her, he'd made it seem accidental, and acted as if he didn't notice.

Now, though: for a moment she panicked; then, almost without volition her right hand reached across to curl around his third and fourth fingers. He was saying something, how he knew she'd come around and be sensible: "—young sprout like you needs a man as knows what's what; that's all." So she tightened her grasp and bent his two fingers back until, abruptly, his words stopped.

Immediately she released the punishing hold. "Chief Houk? A personal question?"

Mumbling around the stressed fingers he'd jammed into his mouth to soothe them, he said, "Ask the hell away!"

"What's your proficiency in unarmed combat?" He didn't answer, so she said, "Before you put a hand on me again, I think you'd better brush up." Her thoughts eddied. *It wasn't me, doing that. Not really. It's what I've got from Rissa, just knowing her all this time.*

She was certain of it; Lisele's unprecedented act was precisely what her mother would have done. Or close...

But Rissa wasn't here, and Lisele was, stuck with Houk's presence for the mission's duration. So she said, "Chief? Truce. Okay?"

"Begging heaven's love, what *for*?"

"Because when we get to Sitdown there's just eight of us and a lot of *them*. If we can't depend on each other, I don't give us much chance."

"So now, you hurting me and all, it's for us to be chums? Houk, stay off me but guard my back? Is that it?"

Actually his statement wasn't unfair. Carefully, Lisele said, "And the other way, too, don't forget. I guard yours. We all do that, every one of us. If we want to stay alive."

She could see him thinking about it, before he said, "All right. We don't need to like, just to trust. I can do that." He made a grimace. "You said I should have a haircut!"

"Yes; I did." Not especially wanting the job, Lisele borrowed scissors from Alina and trimmed deWayne Houk's hair to something like UET-officer standards.

She saw no point in telling anyone about the incident, so she didn't. Houk, she decided, probably thought she had; any time they met in line of duty, he had a way of looking first at her and then at anyone else who was present, as if looking for signs of telltale knowledge.

Well, that was *his* problem.

Near the middle of Lisele's second watch trick, as scheduled, the time came for Turnover. Because this was a short haul, most of the gear had been kept battened down pretty well. Still, Anders Kobolak directed a last-minute inspection before the crew strapped in. He wanted Limmer and Brower on duty with Lisele and himself, so the other four drew lots for the two remaining seats. Looking sulky, as usual, Alys Molyneux followed Alina Rostadt as the two losers went to strap down in bunks.

A fullsized ship, Lisele knew, could make Turnover by pivoting on any chosen transverse axis. All it took was proper

balancing of the three side-thrusting aux-Drive nodes that
made a hexagon with the main ones. A scoutship, though,
carried only one lateral thrustor, so the rotational axis was
fixed.

Out in clear space and on a straightline course, the
restriction wouldn't matter. But now their course was curved,
a geodesic, and to keep navigation simple, rotation had to be
in the geodesic's plane. Well ahead of time, then, she slowly
and gently turned the scout around its long axis, until side-
thrust would be in that plane. Then she looked over to
Anders. "Alignment complete, sir. Ready to swing ship, on
the count."

To her surprise, he was grinning. "Didn't realize you
knew that part. In another five minutes or so, I was expecting
to talk you through it. When did you—"

She shook her head. "I can't remember. On Shaarbant,
sometime, though. Sitting around a fire, probably, done with
eating but too early for sleep. We did a lot of talking, that
way. And some of the best of it was Tregare telling us all
kinds of things. Like this move I just made." Thinking back,
she said, "You have to understand: that was one peacetwisting *long* walk we took, there."

Twenty minutes later, Lisele made Turnover as if she'd
been doing it all her life.

Working different watch tricks, Lisele and Arlen didn't
see each other very much. When they did, it was usually in
the small dining area, with others coming and going. She
knew he wanted a private talk, here on the scout before they
went groundside and had the Uties—oops, the *Patton*'s crew—
to deal with. But the occasion didn't arise.

So during Kobolak's final watch on this journey, when
Eduin Brower joined the two of them just as Arlen had begun
to ask a question, Lisele took the initiative. "Arlen, I haven't
logged a Drive inspection yet. We're supposed to make at
least one. Have you done yours?"

First he looked puzzled; then his expression cleared. It
might take Arlen a little while, she thought, but he did catch
on. He said, "No, I haven't. Should we take care of it now?"

She made a show of checking her wrist chrono. "Might as
well." She stood, saying to Brower, "See you, Chief." Then
she and Arlen went downship to the cramped Drive room.

Entering, Arlen said, "You sure Houk won't turn up?"

"He's asleep. So are Gray and Molyneux. So—" Then he was hugging her, and began a kiss.

She cooperated for a time, then gently pulled back. "All right, Arlen. We've talked about us, some, before. I expect you want to know where we stand. Now, I mean. Before we all get mixed up in the groundside problems."

He nodded. "Yes. It was bad enough, you hedging all the time. But then Chief Houk started hanging around. I can't think what you see in that one, but—"

Involuntarily, she laughed. "I don't. See anything in him, I mean." How to put this? Without telling Arlen what had actually happened? After a pause, she said, "Don't worry about the Chief. He may have had some ideas for a little while, but he must have gotten over them. Hasn't bothered me lately, anyway."

"Well, then." Arlen didn't pull her close again, but his grasp firmed. "Where *do* we stand, Lisele?"

She thought. He was acting more grown up now. More in control of himself, and at the same time, not trying so much to dominate *her*.

She made up her mind. Showing him the bio-age reading on her wrist chrono, she said, "Until I'm a bio-sixteen I won't be lovers with you or anybody else. When I get to that mark, then if we both still want to, we can try it." Brows drawn down, she looked at him, waiting for what he would say.

"*Still* want to, you said."

"Yes."

"That's all right, then." Smiling, he initiated one of the best kisses he'd ever shown her. Then, as Lisele wondered if perhaps she shouldn't have made her terms a bit more flexible, Arlen released her and reached to take two sheets from a bulkhead-mounted clipboard. "Inspection forms. Anders won't expect these, but Comm Chief Brower might."

Again, Lisele had to laugh.

Even if she'd wanted to bed with Arlen just now, the mechanics of the situation would have been too embarrassing. The scout had five single bunks in a dormitory setup, plus a larger one in the more private compartment unofficially known as the "love cubby." As a matter of course, Anders and Alina sometimes disappeared for a time from public view, and Lisele wasn't certain that deWayne Houk and Naomi Gray hadn't been jointly absent now and then. But for herself, circumstances would have to be considerably less public!

Not far short of Sitdown, Anders Kobolak had Pilot seat. When Lisele came in, he moved to the aux position. "You sit First Pilot, but you don't have to do anything for a time. Until we're close to landing I'll run things from here."

She sat, and checked her indicators. "All right." His statements, and the monitors also, she meant.

An idea came; she said, "Anders? We've named this world Sitdown. But we don't live there; they do. I wonder what *they've* named it."

Kobolak shook his head. Eduin Brower said, "That first fella, on the wornout record, mostly called it Hellhole."

Soft-voiced, Alina Rostadt put in, "It hardly matters. People living on a world seldom refer to it by name; they don't need to."

When time for landing came, Lisele worried a little. But the scout behaved exactly the same as it had on simulations. A few minutes short of plowing air, Brower had begun calling groundside, but only the long-ago-recorded voice of Orval Sprague answered. So, homing in, Lisele dropped the scout nearly to ground, a couple of kilometers from the dead ship, and hovered.

Kobolak began a query, but Lisele waved it away. Then, tilting the scout a half-radian but still hovering, she "walked" it a few hundred meters toward the *Patton* before going vertical and landing. Her move blew hell out of the ground below—which was exactly what she had in mind.

As the scoutship came to rest, the terrain she'd blasted lay hidden under the cloud of dust and larger chunks her Drive had blown free; when it cleared, the scout's path showed as a wide, flat-bottomed, smoking trench.

"What the Almighty was *that* about?" said Eduin Brower.

Anders was smiling, so Lisele realized he already knew the answer. But to Brower and the others, she said, "It's another thing Tregare told me about. He used it sometimes, when he had reason. I wanted to know if *I* could do it."

"And if I could—" She nodded toward where the *Patton* sat. "—I wanted them to know, too."

Right out loud, Anders Kobolak laughed.

Then he got down to business. "The time of day it is, here, we can't transmit to *March Hare* for at least the next twenty hours. But let's log some data now, while we have the leisure."

As Alina flipped a switch to Record, he cleared his throat. "Kobolak reporting, captain. Landed shortly before fifteen hundred hours. Instruments show atmo somewhat thinner than Earth's but partial-pressure of oxy makes up for it. Temp, here at late afternoon, is thirty Celsius. Accelerometer puts local gravity at point-eight-two gee." Lighter than Shaarbant's, Lisele thought, but not by much.

Anders continued. "We're less than two kilos from the *Patton*, which is at—uh, I'm not sure of the latitude but it's only a bit north of the equator, so we don't have to worry about Sitdown's excessive axial tilt; days and nights will be roughly equal, and climate shouldn't vary a lot."

Gesturing, Lisele caught his attention. "It will, Anders." He scowled, and she said, "The tilt. In a year—not that we expect to be here that long—incident angle of sunlight swings from sixty degrees north to sixty south and back again, going through vertical both ways, at each equinox. So—"

He nodded. "I get it. Sines and cosines: effect of received radiation, a two-to-one ratio." He looked around. "Anybody get a fix on what part of the cycle we're in now?"

No answers, until Eduin Brower said, "Katmai said some stuff, one time we was talking. Something like: Sitdown, right now, it's about halfway from southern solstice—I think that's what she said—to equinox."

"So we're heading," said Lisele, "into the hot half of the year."

Anders said, "What's the difference? We won't be around long enough to worry. And—" He gestured toward the screen that showed the downed ship. "The groundsiders seem to have managed."

He signaled for Alina to stop recording. "So let's start paying attention to what we're here for."

XII

Viewed on a side screen, the *Patton* didn't look too bad. Dust had accumulated, most noticeably at the nose and then

down as far as there was slope to hold it. Around the upper
airlock, effort had been made to clear the stuff away—but not,
Lisele deduced, for some years now.

Vines grew almost halfway up the landing legs, hiding
the crippled Drive nodes. But not near the bottom of the
main airlock's ramp; that area was clear. Past one side of the
ship's hull, Lisele could see a corner of the cargo hatch,
opened down to its horizontal position.

Around the ship, mostly outside its normal safety perimeter for liftoff, stood a number of buildings. The majority
were small, built of stone, sheet metal, and what looked like
wood. From among the nearest, a group of humans now
approached the scout.

"Hi-mag," said Anders Kobolak, and the pictured image
zoomed closer. "Six men and three women, I make it. How
many are armed? Can anybody see for sure?"

Lisele was still checking when deWayne Houk said,
"Standard energy gun on the man leading; one behind him
packs a heavy-duty. Woman on our right, needler shows out
of a pocket. Whatever's so-maybe hidden, can't be said."

Eduin Brower spoke up. "On ships or any damn place
else, UET never trusted the grunts with guns. Just the
brass."

Kobolak nodded. "Right. Which is why we decided that
a *scout*'s officers are considered brass, these days, when the
scout is on its own." Again he looked at the screen. They'll
be here in a few minutes. Let's get the greeting party geared
up to do its function."

"Officer" assignments on the scout, made solely on the
basis of proficiency with hand weapons, fit reality more than
not. Control officers would be Anders, Arlen, and Lisele: the
first two carried energy guns, but Lisele's weapon threw
softnosed, expanding needles. The difference was that she'd
learned, on Shaarbant, to aim first and *then* fire. With the
miniature projectors a person could pull trigger and sweep
the beam across a target; that was about the extent of the two
men's marksmanship. Naomi Gray's skill was roughly the
same—but since no "officer" slot was available for her, she
would stay aboard.

Eduin Brower insisted he "couldn't hit the broad side of
a barn from inside, with the door shut." While deWayne
Houk, Lisele was surprised to learn, was expert with blasters

and needlers alike. Molyneux had never fired a gun, and
Alina was frankly terrified of handling weapons. Yet she
insisted on accompanying Anders groundside—and surprisingly, he agreed.

So the Kobolaks, Houk, and Lisele would be the team.

Last minute recap: "You know the gen, Brower. We—"

"Yeah, yeah. No matter what comes off, I don't let any
groundsiders in, without you say 'I assure you, Chief.' Anything else, crap on it. Right?" Kobolak nodded, but Brower
wasn't done. "You're doing real dumb here, you know that?"
He'd said as much, earlier, but clearly he was determined to
say more. "Something does happen; they get the squeeze on,
you can't get back in here. So like you say, I stand fast." His
face reddening, the man took a deep breath. "Stand fast to do
damn-all *what*? Not a one of us, left here, knows how to jump
this can. Let billyhell-alone, *use* it. What you expect me to
do, Kobolak? Sit on my big toe, while me and these two take
our sweet damn time starving?"

Seconds passed, before Kobolak's stony expression relaxed. Then he nodded. "All right, Brower. I don't think
there's a chance we'd have that kind of trouble, but just in
case—" He turned to Lisele. "Give him your needler; he'll
come groundside and you sit First Pilot, monitoring the
screen, too."

She and Brower were both trying to protest, but Anders,
now pointing a finger at the Comm Chief, pitched his voice
to override the man. "Don't tell me again how you can't
shoot; I believe you. But if it comes to that, here are my
orders."

Pausing a moment, then he said, "First, no matter what
happens, nobody on this team shoots before *I* do. And now:
you specifically, Brower. I don't care whether you can hit
anything on purpose, or not. All I ask is, if shooting starts,
you do some—just make damn sure you don't hit any of *us*."

Face flushed, clenched fist opening, after a moment
Eduin Brower gave a soft chuckle. "Fair enough. Let's go."

Lisele didn't want to be left aboard, but even if she'd felt
like arguing, there wasn't time for it.

As soon as all five were clear of the airlock ramp, Lisele
raised and locked it. Now then, check comm: "Anders?"

The tiny receiver stuck behind his left ear was working,

and so was the small comm-unit in his shirt pocket, switched
to Send. Because his voice came clear enough. "I read you."

"And vice versa." She flipped a switch. "Now recording."

"Yes. They're getting closer; two-three minutes away.
Lisele—"

"Yes?"

"In case I have to talk something past them, just to you
but with them hearing also, listen carefully."

"I'll do that. Good luck, captain."

Then the five below stepped forward to meet the Uties.

"What's that captain stuff?" It was Alys Molyneux, sitting
to one side in an Aux seat. "Second Hat, that's all he is."

Impatient with the complaint, having no time for it,
Lisele was glad when Naomi Gray said, "On this scout he's
captain."

Below, the two groups were close to meeting; Lisele
waved a hand for silence and strained to see and hear. Six
men and three women approached. All wore standard worksuits,
each embellished with at least one item, however faded or
ill-fitting, of UET uniform garb. Here and there Lisele saw
the shine of insignia.

A tall, elderly man led the nine; he moved more vigorously
than his looks would have indicated. His left cheek bore a
scar: a circle with an X inside. What—?

Anders stepped to shake the leader's hand. "Anders
Kobolak, Captain Malden." To identify the rank, he must
have seen something Lisele couldn't spot on the screen. "I'm
the *Tamurlaine*'s Third Officer, promoted in space. Now
commanding our scoutship here, and of course speaking for
our own captain, Karl Delarov."

Trying not to be noisy about it, Lisele sighed in relief.
Because acting had never been one of Kobolak's strong
points.

He was off to a good start, though. When Malden, asked
about the baldness of all but Houk—"Is that a new reg, or
what?"—Anders ran through their prearranged story about
the *Tamurlaine*'s misadventures, including the story behind
his own in-space promotion. Once those hurdles were passed,
Lisele paid less attention to what was said, and more to what
she saw.

The others, all of them, were considerably younger than

Malden. The man with the heavy blaster, for instance. His name was Goral Craig; he hulked bearlike. Between his short-trimmed beard and the way his side-tilted cap hung over it, she couldn't make out the scar on his cheek—but for certain sure, he had one.

The needlegun-carrying woman: Deryth Mangentes. She'd tucked the weapon out of sight, but the bulge still showed. Her thick black hair was cut straight around at earlobe level; a wing of it now hid her left cheek, scarred or unscarred.

The other six: after a time, because of their unarmed state and the way they behaved toward the dominant three, Lisele wrote them off as flunkeys. So, once again she concentrated on what Kobolak was saying, and the answers he received.

"Not in proper uniform?" said Anders. "Of course we are. We left Earth eighty years after you did; over that much time, things change. Even the specs for uniforms."

With a noise that sounded like "Harumph!" Malden changed the subject. Waving a hand, he said, "Call *that* a scoutship? A peanut, maybe. How many does it carry? And how far?"

Lisele saw Kobolak's brow wrinkle. *Think it out good, Anders!* The Second Hat took his time, then said, "It's a newer model, halfsize; armed ships carry four of them, not just two. Time and distance capabilities are much the same as the earlier ones, but this way there's more flexibility for scouting purposes."

So far, so good. Then Malden said, 'This all of you? Just you five?"

"No, captain. As the regs provide, I left a watch crew on duty."

"Crew? No, you said halfsize; that means your peanut carries six." He wagged a finger. "Don't play games, youngster."

For a moment Lisele was afraid Anders would correct the older man, but his mouth opened only briefly; then he shut it. Malden continued: "Well, maybe you weren't playing. One's a crew if that's all you've got!" He laughed longer than the mild quip seemed to deserve, until all his followers laughed, too. Then he said, "Regs or no regs, you're *all* coming to our welcoming party this evening. First new people we've seen in more than sixty years, you think we're not going to feast you?"

*   *   *

Now *there* was a poser. Even if Anders played on Malden's conviction that the scout carried only six—and thus left two, unsuspected, to keep guard—he'd be letting Malden establish dominance, partial command, over the scout. Lisele crossed her fingers. *Don't give him anything.*

But defying the old man could bring immediate conflict, before they'd had a chance to *learn* anything. Lisele turned to Gray and Molyneux. "Go below. Warm up the Drive, to standby. No more—we don't want those others to hear, if we can help it."

Gray left immediately; frowning, Molyneux followed. Lisele watched and listened. Unobtrusively, Anders Kobolak's right hand had moved back along the side of his hip, nearer to his gun. She'd heard him say he was good at something called "fast draw;" now she realized what the term meant. But he was saying, "—understand your feelings perfectly, sir, and regret being unable to comply. My own orders, you see." He shook his head. "You don't know Captain Delarov, what a stickler he is. I'm sorry, but I won't risk demotion. Not for all the well-intended hospitality on this world!"

Malden himself had made no aggressive move. Now as he made a barely noticeable gesture to those behind him, Lisele saw Craig and Mangentes bring hands away from their weapons. Malden said, "Orders, yes. Autonomous commanders. Always a problem. Well, then," and now he seemed cheerful again, "five of you come, this evening." His scowl seemed programmed, a routine action. "But not this five. Four of you, as you choose, plus the *crew* you've left on watch." Once more he laughed; dutifully, when they realized they were supposed to, his followers chimed in.

Consulting his wrist chrono, Malden punched in some adjustments. "You use Earth-hours, of course. Ours are a little shorter." He looked to Kobolak. "What's the time of day, on your schedule?"

Anders checked, and said, "Fifteen-seventeen. We'll want to log your own time-frames into our Local readout-skeds, naturally, but that takes longer than we have, just now. I—"

"Fifteen-seventeen. All right." Malden nodded. "Then have your group down here, to be escorted to our welcoming celebration, at seventeen hundred. If that's convenient?"

"Certainly. I look forward to the occasion."

Again, as at the first greeting, only the two leaders shook

hands. Definitely UET protocol. Then as the groundsiders left, Lisele put the ramp down, so the five could come back on board.

As Kobolak entered Control, before Lisele could greet him, he said, "The Drive's warm; I can hear it now. Why?"

"It looked like a fight out there, maybe, and—"

"You were going to lift out of here?"

She shook her head. "No. First, I'd have opened the ramp and done some shooting from there. But if we lost—especially if any of you got captured—I'd need the scout warmed up, so I could use it fast. To try and get you back."

His face lost its tautness. "Oh, hell—I'm sorry. Should have known you'd be thinking the way Tregare would, or Rissa." He came to hug her, and she could feel the tenseness still present in his arms. In her side vision she saw that Arlen Limmer wasn't too pleased, but that problem would have to wait. Anders said, "Sure, I can see it. You walk the scout, hovering on low Drive, around to where you can interdict them from the settlement. They *saw* what that trick can do. Then maybe you lift and turn back down to make a pass with the turret, *really* scare 'em loose. Right?" Now he laughed. "Sure it is."

She disengaged from him. "Good luck we didn't need it; you talked everything clear, just fine. Now, though—only an hour and half before Malden's escort gets here. Anders, you have some fast thinking to do. Such as, who goes?"

He looked surprised. "You do, of course."

"Instead of who? The ones who were groundside just now, I mean."

Not for long, Anders Kobolak thought about it. "It isn't the choice I'd rather make, but—" He turned to young Limmer. "Arlen, the same reasoning holds, as did before. While we're gone, you sit First Pilot. And going along with Lisele's hunch, keep the Drive humming on standby. Just in case."

This time Cray Malden sent a larger contingent. Sent, not brought: descending the scout's ramp in time to meet the *Patton*'s delegation a civil distance from the spacecraft, Lisele saw that in Malden's absence the woman Deryth Mangentes led the group. A quick look showed the hulking Goral Craig also missing.

But following Mangentes came nearly twenty younger persons. No UET tokens on these, and except for belt knives, no weapons. Male and female, in their jumpsuits they had a look of sameness, and then Lisele noticed another reason. These wore no caps, and every haircut was much like her own, or the one she'd given Chief Houk. Well, getting along in a new place, conformity might help.

With a harsh downward gesture of her right hand, the woman brought the escort group to a halt. And waited, while Anders and the rest covered the few yards to where she stood. She said, "It wouldn't do to keep the commodore waiting. So as not to have to walk you too fast, let's move now and talk later."

Commodore, huh? Noting how the groundsiders were herding the visitors together—nothing obvious about it, except the result—Lisele decided they weren't in danger and considered the title. One ship, she thought, doth not a commodore make. But a colony—that might be something else, especially to the ego of its commander.

She wanted to share the idea with Anders, but people were in the way; she couldn't get to him without too much pushing. Well, it could wait. Instead she gave attention to the groundsiders around her. To her right, only a half-step ahead, was Deryth Mangentes. Breeze lifted a wing of hair and bared the woman's cheek; suddenly Lisele knew two things.

The exposed scar was in the shape of a UET Second Officer's tattoo. And hot iron, most likely, had burned it there.

XIII

Thinking back, Lisele tried to recall what Tregare had said about officers' cheek tattoos. They consisted of circle quadrants, cut on the diagonal. Third Officer got the bottom sector. For Second, one of the two sides was added; she couldn't remember which one, but presumably Mangentes, with the straight diagonal sloping downward toward the front, had the traditional marking. First Officers picked up the other side, leaving only the upper arc blank; only captains displayed the full circle.

As worn by Cray Malden, yes. Odd that seeing the man's scar, earlier, hadn't triggered recognition. But who'd expect to see officers branded like cattle?

They must have run out of materials, she thought—or perhaps the skills—for tattooing. Looking again toward the marred face, Lisele shuddered.

Has Anders noticed this? She looked around for Kobolak and saw him a few meters away, to her right and slightly behind, with a number of groundsiders between them. She started to move toward him but the others, somehow, didn't let her pass. Lisele stopped her effort; as she walked along, she checked the dispersion of the scout's personnel. Yes; each of the five was isolated, encircled by individuals from the *Patton.*

Deliberate isolation? *Let's find out.* Again she moved toward Anders and again she was blocked. The young man in her path looked at her with an expression that was half smile and half determination. Lisele said, "Excuse me; I need to report to our captain."

He shook his head. "Orders. We walk how we are."

Maybe; then again, maybe not. She gave him her warmest smile, and said, "Orders; yes, of course. But I have my own orders, you know. Not only from Captain Kobolak, yonder, but from Captain Delarov on the *Tamurlaine.*" She shook her head. "I don't think either of us would like it, if I had to tell Captain Delarov that you wouldn't let me carry out his instructions."

It worked. Not only did he step aside for her: leading the way, he cleared others from her path until she reached Anders. Then he stood, all too well within hearing range, until she smiled again, and said, "Thank you. I think it's all right, now, for you to return to your normal station."

Then he left their path of march. Lisele said, "Anders? Have you noticed—?" And she told him what she'd seen and deduced. "It's barbaric."

He shrugged. "UET always was. They've regressed even more here, is all." His hand clasped her shoulder. "Thanks for telling me, though; I missed it. And thanks, too, for coming to talk with me." His laugh sounded shaky. "I'd actually begun to feel lonesome—and restricted, somehow. As if our people were being deliberately kept apart."

"We were. Specifically. Mostly, I suppose we still are. Look around, Anders, at the groupings."

After he'd done so, he said, "Then how did you—?"

The knowledge might be helpful sometime, so she told him.

Nodding, wiping sweat from his forehead, Anders nodded. "Yes. Counter their authority with some of our own. Whether it exists, or not. Damn! Isn't it *hot*, though?"

Lisele was also sweating; it looked as if everyone was. But until he mentioned the heat she hadn't really felt it, much. After thinking a moment, she decided that this, now, was about the same as halfway into the hot season near Shaarbant's equator. When she and Rissa and Tregare and the others could still manage to keep moving all day, well before they had to find shelter and wait out that world's deadly perihelion. Sitdown, here, was hot, all right—but nothing like what she'd survived, there. And this sun, a deeper yellow than Earth's, showed a smaller disc than either Earth's or Shaarbant's.

Coming out of reverie, she remembered to tell Kobolak about the "commodore" thing. He chuckled. "Whatever the man wants to be called is fine with me."

With nothing more to talk about, Lisele began to pay attention to her surroundings. First they'd walked in a dusty patch, the dust rising enough to impede observation, but now they were into greenish-blue ground cover. At first glance it appeared to be grass, but actually the calf-height growth branched quite a lot. It wasn't hard to walk through, though; at the slightest pressure the stuff bent or broke away.

From time to time she'd noticed a form of plant life that looked like a tree trunk with no limbs, bare toward the bottom but with the upper part green-covered, its silhouette bulging to twice the lower diameter. Now as the party neared a group of these growths, Lisele guessed the largest to be roughly half a meter thick at the base and perhaps five or six meters tall. The foliage, from this distance, looked something like moss.

Were these the source of what looked like wood in the

buildings ahead? Until she saw a dead one, she wasn't sure. But that bare trunk, covered with scrawny, equally-dead twigs, was either wood or this world's counterpart.

She nodded; all right, a few things about this place were coming clear. When the scout could next communicate with *March Hare*, there'd be some info to relay to Katmai Delarov.

Until they topped a slight, gradual rise, the stream ahead was hidden from view. More than a stream, less than a river: a creek, perhaps? Not more than six meters wide, but the noticeable current ran smoothly, so the flow had some depth. The crude wood-and-stone bridge spanning the water substantiated Lisele's guess; too deep for wading.

Along both sides stood bushlike growths. Yellow-foliaged, these; a seasonal change, Lisele wondered? Or normal hue? Each bore three branches, diverging at a low height and making loose upward spirals. The shaping caught her attention; she looked more closely. Yes, they all spiraled clockwise. A vagrant datum from her days at the Junior University: this place was north of Sitdown's equator; in the southern hemisphere the things probably turned the other way. Whatever passed for leaves were feathery and hung vertically limp.

Crude or not, the bridge was solid enough; the troop's passage caused no vibration.

Not far ahead, now, the buildings began. No two alike, yet among the smaller ones especially, an overall sameness of stone and wood. For the most part they were built to only one level, with shallow-slanted roofs—generally just two sections, sloping from a fore-and-aft peak. Average ground area, she estimated, was roughly ten to fifteen meters on a side, with a few larger. Bigger families, maybe.

These people provided enough windows to let in plenty of light. Lisele saw no glass or screens, only shutters, most of them open. Now that she thought about it, she hadn't seen anything on the order of insects, flying or otherwise. But from the total lack of barriers at those windows, she decided there must not be any dangerous predators around. Or nuisance-type intruding animals, either.

Either that, or all such creatures were nocturnal; maybe at night the shutters were closed.

* * *

As they passed the first few structures, Lisele glimpsed people peering from windows—looking around one edge or another, showing only parts of faces. They were off to the sides of the line of march, and with all the groundsiders around her, Lisele got no clear view of any watcher. But some faces showed whiskers and others didn't, and certainly the small heads peeking over sills had to be young children.

For some reason, that knowledge eased Lisele's tensions.

Ahead, above the low, nearer roofs, a taller building showed. About three times as high as the others, Lisele guessed. Quite a lot wider, though, and since the party was approaching from an angle, Lisele could see one side as well as the front. Perspective disguised the relative proportions, but a quick count showed that front and side walls had the same number of windows. So the thing was basically square. And how large? Comparing the large structure with the others, she estimated each side at fifty meters.

The group passed the last of the houses; ahead lay the big building. If ever a safety perimeter had been marked around the downed ship, those marks were long since overgrown or scuffed away. But Lisele knew how large the danger zone should be, and this building definitely violated it.

If the *Patton* couldn't lift, the placement hardly mattered. On the other hand, one of Katmai Delarov's possible scenarios involved repair of that ship. Lisele shrugged; no point in worrying about too many things, ahead of time!

Now, closer at hand, she studied the building itself. The front, at least, was faced with stone to a height of about two meters. In the center of it, stone facing also rimmed high, wide double doors. Their height, level with the tops of the first-level windows, indicated an inside structure of two floors only, but the lower was tall enough for two. Most of the wall showed roughly-dressed wood slabs, once painted a color that might have been red but now had weathered to a greyish brown.

A short flight of broad steps led to the entrance. On those steps stood another group of groundsiders, this one led by the big man, First Officer Goral Craig. The rest were younger, and like the scout crew's escort, carried only belt knives. As Deryth Mangentes brought her group to a halt, only a few paces from Craig's, the woman said, "Reporting. Here they are, First. Is the commodore ready to receive them?"

The man nodded. "Report acknowledged, Second. We'll take charge now. Dismiss your group and come along."

After a certain amount of military ritual that seemed to make very little sense, the two officers, plus six of Goral Craig's contingent, escorted the five offworlders inside.

Lisele suppressed either a gasp or a chuckle; she wasn't sure which. Because the interior, although wood and not metal, was painted the dull blue-grey of a UET ship's galley.

Even without the double-height ceiling, the simulation wasn't exact. To one side, the area for preparation and serving of food was fairly standard, and the hierarchal placement of tables for officers, ratings, and unrated crew fit UET's normal distribution. But in no ship did the officers' table stand on a raised platform against a rear wall, with all seats behind that table, facing outward toward the main area.

So, a galley and auditorium combined. And mounted on that wall, high enough for good viewing from the entire room, was a large monitor screen.

Behind the raised table Lisele saw the high backs of ten chairs. Hmmm—all right: the captain and three control officers, a similar allotment for Engineering, plus Drive and Comm chiefs, whose subordinates were ratings, not officers.

Now, though: as Lisele faced that table and those who sat there, the three chairs at the table's right end were vacant. In the next sat a fat, balding man, then Commodore Cray Malden. To Malden's left the row was filled by a man, two women, then two more men.

Craig ushered the group past the tables, now vacant, reserved for unrated crew and lower ratings. The chief ratings' table was well-attended, with only a half-dozen seats empty. On reaching that point, the man said, "Captain Kobolak, you sit up front there. The rest of you—" The man gestured. "—find your places here."

Not liking this separation at all, Lisele took a seat between two of the *Patton*'s ratings and watched Brower and Houk and Alina do the same—each isolated from the others, no two together—as Anders Kobolak was led to the vacant chair at the head table's end. Beside him sat Second Officer Deryth Mangentes; Goral Craig took the remaining vacancy.

Quickly, before any attempt to talk with the ratings at table with her, Lisele looked at the table itself. Each place had a full setting. So this was a relatively formal occasion; they would be served, not rise and go through a serving line.

Several carafes of pale, pinkish wine were on the table, one directly in front of Lisele. *So let's get this show on the road;* she reached for it and poured her own glass full, then handed it to the woman at her right. *Might as well break the ice.* "Do you make this yourselves, or is it from ship's stores?"

Taking the carafe but not yet pouring, the woman said, "Ship's wine is long gone. But before the supply ran out, one of the cooks found several kinds of native berries that work well enough." She made a timid-seeming smile. "This type is stronger than it tastes. If they start raising toasts, I'd advise you drink lightly."

Lisele grinned. "Advice appreciated." Now, while the woman filled her own glass, Lisele had time to evaluate her. In her mid-thirties, Earth bio-years, seemed a good guess. She was lean, with a sallow, lined face, and black hair worn in the standard cut that Lisele's own hair approximated. "My name is Lisele Moray. Comm-nav cadet rating, on the *Tamurlaine.*"

"Elseth Sprague." The woman's smile was missing two upper left bicuspids. Lisele's expression may have looked puzzled, because Sprague added, "Yes, Captain Orval Sprague was my father; I'm his youngest child, and second-youngest of the first generation born here. On the roster I'm a Drive-tech First, but the Cube only needs tuning every week or two, so I spend most of my time supervising unrateds out in the cropfields."

"And I," said a voice at Lisele's left, "am Arnet Kern. I'm second generation, and I have no idea who my father was, because Captain Bull Cochrane threw out the system for keeping track. At least I don't look like *him.*"

Lisele turned. The man was youngish—twenty, maybe—redhaired and freckle-faced. His nose had been broken, and healed bent to one side and partly flattened; if not for that, he might have been handsome. Before she could answer, he said, "If you two aren't keeping that wine a secret, I'd like some."

"Oh, sure; of course." Lisele handed the carafe across to him; Kern poured fast, but with no splash or spill.

"Thanks. I'm listed for Drive, too, but that's a joke. Just something traditional for the records, because nobody's ever revised the Table of Organization to make sense. What I

really do is straw-boss six sheepherders." His grin, breaking
through a rather dour expression, helped his looks a lot. "In
the proper seasons I'm not bad at lambing, or shearing, or
butchering."

"How did you learn all these things? Ship's people—"

He shook his head. "It was the first landers, had to
figure it all out from scratch. By my time we had people who
could teach us."

"It must have been—" But a blare of sound interrupted,
and Lisele saw the big wall screen light up. Picture and
sound quality were so poor that at first she couldn't make
them out. Then she realized: this was an old, wornout
tape of a military band, playing the corporate anthem of
United Energy and Transport. Tregare had a tape of that
composition. . . .

The damned thing repeated three times before someone
mercifully shut it off. By that time, servitors in smocks were
bringing food, serving the head table first and then the
ratings.

During meals, Lisele discovered, it wasn't the custom of
these people to talk much. If at all. Shrugging, she applied
herself to the meal.

XIV

The meat platters were piled with beef, pork and mut-
ton, all three roasted and sliced. For the most part, Lisele
found the vegetables—some raw, some cooked—familiar. Two
strange ones, she decided, must be native here: "empty
calories." The fresh taste of one, she liked; the other smelled
rank, and she passed on it. Cooked berries, served cool in
what was probably their own juice, carried a flavor much like
the wine's.

The situation had her nervous; to calm herself she ate
slowly, and took only nominal second helpings. She was
finished, and sipping a hot liquid that looked like coffee but
certainly wasn't, when Commodore Malden called for everyone's attention.

He stood only briefly, until the room went quiet, then sat again. He was using an amplifier, Lisele noticed, turned high enough to reach the filled tables but not the entire room. The equipment had to be old, she thought, but it worked. Well, solid-state gear could last a long time, and for such items, most ships carried plenty of spares.

"This is a great occasion," Malden said. "Our first visitors here, possibly our saviors. I haven't had time or opportunity to ask Scout Captain Kobolak about the *Tamurlaine*'s intentions and capabilities; perhaps he can tell us now."

Scout Captain? This one's making sure we all know who has the real rank.

As Malden looked to his right, Deryth Mangentes handed Anders Kobolak a microphone. So briefly that Lisele almost missed it, Anders looked startled; then his face took on a self-assured expression. "The question, I suppose, is what you mean by 'saviors.' But first, let me introduce those of my shipmates who came here with me from the *Tamurlaine*." So, having each stand as he gave names and the ranks they'd assumed for this mission, in turn he did the honors for Eduin Brower, deWayne Houk, Alina Rostadt, and Lisele. Brower gestured a minimal wave. "Hi'ya, folks." Houk mumbled, "Pleasure, I'm sure." Alina said, "I enjoyed our dinner very much." Suddenly self-conscious, Lisele finally came out with, "You—you've certainly made this colony a success."

As she sat, Anders spoke again. "You're right, Commodore. We didn't expect to find anyone out here, but since we did, of course we wish to help. And perhaps you can help us, also." He paused. *Thinking fast*, Lisele decided. "The first thing we need to know is: what kind of aid do you have in mind?"

He gave Malden no chance to reply. "Do you want to be taken back to Earth, arriving there more than a century out of your time? You must know we can't do that; our ship isn't big enough, and it's nearly full, anyway." Kobolak's brow wrinkled. "To go—oh, not to Earth, but to the nearest colony from which ships could be routed here—you'd have to allow twenty years, at least, before the first of those could arrive."

He shook his head. "We could take a few of you along, to represent the colony and state your case for further help. But that's about all, I'm afraid, along those lines."

This time his pause allowed Malden to speak. "No, we don't want to evacuate this world. A delegation to go with you—yes, I like the idea. But we have three needs, one immediate and two over a longer term."

Kobolak nodded. "The immediate, I believe, is medical supplies. Well, we brought along as much as the *Tamurlaine* can safely spare. Some of it's new since you left Earth, so we've included the specs on it, too." He made an apologetic shrug. "With the radiation-damage crisis—" He touched fingers to one side of his still-hairless scalp. "—Captain Delarov couldn't spare a medic just now. Some of our people, the complications are rather grim."

He's taking too long at it. As Malden nodded, then said, "We appreciate whatever you can do, medically."

"And your other needs, sir?"

"Reinforcement of this colony! More people, for our working force and our gene pool, both. That's one."

"And the other?"

"Our ship, repaired! The *Patton's* too good a vessel to sit and rust away, for want of six-figures' worth of facet plugs for the Drive nodes."

As Kobolak nodded, Lisele hoped Malden couldn't see how the other man's composure was slipping. This discussion was getting entirely too close to the bone. But Anders said, "We'd need a checkout on how many you'll require. I doubt very much, though, that we could fill you needs and still stay within safety Regs."

Regs. Yes, Anders, that's what to spear them with.

Malden spread his hands. "Your captain will decide the matter, of course. And when will we meet with him? When does your ship rendezvous with you, here?"

Kobolak hesitated. Lisele waited, and finally he came up with UET's magic word: "Security, sir. At this time I'm not at liberty to give that information."

Luckily for Anders Kobolak, frowns and glares weren't lethal. Visibly curbing his temper, Cray Malden said, "You'll do so when you can; correct?"

"Of course."

"And you'll ask your captain, as soon as possible, about all the things we need to know."

"Naturally. At our next comm sked."

"And when will that be?"

"I—" Floundering for a moment, Anders recovered. "By your local time, I'm not certain."

He shouldn't let his ignorance show so much. It was all going to hell, here.

When in doubt, bluff. Lisele stood. "Communications protocol," she said, loudly, "is of course a security matter." She paused, looking quickly from one person to another. All right: "What Captain Kobolak means is that when we get answers from Captain Delarov, you'll receive the info as soon as possible. But we can't predict the timing."

Then Anders picked it up, and fobbed Malden off reasonably well. For a time, Lisele was afraid he was going to tell everything he knew, about the distance and message time to "the *Tamurlaine*," but he didn't. The amplifier shut down; any further discussion at the head table was confined to that area.

So she sat back and sipped on the liqueur that had been served with the latest refill of not-coffee. The strong spirit tasted rather good, more tart than sweet, with an elusive flavor that reminded her of walnuts.

"A century out of our time?" Soft-voiced, Elseth Sprague said it. Turning, Lisele saw the woman shake her head. "The commodore, yes; he's the only one alive here, ever saw Earth. The rest of us? Reckoning Earth years, I was born in NY78. Makes me thirty-four, now. Forty-one and a bit by our own calendar, which is what we mostly think in." Her gaze met Lisele's. "And how old might you be?"

"Well, let's see." *What did we decide? Oh, yes—* "Eighteen bio," because fifteen wasn't even adult. "I started the Academy young and graduated the same way." She tried to think fast.

"Wait a minute." From her other side, Arnet Kern interrupted. "*You* went through the Slaughterhouse? Where's your scars?"

This was all coming too fast, but the digression helped. "Different program." *We've said our ship left Earth in NY91. So—.* "The Tech track has it easier, nowadays." And this UET loyalist said "Slaughterhouse"? *Keep it in mind.*

His next remark didn't need an answer, so she kept figuring. And finally said, "Thirty-six, my chrono age."

Showing the gap behind her upper left cuspid, Sprague grinned. "A little out of your own time, then, when you get back to Earth."

Lisele shrugged. "If we ever do." Now she felt good; the

play-acting was under control, moving well, and she had the numbers straight.

Kern said, "What's that supposed to mean?"

Looking around to him, Lisele said, "I expect things are different now, from when your ship came out. Lots more colonies, for instance. All I meant was, Earth isn't the only place to go back to, these days. Some ships never do return there, or some people. But there's enough traffic that a person can ask for a transfer—and maybe even get it, if the brass is feeling generous."

"Watch it, Moray," Sprague said. "That sounded a little too much like disrespect for ships' officers."

Watch it, yes! Lisele forced a laugh. "No such thing. Groundside brass, I meant. The kind that rides ships in freeze and never even sees space, but runs the whole show anyway." She raised an eyebrow. "Or maybe that's since your time, too. Commodore Malden's, I mean."

The woman didn't seem to have an answer, so Lisele let the matter drop. Since she had no other subject she wanted to bring up, and no one else within intelligible earshot was saying anything, she resigned herself to boredom.

But then two women entered from the back of the room, dragging between them a battered-looking man.

How Lisele came to notice, was that everyone turned to look in that direction. So she did, too.

The belt-knifed guards weren't particularly notable; maybe Lisele had seen them before but she wasn't certain. The man, though: his nose and lips were puffed and bloody; his left cheek bore a raw wound. He walked with a halting, crabwise sidle, and kept his bound hands clasped to his crotch.

"Looks like he didn't confess easy." The bushy-haired woman sitting across from Lisele hadn't looked up from her plate before. Now she was staring, first at the bound man and then toward Lisele. She carried a lot of jowl for the age her dark complexion indicated; the sleeves of her jumpsuit bulged, but the bulges didn't look much like muscle. Her heavy features, previously blank and dour, now showed a grin of large, widely-spaced teeth. "You're in luck," she told Lisele. "You get to see the show."

Repelled, impressed against her will by the other's animal-like vigor, Lisele said, "I'm Moray. You're who?"

"Thela Cochrane, that's who. The Bull's own get. Not that the old bastard ever bothered to set me up in decent rank. I—"

Gesturing toward the approaching trio, Lisele said, "And all this, now. The show, you said." *Keep talking; maybe you won't puke!* "Man looks a little old to be doing Slaughterhouse games. What happened to his cheek, anyway?"

Cochrane laughed; Lisele would have preferred that she hadn't. "Games, hell! That one—his name's wiped from the records, so we can't say it—he was Third Officer. Tried and convicted of mutiny. The cheek? How else get rid of an officer marking, except *skin* it off?" She leaned forward; Lisele caught a whiff of fetid breath. "The execution; that's what you'll see."

The man, whatever his name had been, was brought past the ratings table to face the commodore. As he passed, Lisele smelled the reek of excrement.

Cray Malden stood to face his prisoner. The man's stance told nothing: hope, defiance, or even fear. Malden said, "Traitor, you're in your last hour. Is there anything you wish to say?"

"Only that you'd make the *Bull* look good."

Malden gestured; one of the guards swung a knife hilt to the man's mouth. Lisele heard something break; blood welled. With spasmodic movement the prisoner's hands rose to cup the new injury, as Malden said, "Take him upship. Are the cameras ready?" One guard nodded. "In ten minutes, then." And the man was led away.

Involuntarily, feeling her brows raise, Lisele glanced up to Anders Kobolak at the officers' table, and found him watching her, also. Drawn with tension, his face seemed aged a decade. Frowning briefly, he gave his head a barely perceptible shake, and looked away. *What did he mean by that?*

The way the scout's people were spread out, Lisele hadn't tried to make any visual contact. Now she did. It wasn't easy; too many others blocked her view. But she craned her head this way and that, until she could see persons she knew.

If Alina Rostadt wasn't in shock she was giving a fair imitation; pale, breathing fast and light, staring straight at Lisele but apparently not seeing her. *She needs help, but—*

Eduin Brower was turned toward the *Patton*'s commander; his face betrayed no feeling at all, but his right hand, clenched against his cheek, showed white knuckles.

To see deWayne Houk she had to lean far to her left and raise her head. For a moment she didn't recognize the expression he wore. Then she did: Tregare, during the trek across Shaarbant, hunting prey for food. But Tregare's look had never held this raw disgust.

She didn't have time now, to sort things out. Because once again the big monitor screen came to life.

The show was on.

Malden's comm techs knew split-screen work. The upper left quarter pictured the ship's topside airlock, viewed from just inside and above the inner portal. Upper right, the camera had to be hanging on a boom; it showed an outship view, looking at the airlock hatch plus quite a bit of hull below.

The bottom half was from a groundside camera, set at a fair height above a number of people sitting grouped, twenty meters or so back from the ship and facing it. Making a quick count, Lisele decided that there sat practically all the crew not at the banquet. Well, the tradition of bread-and-circuses went back at least as far as the Roman empire. . . .

When minutes went by and nothing happened, Lisele turned to Elseth Sprague. "What happens to him now? What are they going to do?"

Sprague didn't look happy. Slowly, she said, "Space him, of course."

"In atmosphere? How? Oh—just throw him out?"

Headshake. "No. Run the pressure up, then open the lock. The blast of air—"

"Yes." Lisele couldn't suppress a shudder. She felt the blood draining from her face; vision blurred. Fighting shock, she put her head down and breathed deeply, trying for some semblance of alpha-state calm. Only when she had herself under control again, then heard a murmur of excitement pervade the room, did she sit up and look at the monitor screen.

*   *   *

In the airlock segment, movement showed. The two guards had the man curled up against the lock's outer hatch, his bound hands now secured to his ankles.

One guard turned to leave; the other bent over the condemned man, apparently speaking. Her right arm moved, but from the back view of her, Lisele couldn't see what was happening. She heard Elseth Sprague gasp, and looked to see relief in the woman's expression. "What—?"

Apparently caught out at something, and Lisele had no idea what it could be, Sprague said, "It makes no difference."

Lisele didn't believe a word of it.

The lock's inner hatch must have closed, because now the screen showed a graphic: Pressure In Atmospheres, 1. Then, slowly, the number began to increase. Why not faster? Sheer sadism, prolonging the fear and pain? Until Arnet Kern, to her left, said, "Faster could kill him before the lock blows," Lisele didn't realize she'd said anything aloud. And shouldn't have!

A wine carafe within her reach still held enough to fill her glass. The hell with being polite; she poured herself all of it, but then, as the onscreen number grew, sipped carefully.

Pressure In Atmospheres: 9.5, 9.6, 9.7 . . . Elseth Sprague's hand gripped Lisele's forearm. "At ten, it goes." His face turned away, the man was writhing, slowly contorting within the limits of his bonds. And then, oddly sudden with no sound to confirm the event, the hatch was open and the man gone. The upper outside view, top right of the screen, saw him emerge as though shot from a cannon, then drop from sight.

The screen's top half blanked; the groundside vantage expanded to fill it. Emotions shocked into suspension, Lisele found herself counting seconds that seemed to last much too long; at the count of eight the hurtling figure struck.

When the dust settled, the sprawled blotch looked much too flat, ever to have been a human being.

Holding her dinner down by main force, speaking to no one in particular, Lisele said, "Peace take me if I saw such a thing before!"

"I still haven't," came a strangled-sounding voice, and then Elseth Sprague said, "I always shut my eyes."

To Lisele's other side, Arnet Kern was pushing himself back from the table; hands to his mouth, he staggered toward the nearest exit. And at the far end of the ratings' table, Lisele heard unmistakable sounds of people who hadn't followed Kern's example in time.

On the screen, groundsiders were edging forward to see the body at closer range. "That's enough, I think," said Cray Malden, and the picture blanked. Speaking to Anders Kobolak, but loud enough for the ratings' table to hear, he said, "As you can see, we keep to the Regs. Even improved them a bit, you might say. And now perhaps we can—"

Kobolak stood. "Now my people and I will return to the scout. There's a comm sked coming up soon; you wouldn't want us to miss it." By the time he was down off the platform, Malden trying to talk and Anders paying him some heed but not much, Lisele and the other scouters were there to meet him and form a solid grouping. The thing was, Lisele realized, that Kobolak's words constituted an unspoken order to assemble *together;* by contrast, the *Patton*'s officers and ratings had no such implicit order. So they hadn't moved, soon enough to interfere.

"We know our way back," Anders said now. "If you wish to provide an escort, commodore, of course we'll accept. But it's not necessary, and I'm sure your people have duties to perform."

For no reason Lisele could see, Malden sent fifteen ratings, with Second Officer Mangentes in charge, to walk the five of them back to the scout. Not, this time, isolated from each other—after a couple of half-hearted attempts, the ship's people contented themselves with keeping the visitors surrounded.

The five still couldn't speak together without constraint; on every side, UET partisans were in earshot. Comments were held down to discussions of food and drink, estimates of available facet plugs for the *Patton*'s Drive nodes, and other quite noncontroversial matters.

After several minutes of no talk at all, Kobolak said, "Commodore Malden gave me a voice tape, recorded by him. It's the *Patton*'s history, from an aborted mutiny in space to the present time. He said that to see how things are now, we need to hear it." He cleared his throat. "The man could be right."

Finally they reached the scout. Kobolak and Mangentes exchanged a handshake and a few words; the escort set out on its return journey. When that group reached a distance that satisfied Anders, he waved to the scout and the ramp emerged. "Everybody take a half hour or so to clean up and wind down. Then we assemble in control and hear Malden's tape. Before that, I'll brief the others on what happened over there."

Nearer to an hour it was, before the scout's entire crew was assembled. The three who had stayed aboard, Lisele thought, looked more shocked than those who had witnessed the execution. *But this is UET*, she thought. *UET marooned in a smallish group, inbred culturally if not genetically. How many generations born here?* She thought about the lapse of time involved, and nodded. Three, it would have to be.

With a ringing noise, Kobolak rapped something against a metal panel. "All right. Everybody's up to date now. So let's listen to Cray Malden's story." His laugh came harsh. "You can decide for yourselves how much to believe. Because unless Deryth Mangentes lied to me, whispering at the head table, the man executed today was Malden's own son."

He hit the Start switch; the tape began:

XV

I shouldn't have to do all this. It was in the log once; Orval Sprague put it in and everybody helped, telling what each of us witnessed. But it's not there now, so—

Bull wiped it, I expect: Bull Cochrane, when he was captain. Likely it had some things in it, he didn't want known. Orval never trusted Bull, and it turned out Orval was right.

Up to the mutiny, though, the log's complete. How we lifted from Earth, headed out this way, reconnoitered two fine habitable worlds—all that. The captain named them; that's Captain Edgar Allan Jones, a fine man to his last moment. Big fellow, black as day-old coffee and no cream in the galley. Closer to fifty than forty then, I'd guess, and could still whip any man on the ship.

Except Bull Cochrane, maybe. I'm not sure I ever saw anyone who could stand up with Bull, face-to-face—so when the time came, that's not how I handled the matter.

The captain called those two worlds—no, I don't seem to remember. Someone else found them by now, I suppose, and did their own titling.

The mutiny, I was about to say. The First and Third Officers were in on it; the Second wasn't, so they killed him straight away. Names—they're in the log, and some I've halfway forgotten. All those years...

I didn't see it start. Off watch, asleep. The alarms roused me. Halfway dressed and carrying my needle gun, I started upship. I was a cadet, half officer and half not, training in comm and navigation. Not trained enough by half, it turned out, when it came to trying a landing. But the Drive nodes were already failing; maybe nobody could have set us down right.

I made it up past several decks; three times people shot at me. Two missed but one tagged me with some needles. Not softnosed expanding, though, so I didn't lose the arm. I got that one shooter, because she stopped to reload instead of running before I could get up and aim. And I think I nailed one more, just as he bolted out of sight. I heard him yell and then a slamming sound, like he'd fallen a good distance, but with all the shooting noise from that direction, I didn't go look to see what happened.

I couldn't get as far as Control; they had it, by then, and had interdicted all three accesses. We still held Drive, but I didn't know that until later. Backing off from all the shooting, I came onto some shipmates I knew were loyal, and they knew the same of me, so we retreated down to the galley and began piling tables and such into some kind of barricade.

We had some comm with Drive and other places, but couldn't be sure how much was safe to say over it, with Control in the wrong hands and maybe listening. We did hear parts of what happened, that saved the *Patton* for UET. Not that the saving did much good, the way things ended up—but at least the pirates didn't get this ship!

One minute the intercom would blast out; the next, voices so dim you had to turn it up to hear at all. We couldn't tell what was going on, didn't know what to do. Coffee—

three cups in a row I poured myself, found they'd gone cold without my noticing.

Then the captain's voice cut through all of it. He was hurt; to this day I'm sure of that. You could tell by his breathing. Not by his words, though, or tone of voice. He said, "We will stop this slaughter. Now!" And all the chatter ceased; when the captain talked, he had that effect.

He was holed up in the topside airlock and he had secure comm to Drive, where the Chief was loyal. If Captain Jones said to blow the Drive and the whole ship with it, goodbye the *Patton* and hello a cloud of plasma; that's how it was.

The First and the Third, thinking they had it all their own way, now knew differently. He set his terms and they agreed.

He knew he couldn't win, he said. But to save lives, he offered to surrender and be imprisoned, and guarantee surrender of the Drive room, if the damned bandits would grant amnesty to all us loyalists. But he'd only give his surrender to those two mutinous officers, and to get it, they had to go to him.

Without the captain's control of Drive, they'd have laughed at him. But the way it was, they couldn't dare. So they agreed. They went up to the topside airlock, looked through the transparent port to be sure the captain wasn't armed, and went inside to negotiate his surrender.

That's where they made their last mistake.

Jones wasn't armed; the airlock was. He'd programmed it; Orval Sprague figured that out later, trying to make sure the thing wasn't a death trap any more. It wasn't; the captain had set only a one-time deadfall.

When the lock closed, you see, with the captain and First and Third all inside, it went into a programmed cycle that allowed no changes until it was done. The inner door closed and couldn't be opened from within the lock. Air pressure inside began to rise, the pumps boosting it at what must have been a terribly painful rate. The pressure distorted the captain's last words, when he yelled, "I've cut the heads off this snake! Now you deal with the rest of it!"

Not more than ten seconds later, the lock pressure triggered the next part of the captain's program. The *outer* port opened. All three men were blown free of the ship, into vacuum, with no suits.

They were the first to go that way. With the mutiny's leaders gone, nobody to run their wagon for them, and Drive still solidly in our hands, we gutted them.

Topside airlock, besides not being checked out yet, was too inconvenient for spacing the pirates. So we used the main one. I don't recall how many we put outship. More than twenty, though, were still alive to breathe vacuum.

There's a thing I remember now, that Bull Cochrane would have wiped the log for. His trial, on charges of spacing two of our own because he plain disliked them. And one, Bull wanted the man's woman. Never got her, though, except on schedule like everybody else.

The verdict said there was a reasonable doubt, so Bull lived and kept his rank.

Taking stock took some time. We had less than fifty live aboard, out of over a hundred. No officers for Control. Orval Sprague, Comm-tech First, was the highest rating who worked there, so that made him captain. Orval was a quiet man. So quiet that most people didn't realize one thing about him: when Orval made his mind up, about anything at all, the decision was over and done with.

The bandits had left us in the worst mess they could. They overrode from Control and threw the Drive on all-out max, way past redline. The lurch put the Drive Chief down with a concussion and he never did come out of it, really. And it took Bull Cochrane four hours to work a disconnect code and get the Drive down to normal. That may have been what hurt the Drive nodes: the damage we didn't know about until later.

They'd skewed our course, too—flung in changes, while the Drive was going fullbang, and then wiped the numbers off the log. So we were heading someplace we didn't know, faster than we should be, and not knowing how to locate ourselves. No landmarks ahead, was the problem. And trying to spot something on the rear screens, past the Drive field's bulge, was a job for experts.

We didn't have any. The captain and all three Control officers were dead. There'd been one other pilot-nav cadet with us, but she went bandit and got spaced, so I was all the ship had. I wasn't much and I knew it.

I told our new commander, Captain Orval Sprague, the only way I could tell where we were was to see back behind us. In other words, do Turnover and point backwards, doing decel. I'd never done it except on sims, but I thought I could.

I was wrong. If the nodes had been working balanced I think I'd have made it. But the way it was, we didn't straighten up right. The ship went into spin around two axes at the same time, and it took almost two watch-periods to get it stopped. With nearly everyone throwing up all over the place. Not me, though. The way Orval Sprague was looking, I didn't dare.

We discovered where we were, all right: too far out to get back to anyplace. The mutineers had messed with the fuel-mix, too, wasting a lot of our supply. All this after they knew they'd lost, of course; anything to hurt our chances.

Since we couldn't go back, there was nothing for it but to turn again and look for a habitable world ahead. That time, knowing about the node imbalances, I took Turnover slow and easy, about four times as long as normal, and it worked better.

I'll skip the search routines and the places that didn't pay off, because here is where we came to. By that time I'd done several Turnovers, gone in to look and then away again, so I wasn't too bad at it.

What I hadn't done was landings, and what nobody at all had done was make a good assessment of a world's conditions, from space. Not that there was much choice about where to try to land. The way the Drive was sputtering, I had to set down where I could.

The main thing none of us realized was the meaning of this world's axial tilt. I brought us down, not much below latitude sixty. Into a true hellhole.

I don't know how the tropics can be thirty degrees above the Arctic Circle, but here on Hellhole they are. If we'd hit that place in winter we'd have all been dead before spring. As it was, summer nearly did us in; only the meat tank kept us alive. We couldn't use cargo seed to plant crops, or force-grow frozen zygotes of meat animals; none of those things could have survived, outside. And native animals were poison to us. The plants—

well, some we could eat, but only for "empty calories."

Then the tank began to unstabilize. The only Tech who knew much about it said she could hold it for a while but not forever. So Orval Sprague and Bull Cochrane had a big argument.

Bull was Drive Chief by then; the old one had died. Except for ship command itself, this put Bull and Orval at the same level of rank, along with—oh, never mind; he's long dead.

Anyway, Bull said we had to move the ship. Orval said it couldn't be done: number two Drive node was in good shape, number three about halfway, and number one as close to dead as made no difference. Too many facet plugs burned out. And no ship can lift with that kind of imbalance; it would spin over and crash.

I remember that argument word for word. Sitting there in Control, scared somebody would get killed and likely me. Bull with his head cocked forward, that heavy jaw, eyes could drill a hole through you: "We got to *move*, Orval."

Orval Sprague shakes his head. "Can't be done; you know it."

Bull leans forward more. "No, I don't. I've been reading the manuals, Orval. I can fix this ship to lift."

"What for? We can't get off this planet."

Bull's fist slams the table. "Who said *off*? It's south of here, I'm talking. Down where we can raise crops, and such."

I remember the rest, too, how Bull convinced Orval. The thing was that Bull had studied. It wasn't his usual way of doing but that time he did it. He said he knew how to test Drive-node facet plugs for good or bad, and how to pattern what good ones he could find, into each node, to get the best push and balance. "Can't lift us up and away from this mudball," he told Orval, "let alone set us back down from that kind of speed. But with node balance we can lift *off this spot* and come down safe again. Still on the rock here, sure, Orval. But down south, far enough where we can grow some crops. Food beasts, maybe."

If Orval Sprague hadn't agreed, then, I might have shot him. Maybe he knew that, sensed that under the table my needler pointed at him. He did concur, though, and my potential action horrified me. What had happened to my respect for authority?

The only answer I had was that Hellhole's authority was beginning to supersede Captain Sprague's.

We moved the *Patton,* else we wouldn't be here where you find us. I made a fair lift and a good traverse to the south. Even my landing was tolerable; the ship does stand upright.

That was when the technical problems began to ease off and the social ones took over. These latter are what you may find hard to understand.

But you'll have to. Because now you're part of them.

When the contraceptive implants began wearing off and the women became fertile, Captain Sprague set up a breeding system. With only ten men and twenty-eight women, we had a limited gene pool. It was essential, he said, "... that parentage achieve a maximum variation and that we keep full track of it. To avoid inbreeding in the first generations. After that, everyone will be descended from all of us, so it will make no difference. For now, though, my plan will safeguard our descendants' future."

Orval's plan was simple enough. First, out of stone and mud and this crazy wood we have here, we built ten houses. One per man. With two or three women arbitrarily assigned—by Orval, of course—to each house. Once a woman finished an estrual cycle and hadn't conceived, she moved on to where Orval said she should go next. I have to admit that as an eighteen-year-old cadet I did enjoy Orval's system a lot: two or three women in my house, and duty said to service them the best I could. Since we all, simply by surviving together, had what you might call a kind of team spirit, there wasn't as much trouble as you might expect. Sure, some of the pair-bonders raised a storm, for a while. But all in all I think that system worked as well as it could for as long as it could.

But of course, Orval never ever changed his mind. Only the once, all the time I knew him. To let us move the ship.

The meat tank didn't fail completely; just the output went down, the recycling took longer, and don't even ask about the taste. But here the food crops ripened fast, and we force-grew the young animals from the frozen zygotes. So we skinned by that crisis, barely, being at our lowest numbers then. By the time babies started coming, we were past the worst of it.

Anders stopped the tape. "I could use a snack; what say we take a short break and discuss what we know?"

"I'm primed for that," said Eduin Brower.

XVI

Aside from Anders Kobolak, only Brower was hungry. Alina Rostadt and Lisele took some reconstituted fruit juice, and deWayne Houk sipped bourbon poured from a bottle that seemed to be lasting phenomenally well. Limmer, Gray and Molyneux all passed.

Since the dining cubby was too small for the group, Regs went by the board; refreshments were taken in Control. Between bites, Anders said, "Before we report to Captain Delarov, we need to sort out our opinions of this setup."

"She can sort a large part out for herself," said Alina. "While the tape runs, I'm transcribing all of it to fast disk, for wide-burst transmission."

Smiling, Anders nodded. "I noticed. Good move."

Arlen Limmer scowled. "We hoped to make some arrangement, some trade to get a Nielson Cube for *March Hare*. But how can we treat with these rotten savages? Or trust them?"

Clearing her throat, Lisele said, "Tregare had to deal with a lot of people he couldn't trust. The way to do it, he always says, is don't ever put yourself in a position where you *have* to depend on them. I think that's about where we are right now."

"Beware the enemy behind you," said Houk.

"What I don't understand—" Lisele began. "Those people, back when their ship came here. Sure, they were on the wrong side, and working under a rotten system. But with all the troubles they barely lived through, don't you have to admire the way they managed? There at first, anyway? So what bothers me is, how did it all go so *bad*?"

Brower shook his head. "How don't matter; it's *what*, that counts. Malden's a mean sumbidge, a real weasel; we saw it today, and there's hints on the tape, too. I say we wait 'til we hear the rest of it. *Then* try to figure if there's any way we can work with that little self-made tin god. Or whether he's worth the piss to drown him."

Kobolak said, "If we want cooperation out of Malden's gang, we have to make it worth their while."

"Or that they see it so," said Houk.

Lighting his first cigar since the scout had landed, Brower said, "Wouldn't try to crap that Malden, myself. Slaughter-house grad, no less. The ones born here—" He shrugged. "All they know, come to 'em secondhand or worse; they'd be easy. Malden, though: he's the one, makes it tough."

Houk leaned forward. "Dead, then? You want that? How, I think, makes a problem."

After a moment of silence, several tried to talk at once. Then Kobolak got the group's attention. "Nothing of the sort will be attempted. Not unless Captain Delarov orders it, and I doubt she would." He rubbed his chin. "Granted, the commodore's our biggest roadblock here."

"Do you feel," said Alina, "that the other officers might be easier to deal with?"

He nodded. "The Mangentes woman seems straightforward enough. And Craig, the First, isn't a bad sort. For all that he's Bull Cochrane's son."

"Now how'd you skin *that* out of somebody?" Eduin Brower squinted. "Or is it a wildass guess?"

"No guess," said Anders. "And nobody said it straight out, all in one package." He shrugged. "But putting a lot of hints together, things said in casual talk, the man is called Craig by courtesy only, because his mother was living with somebody-Craig when Goral was conceived."

"Considerable to deduce, only from hints," said Houk.

"Well, maybe a little more. Something about him being second in command, and that it's lucky he has only his old man's looks, not his disposition. In context it seemed clear enough."

"Fat lot of good," grumbled Brower. "Doesn't get us past that prick Malden. And say we can't; *then* what the hell?"

Kobolak spread his hands. "One thing at a time, Brower.

First we need to confer with Delarov. When does the signal window open? How long from now?"

Exhaling cigar smoke, Brower said, "Rough figures only; all right? The way we're set now, planet's orbital position, Jumbo and Goal Star are at right angles from each other. Means Jumbo's in line of sight from midnight to noon, local times. Given an hour and a half either end of that period, when Jumbo's too low to the horizon, leaves us about twelve hours out of every thirty, that we can get solid signal through." He shook his head. "That damn transit time, an hour each way, don't help for crap. But anyway, it's something like another four hours before we can start talking and expect Katmai to hear us. Dunno for sure, until I have local time on my chrono."

"Let's fix that right now," Anders said. "Deryth Mangentes programmed the local-time display on mine, before we started eating." So talk ceased, mostly, while he showed the others how to set the circuits. "Local and ship's times won't correspond in any permanent way; we'll just have to check back and forth."

Alys Molyneux hadn't talked much; now the lately-sullen woman said, "Brower had a good point. Supposing this Malden, commodore or whatever, won't help us. Then what?" She turned to Lisele. "I heard your idea: point the ship toward human space, turn the beacon on, and put everybody in freeze." Scratching her bare scalp as though she wanted to punish it, she said, "As far as I'm concerned, that's just one step better than dying and be done with it. I'd sooner jump ship and join the colony."

"And be chattel to the *Patton*'s brass," said Houk. He turned to Anders Kobolak. "What Brower said, the hours we spend waiting signal transit. Enough of us awake at once, time to think instead of rushed so much, we wouldn't have to do that."

Anders frowned. "I don't follow you."

"The ship, could have brought it here."

Lisele protested, "But *you* said we couldn't land, or even get into orbit!"

"Not then; too much speed. Jumbo had been right here, we couldn't orbit, even. But out there, slowed down more, we could. Did. Don't have that speed now. Could have eased away, coasted in, made orbit here. Synchronous, even."

"Well, if we could have, then, why not *now*?" To Lisele, it sounded as though Houk had a good idea.

"Who tunes the Drive? Fredericks? Hassan? Never manage it. Me, I'd have to be there."

Before Lisele could speak, Anders said, "That's another item to ask our captain about. Taking the scout back to *March Hare* and bringing the ship to a Sitdown orbit."

"Making a new start on the problem?" said Alina. "With better comm this time?"

Naomi Gray cleared her throat. In her soft voice, she said, "If we overlooked one option, maybe we're missing a number of other possibilities."

Brower chuckled. "You got some? Name 'em."

"All right, I will. The *Patton*'s crew survived here. What makes them any better than we are?"

"But they're a danger to us!" Alina Rostadt looked startled. "You'd want to live with enemies at hand?"

"Of course not. But there's a lot of habitable space on this planet, and—"

Lisele couldn't stop herself from interrupting. "And if we set up camp somewhere else, these people wouldn't even have to know we were on the same world with them!"

Arlen had been scowling; now he spoke. "Food. Sitdown's animal life is poison to us. And the *Hare* didn't come equipped with a meat tank."

"*Or* with Earth meat-animals in zygote form," said Alina.

"Just a minute!" Lisele was getting excited. "Earth animals, no. But we do have lots of samples of *Shaarbant* animal zygotes, the ones we found fit to eat when—oh, you know."

"Yes," said Anders. "When you walked a long, long way on that world." He nodded. "And—I remember now—the ship also carries considerable in the way of seeds and cuttings from Shaarbant's edible plant life. We could—"

"Could starve the hell to death," Brower put in, "waiting for all those things to grow enough to feed us."

Kobolak's hand pushed that argument away. "Not so fast. I don't have all the supply figures, but the captain does. How many people, I mean, who could stay alive for how long, until the new foods grew enough to support us all. With some of us in freeze, I'd expect, until that time."

Looking interested again, Arlen Limmer said, "That's not the only food on this world." As everyone turned to look at him, the young man grinned. "Is my father the only person who likes holos of Old West fiction? The western part of Middle North America, about two hundred and fifty years ago?"

He peered around; when no one spoke, he laughed. "Hasn't anyone else here ever heard of cattle rustlers?"

Lisele had, vaguely; most, it seemed, had not. Arlen explained; from a distant groundside base, lift the scout, all cargo space emptied, "—and raid Utieville, here. At night, I suppose. Load up with sedated meat animals and as much grain as we could grab in a hurry. The animals—eat some and breed some." He grinned. "Anybody see anything wrong with it?"

On ethical grounds, several did. Lisele spoke up. "Stop it! If these people are willing to help us and be helped, none of this would have to happen. But when it's our lives against their meanness, Arlen's right." She looked at him. "Even for Tregare, that'd be a good idea." And saw, how in him the pride glowed.

Houk gestured for attention. "Fuel's the problem. Bring the ship here to orbit—synchronous, away from UET's sight? Scout goes up and down many times, getting supplies groundside. How much fuel? When all is gone—" He shrugged. "*Hare* has fuel-refining equipment, of course. But can't be disassembled into parts, small enough to bring down with the scout. So—"

Anders laughed. "We wouldn't need it. The *Patton* has one; we don't know where they've set it up, but they had to. Because—" He paused, thinking. "Fifty-two years. Of course they've shut down all unnecessary power drain, but still there's a minimum requirement. Let's see—" Not aloud, he counted on his fingers, then nodded with vigor. "They'd have run out. And besides—lights weren't needed in the big hall today, but the fixtures were there. I suppose the houses use ship's power, too, for whatever amenities these people have managed to keep going."

With a wave toward Arlen, he said, "In terms of poker, I'll see your cattle rustlers and raise you some claim jumpers."

"If we need to, of course. And after we do a little looking around, to spot where the claim is."

*   *   *

Anders stood. "Let's doss up after ourselves now." He first, then the others, cleaned and put away their own utensils. Then he said, "We've heard only part of Malden's story. I realize we all need sleep, but until I have better knowledge of this situation I don't think I could rest very well, anyway. So after everyone's; had a john-break, anyone who wants to can join me in hearing more of the commodore's tape. Maybe all of it, if it's not too long."

A short time later, with no one absent and all seated, Kobolak signed to Alina. She pushed the Start button.

XVII

One problem we had at first, there, was a shameful thing I hate to mention. I suppose any ship has a few unnaturals, sneaking off to do dirty things with their own sex. But any time they got caught, it was out the lock right enough!

Here, when Orval Sprague set up his breeding schedules, two of the women said they wouldn't, and why. I thought Orval would kill them on the spot. But of course he couldn't, with so few of us left.

He let on, though, that he just might, if they didn't give the minimum of cooperation. So he got a compromise: those two only had to be with men long enough to conceive; the rest of the time they could live by themselves. One other thing he put on them: they had to build their own hut.

It wasn't any fun, I tell you, being with either of those; they'd just lie there and hate you. I was always glad if they caught before it was my turn.

Orval didn't try to set up a nonstop baby factory. He would have, except that our only remaining medic told him that two years apart was better, for health reasons. So every time a kid was born, the mother got a one-year contraceptive implant. And the way the conceptions and births spread out, not happening all in a hurry as you might expect, after a while nobody was in step very much.

We didn't build more houses right away; first we added

onto the ones we had. Women not on breeding-sked at the time, and their kids, generally lived with one or another of the fathers. Of course, some of that paternity was nominal; even then, Bull Cochrane took some chances, and I'm not sure he was the only one.

Orval and the medic—Sheila Farnol, her name was— set up a chart: considering all the women's ages, how many first-generation births we might get. If events had followed the chart, we'd now have a considerably larger colony here.

But too many of the kids didn't live very long, and some of the women went sterile early. We wound up with about half of what Sprague and Sheila had figured on. Still, by NY76 when the first born-heres were getting nearly grown-up and we'd had only a few deaths in the landing group, our population curve was on a safe rise.

And that was when the first real trouble started.

The thing was, Bull Cochrane always wanted his own way. He'd never liked Orval's breeding schedule because it gave Bull no special privileges; he had to take turns like everybody else. What he wanted was precedence according to rank, and Orval wouldn't agree to that.

Bull couldn't complain on grounds of fairness. One thing I'll say for Orval Sprague; any rules he set, he followed them himself, too. I've tried to do things that same way, but it isn't always possible.

So Cochrane tried another angle. First he said that adult status, by which he meant breeding eligibility, should be sixteen of *our* years, not Earth's. He brought the question in Council, which by then meant all the survivors from the *Patton*. I was the newest and last to be admitted, so I listened a lot and kept my face shut.

Never one to be hurried, Orval punched numbers on his calc. "No. Too young. That's barely thirteen, by Earth age."

Bull punched some keys himself. "Seventeen, then. Fourteen Earth years." While Orval was still checking the figures, Bull stood. "I so move."

I don't remember who seconded; I wasn't the only one looking around to see what everyone else thought, and what I saw made me think I didn't want to be the only one to vote No.

Seven, it turned out, were braver than me. I can't recall how they all died, when the time came.

Bull wasn't finished. Feeling cocky, I suppose. So for the first time he went official with his precedence idea: spelled it out and then said, "I so move." This time, peering around, I saw more people than not looking stubborn, so I got my nerve up and did vote No. Bull lost by five votes, and I felt better.

For some time, then, Bull seemed to keep his head down. The first two girls and one boy to reach the new age for being adult, they went into the breeding sked like everybody else. The boy didn't need a new house built for him, because by then we had some deaths and thus some empties. Orval turned out a crew to clean the place up for the kid, too; things like that, he was always good about.

What Orval wasn't good at, was spotting trouble. I've tried to learn from his mistakes.

It was at the first Council meeting in NY78, that we found out. On Earth—northern hemisphere, I mean—that would have been the middle of winter. Here, it was a week after we had most of the grain harvested. Lots of work, that was, and still is; we've never managed to get much tech into those chores.

People do die; over the eighteen years we'd been here, the Council kept getting smaller. But still I wasn't expecting, walking into the big hall you saw today—

When was that built, now? NY66, I think. When the crops and meat were going along well, and we could spare the time.

Anyway, we went in, and Captain Orval Sprague wasn't there yet. Unusual, for Orval. Bull Cochrane was sitting in Orval's chair. And behind Bull, one to either side and carrying energy projectors, stood two of Bull's strongest supporters. I wasn't sure how he'd got those women on his side, but they were the two who lived together most of the time, so I had a fair idea.

Well, it doesn't take a house to fall on me; a small shed is plenty. Along with everyone else, I found a seat and sat in it. When everybody was quiet, Bull stood. "'smy sad duty to announce, Captain Sprague met with an unfortunate accident. Therefore—"

Garr Albride, senior remaining Engineer—*that's* the name I couldn't remember, earlier—stood up and said, "If you mean that the captain's dead, what are *you* doing up there, Cochrane? I'm senior to you and you know it. I—"

Albride wasn't exactly in line with me, from the head table, but people using energy guns are apt to wave them around too much. So I was on the floor when one or both of Bull's guards cut the Engineer apart. When I sat up, I saw that two other people hadn't thought fast enough.

I also noticed that it would be just plain silly to ask who was captain, now.

When it came to making changes, Bull didn't waste time. He had a printout with him, things he'd worked out beforehand; now, after looking to see who the two extra corpses were, he scribbled some corrections on the paper.

Of the thirty-eight who had come here in the ship, only twenty-one of us were still alive: seven men and fourteen women. I think Bull had planned further culling, but decided against it so as not to weaken the colony's spacer contingent too much. Because at that point there were over twenty youngsters nominally in adult status or nearing it, and pretty soon some of those would have to be admitted to the Council. So for once, Bull held his fire and just talked.

First, after sending one of his guards out with some instructions we couldn't hear, he made some promotions. The only one that still means anything, I suppose, was me to Third Officer. But he named a new Drive Chief and a Chief Engineer, and boosted some ratings to fill out supervision in those groups. Comm still had a full quota, people appointed earlier by Orval Sprague. I know Cochrane wanted to get rid of Leah Pendleton, the Comm Chief, because unlike Orval he stuck to UET's policy of never making a woman Chief of *anything*, and besides they didn't like each other much. But not even Bull dared execute a female who still might have a couple of fertile years to her.

Next he started reassigning quarters. He took Orval's digs, of course, and all the bigger houses went strictly according to rank. My new residence was nearly twice the size I'd had before.

"We need five or six new places, too," he said. "Having

several young studs *and* their quota women all sharing quarters together is bad for morale." The new Chief Engineer nodded and made some notes.

Then, as we all knew he would, Bull got around to the breeding schedule. His version was quite simple. In order of rank and seniority, each man chose as many women as he wanted, for as long as he wanted. And a man could preempt a lower-ranking man's woman at any time. Disputes, if any, would be settled by the captain, whose decision was final. And, I thought to myself but not out loud, most likely fatal, too.

"One more change," Cochrane announced. "No more of this contraceptive implant stuff."

"But, Captain—" Farnol, the medic, rose to her feet. "The health factors. We can't—"

"Siddown!" Like an emptying balloon, Farnol slumped back into the chair. "Comes to health factors, we're running low on implants and you know it. Only reason they've lasted this long is that the ship stocked for a full crew; plus, we only use the things half the time. So I say, we save 'em for where there's a *real* need."

"Such as what?" Farnol was stretching her luck.

Bull shrugged. "How do I know? That's your department."

"And meanwhile all of us women just have one pregnancy after another? Is that what you're saying?"

"You don't want to catch a kid, do it some other way." Cochrane glared. "I have to draw you a picture?"

In order of rank, then, the men picked their initial quota of women. Bull took four of the brand-new adults—including one that didn't quite meet the age standards, but nobody objected. After that, Engineering and Comm and Drive Chiefs got their turns. And then, in the same order, the Firsts and Seconds and Thirds.

Males only, of course; women were chosen, not choosers. So instead of being thirteenth in line, I had seventh pick. Of the three women I'd been living with, the new Chief Engineer had taken one; a second didn't like me much, and it was mutual. I kept the third, because we'd had several times together and two of her children were mine. Including, unfortunately, the one who turned on me, tried to kill me.

The man I have to execute, tomorrow.

*   *   *

From the list of females I picked two others. First a young one, a groundborn who was newly pregnant; I'd wanted her earlier but Orval's schedule hadn't brought her to me.

Then I had to think, some. And finally picked an older woman, probably past bearing. A Drive tech by title, actually a field hand. But soft-spoken, and probably the best cook who'd ever shared my quarters. Food's important, too.

The other choosings didn't take long. There weren't quite enough women left to go around, even one to the person, for the younger generation of adult males. But they weren't voting, and it didn't seem to be the right time to bother our new captain with details.

Then the guard Bull had sent out of the hall a time ago, came back. She was carrying something that sent smoke up, but at first I couldn't see what it was.

We all found out soon enough. She had there a bucket half full of hot coals, with two handles sticking up out of it. Bull took hold of the handles and lifted; at the other ends were little pieces of red-hot iron. One was in the shape of a quarter-circle, the other a straight bar, just right for the radius of that circle, and each about four millimeters thick.

Without having to ask, I knew what was coming, and wished I dared to turn down my new promotion. Bull said, "You've practiced with these, Varda?" And the woman, Varda Claiburn, nodded. Bull said, "Let's see you do one on this stool. The full circle. I want to see you can line it all up right, and not burn too deep."

So then we smelled charring wood. She applied each iron, the arc and the spoke, four times, reheating when the color dimmed. Then Bull held the stool up for us all to see. From where I sat, it looked as if Claiburn had aligned the marks well.

"All right," said Bull Cochrane, "it's time we had Control officers who *look* like Control officers. Let's get to it."

My gut felt clenched around a block of ice; I figured he'd make me, the junior officer, go first, and I wasn't sure I could hold still for it, let alone stand and go up there.

But he fooled me; *he* went first. Claiburn asked him if he was sure, and he said he was captain, wasn't he? "So shut up and do it right. Or I'll use that thing on your whole face."

She could have killed him then, easy; the hot iron would have gone through his throat like butter. For a second or two I thought she'd do it. But she took a deep breath, and moved the arc-iron up and put it to Bull Cochrane's cheek.

His eyes went tight shut; sweat came out on his face. But except for an insuck of breath he didn't make a sound. Then, putting one iron in the bucket while she used the other, Varda Claiburn put the full circle-and-X on Cochrane. From where I sat, all the red, angry marks looked about the same, and so well placed they could have been made by one touch of a bigger iron.

He looked in a hand-mirror, nodded, and said, "Thanks. Good job." From a bowl he took a handful of ice to hold to his burns. And said, "All right. Next!"

The First couldn't maintain silence, and Bull had to hold the Second's head immobile because she kept flinching, but Claiburn managed neat jobs anyway. I was numb now; I stood and walked on dead legs to sit in the chair; I shut my eyes and went rigid. I swear I don't remember how the irons felt, searing into my flesh—only the sweet relief of the ice, afterward.

Bull wanted rank signs burned into the other officer groups, too—Comm and Drive and Engineering—but there wasn't any UET precedent for that, so when the vote went against him he had to abide by it.

Anyway, that's how the custom began. In a way it's not a bad idea; if you want rank in Control, you have to pay for it.

Once Bull had most of what he wanted, he eased off, some. Those of us with any rank to speak of had no real complaints, and any who did were keeping quiet about them. Partly because nobody except Bull and Claiburn, and Rait Oliver, the other bodyguard, had guns. It's safe to say that Oliver was the most purebred rat I've ever met. Bull boosted her from unrated to a Chief's rating, just below officer grade, in one jump, because that way he owned her.

Neither Claiburn nor Oliver were real weapons people. Like anyone else, they could trigger an energy gun and sweep the beam across a target; that was all. Bull, now, carried a needler; he was a good shot, aiming, and proud of it. I wasn't too bad in that line myself, back when I'd had the chance to practice.

*   *   *

So things ran smooth on the surface, but not for very long. The young men resented having to share women, and only the Councilmen's leavings, at that. They kicked up enough fuss that Bull Cochrane had four of them whipped, and executed the ringleader. Well, the one Bull said was ringleader, anyway. He based his method on the sacrifice of Captain Edgar Allan Jones, but he added something: a four-meter tether, tied to the kid's balls. You won't see that tomorrow; I used it on one drastic occasion, but it's not something a man does to his own son.

Then Bull instituted the submissuals. None of the young men had been through Slaughterhouse training, of course, the way we Earthborn had. So they'd never had to fight free-for-all, keeping at it until one of the group was killed.

Well, now they did have to. Bull divided the born-here male adults into sections by year of adulthood, and each section, one after another, was forced to fight to the first death. You might think they'd refuse, not being Slaughter house broken-in, to do such a thing. Well, the first batch did—but then Bull's needle gun splattered the loudest one's head all across the fighting area he'd marked off, and the rest changed their minds. I never liked those fights, then or earlier. But I guess they were necessary, so I've continued the custom.

Bull called the fights "submissuals" because after that first time a young man could either submit himself to them or not. If he didn't, Rait Oliver turned him into a non-breeder. The first two didn't know what the choice meant until it was too late, and after that, no one failed to volunteer.

At any rate, the first submissuals took care of the woman shortage. Not for long, though, because a little later came the women's rebellion. In a way I couldn't blame them for it, and in Bull's place, once their attempted coup had failed, I wouldn't have killed more than one or two. Bull, though, never had a sense of moderation. I did notice that he got rid of more older ones, than younger. And some older men, as well, that he accused of being sympathizers.

I think he had me pegged to go, too. The reason he didn't manage it is that in the fighting, one young woman put an icepick in the back of Rait Oliver's neck, and I got to the energy gun first. I didn't use it on Bull, when we met a few minutes later, because Varda Claiburn was with him, and two to one was more than I felt I could handle. But at the same time it wasn't good enough odds for them, either.

So we pretended we hadn't had any crisis between us, and Bull named me First Officer, replacing the deceased incumbent. So I got the burns of two promotions over with, all at once.

There weren't many of us left then, from the *Patton:* just Bull and me and Elroy Fisk, who succeeded to Chief Engineer, and Varda Claiburn and Sheila Farnol. Bull had already started bringing some born-heres into the Council and now he had to load it up some more. Usually he started favoring his candidates first, getting them firmly on his side before admitting them. But now he had to make choices in a hurry, which meant doing some guessing. Almost always he picked males, so that he'd have them in line for promotion to the Chief spots. He liked to keep the Council at about two dozen: the sixteen officer slots plus a few in waiting, and at the point I'm talking about, we were nine short.

Officially, Bull didn't pick these people all by himself. He or Claiburn would nominate, and everybody voted Yes.

Things went along that way for longer than you might expect. Nobody liked it much, but nobody wanted to do a Captain Jones, either. The way Bull took pick of all the new women, he was siring a lot more kids than was good for the overall gene pool, though I don't know if anyone but me worried about that part.

What set my mind to do something was when my oldest daughter was closing on adult status, and Bull Cochrane could hardly wait to claim her. So a few days before he was going to do it, I put on a dinner for him and Elroy and Varda and Sheila. Just the five of us left, from the *Patton,* to celebrate however many years it was by then, that we'd been on this planet.

I was sorry about Sheila Farnol, but there wasn't any way to leave her out.

How it was, is that I remembered some experiments from the early days. Trying to learn if we could adapt to the native meat without getting poisoned. Well, by taking very small amounts, building your intake slowly, you could get to tolerate it and not even feel very sick. When we passed our meat crisis, and it turned out that the native stuff was only empty calories at best, not really worth it, Orval dropped the whole program and everybody forgot about it.

Except me. Three months before Bull was due to take my daughter Clairi, I started building tolerance for native meat. I had to be careful nobody knew about it, and that was the sickest three months I ever had. Terrible ordeal, just getting around to perform my duties.

But when the time came, I was ready. I sent my women off on some pretext or other and fixed the ceremonial dinner myself. Main course was a nice spicy stew that I knew Bull loved.

I came close to putting in too much of the poison meat; it made me so sick that if Bull had realized what was happening, before he died, I couldn't have defended myself. But he didn't, so a time later I cleared the house of my personal belongings and those of my women, and with Claiburn's energy gun I flamed bodies, the house, all of it. Because now I was moving into Captain's digs.

Since that time, I've tried to adhere to the Regulations without need for such extreme measures. And most of the time this has been possible. Why, tomorrow's execution will be the first in nearly a year.

But running a colony, with nobody but yourself to back your authority, is harder than you might think. I hope you understand that.

End of report. Cray Malden, commanding the *Patton*.

XVIII

"Satan on the half-shell!" Eduin Brower slammed one fist into his other palm. "Worse'n I'd thought, that bastritch is."

"What I don't understand," said Alina, "is why he'd tell us all those horrible things about himself."

"When he didn't have to, you mean?" Lisele said. And

for that matter, why had he shown them the execution?
Trying to scare us?

Naomi Gray spoke. "I think I see. Malden's alone, the
only one left who came from Earth. Maybe he simply needed
to unload, to somebody from outside."

"And what he thinks," said deWayne Houk, "is he's
talking to UET, anyway. UET brass not likely care much, how
a man keeps himself boss. Just so he's on *their* side. Or else
he wouldn't of showed us that killing, either." Yes; that made
sense.

Anders Kobolak nodded. "Like as not, you're both partly
right." He stood. "Almost three hours until our comm-window
opens. I'm going to grab a nap, and suggest that most of you
do the same." He looked around to all the group. "Who's
slept most recently?"

"Me, I guess," said Arlen Limmer. "And Molyneux."

"You two take the watch, then. All right?" Both nodded,
and Kobolak said, "No one's obligated to join me when I
transmit to *March Hare*, but anyone's welcome."

Then all but Limmer and Molyneux headed for their
bunks. Lisele thought she might be too nerved-up for sleep,
but she was wrong.

She woke to hear Arlen quietly rousing others who
wanted to be present at Kobolak's transmission to the ship,
and felt refreshed enough to get up and join them. She found
Anders taping some comments. "—forget the option of repairing
the *Patton* and going home STL; colony population's too big
to ride the ship, and they don't want to abandon the place,
anyway. What they do want is to get their ship repaired,
which I doubt we could manage, and more people to reinforce the colony.

"So, keeping in mind that these people's willing cooperation begins to seem quite unlikely, we'll have to concentrate
on the other possibilities we've considered. In fairness, if we
do get their Cube, one way or another, we'd have to leave
them the scout's, if possible. Otherwise the colony would
have no power source at all. Now you can listen to Cray
Malden's account of his ship's history."

Cutting his Talk circuit, he looked around at the assembled group: Lisele, Alina, Arlen, and Eduin Brower. "I think
I've told her most of what happened here, and our thinking;
it's on fast disk as well as tape. Shall I play it back for you?"

He did, and consensus had it that his coverage was thorough. Brower said, "Damn all! More and more, it looks like we're stuck with setting up our own colony, other side of this mudball. With the *Hare* in orbit 'stead of groundside, and granting our beacon has more power than the *Patton*'s, there's a chance of rescue someday. But if it don't happen—" He gestured futility. "Gene pools, Malden said about. They had ten men, twenty-eight women. Seven each, *we* got."

Suddenly Lisele felt nausea. Not only at the idea of living as a groundside farmer and—well, she'd *have* to—a breeding machine. Though she wasn't sure that Orval Sprague's idea of variation in the siring of each woman's children made any sense, genetically. But now it struck her—after all her blithe talk of riding in freeze for years and years, or STL in the *Patton,* or of colonizing this world themselves—none of these alternatives would ever let her see her parents again. Or anyone else she'd known, on Earth or on *Inconnu Deux,* who wasn't here.

For long moments she simply didn't hear what anyone said; she was too busy fighting despair. Then Kobolak's words came through to her: "—older than cattle rustling, Arlen. Tribes raiding each other for women. And we could, you see, with the scout. But the ones here couldn't get back at us."

Lisele expected Alina to be shocked; instead, Kobolak's children and wife said in calm tones, "Not for women only, Anders. For adolescents, of both sexes. If you're really concerned about genetic resources. And of course the younger people would be less rigidly set in UET's ways, more flexible in adapting to ours."

I don't want to hear any more of this! Lisele said, "Stop it! You're talking about us getting to be like *them*. Well, we're not going to. Captain Delarov won't let you. We need a Nielson Cube, is what. So let's talk about getting one."

"Certainly," said Anders Kobolak. "You first, Moray."

Unable to find any answer at all, Lisele stood and left the group. In her bunk, this time, for a long while she *couldn't* sleep.

When she got up, dawn was breaking; Anders and Alina had the watch. As Lisele made breakfast for herself, Kobolak told her the duty arrangements he'd planned. "Like it or not, we have to adapt to this planet's thirty-hour day. That means four watch teams. The way I've set it up, if no one objects, is Alina and me, Limmer and Molyneux, you and Houk, Brower and Gray. Rotating in that order. All right?"

Peace take the man! Well, how to say it? "The order of rotation doesn't matter, one way or the other. But couldn't Arlen and I—?"

He shook his head. "You're both pilots, the only two aboard here, besides me. It's bad enough having one shift with no pilot, but two of you sleeping the same hours—no, it won't do."

She saw what he meant; with the three of them working separate watch tricks, at least one would always be awake and available, if needed. But *still*—! "How about if Gray and I swap? She teams with Houk, me with Brower? Could we do that?"

Anders frowned. "Maybe. If you give me a reason."

In peripheral vision she saw deWayne Houk entering the Control area. She moved her head slightly, to call Kobolak's attention to the man, and said only, "Compatibility. Tell you later, if you really need to know."

Startled for a moment, Kobolak nodded. "I think maybe I do. Meet me—let's see—" And that, Lisele realized, was a stumper. Where and when, in this crowded little can, could a confidential meeting occur without drawing attention?

"Anders," said Alina Rostadt, "don't be stuffy." As her husband began to muster protest, Alina's eyes narrowed into a look of determination. She turned to greet Houk. "Good morning, Chief. You'll be pleased to know that you don't draw duty for nearly twenty-four hours. You and Gray have fourth watch." She gestured toward Kobolak. "Anders and I are nearly done with first shift; when you've breakfasted, you might go wake Chief Brower. He, and Moray here, are due to relieve us soon."

Kobolak was glaring at her, but she showed no sign of noticing. "So Limmer and Molyneux are the team you'll be relieving. All clear?"

Houk frowned. "No pilot on our watch. *Or* Comm."

Making the best of things, Anders shrugged. "With only three pilots, one shift has to come up short. There'll always be one handy, though."

And Alina said, "And it's the same with Comm personnel. But only first and second tricks have the communication window with *March Hare*, anyway."

Lisele stared at Alina. Why, the woman had figured it out perfectly, even to reshuffling the order of rotation.

And to top it off, Arlen and Lisele were on adjacent shifts, not opposite. Had that choice been by accident, or purpose?

Lisele began to see how and why, so many years ago, Alina Rostadt had been chosen in a very dangerous situation to impersonate Lisele's mother, Rissa Kerguelen. She could think in a hurry, Alina could.

Watch change ran a little late, but no one seemed to mind. Arlen, not on duty but up and around anyway, sat for a leisurely breakfast. Brower, roused by Houk, ate briefly and joined the group in Control. "What's Katmai had to say yet? Anything?" And Lisele realized she hadn't even thought to ask about Delarov's reaction to events, past and present, here on Sitdown.

Kobolak made a minimal shrug. "Acknowledged, was about it. She was late in answering; we got worried. But she felt she needed to hear Malden's story in full before making any comment. And then what she said, basically, was that she wanted to give all the factors more thought, ahead of deciding on any recommendations to us."

"And that we must be very careful," Alina put in, "to do nothing to close off any possible course of action. As well as using extreme caution in dealing with the *Patton*."

Anders grinned. "I liked her signoff. She said 'Having a very dull time. Wish I were there.'"

He stood. "All right. Brower, Moray—it's your watch."

Before he and Alina got away, though, deWayne Houk wanted to talk with Anders. "Like to have a looksee groundside, if it's all right." He gestured toward the monitor screens, then patted the needle gun at his side. "Nobody out there, in sight. And I can take care of me, all safe."

Kobolak shook his head. "One person alone—I don't like it."

But Arlen Limmer, pushing his emptied plate away, stood in the dining cubby. "I'll go with him. Wait up, Chief Houk, while I get my blaster."

"*After* you wash your dishes," said Anders Kobolak.

*   *   *

Bound for either a bunk or the cubby, Alina left Control. Anders lingered. "Chief Brower? The matter isn't urgent, but the commodore would like to get direct communication set up. Groundside frequencies, straight voice at least, and maybe scramble. To save time."

Looking up from his comm-panel, where he was setting up a screen to follow the outdoor progress of Houk and Arlen, Brower grunted. "Save his troops a lot of walking, sure. You buy it?"

"I said we'd cooperate. On the *Patton*, none of that gear's been used since their last aircar blew out, maybe forty years ago." As the Comm Chief's eyebrows rose, Kobolak added, "In the colony itself, all local comm is by way of cables."

"Damned if I want that swine any closer than he has to be." But he hauled out a dog-eared tech manual. "Any idea what his frequencies are? Bandwidths? Modulation systems? Over—what is it by now, a century at least?—those things change a lot."

Anders shrugged. "He has two of his best people, the ones who know where the switches are on the panels, mostly, trying to get signal on the air. Wants us to search the bands and find it. If we can't, he's asked that you go there and see what you can do. And also help if they can't read *our* sigs."

Brower's fists clenched. "That'd be a goddamned order, would it, captain? Scout captain, Malden said. What if this Comm Chief, me, tells *Hare*'s Second Hat to bugger off?"

Kobolak's stare did not waver. "Alina's our only other Comm expert. If you want her to go in your place—"

Eduin Brower blinked, then said, "Ah, go piss up a rope! It's not I'm *scared* of that turd, and you know it."

Saying nothing, Anders waited. Finally Brower nodded. "You say go, I'll fuck-aye do it." He made the meanest grin Lisele had ever seen. "How much good it'll do the bastard— that, I'm not promising."

Kobolak's own smile looked less than amiable, but he said, "The bluff won't work, Chief. In your own specialty, you couldn't do a bad job if you tried."

He left; when he was well out of earshot, Brower turned to Lisele. "Trouble with that young man, sometimes he's right when I wish he wasn't."

Moving west, away from the UET ship and its colony, Arlen Limmer and deWayne Houk had climbed a low range of hills and were out of sight behind them. Nearly two hours later they came into view again, headed back to the scout. Arlen carried something not identifiable at a distance, and Houk had a bundle of native plants.

After a time the two men passed the lower limit of the monitor's range, and Houk, giving the "I assure you" password, called in for entry. Brower hit the Come In switch, which opened the scout's airlock and lowered the ramp. Receiving the Have Entered signal, he resealed the scout.

Lisele expected the exploring party to come directly to Control, but not for another half hour did they do so. Then Arlen, carrying some sort of cage, came in. And Houk behind him.

Limmer's smile was broad. "Wait 'til you see *this*!" He set the cage on the shelf of an idle console, and both Lisele and Brower peered inside, to see a small bundle of grey-brown fur, moving slowly and tentatively in its confined space.

"Welded the cage up out of exciter-lead wire," said Houk. "Loose odd ends only; waste stuff. Is why, took so long getting up here. Making the door work, mostly."

Any chance to ease tension with Houk was welcome, so Lisele praised his handiwork and even meant it; Brower added a few words in the same direction. Then Arlen opened the cage and removed its occupant, cupping the creature in his spread hands. "See?"

Lisele squinted. "What is it?" Roughly the bulk of a medium-sized gopher and much the same color, the animal looked to mass about a kilo. Though maybe much of the apparent size was merely fur.

Arlen smoothed back some of that fur, and a head appeared. No gopher, this: three peach-furred arced flaps of skin lifted to expose black, tiny, opaque eyes. And in the lifted position it was obvious that the flaps also served as ear-cups.

"Everything straight ahead," said Houk. "Beats all."

With apparent nonchalance that Lisele wouldn't have felt in dealing with a strange life form, Arlen probed a finger into the area below the eyes and ears, to expose a vertical slit. "The mouth," he said, and nudged it open.

No gopher, for sure and certain! Both sides of the opening, as far inside as Lisele could see, carried solid

groupings of rounded, irregular things: probably teeth of a
sort, but nothing like rodent incisors.

Herbivorous, then. And Houk had carried a bundle of
plants. Now he said, "Saw it eating, we did. Brought some
fodder along."

Eduin Brower shook his head. "And with all the other
crap we got to handle here, what good's this thing doing?"

Looking hurt but not sounding at all apologetic, Arlen
said, "Anything we can learn about this place, I think we
should."

Saying nothing, Brower shrugged. After a pause, Arlen
looked over to Lisele. "Want to know his name?"

"How do you know it's a he?"

"Well, I *don't*. Or even whether he and she *apply* here.
But—" Then, "All right; you want to know *its* name?"

Not particularly. But she said, "Sure; what is it?"

"Extra Sensory." When Lisele didn't respond, he said,
"Don't you see? Three eyes and three ears. Extras."

She guessed it made sense if you didn't pay close attention, so she tried to sound enthusiastic.

For three of Sitdown's long days, Eduin Brower let the
Patton's excuses for Comm techs stew in their own juices.
Then, under no direct orders from Anders Kobolak but
(Lisele noticed) after quite a lot of glowering from Anders,
Brower accompanied a *Patton* escort to that ship. He'd been
aboard less than an hour when full two-way comm was
established. "We can't get picture for sour owl crap, Kobolak,"
he said. "And forget scramble; our codes stack three levels
past theirs and damn if I bust my balls trying to sort *that*
out."

Kobolak gestured; Alina cut Talk. To his own group
Anders said, "It's a good compromise; we have minimum
comm to Malden, and Brower's over his sulks." He nodded;
Alina activated Send. He said, "I'm sure you're right, Brower.
Good job; captain out."

But as Rostadt reached to cut the circuit, a voice came.
"Malden here. Commodore Malden. While we're talking,
let's get to the next item on our agenda."

Alina moved her hand back from the switch. Looking
puzzled, Anders said, "Next item? I didn't know we had one
set up."

"If you listen, scout captain, instead of talking, in a moment you will be informed."

Kobolak's face went stubborn; Lisele knew he wasn't going to answer, and he didn't. He waited, until Malden said, "Our next item of business, then. It is how and when you and your other two men come here, so that over the necessary period of time, all four of you may contribute to our colony's gene pool."

XIX

His brows raised to their utmost, Anders Kobolak said, "Maybe you'd better explain that a little more."

"It's simple enough. We'll provide a house for each of you, and of course your food and so forth will be furnished. You each choose as many non-pregnant women as you like— and the more the better. At the time when any one of them should be fertile, she will stay with you for three days. For faster breeding, this system is obviously more efficient than Orval Sprague's. Naturally we don't want to keep you from your other duties any longer than need be."

Stretching his reach, Anders cut the Talk switch. "The man's crazy!"

DeWayne Houk nodded. "Not to tell him that, I think."

Unexpectedly, Alys Molyneux giggled. "*All* of it, insane. The black hole almost got us, then the radiation took my damn *hair*, most of what looks I ever had. The ship's Drive gone. Us stuck here on a stupid world with a lot of Uties, and no way off it. Now they want stud service!" She spread her arms wide. "I say the hell with all of it! I say—"

As Alina Rostadt's slap reverberated and Molyneux went silent, Lisele thought, *she doesn't even realize she's still handsome, hair or no hair*! But Naomi Gray was saying, "You can't all go stay in their area of control, captain. You—"

Anders swung a hand against any talk at all. "I know that. And more, too. But I need to *think*."

Leaning forward, Naomi Gray touched his shoulder.

"Tell that man—just tell him the matter is under advisement, and that you'll get back to him."

Kobolak's expression was a mixture of gratitude and surprise. He nodded, and on the circuit to Malden, phrased his answer rather closely to Naomi Gray's suggestion.

Cutting the circuit, he said, 'Now what?"

"This doesn't affect me personally," said Gray, "since they're not asking us women to breed for them. Not that we could, anyway, with our implants working. So I think I can speak impartially."

She paused; Kobolak said, "Well then, do it!"

"All right. I think you're going to have to do something along the lines Malden's asking. You want his cooperation, and here's your first hint of a bargaining tool."

DeWayne Houk smothered a laugh. "Tools; oh, yes!" Sobering, he said, "Father a few colonist brats, no skin off mine." He looked sidewise to Naomi Gray, as if gauging her reaction; when she showed none, he added, still looking at her, "But right, you have it. Not to go to them; they come here."

"No." Anders shook his head. "Whatever else we decide, there'll be no Uties—colonists, I mean—on this scout."

"And what *will* we decide?" said Alina Rostadt. Anders looked distressed, as his wife said, "If all this officially-mandated rutting gives us a chance to get our ship working again, I for one won't raise any prissy objections. I don't pretend to like it, but—" She clasped Kobolak's hand. "I know it's not your doing, and I won't hold it against you."

"I don't like it either," Arlen blurted out. His flushed face, Lisele thought, belied his words. "But if we *have* to—"

"If we have to," Alys Molyneux put in, "I want *my* share." Her head moved, tossing the hair she no longer had. "They don't have to know we're contracepted, or that none of us plan to be here any damn' nine months. So the hell with bald and ugly; they'll want me anyway!"

Kobolak glared at her. "Are you calling my wife ugly?" Her gaze dropped; he said, "I'm sorry you feel the way you do, but on top of everything else, Malden doesn't know that you and Gray even exist. And he's not going to; that's an order."

Houk grinned. "Hey, Molyneux. Wasn't you all the time so stuck up, might have asked you." She looked at him as though he were spoiled food, and his grin died. Then her expression softened, but Houk had turned away.

Angered, Lisele said, "If you're all done sniffing each other, can we get back to the problem?"

When a tentative solution emerged, it was Naomi Gray's suggestion. In final summary she proposed, "All right, then. Our territory, not theirs. Tents, pitched outside our safety perimeter. To include portable latrines and showers and a dining space. Logistics—" She shrugged. "We're bound to miss some problems, but to start with, they bring food and a water cart, every trip. And—"

As Gray continued, Lisele realized the woman's organizing talents. One oversight, though: Lisele interrupted to say, "We need some scheduling here. We don't ever want to have more than two men groundside at once. Only one, maybe." Anders agreed, and Lisele returned to brooding over Arlen Limmer's futile efforts to pretend he wasn't panting at the whole idea. *Oh, well; maybe he could do with the practice!*

A little later, Anders said, "I think we have everything settled now."

"Not exactly," said Lisele. "You still have to sell it to Cray Malden."

As Kobolak recorded a summary of the newest problem, for transmission to *March Hare*, Arlen Limmer stood and came to where Lisele sat. Leaning over her and speaking softly, he said, "I'm off watch now; going to grab a nap. Call me if anything happens?"

"Sure," and he left.

Anders taped his signoff and sat back. "Well, that's that. Too bad we can't send it for another seven or eight hours." Frowning then, he said, "It's getting dark. Brower should be here by now."

"Staying over, maybe?" said Houk. "Getting his licks in first?"

"But he—" Lisele began, and then shut up. It wasn't her place to point out that Brower and Delarov seemed quite devoted to each other—and besides, she could be wrong about the terms of that devotion. Meanwhile she noticed that Alys Molyneux had left and gone toward the sleeping space. To a bunk, or she and Arlen to the cubby? *Peace take me, I will* not *spy on them,* and she put her mind back to more important matters.

"Get me the commodore," Anders said.

"Right," said Alina.

She had to talk her way past two people who tried to stall her, but then, "Commodore Malden here. I trust you're calling to affirm our agreement?"

"Not exactly." Anders, Lisele noticed, had a rather good growl when he cared to use it. "I spoke our ship, of course, and the matter's being decided by Officers' Council. When they—"

"Then why, scout captain, are you interrupting my dinner?"

"My man Brower; he's overdue here. Why?"

Malden chuckled. "I thought that until the rest of you arrive, Brower might as well go ahead with our breeding program."

"I told you, that question hasn't been decided yet. Until it is—"

"Until it is, your man Brower waits here for the appearance of you other three."

Cutting the Talk circuit, Alina shook her head. "No. If he can hold one hostage, he could hold four. Then what would he demand? Our scout, here?"

And Lisele put in, "Tregare always said, don't give a blackmailer *anything.* There's no end to it."

Kobolak nodded; Alina reopened the circuit. "We don't negotiate on such a basis; that's firm policy and you should know it. I want my man back here in—" He checked his chrono. "—in one hour, or—"

"In the dark?" Malden's voice showed honest surprise. "Our handlights—even the rechargeables wear out eventually. We have to conserve what's left. And you may have noticed, this world has no moons of any size, to give light enough to matter."

Anders looked fit to bite porcupines! "At dawn, then, he starts for here. That'll still make him late for watch, but since it's not his fault—"

A pause then, with only noise crackling on the open channel, before Malden said, "We have one minor problem. On the schedule you demand, I'm afraid we can't spare an escort. And certainly we can't let a guest risk himself here, on a strange world, without protection."

* * *

All sign of blood left Kobolak's face; without it, his normally-fair skin showed deathly white. Whether from rage or the frustration of helplessness, he seemed paralyzed.

Looking around, Lisele saw decision on no face at all. Lunging, she got herself to the main comm panel. "Commodore Malden!" Somebody was trying to pull her away; she kicked her right heel back and heard a groan. "Commodore? Are you saying that Mr. Brower is a prisoner?"

"Of course not. It's—I said—no escort available, and—"

"Then you won't mind if we come pick him up."

Alina cut the circuit. "We can't send people into possible ambush!"

Lisele shook her head. "Course not. Open communications." When Rostadt did, Malden was saying, "wouldn't want that."

"No," Lisele said; the commodore's words, whatever they might have been, simply didn't matter. "Turn on your lights. So that when we move this scout over there, in about twenty minutes, we won't blast any more of your buildings than we can help."

As Cray Malden spluttered, Kobolak leaned forward. "And in the interests of safety I suggest you evacuate your people from this side of the colony."

Good; Anders had his brains back. His face regaining color now, he patted Lisele's shoulder. "I'll sign off now, commodore, so that you can make the necessary arrangements."

Malden's resigned sigh was quite audible. "Your impatience is raising hell with our normal schedules, Kobolak. But I suppose it's simpler to provide the escort, after all. I doubt that your Mister Brower will appreciate being dragged away from present company, but since you insist—"

Fifty-six Earth-standard minutes later, Eduin Brower came aboard the scout.

"Arlen, there wasn't time to wake you earlier. Everything happened too fast." For what it was worth, so much later, she'd found him in a bunk, alone.

After a moment his sulky look faded. "Sure, Lisele. Fill me in later, though?"

"Yes. But now, let's listen."

Sipping unwatered whiskey from Houk's bottle, Eduin Brower looked even messier than usual. "Friggin' well raped me, the bitches did—held me down while one straddled. Didn't think they could make a damn thing happen, that way, but then they started *pinching*." Scowling, he took a larger swallow. "I got bruises where nobody ought to. And that was just the *first* goddamn time." He shook his head. "Would've bet gold for shit against three comes at my age, but they got it." He drained the glass and gestured to Houk for a refill. "Gimme some more; I ain't burned so bad, all the way down the tube, since I was sixteen."

Alina said, "Since it's fertility they're after, that was stupid. The second and third discharges, so soon afterward, would be essentially sterile."

Brower's grin was half a snarl. "Too pissing bad you weren't there to tell those Utie sluts!" Then he paused. "Hey, sorry. None of it's your fault. Just, damn and all—"

Before Alina could answer, Houk cut in. "Put up, did you, a fight for virtue? At such an offer, not me. Why—?"

Eduin Brower's stare pinpointed Houk until the other man looked away. "Aaagh! Think you know it all, and don't know turd from biscuit. Screw virtue. And the same to caution; no ship ever lifted with fuck-diseases aboard. What you don't understand is—" His voice went plaintive. "Nobody asked. They just *told* me."

Houk nodded. "Apology, if you like. Hadn't considered that part. But I agree."

"'sall right, Houk. Surprised hell outa *me*, too."

Dodging Arlen's obvious wish to talk with her, Lisele got some sleep, setting her wrist-alarm to wake her two hours after the comm-window opened. This thirty-hour day, plus all the disruption, confused her time-sense, but so far she was keeping up. She rose and fixed a snack, sharing the table with Naomi Gray who was off watch now. Nothing new as yet, Gray told her.

Seeing the offship comm-screen light, Lisele went over to take a seat in the Control area; on the screen, Katmai Delarov appeared. "I've considered the events you report from your visit to the colony, and the tape from this self-styled commodore. I wish I could give you a plan to follow, a solution to our problem. But I haven't one. All I can suggest is that you gather further data as best you can, in hopes of finding a handle on the situation, and—" The woman leaned

forward; her image filled the screen. "And tell that man as
little as possible, of our true condition."

Moving back again, Delarov shrugged. "We may as well
be planning for several contingencies. I'm assuming you're
not in immediate danger there; if at any time you are, lift
scout and come home. Otherwise, if in another week—seven
of *your* days, I mean—you've made no progress toward an
agreement for borrowing their Nielson Cube, return here. In
that case we'll rouse everyone and hold briefing sessions, in
order to make an informed decision, by vote, as to what we
do next."

In the order they'd been proposed to her, she specified
choices. First, to put everyone in freeze, turn on the beacon,
and head *March Hare* for human space. Second, to bring the
ship to orbit around Sitdown, use the scout to bring people
and supplies groundside to start their own colony, out of
reach of the existing one. Then she cleared her throat.
"There's one other way. But I won't approve it unless every
single person in my crew votes to do so."

In the pause that followed, no viewer said a word. Until
Katmai Delarov continued. "Between the scout's projector
turret and its Drive blast, you could destroy that colony.
Enough of its two hundred fifty people, at least, that the
remainder wouldn't give you any trouble."

She blinked, and Lisele saw tears emerging. "But if I
have to give that order," said Delarov, "I refuse to live to see
it carried out."

The screen blanked; instead of human voice, star noise
hissed. Eduin Brower said, "Too good for this crappy world!
Damn blanketweaving squaw!" One hand wiped his eyes;
then he glared around at the group. "Don't nobody else call
her that, y'hear? *I'm* the one, loves her."

XX

The problem was that Delarov was two jumps behind
events. And as long as *March Hare* orbited Jumbo, she

always would be. Anders turned to Houk. "Are you *sure* your helpers, in Drive, couldn't get the ship here safely?"

"Sure of nothing." The man shrugged. "Ride that trip, though—I wouldn't care to."

Kobolak shook his head. "Then we won't suggest such a move. But there's not much we can do now, until the captain's been brought up to date."

The discussion seemed futile, with people talking in circles and ending up where they started. Lisele left.

Wanting to be by herself for a time, she went down to the Drive room and sat, staring at instruments that told her the Drive was quiescent, but ready on short notice. One light, blinking slowly and changing color at each appearance, had her almost hypnotized. So until Arlen Limmer said "Lisele?" she didn't notice that he'd entered.

Shaking free of her fugue state, she turned to gaze at him. "Something on your mind, Arlen?"

Fidgeting, he looked uncomfortable. She motioned him to a seat not far from her, then said, "Don't play games. If anything's bothering you, just say so."

Briefly, his forehead wrinkled. "It's this—this *breeding* program. I—"

Carefully she stifled her urge to laugh. "You'd like me to think you don't want to, but you really do. Right?" Not giving him time to answer, she said, "I don't blame you, Arlen; really I don't. You—" She paused; *mustn't condescend*.

"Lisele—if you and I were lovers, I'd say go to hell. To all of them."

"If you were ordered?" She shook her head. "No. You couldn't. Not when it's for the ship."

His face reddened. "I could try. I—oh, hell! I'm not saying this right—not what I *want* to say."

"Then why don't you?"

Arlen nodded. "Alys Molyneux asked me. I said no."

"Because she's bald and ugly?"

"Of course not!"

"Well, that's what *she* thinks."

"No. I told her that you and I—"

"Are lovers? Arlen—"

"Are going to be—I hope. That I'm waiting for you."

"You didn't have to. Say no, I mean."

His brows raised. "You wouldn't have minded?"

"Course I would've! But I don't own you."

Arlen's laugh held little humor. "I wish you did."

"Oh, Arlen!" Lisele hoped her exasperation didn't show, but the talk was going nowhere. "Owning isn't what I want." He didn't answer, so she said, "And neither do you, really."

Slowly, low-voiced, he said, "What I want is you. Us. Ever since Shaarbant, when you came back grownup while I'd been in freeze. But you keep putting everything off."

"I told you why. And it's not so long, now."

"Too long." His mouth twisted into a grimace. "I don't know what you think I've ever done. Well, nothing! And what I can't stand is, when I do start, it'll be with a damned Utie."

It's not their fault, but she didn't say it. Trying to think, for a time she said nothing at all. It wasn't his fault, either; the situation was none of his doing. So, what was the right thing to say? Tentatively, she spoke. "It's the way Alina said. I won't hold it against you."

He wanted to talk, but she kept going. "You think Tregare didn't have other lovers before he and Rissa met? I only know about two in particular: the Utie captain on Tregare's ship spaced one of them out the airlock, and that's what set off Escape. Another turned out to be an undercover Utie and tried to betray him. He spaced her himself. Others, I suppose—"

"It's not the same. He and Rissa *hadn't* met. You and I, we've known each other all our lives, practically. I—" His gaze dropped; he gestured futility.

"Yes. You're right; we have." Looking long and hard at Arlen Limmer, she tried to make up her mind: for him and for herself, in this crazy mess, what was the right thing to do?

Finally she stood. "I think you'd better dog the hatch, Arlen. We won't want interruptions."

All that Lisele knew of sex with another person was at second remove, from reading and discussion. But she did know it should be better than *this*. Her guess, that Arlen could use some practice, had been all too correct. Oh, he must have read or heard a few things, and he did try; from his words and voice-tones she knew he truly wanted to pleasure her. The trouble was, he didn't seem to know how.

He wasn't hurting her or anything; that much he did know, and was careful about. It was mostly that his rhythms didn't hold, that his movements were clumsy—and just when

her body had begun to make automatic adjustments in response, he finished.

Well, next time couldn't be anything but better.

As he sat beside her, Arlen's smile wouldn't quit. Feeling
somewhat less cheered, nonetheless Lisele patted his shoulder. After a time of silence he said, "I bet if we asked Anders
to marry us, he would. As scout captain he has the authority."

She thought about it. Why not? She'd committed herself
to Arlen now; might as well make it official. And this had
been only his first try at making love; surely he'd learn better.
So she said, "All right. Which style?"

"Huh?"

"Old, new, or free?" Oldstyle meant strict monogamy;
free was totally permissive. Newstyle allowed outside activity,
but only with specific sanction from the other spouse.

She waited, and after a time he said, "Does first choice
have to be permanent? Because I'd like oldstyle, but in this
setup we can't stick to it, right now."

Lisele nodded. "Too peacefixing true. So what about
newstyle? And then when this mess is over, have us an
oldstyle ceremony. That should take care of everything, don't
you think?"

"Mmm, yes, *Hey!*"

Well, maybe she'd let her hand get a little bold, but it
showed her that Arlen didn't need too long between times.
Feeling an excitement that surprised her, she said, "While
we're here?" He nodded. "This time, Arlen, why don't we do
everything very, very slowly?"

Oh, yes! Arlen could learn, all right!

They were lucky, she thought, that the intercom didn't
blare a minute or two earlier than it did. Because Eduin
Brower wasn't sounding very patient. "Limmer? Moray? Where
the hell are you? The skipper's on circuit."

Up in Control, most of the group were listening to
Katmai Delarov's comments on Commodore Malden's latest
demand. "Breeding program, eh? Typical UET thinking. In
fairness, though, if we're reduced to forming a colony—well
clear of Malden's, of course—we'd have to think much the
same way. Even to the suggestion someone made, of kidnap-
ping some of his younger people to augment the gene pool."

Frowning briefly, the captain paused. "Meanwhile you

need to answer the man, and I have no illusions that your choices will be easy ones. Eduin, you know that in this necessity you have my leave, freely given." Brower's face made momentary contortion; then he nodded. Delarov continued, "Anders and Alina: you'll have to decide for yourselves; we've never discussed how important exclusiveness is to your bonding so I have no idea. Mister Houk has no such problems, I'm sure. And Mister Limmer—" She chuckled. "Young men seldom argue against their gonads."

Arlen, Lisele saw, wanted to argue with *somebody*. Probably to back up his earlier brag to her, that if they were lovers he'd refuse to play Malden's game, orders or no orders. But that was unrealistic; she patted his arm, and he subsided.

"—temporary quarters nearby, as you suggest," the captain was saying. "So whatever you decide, individually, as to who participates and who doesn't, I suppose you'd better begin to make arrangements with Malden. Unless you've already done so, and in that case you have my retroactive approval."

She cleared her throat. "More importantly, we need data on the condition of the *Patton*'s Drive. I suggest—"

As Lisele listened, the captain's ideas sounded good. With the scout's people cooperating, Malden wasn't likely to get tricky again. Not for quite a while, anyway. "So for the moment I'm extending that one-week deadline I set. Just keep me posted.

"Delarov out."

The screen went blank; Brower cut the circuit. Anders Kobolak said, "She's right. I'd better call the commodore."

Cray Malden wasn't immediately available. Feeling restless, Lisele went into the sleeping area and sat on her bunk. She wanted time to think, but the place simply wasn't private enough. Go groundside? No; she wouldn't be allowed out by herself—even though, with someone on watch checking the outside monitors, there was no possible threat. What, then?

The love cubby. Its indicator showed Vacant, so she went inside and punched the Occupied button. Then, in the narrow space beside the doublesized bed, she stood and looked around.

Not exactly a bridal suite, this place, but minimally comfortable: soft colors and lighting, a few necessary facilities and conveniences; it would do.

Trying to get her thoughts in order, Lisele sat again.
What was bothering her? Did she regret anything she'd
done? Then she realized: it wasn't guilt that plagued her, but
a lack. She needed *Rissa;* this was a time when Lisele and her
mother could have talked together, the one's knowledge
making better sense out of the other's new experience. It had
happened so often, and always helped. But now, of course, it
couldn't.

Once again it came to Lisele that all her life, even during
the long harsh trek, thousands of kilos around the arc of
Shaarbant's surface, she'd had the comforting support of Rissa
and Tregare. And now it wasn't there.

Oh, she'd been alone when she and Elzh, of the Tsa,
broke through into communication. But she hadn't gone into
that situation on purpose; it fell on her, was what.

And so had this one. All right; Lisele nodded. She'd just
have to get used to being on her own. With a sigh, she lay
back onto the bed and dimmed the lighting near to dark.

Sleep came soon.

From outside the cubby, it was a voice that woke her.
"We've raised Malden. Let's go hear what he has to say."
Unwilling, for reasons she couldn't define, to have anyone see
her emerge from this place, she waited until no more sounds
came, then came out and went to Control.

Malden didn't like the arrangements. The colony's wom-
en to go to the scout? Only four at a time? Colony to supply
food and water? Escorts not to approach the scout, and rather
than staying, to return to the colony once they'd done their
job?

He argued nearly every point, but it got him nowhere.
Because Anders Kobolak, clearly enjoying himself, made it
plain who was on which end of the handle. As he worked
from reminder notes, Lisele thought he improvised very
well.

Sounding more plaintive than not, Malden said, "If we
make all these concessions, what do *we* get out of it?"

"Exactly what you asked for: four new chromosome-sets
into your gene pool, and distributed as widely as possible in
whatever time we have. Plus—" Lisele heard the faint tension in Kobolak's voice; *here comes the kicker!* "Plus, looking
ahead to possible recommissioning of the *Patton,* I offer the

services of two expert technicians. With your permission they'll inspect your Drive and make what corrective adjustments can be done with materiel at hand, while gathering data on repairs that can't be managed until the *Tamurlaine* arrives." He cleared his throat. "I'd think these benefits outweigh the minor inconvenience caused by our need to follow our standing orders."

Stammering, stumbling over his own words in the rush to express gratitude, Cray Malden bought the whole package.

"Married? Now?" "What on earth for?" Anders and Alina seemed puzzled by Lisele's request; Arlen, beside her, wasn't being much help.

"Because we want to. And you're authorized, Anders."

Aline reached across the small dining table to touch Lisele's hand. "You're not sixteen yet, not quite. And your parents aren't here to give consent."

Lisele didn't let herself laugh; it came out more like a snort. "You two have known Rissa and Tregare since before I was born. Do you think they'd say no, if I asked?" Glancing to the side she saw that Arlen's look was accusing; this wasn't what she'd told *him*, earlier. Well, things had changed, was all.

She said to him, "I did want to follow the formalities, Arlen. But now's not the time for that."

Kobolak nodded. "All right. What style?" Arlen told him, and he said, "I don't remember all the words, and I doubt we have any such book aboard, but I'll do the best I can."

So a little later, in the Control area because Lisele was on watch, Anders spoke a reasonably clear version of a newstyle marriage rite. Except for deWayne Houk, who was sleeping, all the scout's complement attended.

Not until Lisele's watch was done, and then Arlen's, did they go to the love cubby. To her relief, and—she supposed—Arlen's, too, the indicator read Vacant.

Having had time to think about such matters, she did try a little unobtrusive coaching. Definitely, it helped.

Two watch tricks after Malden agreed to Kobolak's terms, he called to announce that his first group, with escort, would soon be ready to leave the colony. Logistics had caused some delay; the scout simply didn't stock a number of items needed to set up the proposed facilities. Grumbling, the commodore had arranged to provide whatever was necessary.

Now, a good twenty meters farside of the safety perimeter for the scout's Drive, stood seven plastic tents: four "residential" and one each for dining, bathing, and excreting.

When Malden's call came, Lisele was having a light meal while she waited for Arlen's watch to end. Finishing quickly with food and utensils, she hurried over to the Control area in time to hear Malden say "—did tell you, you could choose individuals by priority. But from there, since we can't get picture over this circuit, I don't see how."

Obviously wakened on short notice, Anders said, "Doesn't matter. Look—have you figured out yet, how many you'll be sending here? In all?"

"It's not certain. If we follow our usual rules, the age for adult status and the two-year schedule, there aren't too many eligible. And three of those, we won't know for a week or two whether or not they've already caught. So—"

With evident effort, Kobolak relaxed his scowl. "What if we discount the three and you do stay with your normal rules?"

"Strictly speaking, only fifteen. But with a little fudging, less than half a year in any case, perhaps two dozen."

The scowl again. Anders said, "Fifteen then, for now. Four at a time." Well, under Delarov's current orders, the scout might be groundside long enough to take care of that minimum group. Not that Lisele cared two raps about the impregnation of a bunch of peace-wasting Uties, especially by the agency of Arlen Limmer! Now Anders said, "What time should we expect the first four?"

"In about an hour." Oh, damn! Before Arlen got off watch. So there wouldn't be time—"I wish you good luck, scout captain."

"Thank you, commodore." Anders cut the circuit. "Well, people. Let's use this hour to recheck our schedules."

No chance, then, of getting Arlen free of the last part of his watch shift. Lisele shrugged; only a few days ago, nothing like this would have mattered to her. And not too far in the future, one way or another they'd be out of here. But right now, she really wished the commodore wouldn't be quite so prompt.

But other matters caught her attention, as Kobolak said, "The important thing is to give deWayne Houk a good look at the *Patton*'s Nielson Cube. So that we can begin to decide what can be done, and what can't."

XXI

For this first of several less-than-romantic assignations, protocol was important. "Because," said Alina, "once we've set up a routine, we'll be pretty well stuck with it."

They talked matters out. When the *Patton* group arrived, all four men would have to meet them groundside. "To make choices, yes," said Naomi Gray, as deWayne Houk shrugged and Arlen's face went red. Then, on the principle of having only one man at a time in the temporary camp, three would reenter the scout.

Kobolak said, "We'll go unarmed; I think that's best. But, Lisele—just in case, you cover us from the airlock."

"Just in case," she said, "is what wins arguments. I remember Tregare saying that." She paused. "But why me?"

"Because," said Anders Kobolak, "you'll be the only one left aboard here who really knows how to shoot. Who's ever shot at much of anything—and hit it."

Small animals, yes, back on Shaarbant, for food. This was different, a *lot* different, but—all right; she nodded. "I'll carry my needler, then. Not an energy gun."

Houk grunted. "Both, you should have at hand."

He was scheduled for first duty in this bizarre assignment, so as to free him, as soon as possible, to go inspect the crippled ship's Drive. "Love 'em and leave 'em!" was Brower's comment, to which he added, "Flowers and candlelight ain't exactly what they'll expect. Not being used to it, anyway." Brower himself would be last in the ordering: "When I ain't quite so sore, maybe." Leaving Anders second and Arlen third.

With each man in turn merely going down to the tents once a day to perform stud service, and returning promptly to the scout, the breeding program didn't strike Lisele as being much of a social event.

*   *   *

Commodore Malden's escort service kept getting skimpi-
er; when the outside monitor showed a group approaching,
Lisele saw only three semi-uniformed persons with four
civilian-clad women. Second Officer Deryth Mangentes was
easy enough to recognize, needle gun and all. Whether
Lisele had previously seen the two young men carrying only
belt knives, she wasn't certain; they all tended to look a lot
alike.

"Well, gentlemen," said Anders Kobolak, "let's move."
He touched the tiny receiver behind his right ear. "Comm
same as at our initial contact, Moray," he added, "except that
we'll relay through Alina's board. So she can tape everything." Checking to see that her pocket two-way showed
operational, Lisele nodded. "All right then," Anders said, and
the four men, heading for the airlock hatch, left Control. As
far as that hatch, Lisele followed, watching them go down the
ramp. Then she brought the hatch back halfway-closed. So
that she could observe—or if need be, fire from a shielded
position.

So strange! Never in her life had Liesel Selene Moray
fired on a fellow-human. *What am I doing here?* But as
Anders had pointed out, of the four women present she was
the only one who could be depended on to hit anything,
reliably, with a needler. And regardless of Houk's advice,
a projector beam wasn't something, a person wanted to shoot
toward a group that had friends in it.

Her main hope was that she wouldn't have to do anything of the sort. But if she did have to, peace take it, she
would!

As the meeting began and continued, Lisele relaxed.
First Mangentes introduced her charges: only the four wom-
en, not the two escorting men. The names weren't important
to Lisele so she paid no heed to them; all she noticed were
appearances.

All right, then. The first woman small and dark, trim-
figured, presumably young. A second was tall, ruddy-faced,
sandy-haired; her jumpsuit's bulge indicated large, sagging
breasts. Grossly overweight, the third was; Lisele squinted
and saw that although the slanting light didn't show it clearly,
she did have a close-clipped fringe of pale blond hair. Her
face looked quite youthful.

The fourth woman was of medium height and very thin.

She looked at the ground, hiding her face; of her head, only the short black hair was visible, and smallish ears.

As Lisele ended her quick scan of the four, Mangentes said, "Well, it's time for strip and choose. But we'll do that inside a tent, if nobody minds. Or even if they do. This is bad enough on our women, without people watching from your scoutship."

"Stripping won't be necessary," said Anders Kobolak. "We'll decide now." Even as he spoke, Lisele had the thought that Utie or no Utie, she rather liked this scar-cheeked woman.

In order of the fictitious ranks assumed for this mission, the men chose. Anders took the skinny one; Lisele hoped the choice wasn't meant as criticism of Alina's excess bulk.

Eduin Brower surprised Lisele by nodding toward the obese blonde; then Drive Chief Houk opted for the tall, rangy woman with the oversized, sagging breasts.

Which left Arlen with the small, dark one—the youngest and only really attractive person in the lot. *On purpose, they did that? Oh, peace take it—who cares?*

On Lisele's comm set, Kobolak's voice came softly. "Moray? Skeds are set; we're coming aboard. Make ready to accompany our Drive tech to the *Patton* in an hour or two. Their escort group will wait to take you there. Acknowledge?"

"Yes, *sir*." Maybe the Uties could hear, maybe not. Either way, it wouldn't hurt to talk as if they could.

So she waited until everyone except DeWayne Houk came back into the scout, and the ramp was sealed again. On the screen, Mangentes and the two men could be seen retiring to the dining tent. When everyone on the scout gathered in Control, Lisele asked, "What happens next?" Working inside her she could feel more adrenalin than she liked; alpha-wave peace, now, was more than she could manage.

"It's not the way I'd prefer to do this," said Anders Kobolak, "but the *Patton* needs reconnoitering, in Drive and Control both. And while I think we have Cray Malden on hold for the time being, I can't send anyone who might be helpless against armed threat."

"Like *me*, you mean." Brower growled the words. "So

you're sending the kid, are you? Why'n't you go yourself, Kobolak?"

Before Anders could speak, Lisele found herself protesting. "Because he can't! Somebody has to be here, in charge, and he's the one who's stuck with it. Don't you see?" Half-standing, she sat back again. Brower was sitting open-mouthed; Lisele shrugged, and said, "Nobody ever put it that command was easy." *Now, when did I hear Tregare say that?*

Eduin Brower nodded. "Sorry, Kobolak. Never said I was *always* right."

After a longer time than might have been expected, Drive Chief Houk emerged from a tent and walked toward the scout; Anders had the ramp down before the man reached its foot.

When Houk came into Control, his face gave no clue to his feelings. "Have you a good time?" Grinning, Brower asked it.

Sitting, pouring coffee for himself, Houk shrugged. "Had better, had worse. Nice big cans on her, though." And was that all that mattered to this man? Fuming, Lisele said nothing.

Brower wasn't done. "That why you stayed for seconds?"

Houk shook his head. "No such happened." His face showed the beginning of anger, as he said, "Slow and easy, I like. And then—to leave right away, no talking after, not polite." For a moment he half-smiled. "What it's like elsewheres, she wanted to know. Hard thing to try to tell. Out of so much, what to say?"

In an abrupt reversal of feeling, Lisele realized she'd just seen an aspect of the Drive Chief that she could like.

He and she had a light meal before getting their gear together; that chore gave their stomachs time to settle before the hot, late-afternoon hike.

Loading the standard lifeboat-kit knapsack brought back memories. How far, back on Shaarbant, had Lisele toted one of these, before she had the weight and strength to pull a travois?

This one, she noted, wouldn't have taxed her even then, when she was so much smaller. Ration packets ("just in case") and personal items made up little space or weight; the main load was deWayne Houk's instruments, the ones he couldn't cram into his own pack. She hefted hers: well under ten kilos.

Plus, on her belt, a canteen and the needler.

"All right, Chief. I'm ready when you are."

From the dining tent someone must have been watching, because as Lisele and Houk started down the ramp Mangentes and her two subordinates came out. They stood there, waiting.

Mindful of UET's ideas about women and about rank, Lisele let Houk have the lead. He and the Second Officer shook hands; without further preliminaries the woman said, "Let's go." But she beckoned for Lisele to walk with her, leaving the three men to follow.

Not wanting to be first to speak, for a time Lisele walked in silence. After a minute, maybe two, the woman said, "Which of the men do you belong to? The young one?"

Belong to? Lisele said only, "We're paired, yes." Then, deciding that questions could go both ways, "Will you be part of this program?"

"I don't know yet." Looking aside, Lisele saw that the other's face showed no feeling. And how old was she? In the bio-thirties, Lisele guessed. Except for the scarred cheek, her skin showed relative youth and health. Now she said, "Goral hopes he already has me pregnant. He won't like it much if—" She shrugged. "But he won't buck the commodore's orders."

Silence again except for talk from behind, too low-voiced for words to be recognized. Until, "Moray? That's your name, isn't it?" Lisele nodded. "Are your people really going to get the *Patton* into space again?"

"I don't know. If we can, I suppose."

She felt the woman's hand on her shoulder. "Don't ever repeat this, but I hope you can't."

What—? "I don't understand."

"Here, I'm Second Officer. I worked for it and hurt for it, and I do the job. But say we get the ship to a UET base. I'm not really qualified and they'll know it. I'd be lucky to be no worse than unrated; Welfare's more like it." Her laugh came harsh. "Even the *commodore*—" and Lisele heard contempt in the word, "he's trained only as a rating, and too old for that, now."

No point in asking why no one told him so; topside airlock said it all. Lisele frowned; giving this woman any real facts was entirely too dangerous. But still—she said, "I don't

know how things were when the *Patton* left Earth, but in
these times ships' people with good records are *never* Welfared."
True, and yet she'd given no hint of the great changes back
on Earth.

Mangentes looked more cheerful; Lisele ventured a further question. "Is it because you're Second Officer, that you
don't wear the standard haircut?"

After a moment, the other laughed freely. "Not exactly.
It's because I wouldn't take the promotion unless I could
screen the scar a little. Well, it helped that I'm Goral Craig's
woman." She hesitated. "Mostly, that is. Once or twice a
month the commodore wants to see me. His ideas, you
understand, are a little different from most men's. Except
when he initiates the new adults. But he's not hung big
enough to really hurt much."

Why is she telling me all this? The grim thought came,
that maybe Lisele was intended to have no opportunity to
repeat any of it. Tentatively she said, "I wouldn't think you'd
talk about him this way. I mean—"

Another laugh. "Oh, everybody knows it; why shouldn't
you? So that in case you get invited, you'll know ahead of
time. I'm sure you have the sense to keep all this to yourself."

Strange. But maybe not so dangerous, after all—barring
this business of a possible "invitation" by Cray Malden.
Lisele said, "The cheek. Did it hurt a lot?"

Mangentes shrugged. "Afterward, one *hell* of a bunch. At
the time, though, Goral had me so drunk, they could've cut
my head off and I'd just have asked them not to lose it!"

Surprising herself, Lisele couldn't help but laugh.

Not for long, though. Another question itched at her,
and finally she said, "The man who was executed. Was he
really the commodore's own son?"

Stopping abruptly, Mangentes grabbed Lisele's elbow.
Then, shaking her head, the woman released her grip and
moved ahead again. "He told it, did he? Kobolak, I mean.
That was *officer* talk, damn it!"

"Malden told us himself, in the tape he gave Anders,
bringing us up to date on the colony's history. We found it
hard to believe, was all. And the commodore didn't say *why*."

She paused, hoping the Second Officer would answer
the question Lisele didn't want to ask. "All right. The son
tried to kill his father. Mutiny. Not going directly for com-

mand; he'd've had Goral and me to deal with first, and he knew better. Just to kill the commodore."

"For what reason?" This was pushing, but maybe the answer was important.

After several silent paces, Mangentes said, "His full sister was turning new adult. He objected to their father's plans for initiating her. What he didn't know, soon enough, was that she objected, too. Enough to walk out there—" Toward the horizon, the woman's hand waved. "—and not come back. She was already gone when he made his try."

Subdued, Lisele asked nothing more.

The talk had distracted her; suddenly she realized they were nearing the colony. Before she could notice much, Mangentes touched her arm. "You're only eighteen, Earth-bio; that's what Elseth Sprague told me. But you talk like older."

And why was that? Because she'd spent her growing-up years on the trek across Shaarbant, with Rissa and Tregare and Jenise Rorvik and Hagen Trent, not to mention the two alien Shrakken. Lisele said, "Since I was little, I haven't been around kids, to speak of. I didn't know it showed."

"It does." Mangentes pointed ahead. "Well, look now, would you? The commodore himself, he's out to meet us."

Lisele would just as soon he wasn't.

But sure enough, waiting outside the large galley-cum-meeting-hall was Commodore Malden, flanked by the hulking Goral Craig and two flunkeys—one male, one female. "Welcome," said the commodore. "I'd suppose you're hungry?"

Before answering, deWayne Houk moved into lead position. *He does understand these things.* "Not the case, sir," he said. "Fed before departure. But sit and have a bite, a drink maybe, talk while yourself dines—a pleasure, would be."

Malden smiled. "Fine. That will give us time to make arrangements, settle terms, for your stay here."

Only the commodore and his two officers escorted Houk and Lisele into the building. Inside, she saw a few people who were obviously there to provide service. The long, raised head table had no place settings, but in front of it, on the main floor, sat a smallish round table. Arranged for six, it could have accommodated perhaps two more in reasonable comfort.

Malden went to a chair, stood behind it, but made no move to sit. *Why six chairs for five people?* But then, hurrying, Elseth Sprague came in. "Sorry I'm late, commodore."

"Not enough to matter," said Cray Malden. "Now then." He turned to deWayne Houk. "You're the Drive man. Only a tech, I'm told. How skilled?"

"Up for Chief, next time home. To officer grade."

"That's good." Malden nodded. Then, to Lisele, "Cadet, aren't you? To check out our Control? Why couldn't they send someone better?"

He's dangerous, but— After one deep, calming breath, she said, "My training's good, sir. I don't know *all* the ins and outs of your circuitry on fullsized ships, but I can vet everything that's really important." He didn't look convinced, so she added, "When we came here, I landed the scout. I'd done that before: quite a lot, in fact.

"*Sir,*" she remembered to add, and was relieved to see Malden nod, then begin to assign seats. So far, so good . . .

The commodore put Houk directly across from him, with Deryth Mangentes and then Goral Craig to the Drive Chief's right. In the chair to Houk's left, Lisele had Elseth Sprague between herself and Malden. Once they were seated, the commodore raised a hand, signaling for delivery of food and drink.

Lisele (and Houk, she noticed) declined any part of a regular meal, preferring to sample snack trays and sip wine instead. Too nervous to be hungry so soon again, Lisele listened as Cray Malden rambled along in reminiscence.

"—hurt us a lot, yes. But hadn't been for Bull Cochrane, we'd all be dead that first year." His gesture swung wide. "On my tape, you've heard that." Coughing to dislodge something he hadn't quite managed to swallow, after some seconds he said, "Some of Bull's ideas, I've never liked too much. But they work, y'see. And—" He grinned. "If it ain't broke, don't fix it."

How she got through that seating, Lisele wasn't sure. Skipping between humorous incidents and others with grisly connotations, Commodore Malden held the floor. The scary part was that going from funny to nasty and back again, the commodore didn't seem to know the difference! Finally Lisele figured the problem out: *it's been too long since anybody told him "No" and made it stick!*

And in the heat of the place, the meager supply of wine had just enough sweetness that a sip of it made her more thirsty, rather than less.

But eventually Cray Malden, gulping the remainder of his own latest glass and then belching loudly, rose to his feet. "Well, then! It's getting a little late today, but at least we can give our guests a brief look into the *Patton*, to set their thinking before the real work starts."

Good enough, Lisele thought. But as Goral Craig began to lead the way out of the main hall, through a back door that faced toward the ship, she heard Malden say to deWayne Houk, "Craig can put you up with him and Mangentes and his other women; you'll do fine. And I'll take care of your colleague in my own quarters."

XXII

Anger fought with shock, and won. This peace-twister hadn't bothered to "invite" her, or even *tell* her directly; he'd simply assigned her to himself and informed her superior officer of the fact—as, presumably, a matter of courtesy!

Until peripheral vision showed Elseth Sprague pale-faced, shying away and shaking her head, Lisele didn't realize her right hand held the butt of her needler in an aching grip. The two women were behind the others; a quick glance told her no one else had noticed. With a nod toward Sprague, hoping to reassure her, Lisele moved her hand free of the weapon. *Was I going to shoot that man, for saying some words? What's happening to me?*

She had no idea what her face showed, but any kind of smile was out of the question. Quietly, from the side of her mouth, she said, "Just checking. Riding up loose, it felt like."

"Yes. Of course."

All right. But the problem hadn't gone away; what was she going to do about it? Up ahead, Houk was speaking, and belatedly Lisele realized she'd experienced adrenalin time-

stretch: while minutes had seemed to pass, only seconds
really had. "—regret, I'm sure," the man was saying. "Orders, though. The *Tamurlaine*, Captain Delarov's—only obeying,
is our scout captain."

What was this all about? Cray Malden looked angry but
not quite furious, as he said, "Can't be separated, eh? Quartered by yourselves; not very sociable. Well, we don't have a
spare house for just the two of you. What do you say to that?"

They were nearing the *Patton*'s ramp; Houk pointed up
it. "Quarter aboard, we can. With the work, it saves time."

"On the ship? No one lives there; haven't for years. Only
people allowed to board at all, nowadays, are me and my
officers and division chiefs. Well—Sprague, there, too. My
Drive Chief's too nearsighted to do a good tuning job, lately;
sends her instead. If it weren't that women don't have charge
of things, I'd space the idiot and give her his rank. She'll be
helping you with your checkup, by the way."

As they started up the ramp, Lisele didn't hear deWayne
Houk's answer, but Malden said, "Galley's been shut down
for ages. Take weeks to get it working, you understand. So—"

Since they'd brought rations along, Lisele expected Houk
to soft-pedal the matter. But he said, "Someone can bring
food: whoever's in and out. Sprague, you said?"

"Well, I suppose—" Malden's voice carried the whining
note Lisele had heard on parts of his "history" tape. "But I
look forward to meeting your Captain Delarov. He needs a
little instruction on intership protocol."

"Always willing to learn, the captain," said Houk. "But a
time, it may be. Sooner we check and report, shorter the
time."

Lisele regained calmness. *Chief, I owe you one!*

Inside, the *Patton* didn't really look its age. Stair treads
were worn, but not much worse than those on Tregare's
original *Inconnu*. From what Malden had said, Lisele supposed that shortly after the ship was brought here, most
activity had been taken groundside. And if only a few ever
came upship, and those few seldom—yes, that would account
for it.

Very little dust showed—but then the precipitators, used
occasionally, would take care of that.

When the galley level was reached, it was obvious that

the commodore had told truth; not even the glow of standby lights showed any indication of power in the darkened place.

Climbing past officers' quarters, the group reached Control; the large double doors to the area sat open. Lisele knew vaguely that UET ships' Control areas used to have doors at the entrances, but this was the first time she'd seen any. Something else about them nagged at her: some crudely-done repairs.

But again the commodore was talking. "You'll want to check for yourselves, of course, but the main intercom channels are working. At least, between here and anything that's important: the Drive room, officers' quarters, both airlocks, the cargo hatch." He paused. "That hatch needs fixing, by the way. Some imbecile, I forget the name, tried to close it when it wasn't clear. Burned out the motors *and* smashed our last aircar, that we wanted to uncrate and commission." Scowling, he said, "Spacing the fool didn't fix the aircar!"

Control was Lisele's assignment, so detouring around the commodore and his satellites she went to the main Comm position and began checking monitor functions of the main and aux screens. The funny thing was that although this console wasn't the same as those she was used to, it gave her no problems. Because it was simpler; it lacked some refinements she knew, but the basics didn't vary much.

Working fast, she began to run elimination sequences based on the principle that either end of a two-way circuit can be good or bad: if a given hookup didn't work, she switched to a Control component already proven out.

So rather quickly she ascertained that the main screen and five of eight aux screens worked; the other three didn't. At the far ends, enough outside monitors were operational to cover more than three-fourths of ambient space (assuming the ship ever got out there) and nearly all of groundside. She had no idea of those inputs' physical placement on the ship's hull, but that knowledge wasn't necessary.

Yes, the airlocks and cargo hatch all came onscreen. The latter puzzled her. Not the obvious charring of the motor mounts and some evident damage to the closing mechanisms—when you hit power-override hard enough to tear apart a ratchet of that size, it slings hot metal all over! But the hatch itself stood out flat-level from the hull, and as near as Lisele could estimate, it hung more than ten meters above ground level. And on *Inconnu* the extended hatch had been only about a fourth as high.

Well, of course! This was a simple flat loading gate. On ships like *Inconnu* the design had been improved; the gate swung down from above and had a stairstep right-angle bend in it. When you cinched the crates on solid, the gate *pivoted* the cargo up to the hold's true entrance.

"How does it look, so far?"

She hadn't heard the commodore come up behind her, but managed to suppress any physical start of surprise, and kept her voice calm when she told him what she'd learned. "Now the other internal circuits," she said, and began on them: quarters of officers and division chiefs, galley, the four cargo holds.

Except for captain's digs, those circuits responded only with "Power Off" indications. "Yes, that's right," said Malden. "A long time ago we shut those down. Sprague? Go turn them on. One at a time. Wait for a call and acknowledge it. Then move ahead to the next one."

He gave the order of locations for testing; Lisele tried to memorize it at first hearing and hoped Elseth Sprague could, too. Because she'd hate to see the woman suffer Malden's casual, deadly wrath.

Except for Chief Engineer's quarters, all stations responded. For a time Lisele worried that Sprague wouldn't know what to do next, but when the next stop was called, the woman answered. And, completing the list, returned to Control.

"Well, that's a good start," said Cray Malden. "You want to see Drive now?"

Houk shook his head. "Tired. Tomorrow, soon enough."

"By this time, maybe you'd like something to eat. Come groundside for it, or Sprague can deliver. Whatever you like."

Actually Lisele did feel hungry, but the Drive Chief said, "Tomorrow for that, too." No question about it, he wanted free of the *Patton*'s contingent. Lisele didn't know why, but he was playing the hand so she asked no questions.

Still Malden talked. Rather than saying merely that captain's quarters had the necessary conveniences, he explained in detail about bedding and running water and latrine facilities. But finally he motioned to his cortege and turned to leave. "In the morning I hope you'll join us groundside for breakfast. Two hours after dawn?"

Houk nodded. "Obliged," and the Uties went offship. Lisele, watching an aux-screen monitor, confirmed their leaving. She turned to Houk, but he spoke first. "Captain's digs. Work to do, and we need to eat first."

"But we could have—"

"Not with *them*. Need to talk, too."

As on any ship, the captain had certain minimal cooking arrangements. Houk heated two ration packets and made coffee. As they began to eat, Lisele tried to sort her thinking out. Well, first: "Hey, thanks for unhooking me from the commodore's plans. I didn't quite know how to handle it, myself."

Swallowing, he nodded. "Sure. Couldn't let that happen. Myself, need you here."

"Now just a minute! I'm not *your* cozy little bed partner, either. I can take some bedding and sleep in one of the unpowered rooms. I—"

"You. You don't listen, long enough." Surprisingly, for long moments he looked really angry; then his expression calmed. "Work, still tonight, I need you for." She must have looked puzzled, because he said, "Clear your head! Wanted you, a time back, yes. That youngster! I'd do you better. But now—"

He didn't seem to know what to say next. "Yes, Chief?"

Never before had she seen such a sheepish grin on the man. "First thing. To Brower I lied. *Did* stay and do a second time, with that woman. The rest was truth; also we talked. Needful, that was." His scowl, then, seemed to denote only concentration. "Forget other room. The big bed here—share it with me and fear nothing. As friends, only, we sleep. More important, though—"

"Yes?"

"Done eating soon, we check the Drive. Things we can't do with *them* around."

"Like what?"

He leaned forward. "Node power—how much is left? And the balance. Slight tilt, this ship has. Not much, but caused how? These things, we have to know."

"We do? Why?"

"A plan. Alternative. Nobody else—not Kobolak, not you, not anybody—says it. A way to save *March Hare*."

"What *is* it?"

With both of them done eating, he stood. "Once I find will it work, I tell you."

Scoutship routines persisted; before Lisele and Houk began the job the man wanted done, they cleaned up after eating. Then, up in Control, he told her what he wanted: between the two of them, calling indicator readings back and forth between Drive and Control, to bring the *Patton*'s Drive up live, to idling level and a bit more. "The thrust part, not," he said. "That, they'd hear, groundside. So just the power acceptance, by nodes and by numbers of facet plugs in each node. The push switch, we call it—that, I'll keep Off."

"What good will this do? Any of it?"

His shrug came onesided. "Balance."

"And what does that mean? Here, in this situation?"

"Later, we talk that. Now I go down to Drive."

He did, and for more than an hour they fiddled back and forth with Drive controls. First he wanted readings on the transverse thrustors used for Turnover and sometimes for course changes; those units seemed to be in good order and needed only minor adjustments to satisfy Houk's criteria. Whatever those might be, thought Liesel Selene Moray.

Then for an interminable period he had Lisele making adjustments and taking readings on the ship's major Drive nodes. From hearing Malden's tape she knew all three had lost function in too many facet plugs, ever to lift and reach another world. But Houk kept asking for shifts in power feeds; as she made adjustments in answer, she saw the three indicators show a smoother pattern, the separate phase relationships making smaller and fewer peaks and valleys. Whatever power/thrust level the man had achieved, and for whatever purpose, at least he had a more stable power distribution.

And finally he called over the intercom to say, "Gradual shutdown, let's do now. Around the board, all even." She followed his countdown, and the system settled to quiescence.

She met him in captain's quarters; nude, he sat with a glass of iced spirits and offered her another. "The skin, don't mind it. With friends we never do. Correct, not?"

She laughed. "I'm too pooped to care." She took the drink from his hand, and then a great cold gulp of it. Sitting heavily, she decided that the reason she didn't shuck her own sweaty clothes was that just now it was too much work.

"All right. What did you learn? About your plan, that is?"

His eyes narrowed. "It could work. But how to make it happen, may not be possible."

And peace take the man, she couldn't get him to say anything more, that made any sense.

So after a time she stripped and used a flagrant amount of the ship's water to wash herself in the captain's shower, and joined deWayne Houk in the huge bed.

Somehow, after the experiences of that particular day, she wasn't at all surprised that he stayed on his own side.

His chrono alarm woke her. Sitting up, she checked her own, and said, "It's barely dawn. Why—?"

"Two hours before we meet with them. Time we can use."

"Sure." She took first turn in the bathroom and came out to find coffee at hand. When he, too, was ready, they sat drinking it. She said, "Tell me a little more, can't you? What it is you're trying to do?"

"For now, balance Drive nodes, estimate thrusts. Power I've balanced, yes. Thrust—that's different. Darwin Pope were here, he could monitor facet plug leads and integrate results by computer. Me—" He shrugged. "Have to take individual readings, enter them, add them myself. Long job. Several trips here." Draining his cup, he stood. "Ready, are you?"

"Yes. But you haven't said—"

"Not now. When I know more." And that was that.

Houk kept them working until Lisele worried they'd be late and irritate the commodore. But this time he ordered a faster shutdown, and by hurrying ("on the high lope," Tregare would have said) they entered the large building about thirty seconds ahead of the ship's group. Except for a few servitors, the place was empty; Lisele decided it was used only for official occasions.

Standing behind the chairs they'd had previously, she and Chief Houk waited until Malden's people, the same ones who had been here yesterday, arrived. The commodore waved a hand. "Sit down, sit down"; when that was done, he said, "What can you tell me, Drive tech?"

Hungry, enjoying eggs and bread with the not-coffee and some tasty but unfamiliar juice, Lisele heard deWayne Houk tell a slightly different story than he'd told her. In this version he was merely assessing, unit by unit, the capabilities of the nodes and the facet plugs that comprised them. Of balance, he made no mention. *So he thinks he may have a way to* use *this Drive.* But what could it be?

The commodore seemed satisfied, so at this point the question didn't matter.

Done with breakfast, the six walked over to the *Patton* and went upship. Sprague wasn't there for long; Houk handed her a long-handled instrument and a short-range comm set. With instructions to go groundside, hold the instrument's sensor head against one facet plug after another at Lisele's orders, and report each reading back to Control. Lisele didn't know how the plugs' numbers were arranged on each node, but apparently Houk and Sprague did, so all she had to do was call out and report on the numbers as given to her.

She found the routine dull and boring, and was happy that the commodore seemed to feel the same way; after about twenty minutes of it he signaled to his officers and all three left. Lisele checked an aux monitor screen and confirmed that they did indeed go offship.

Four hours later the Chief called halt; he and then Sprague joined Lisele in Control. "A rest and some food now," he said.

"You could have told me that when I was still groundside!" For the first time, Lisele saw the woman show anger. "Now I'll have to go all the way down and back again, to bring the meal."

Looking startled, Houk said, "A better way, must be." He suggested that Sprague use an intercom circuit to the galley part of the large building, and order a lunch for three. Which someone else could deliver. When Sprague protested that "someone else" wouldn't be allowed to board the ship, he overrode her. "Top of the ramp, only. Where *I* meet, and accept the food." He paused. "Standard routine, from now. Acceptable?"

Eyes downcast, Sprague nodded. "Thank you. I'm sorry—"

"Don't bother. Should have thought, me."

The lunch was nothing special, Lisele decided, but hunger and a certain amount of fatigue helped it a lot. Again she passed on the rank-smelling local vegetable—and this time, also on the other "empty calories" entry. When they'd cleaned the utensils, it was back to work again.

Three more hours, only. Then, from Drive, Houk said, "For today, enough. Moray—the woman Sprague, tell her she's relieved. The equipment, no need to bring upship; take it with her, bring it back next time she's needed."

"All right. Anything else?"

"Escort back to the scout, if they think we still need one, ready in fifteen minutes."

"What's the hurry, Chief?"

"Tent duty I'm on, don't forget. Before that, after we walk to there, a little rest."

After Elseth Sprague acknowledged the instructions Lisele relayed, it didn't take long before a group headed back toward the scout. Without Houk's instruments, Lisele's pack seemed to weigh hardly anything.

She was disappointed that Deryth Mangentes didn't head the escort party. Instead Lisele walked beside Goral Craig, with one female and one male flanking deWayne Houk.

XXIII

As soon as they'd passed the last of the outlying buildings, Craig said, "Moray? The commodore asked me to get a report. How's it look, so far?"

The big man sounded friendly enough, *but with Uties, you never know*. She said, "About the Drive, you'll have to ask Mister Houk; that's his department. But probably he couldn't tell you much, yet. I think his testing's still in the early stages." True enough. "The Control circuits—well, you were there. A few failed units, but nothing serious." Would they have spares, and anyone who knew how to install them?

"Ummm." A few paces in silence; then he said, "You and

Deryth talked, she tells me. Her filling you in, some. I was
wondering, do you have any questions, just now?"

Was this a trap or an opportunity? She gave the man a
sidelong glance; he looked serious, but without the tension of
attempted deceit. So she took a chance. "If I'm out of line,
just say so. But I'm a little curious about your woman's
arrangements with the commodore."

His hand jerked, then, but not toward his gun. Walking
at Craig's right, she saw the move, and realized her own
weapon was out of his view. Briefly she thought, Tregare
would have figured that out ahead of time, not observed it
later. The officer's face darkened, and he said, "She told you
about *that*?"

"And with people who didn't already know, to keep it to
myself." He nodded, so she went on. "I was wondering how
you felt about it, is all."

His anger faded, gave way to a look of resignation.
"How'd you suppose I feel? Him doing her that way, any time
he wants." A great sigh, Goral Craig made then. "My father—
and that's Bull Cochrane, if you haven't heard or guessed—
he'd've slaughtered the man out of hand. But it happened
'tother way 'round."

There was no safe answer, so Lisele waited. Until Craig
said, "Knowing the history of this ship, you probably wonder
why I haven't done it. Well, I can't. Even though he killed
my father, I can't. He's a symbol, you see—the only living
person who came here with the ship. Crazy as he is, he holds
this colony together. I don't think I'd be able to manage that;
things could go totally to hell. And every bit of it would be
my fault."

Trying to find a response she could make, Lisele decided
that to say all this, Goral Craig must have really needed to
talk to someone.

And that probably he took after his mother a lot.

It seemed a good time to open a new subject; wiping
sweat from her forehead, Lisele said, "The days are getting
hotter, aren't they? How much worse does it get, here?"

His look showed faint surprise. "I hadn't thought. You
people aren't used to this, are you? Must say you're doing
well, Moray."

"Thanks. But we've had heat before. On—" Oops!

Shaarbant wasn't in "the *Tamurlaine*'s history!" "On Franklin's Jump; we got there a time after perihelion, but it was still pretty bad." Far as she knew, the Jump's climate was moderate, but these people couldn't know the difference.

"I keep forgetting you've been to other places. I wish I could. Well, maybe—"

Time to push a little? "Deryth was concerned about that. Maybe reaching a colony and not measuring up to modern-day officers' standards. How do you feel?"

He shrugged. "She worries too much. If we got the *Patton* someplace, safely, I'm sure we'd be allowed to study up on anything we needed to know."

It wouldn't do to say anything against UET; Lisele made a shrug of her own. "I expect so."

"I'd bet on it. Given the chance, I will." He looked ahead. "Not much farther now, to your scoutship. Excuse me; I think I *will* ask your Drive tech a few questions."

So he moved to join deWayne Houk. With no signal Lisele could notice, the other male escort came to walk with her. She hadn't taken a close look before, but now she recognized him—the young freckle-faced redhead with the sideways nose. "Hi," she said. "You're—I almost remember— Arnet? Arnet—" His other name refused to come to mind.

"Kern. I wondered if you'd remember me."

"Sure I do." And what else had he said? Oh, yes. "How's the sheep?"

He grinned. "Somebody else's problem, this month and next." Lisele hadn't heard or else couldn't remember how months worked on this world; she decided not to ask. "With the chance that you people can do something for our Drive, the commodore decided I should come in and really learn about it."

She nodded. "It can't hurt." They were near the plastic tents now, to the point where escorts stopped. She turned to shake the man's hand. "Nice to see you again."

"Yes," he said. "Next time on the ship, maybe."

"Might be. I hope you like to study hard."

"Wouldn't know. Never had to try."

She laughed, and turned to follow Houk to the scout's ramp. The trouble was, why did some of these Uties have to behave like real people?

*　　*　　*

Up the ramp and inside, Lisele opted for a quick cleanup and changed her clothing. Noting that she'd allowed used garments to pile up, she found the laundering machine idle and put a batch through it. Then, before joining the group above, she stowed her things away.

Several people were grouped around the Control consoles; Arlen was one, and not looking in her direction. In the dining nook sat Houk and Anders and Naomi Gray; as Lisele collected a light meal and some coffee for herself, Gray slid over to make a place to sit. "What do you think of the Chief's idea?"

With an accusative glare toward Houk, Lisele said, "How would I know? He hasn't told me what it is."

The man gestured appeasement. "Would have, were you here. To tell things twice, a waste."

But he had to tell it twice, anyway. Parts, at least, with the others filling in details. What it boiled down to was that if they could find no other way to get possession of the *Patton*'s Nielson Cube, that ship's own Drive could be used to "liberate" the device.

How? Two possibilities. Possibly the Drive could be balanced and fine-tuned well enough to lift the ship into low orbit. Then the scout could go to *March Hare*, and with deWayne Houk's help, bring that ship to dock with the *Patton*.

And if this couldn't be done? Kobolak said, "There's a way that's easier in terms of Drive capability, but riskier. Simply firing the Drive, fully hot but short of lift, could interdict the area. So that no one could come near the ship, while we disconnected its Cube and transferred it to the scout."

Lisele had a question. "To the scout? In that interdicted area you have in mind, where would the scout *be*?"

Then, seeing Houk grin as he held one palm out horizontally, she had the answer. Before he could speak, she said, "The cargo hatch door! It's flat, and big enough. With a soft setdown, it could take the weight."

Anders nodded. "I'm glad you see it." But Lisele frowned, and Kobolak said, "What else troubles you?"

She thought, *I don't like that interdict thing; no matter how it went, we'd kill people who don't deserve it*. But she said, "Low orbit, you're suggesting. Anders—except for Chief Houk and myself, none of us are allowed on the *Patton*."

"So?" Kobolak had his eyebrows up.

"So," said Liesel Selene, "I don't think we could do it, by ourselves." She pushed fingers back through her short hair. "Talk sense! If I thought I could manage orbit in a strange ship, you know I'd try. But I don't have the *training*. You're the only one, on here, who does. And the Chief would need someone watching the aux monitors, to pick up Drive corrections for him." She paused. "So tell me one thing. How do we get you extra people on board?"

He gestured. "Naomi? It's your idea; you tell it."

The woman, still gaunt-faced but looking healthy now, cleared her throat. "The little animal gave me the notion. To find out why the native meat's poisonous, I mean. I tested—"

Sure; scoutships sometimes had to serve as lifeboats. If you landed on a strange, habitable planet you had to be able to test the native plants and animals before you tried to eat any. Back on Shaarbant, marooned in the swamp with Tregare's crashed scout, Jenise Rorvik had done the testing in a more primitive way, because someone had borrowed the scout's kit.

But— "You killed Arlen's little pet? Does he know?"

Headshake. "I took samples only, blood and tissue." All right; Lisele nodded. "And the answers," Gray continued, "weren't all that hard to find."

"Then why didn't the *Patton*'s crew find them?"

Kobolak shrugged. "Maybe the mutineers destroyed the equipment. Or possibly, when that ship left Earth, the techniques simply hadn't been developed. Anyway—"

Naomi Gray nodded. "Anyway, the lethal factor in native meat is nothing fancy. Strictly chemical. The compound's name is too long to pronounce and if I did you wouldn't recognize it. Unfortunately, heat won't break the stuff down or boil it out. *But*—" For a moment, she paused, then said, "In our medical supplies we have something that makes a fairly good antidote. Not very much of it, but enough."

Lisele scowled; she didn't understand what all this had to do with anything. Before she could say as much, deWayne Houk slapped his hand down on the table. Grinning, he said, "Malden's tape! The main Uties—for dinner, feed them Sit-down stew!"

The "main Uties"? Including Deryth Mangentes and Goral Craig? But for Lisele to mention her reluctant liking for those two would do no good at all. She said only, "You think you'd catch the commodore in his own trap?"

"Why not?" said Gray. "It took him months to build his tolerance; we haven't been here a week. So how could he suspect anything?"

Lisele shook her head. "I still don't see how it works. Where does all this happen? Here? That still leaves more than two hundred colonists to get past, to reach the ship."

"Easy, now." Kobolak said it. "Here's how we've figured this, Moray. You and Houk, when you're at the *Patton*, you use captain's digs. So when we're ready, you host a dinner there for Malden and his officers and his division chiefs. A real treat, out of scout's supplies. Only with a little something extra in the stew." Her attempted protest, he waved aside. "Oh, it won't be stew, actually; that'd be too obvious. But some kind of meat dish with enough flavor to mask the native stuff."

"How *much* native stuff? Enough to kill? And how could you know what amount to use, to make them sick enough to be helpless?"

"It's all guesswork," said Gray, "except that I *can* measure the antidote to counteract the poison dosage you'd be getting. So to be certain that the plan works, we have to put that dosage on the high side."

When Cray Malden had poisoned his contemporaries, he'd killed only one he hadn't wanted dead, and in his tape he had expressed regret about that one. Were these people, here, even worse than Malden?

No, that wasn't fair. Malden's treachery was against his own shipmates, for personal gain. This Borgian plot was, at least, directed toward a threat to *March Hare* and the ship's entire complement. So Lisele said only, "So let's say this plan did work. Now how does it get you past all those colonists?"

Anders grinned. "Why, we're already there. Helping you honor the commodore. How else would he allow us aboard?"

I don't like any of this! But what could she say?

With the discussion at apparent end, Lisele stood, ready to leave. She turned toward the latrine and found herself facing Alys Molyneux. "Well, Moray. You and Houk have yourselves a good time, over in Utieville?" The woman's mouth tightened; then she said, "Since I'm not allowed groundside, I can call them anything I damn well please." She shouldered past, to the seat Lisele had vacated. Shrugging, Lisele stepped away.

As she neared the facility she sought, the door opened and Eduin Brower came out. "Hi'ya, Moray."

"Hi'ya, Chief."

She moved to step past him, but he said, "Ain't you gonna ask me did I have fun, down there in Tent City?"

Her smile didn't seem to want to work; she said, "Hadn't thought that was any of my business, Chief."

"Oh, everything's *everybody's* goddamn business these days, kid. All you got to do is ask."

"Sure. Did you? Have fun?"

Some of the man's obvious tension relaxed. "Better'n I'd've thought. I took the fat one so's she couldn't be as good as Katmai, no matter what. Accommodating woman, though—didn't expect more'n I could do, comfortable." His expression twisted, then eased again. "What the piss am I doing? Old renegade like me—she said it herself, Katmai did, and she's right—why's it knot me up like this, to hump somebody besides that damn fine squaw I got?"

"I don't know. She told you it was all right; remember?"

"For hellfire sure, she did. But—" He blinked hard. "Maybe it's—I cheated, sometimes; she never knew. Now she hands me a *license* to fuck. It just don't feel right."

Don't tell me about it; tell her. Not until Brower said, "You got you a good idea there," did Lisele realize she'd said it aloud.

After the delay with Brower, Lisele's need was urgent; her relief was also proportionately greater. As she emerged from the cubicle she found Arlen Limmer waiting. "Your turn," she said, but by the doleful look of him she knew that wasn't what he wanted—and that she was by no means done with listening to confessions.

"Oh, peace take, it, Arlen! What's *your* problem?"

"I can't tell you here. The cubby. All right?"

With a spitefulness she couldn't quite hide from herself, Lisele said, "Aren't you supposed to save yourself for the brood mares?"

His headshake wasn't negation. "To talk, I mean! Please."

She relented. "All right, Arlen." But when they were down there, the door closed and the "Occupied" light turned on, her irritation surfaced again. "So talk." *If you have to.*

On the side of the bed they sat well apart. He said, "It wasn't what I expected."

No possible answer to that; Lisele waited, and Arlen spoke
again. "She's pretty, you know. About your own age, I think."

"Naturally I needed that information. Go on."

"But she doesn't know the things we know." And hadn't
Houk said much the same? "Other things, though—"

He was stuck, but she was tired of that. "Like *what*?"

Arlen looked down, then to each side, anywhere except
directly toward her. "At first I couldn't. I don't know why."

Lisele neither knew nor cared. Arlen said, "Then she did
something for me, so I could."

If he thought she was going to ask for details, he'd have a
long wait! Finally he said, "Her mouth. I hadn't—"

Oh, peace take the man! She started to say something
scathing, then paused. Wait a minute— "On Stronghold,
when you were a kid in school, didn't they have the tapes
that showed all the different ways?"

He shook his head. "You mean, you already knew about
that?"

"From the tapes, sure."

"You never said anything."

"Didn't see any need to."

He sighed. "I wish you had. I hate it, learning something like that from a damned *Utie*."

She didn't bother to correct his terminology. "What's the
difference? You liked it, I expect."

"Yes, but—Lisele, would *you*—?"

For no reason she could identify, she felt embarrassment. "I don't think so." Because the tapes showed only what
happened, not the details of how it was done, and Liesel
Selene Moray disliked being awkward at *anything* she tried.

He couldn't seem to find an answer. She reached out, patted
his shoulder in vague effort at reassurance, and left the cubby.

To hear, on the intercom, "Captain's message coming in."

XXIV

There couldn't possibly have been time, Lisele thought,
for round trip comm with the *Hare*. But checking her chrono,

she found she was wrong. Houk must have taped his plan—
his and Gray's—immediately, and sent it out.

Quickly she climbed to Control and found a seat off to
one side, next to Alina Rostadt. To hear the voice of Captain
Delarov saying, ". . . condone the poisoning, except as an
absolute last resort." Well, *that* was good. "Now for the
alternate plan, using the *Patton*'s Drive emissions to chase
the colonists a safe distance away, so that you could load the
Cube onto the scout. I have no objection to this, provided
that you first interdict the ship's immediate area and then
warn the colonists that for their own safety they'll have to
move clear, to a considerable distance. Of course, that also
holds true of the low-orbit option. Taking their power source
and burning some buildings, if we have to, is one thing.
Frying people is something else."

The captain paused. "Not having seen a ship of that
vintage, I can't visualize this cargo hatch. But I'll take your
word that it's substantial enough to hold a scout, soft-landed.
Now of course you realize, though nobody mentioned the
problem, that you'll need to land with your airlock facing the
open hatch. So—is there room, once you're landed, to maneuver an object the size and weight of a Nielson Cube,
between the ship's hull and the scout's? To hoist it, insulation-
wrapped, and lash it firmly to the scout?" Her voice gained
intensity. "Be sure you *check* all these things first, is what I'm
saying. Because nothing's worse than a plan that breaks down
in the middle, because of some small overlooked detail."

So far, Lisele thought, Katmai Delarov was right on top
of things! Now the woman said, "Your area of interdiction
must keep the colonists out of effective, accurate handgun
range, including heavy-duty energy weapons. You've mentioned
at least one officer carrying that model." Goral Craig, yes.
"The dust and churned-up debris from the Drive will shield
your activities visually. Which also means, I suppose, that if
you intend to breathe while the Cube's being transshipped,
any of you working outside had better be suited up." Another
pause, then, "Oh, hell! The scout carries only two suits, if I
recall. The utility model—the one that fits most people, but
nobody really well. And to secure that Cube you'll need at
least three of you working; four would be better. So, Houk
and Moray, you'd best check to see if the *Patton* still has any
spacesuits that might function for perhaps an hour." Well, for

that matter, unless the cargo hatch could be closed and sealed, they'd need suits for any try at low orbit.

What had sounded fairly simple, at first, was getting more complicated all the time! And the captain wasn't done yet: "Even if they can't see you, and have no idea what you're really doing, they can still shoot into the area where you *have* to be. Which is on and above the cargo hatch, between ship and scout. They can sit off to each side, keep shooting, and hope to get lucky. Because to anyone with the slightest indication of brains, that's the only thing they *can* do."

From the sounds that came next, Lisele decided the captain was swallowing some liquid; then Delarov cleared her throat. When she spoke, Lisele's own train of thought predicted the words to come. "The way you handle that problem," said Katmai Delarov, "is with snipers, working from the ship's topside airlock. One covering each side."

One more brief pause; then, "Delarov out."

Lisele said to Alina, "Well. She certainly picked up on the possibilities, fast."

"I thought she was against killing. Certainly didn't sound like it, this time."

Lisele shook her head. "Then you weren't listening. She was talking about shooting *back*."

Alina's expression cleared somewhat, but she still looked worried. She said, "Our men's groundside duty. Are you and Arlen handling the situation all right?"

In no mood to bare her own feelings, or Arlen's problems, or any of it, Lisele said, "Well enough. And you?"

Looking chagrined, Alina made a faint laugh. "About the same, I'd expect." She shrugged. "It didn't pass my notice that he chose the slimmest one. Do you think he was hinting to me?"

Enough of this! Lisele stood. She did like Alina, but— "You could ask him, I suppose."

The woman sighed. "I really should cut down, shouldn't I?"

"If you want to," said Lisele, and left. She could use a bite to eat, herself. And then a little sleep wouldn't hurt.

What with "tent duty," along with Lisele's and Houk's work at the *Patton,* watch skeds had become a total hash. Next morning, after readying herself for the day, Lisele filled in for half a watch, relieving Alys Molyneux. It was no surprise that the woman didn't bother with thanks.

People came and went. DeWayne Houk had breakfast, disappeared below for a time, then on the monitor could be seen arriving groundside and going to one of the tents. Well, he'd be there for an hour or so, at least.

Anders Kobolak, over at the dining nook, caught Lisele's attention as he raised his eyebrows and a cup. She nodded, so he brought coffee for each of them. Sitting alongside, he said, "Did a night's sleep give you any good ideas?"

"Not really. Except that low orbit looks tougher all the time. Even if we didn't need the cargo hatch to land on, I don't think we could raise and seal it." Against his protest, she shook her head. "You haven't seen what's left of the mechanism."

He nodded, then. "If you say so, I believe you. I hadn't really considered the matter. Maybe because I've never been inside the ship, myself. So what do you suggest?"

"Up above atmosphere, you'd have to bring the scout to rendezvous before we run out of tanked air. Can you?"

"I'd think so. Once Houk gives us his evaluation of the *Patton*'s Drive. When do you think he can do that?"

"Don't know. I doubt if he does, either, this early. After he's finished for today, groundside, I expect he and I go back for more testing?"

"Yes. If we knew when that would be, I could call the commodore and schedule his escort service."

Lisele checked her chrono. "It doesn't matter. I promised to sit watch for four hours, and there's more than two of those left. Twenty minutes after that, we could leave, and the Chief should be here well before then."

So Anders put the call through, reaching Deryth Mangentes at the other end, and they made the arrangements. Houk came aboard forty minutes before Lisele's watch trick ended, and an hour later the two of them stood groundside.

Today only Arnet Kern had come for them—the freckle-faced man with the skewed nose. Carrying, this time, a smallish, well-worn energy weapon. "Greetings! From now on I'm supposed to work with you. So I guess the commodore thought I could be asking some questions, while we walk. If I knew what to ask."

"The asking, I'll do," deWayne Houk said. "What you already know, is good place to start."

"Hi, Arnet," said Lisele. As they began the hike she stepped to Kern's right, leaving the other side to Houk. After only a few steps she paused and knelt down, pretending to adjust her shoe's fastenings but sneaking a glance at the man's gun.

The charge indicator showed practically zerch. Not that it mattered, probably, but it didn't hurt to know these things!

About the *Patton*'s Drive, Kern knew even less than Lisele did. So whatever Chief Houk was trying to do with that Drive, the young man's observation of the process could be no danger. Still, after a few minutes of questioning, Houk said, "Below, groundside, you'll start. Helping Sprague," and explained that the sensing instrument was a little heavy for her to manage, while taking readings at the same time.

"Whatever you say," said Arnet Kern. And then, "You the one who's siring on Ardissa?"

Houk frowned and shook his head. "That name I don't know. Just Urline, the one I go to."

Kern looked at him. "For a woman, she has brains. If that's what you like." He shrugged. "I expect your scout captain picked Ardissa off. Being as she's the prettiest."

Watching Houk figure it out, suddenly Lisele wanted to tell him to shut up. But she couldn't do that, not in a Utie's presence. He said, "The one young Limmer has, that'd be."

Suddenly Kern's face wore a tight grin. "The young one, eh? Then I'm not outranked! Or not by much. I can challenge him!"

"Challenge?" Lisele didn't understand, and said so.

"The Submissuals. Maybe he's been through them on Earth, but not here, and when it comes to rights with women, here's what counts!"

Flat-voiced, Houk said, "This challenge means what?"

"It means I get my chance—hand-to-hand, of course—to kill him. And have Ardissa back."

Peace take it! Arlen, Lisele knew, had practically no combat training. Armed, or unarmed. This colonist's fighting techniques must be decades behind current training, but they'd be better than none at all! The man could kill Arlen—and for something that wasn't even Arlen's fault.

When in doubt, bluff! Lisele said, "I'm afraid Captain Delarov won't allow such an obvious mismatch." As deWayne Houk looked at her, his puzzlement obvious, she said, "If Arlen Limmer were to kill you in unarmed combat, his advantage in skills would make it murder. The captain wouldn't care to have to prosecute such a charge."

As Kern, frowning, tried to find an answer, Lisele knew what she had to do. "I'll show you what I mean. In real combat, Limmer could kill me in less than a minute. But I'll bet that if I fight *you*—to first disablement, say, or a no-escape pindown—I'll win."

As she and Kern stripped to basic briefs, ignoring the protests of deWayne Houk, Lisele put her mind to what she intended to do. She had no formal combat training; what she knew, she'd learned from working out with Rissa, her mother, during the long stopovers in the trek around Shaarbant. Not the hot-weather stops, but the rainy ones. Rissa had taught her a lot. Of course she'd never tried the killing moves except as "pulled punches," but this wasn't going to be a death bout. And she had three things on her side. She knew advanced, modern techniques Kern couldn't know. She'd spent four (or was it five?) years in strenuous physical activity. And she'd done it in a gravity field appreciably stronger than this one.

Still her breath and pulse speeded; alpha-state calm was hard to attain. "Ready?" she said, and moved toward Kern.

Wanting to know what the man could do and what he couldn't, she held her first moves to feints. Then, nodding, she stepped forward in wide-open stance and caught his outflung arm to make a hip throw, sending Kern to the ground with a satisfying thud.

So far, so good. She moved back, but still he rolled and sprang up faster than she expected; his foot came at her like a projectile, and only fast reflex got her head out of the way in time. At that, his shoe grazed an ear.

He was off balance now. Without thought, Lisele went to ground, hooking one instep behind his ankle and launching her other foot straight at his kneecap. But in midthrust she eased the strike; instead of a knee-breaking kick, she caught him with a push just hard enough to pivot him backward. Since he didn't get his arms out soon enough to break the fall, he landed flat and hard.

Scrambling to her feet, Lisele stepped back to catch her breath and was surprised to see Kern in starter's-blocks position, ready to charge at her.

"Hold it!" and he paused. "I could have wrecked your knee there, if I wanted to."

"But you didn't. So—"

"Don't you understand? I *chose* not to lame you for life."

He nodded. "And now you're stuck with that choice." Slowly, he moved forward. "Ready, are you?"

"No!" Frowning, she said, "We better get our rules straight first. The ones I'm used to, when it's not to the death, then demonstrating that you *could* disable counts for the real thing."

He looked puzzled; she said, "By those rules, I won. If that's not good enough for you, then I guess I'm ready again."

"You wouldn't catch me the same way twice!"

"What makes you think I'd have to?"

Uncertain now, he moved forward again. Until deWayne Houk stepped between them. "Hold. Matter of rules, we vote."

"Vote?" Kern's voice, protesting, went high.

"Sure, vote!" With a grateful look to the Chief, Lisele continued. "Among people from different worlds, different customs, that's always how it's done."

"What's the use? You vote your rules, I vote mine. We're still stuck."

"Witness," said Chief Houk, pointing to himself. "Votes, too. Temptation, though, to vote your side. Let her show you."

Lisele glared at him. After a moment, with a lopsided grin Houk shrugged and cast his vote with Lisele's. Unable to discern whether Arnet Kern was more frustrated or relieved, she said, "You still mad about anything?"

"No." Looking very serious, he said, "Because I think you just saved my life, didn't you? If that Limmer—! Thanks, I guess."

"How do you feel about Limmer, now?"

Kern shrugged. "It's like with the commodore. If you can't do anything about it, you don't."

Sometimes, thought Lisele, a bluff does work.

Fully clothed again, the two walked along with Chief Houk. That man kept looking over to Lisele, but whatever questions he might want to ask, they couldn't be spoken in Kern's presence.

At the colony Deryth Mangentes met them. "The commodore's busy. I'll let you aboard, and Sprague's ready for duty."

At the foot of the *Patton*'s ramp Elseth Sprague waited, with one end of the sensing instrument on the ground like a rifle at "parade rest." After greetings, Houk said, "Kern, you help Sprague. Just what she says, you do."

Then, as Mangentes left them, he and Lisele climbed upship to Control, where he unfolded a partly-finished chart. "The Drive nodes, Moray. Thrust-percentage figures on the facet plugs." As he explained it, all Lisele had to do was give instructions, which plug to read next, and enter Sprague's reported figure in the proper space. "To make no mistake, is crucial."

"All right, Chief. But *you* did all this, last time. So why—?"

"Down below, I'll be. With the tools, a ladder. To remove plugs, somewhere else place them."

"You're going to balance the nodes, aren't you? For best max thrust all around. But when somebody asks us why, what do we say? That makes sense to *them*?"

"A thing not true, so not necessary you understand." He coughed once; Lisele took it to be only a hesitation. "I am, what we'll say, best-matching plugs to power feeds. For, when—uh, the *Tamurlaine*—lands, least work remaining."

"You're right. I don't understand it at all."

"The commodore also, I hope."

Houk didn't go groundside immediately. For the first hour or so he called instructions down to Sprague and checked the figures reported, plus Lisele's placement of them on his chart. Then he said to her, "Down there, I go now," and explained that although less than half the facet plugs had been checked, from the overall power draw of each node he already had enough data to begin relocating a few fully-operative plugs from the best node to the weakest one. "Fine-tune it later," he said. "For now, save time on preliminary balance."

"Makes sense." So he left Control; following his listings, Lisele called down plug-position numbers and recorded Sprague's readings on them.

Shortly before the local-time readout on Lisele's chrono reached Sitdown's midday, Houk called her. "For lunch, break now. Down here, I'll eat. You also, or a meal delivered?"

From the contest with Kern and the walk afterward, one leg hurt. "Neither, thanks. I'll heat rations."

So she went down to captain's digs. And opened the door to find Cray Malden inside.

"Welcome," he said. "I've been waiting for you."

XXV

A step past the entrance, one hand still on the door's handle, Lisele froze in place. "Commodore."

She didn't like the expression on his face, his presence here, or anything about him. "You—" She wasn't sure what she intended to say, but she had no time to say it; looking a bit to Lisele's right, Malden nodded.

The door was jolted from her grasp; someone pushed her from behind. She felt a hand brush her side, and turned to see the big woman, Thela Cochrane, holding Lisele's needler.

The dark-faced, heavy woman had the gun, all right, but not in a firing grasp. The door hadn't closed fully; Lisele grabbed and swung it open, as hard as she could.

Its bottom edge, perhaps five centimeters above the room's floor, raked the instep of Cochrane's sandaled foot and jammed against the ankle. With a high-pitched, cursing scream, the woman crouched to free her injured foot. Ignoring that problem, Lisele reached across to Cochrane's other hand and retrieved her weapon. Pointing it perhaps three decimeters to one side of the commodore, she said to the moaning woman, "I'm afraid I was clumsy. Thanks for catching this before it hit the deck."

Things had happened too fast for any emotional reaction, yet without the special urgency that brought adrenalin time-stretch. Now as her pulse slowed, Lisele looked at Malden and saw no visible weapons. The commodore said nothing, so she took her time before saying, "I wasn't expecting you. Mangentes told us you were busy."

Temporarily chalk-faced and expressionless, Malden began to regain color and essayed a kind of smile. He gestured toward the gun. "Would you mind—?"

As though her aiming had been accidental, Lisele nodded, then let the weapon hang at her side. "Sorry. I forgot I had it." He wouldn't believe her, but why should he?

In peripheral vision she saw Cochrane stand and take a limping step, before saying, "Commodore?"

Malden frowned. "Go get that foot looked after. Bennings is staying with Craig this month; she may be there now."

"But shouldn't I—?"

"You bungling fool, I said get out!" Bungling fool, eh? The commodore certainly wasn't good at covering up! Edging past Lisele, the woman went out, and closed the door behind her.

Now Lisele cased the gun. "What are you doing here? Sir."

"It's my ship, isn't it?"

"I mean, you said you were waiting for me. Why?"

His grin had a nasty look to it. "Your men are enjoying our women, aren't they? So—"

"That was your idea, not theirs."

"And so's this. Things should go both ways."

So *that* was the peacetwister's aim. Holding to calmness with almost-gritted teeth, refusing panic any hold on her, she said, "Well, they don't, commodore. And I couldn't breed now if I wanted to. My implant—"

As though brushing her argument aside, his hand moved. "No thought of breeding—Moray, isn't it? Simply enjoyment."

"Enjoyment?" With Thela Cochrane there to hold her down, to make certain she "enjoyed" the man's special ways? No point in saying any of that. "I'll have to decline. Now—" She paused, because she couldn't very well order Malden around on his own ship. But she wasn't going to eat while he was there. So she said, "Now I'm going groundside and have lunch with Mister Houk."

He tried to smile, but his glare betrayed his anger. He stepped toward her; deliberately she halted her hand's involuntary move toward the needler. He must have noticed the brief twitch, for he stopped moving. "What's the trouble, Moray? You're not afraid of me, are you?"

As soon as he said it, she knew she *had* been afraid—but that now, with the man unarmed and lacking his female gorilla, she had no cause for fear. "No, commodore. I'm not."

He went past her, almost close enough for garments to brush together. She moved to open the door for him, then closed it when he was gone.

Well, she might as well eat here after all. And in a hurry: the commodore's little games had used up most of her lunch break.

Late or not, she finished cleanup before she left. As she entered Control, Houk's voice on the intercom sounded peevish. "To eat a bite, how long? Moray—?"

She punched the channel switch. "I was delayed, Mister Houk, by a visit from Commodore Malden and—and one of his crew. We can talk about it later. Now we left off in Node Three, fifth circle, plug number two, clockwise on ship's axis as seen from below. Ready on number three."

The brisk recitation of full data, even though Houk already knew it, shut off his complaints. "On three, ready. Your reading, Sprague?" And when Lisele reported the reading entered on the chart, Houk added, "That visit. Later, yes, tell me."

During the morning stint deWayne Houk had relocated only a few facet plugs; now he was doing so after every second or third reading. Each time he did it, Lisele's work stopped, because the task needed physical help from Kern, and Elseth Sprague had to keep out of the way. A facet plug, Lisele recalled, massed about ten kilos.

Each change meant removing two plugs but relocating only one; the "dead" units were to be brought upship, where the Chief would test circuitry and see if any could be repaired. Arnet Kern, Lisele thought, was going to be stuck with a lot of carrying!

The pauses bored her, so she began using them to check other data on the Control consoles. After a time she also began making notes. Some of this stuff might be important. . . .

When deWayne Houk called a halt to the workshift, he and Kern and Sprague each carried a plug upship. Lisele, too, was pressed into service; all four of them made three trips down and back. Total of plugs for the Chief to check out: fifteen.

Having done the least carrying, Lisele drew the chore of meeting someone at ramp's top to accept the meal Houk had ordered. She had no idea why he wanted Sprague and Kern to dine with them, but there was no way to ask, so she accepted the fact.

At the airlock she was surprised to find Thela Cochrane delivering dinner. The woman glowered. "Think you're pretty good, don't you? That trick with the door." Looking down, Lisele saw bandages sheathing a swollen foot; traces of blood had seeped through to the surface. Cochrane made a snort. "The commodore didn't tell me not to, I'd show you different."

Pure malevolence, this one; at the banquet, with a man's death as entertainment, Cochrane had shown it. Carefully, Lisele stepped back and gestured for the woman to set the dinner trays down, off to one side. Then she said, "I didn't hurt you on purpose. You surprised me and my reflexes took over. I—"

Cochrane turned to go back down the ramp. "From now on, you keep out of my way!"

Gladly! But the ultimatum couldn't be left unanswered, or Cochrane would hold advantage. "And you out of mine!"

The woman looked back; whatever she may have thought was hidden behind the blackest of scowls. Then she went groundside.

The food—roasted meats, vegetables both raw and cooked, a little fruit—was tasty enough, but much the same as previous meals from colony supplies. It could, Lisele decided, begin to get monotonous. At least it wasn't spicy; had it been, after having been in Cochrane's hands, Lisele wouldn't have taken a second bite, nor allowed anyone else to do so. Not after hearing Malden's tape, she wouldn't!

As they ate, Chief Houk asked questions of Elseth Sprague, mostly concerning the *Patton*'s Drive. Since these were things he must have known already, the motive had to be learning the extent of *her* knowledge. As near as Lisele could determine, the woman was sketchy on theory but solid on operation.

Along with the meal, the four finished a bottle of the colony's wine: not as sweet, this, as the stuff the commodore had offered on their previous trip here. Then, from scout's

rations, Houk offered Sprague and Kern real coffee. The
gesture may have been well-intended, but the fact was that
neither colonist *liked* the unfamiliar drink. After one cup
each, they both switched to not-coffee from the trays Cochrane
had brought.

Daydreaming for a moment, when conversation had
lapsed into quiet, Lisele heard Houk speak, and realized he
was breaking new ground. "—so about your life here, tell
me."

"It's good, mostly," said Kern. "The everyday work and
all, I mean. The really bad parts happened before I was born,
but the crew managed to live through it. Enough of them to
keep the colony going, anyway." He broke his brief scowl
with a grin and shrug. "Some of the official stuff—well, rank
has its privileges and most of us don't have that much rank.
And the Submissuals—"

Sprague put a hand on his wrist. "Arnet—"

He pulled his arm free and gave hers a brief pat. "Oh,
everybody knows how I feel! Which isn't too different from
the rest of us. If the commodore spaced everyone who griped
a little, he could get pretty lonesome."

That bad, huh? As Houk turned to Elseth Sprague. "And
in your view, things are how?"

Looking embarrassed, she waited long seconds before
saying, "I have a good job, more rank than Arnet." Her face
went taut. "But still I'm property and he's not. Me, along
with every woman in this place. We live with whatever man
the commodore tells us to, whenever he says so. You didn't
know that, did you?"

Houk and Lisele did, of course, from Malden's tape. But
the Chief's face showed no expression as he said, "Stretches,
a bit, the regulations. In emergency, though, I suppose . . ."

"Fifty-two peacefucking *years* of emergency!" Sprague's
face had gone red. Now, shaking her head, she sat back and
took deep breaths. "No. I'm not saying any more. Living the
way we do is better than not living at all."

She stood. "I think we should go, Arnet." Then, to
Houk and Lisele, "Thanks for having us here, for the
dinner."

And after a few more words of ritual politeness, the two
were escorted to the ramp and left the ship.

*   *   *

Back in captain's digs, finishing the coffee Kern and Sprague hadn't wanted, Lisele and Houk looked at each other. "Now," he said. "The commodore, tell me of."

Flat-voiced quiet, as though it had all happened to someone else, she told it. And was surprised to see deWayne Houk flush with genuine anger. "Killed him, you should!"

Oddly, his reaction collapsed her tension. "Don't be silly!" was the first thing that came to mind, but that would be an insult. She said, "He didn't touch me, Chief. There was no reason to risk everything we're trying for."

Houk's fury dissolved into a sidetwisted grin. "The right of it, I suppose you have. But—" He paused. "That one's death, *any* excuse."

Looking at the Drive Chief, the man whose own crude advances had bothered her more than a little, Lisele felt puzzlement. What had changed his attitudes? *Maybe it's just that now we're on the same side all the way. And before, we really weren't.*

She said, "I don't like him much, either. But—" She thought back, to what Goral Craig had said. "For good or bad, he holds this colony together. So while we're stuck here—"

"For now, yes." He nodded, then stacked some dishes and stood. "Cleanup, we do. Then more work."

Gathering whatever utensils he hadn't, she moved to help with the chore. While they shared it, she said, "Up in Control, while you were moving plugs, I checked some things. Maybe, before you start working on the dead units, you'd like to have a look, yourself."

"Or simply tell me, you could."

"What I know, yes. You might need to check further."

He didn't answer, so she said, "First place, some of the Drive functions can't be handled from Control; those circuits feed back an Outage signal and so do the backups."

"Hmm." After a few seconds his frown cleared. "For that, if on purpose, only one reason."

"Such as?"

"Mutiny, they had. Against another, they made precautions. Taking of no one station can rule the ship."

She thought about it. "Maybe you're right."

"And you found what else?"

"Well, for one thing, the fuel tanks are chockfull. If we could get the scout here and hook up a pump and feedpipe, then no matter what we decide to do, we wouldn't need to raid the colony's fuel refinery."

"Unfortunate." He shook his head, and all Lisele's asking couldn't get him to say what he meant.

The chores were finished. Houk said, "A look around Control, you said. As our next step, a good idea."

So they went upship. At the entrance to Control, Lisele gestured toward the heavy, opened doors, with the crudely-welded additions that puzzled her. "Can you figure what *this* is all about?"

Pausing, he looked at those doors and at the bulkhead around them. One door he freed of the latch that held it open, then pulled at the massive thing. It moved easily; he pushed it back and relatched it. Then he pointed to that door's crudely welded attachments. "From inside, to seal Control. Manual lock; no override from any other place. After the mutiny, someone did this."

Yes. Noting a switch, placed to operate when the door closed against the bulkhead, Lisele pushed it. For a moment she thought nothing was happening; then she heard a faint background hum wind down and stop, and she looked over to Houk. "It cuts off the air circulation, in and out of Control."

He nodded. "The same, I noticed, in Drive."

Lisele shrugged. "I suppose they had their reasons."

The two looked at a few other unusual things Lisele had noted. The topside airlock control was relayed through to an offship channel. "Sure," she said. "So the commodore can push the button, when he's executing someone, from his banquet hall."

"On the other end of that, I'd like to see him."

"Who wouldn't?" Yet she knew *she* couldn't push that button.

They went down to Drive, and Lisele helped the Chief with the horsing of facet plugs up onto his test bench—and then, as he tested one after another, down again. He found three in good enough condition for immediate repair, four more that might be fixed if he could find the parts, and eight useless ones. When he got to the repairing stage, she went upship and brewed fresh coffee, bringing back the pot and two cups. No sidearms; neither of them used sugar, nor what passed for cream.

After they'd had that break, the Chief said, "Another hour I'll be, on these. Two, maybe. Go sleep, you may as well."

"Sure. Thanks." Up in captain's digs, her mind replaying the day's events, she didn't expect to sleep soon.

She was wrong. And whenever Houk came in, she didn't wake.

XXVI

"One thing for certain," Lisele said. An hour past dawn, she was making coffee while Chief Houk tried for originality by mixing last night's dinner leftovers with the contents of assorted ration packets. "From now on, we won't be invited to breakfast with Commodore Malden."

"As well, that. A man to avoid."

Lisele couldn't disagree, so she didn't. After breakfast and cleanup, she went to Control. The Chief wanted to go downship and root through the parts bins for components that might make a few more facet plugs operable; when Sprague and Kern showed up for work, somebody had to be on hand to answer.

Almost precisely on time, those two arrived at groundside and called upship via the assigned channel. "Yes. Good morning," Lisele said. "Mister Houk should be down to join you in a few minutes." He answered the intercom immediately; not long after, the testing program resumed.

Because she was too often left waiting with nothing to do, Lisele knew the results had to be encouraging; today, Houk was moving more facet plugs than before. Looking at his chart, she could see a pattern forming: each time he moved a working plug it went into an outer area, relative to the ship's central axis, of whichever node showed weakest.

Leverage, yes: thrust from the outer edges put more lateral torque on the ship, so balance there was essential. Well, the man did know what he was doing, or else the whole

effort was useless. She wished *she* knew more, but now
wasn't the time to try learning it.

At lunch break she went groundside to eat with Houk
and Kern and Sprague, of food delivered from the colony. For
taste, it wasn't up to previous meals. Would the commodore
be so petty? Yes, Lisele decided; he probably would.

How to find out? Deliberately fishing, she said, "I guess
the kitchen's having an off day."

Kern's chuckle was half snort. "Not exactly."

Lisele waited, but he said nothing more. While she was
trying to formulate her next question, Elseth Sprague spoke
up. "Before, you've eaten ratings' food. This stuff came from
the unrateds' tables."

Fixing the woman's gaze with her own, Lisele said,
"That's interesting. I wonder why. Whose decision, I mean."

From Arnet Kern, another snort. "Who do you think?
And the why, I'd guess, is that the commodore came offship
yesterday carrying a real fume. Worst I can remember since—"
He paused. "—since the one who no longer has a name, tried
to kill him."

"You're talking too much," Sprague said.

"Not so, that," said deWayne Houk. "To us, safely you
can speak. And—appreciated, is this information."

So now she knew. Putting her utensils neatly on the
delivery tray, Lisele stood. "I'm going upship. When you're
ready to start work again, give a call."

As she began to climb the ramp, she saw Houk walking
off with the other two. Well, if she were working groundside,
she wouldn't want to go all the way upship to a toilet, either.

The afternoon's testing went smoothly enough, with
even more pauses while Houk relocated plugs. After two
hours he called a break; after another two he ended the
workshift. This time he asked Lisele to come down and join
the others on the first trip, carrying dead plugs up to Drive.
In all, there were eighteen of those, but on the second climb
he and Kern each carried two: one in arms and the other
slung into a backpack. From their breathing at the end of that
climb, Lisele saw why they wouldn't want that much load as a
regular thing.

Then, to announce that he and Lisele were leaving, the
Chief called Malden's comm center. The man who answered

said that an escort would be on hand shortly, so all four went downship and groundside, walking to the front of the large hall before the two colonists went their own ways.

Now and then various people walked past, going one place or another, some nodding or speaking and some not, but no one seemed to have any specific interest in Houk or Lisele. The man said, "Waiting, he keeps us. Like the food, another affront."

Lisele shrugged. "We know the path. Why wait?"

"Yes." But as they began to walk away, a shout came, and Lisele turned to see Malden standing in the huge doorway. Saying nothing, she and Houk paused.

Cray Malden marched out to them. "Where do you think you're going? My comm man told you there'd be an escort. Don't you have the common courtesy—?"

With this man, no apology would help. Lisele said, "While we waited, we thought we'd stroll a bit. Of course we wouldn't want to violate security, sir, but there aren't any signs here, saying to keep out or anything. So we—"

She was running out of words; the redfaced man's explosive answer came as a relief. "You'll go where I tell you and when I tell you. Not any place else. Understand?"

"Of course, sir." She thought Houk looked amused, but with the Chief she could never be certain. She was going to ask if the escort would be along soon, but following a gesture of Malden's she looked to see Deryth Mangentes approaching. Followed by a limping Thela Cochrane. Both were armed.

After saluting the commodore, Mangentes shook hands with Chief Houk. "Ready to go?"

He nodded, but as everyone turned to leave, Lisele stopped. "Just a minute, commodore." Pointing to Cochrane, "Her foot. She shouldn't be walking that far, so soon."

Smug was the only word for Malden's grin. "Teach her to tackle someone like you. Or maybe *how*." Turning away, he went into the large building.

There was nothing to say, so Lisele made a mental shrug and joined the other three, beginning the walk to the scout.

Houk and Mangentes took the lead; the woman's movements seemed oddly stiff. Lisele was left to walk beside the glowering Cochrane. "I tried."

"Save your breath. Next time—!"

And that was too much. Holding her voice flat, level, Lisele said, "Next time you're behind me? It won't happen." The woman didn't answer.

When they topped the nearby rise and were partway down the next slope, Lisele looked back. From here, the colony was hidden. And so, from its view, were the four of them. "Everybody? Let's stop a minute."

"Tired already?" Cochrane.

"Listen first." Then, to Mangentes, "I don't know what the commodore's doing, but this woman isn't in condition to walk to our scout and back."

Mangentes frowned. Looking closely for the first time, Lisele saw swelling at nose and lips, and on the unscarred cheek, a bruise. "The commodore's orders—"

"What the commodore doesn't know won't give him ulcers. On this trip you don't need Cochrane's help and you know it. Why can't she sit down here in the shade in one of these bushes, out of sight from the colony, and wait for you to come back?"

The Second Officer looked toward Thela Cochrane. "Can I trust you not to tell?"

The heavy woman nodded. "I'd get punished worse than you."

"All right, then. You have water, and so forth." She turned, ready to leave. "Let's go."

"One thing," said Cochrane. "Miz Fancy Fighter, there. Don't think this buys you anything."

Angered, Lisele said, "I'm not *buying* anything! Not from you, anyway. Keep your stupid grudges and peace take you!"

The three moved along. In the middle, with Lisele to her right, the Second Officer's gait definitely showed impairment. When they were past Cochrane's hearing, Mangentes said, "Her job was to spy on us, tell the commodore everything we said." Briefly, she laughed. "I wonder what she'll make up."

"You don't have worry?" said Houk. "I would."

"Oh, what's the difference? He can't kill me and he knows it. Goral's a gentle man, but his patience has limits. And yesterday Malden came close to breaking them."

Gesturing to the facial bruises, Lisele said, "*He* did that?"

"Who else would?"

"But why? What did you do—?"

Mangentes made a rueful snicker. "Me? No. It's what *you* did. Or didn't, rather. The commodore doesn't like rejection; he's not used to it."

"So he made *you* pay!" Even knowing that Malden's cruelty was none of her own fault, Lisele felt guilt. "He hit you in the face. And what else?" As the woman raised her eyebrows but gave no answer, Lisele said, "You don't usually walk like a cripple."

For moments Lisele expected to be hit, herself. Then the woman shrugged. "I already told you the man likes his sex a little different. Well, to work right, that way needs some extra lubrication. Always before, with me, at least he's been good about that part. Yesterday, though—" Watching the face change expression, Lisele felt relief that Deryth's anger wasn't toward herself. "—yesterday, he opened the way with two fingers, nails and all. Blood lubricates just fine.

"Especially if it's not your own."

Trying to find a better answer than a mere "I'm sorry," Lisele heard herself say, "Have you ever killed anyone?"

"No. And didn't think I ever could. But—"

"Neither have I."

"With me, different," said deWayne Houk. "Holding the colony together or not—Goral Craig's assessment of Malden, I cite—my fourth, he'd be. And after doing it, sleep well."

The concept stopped Lisele's thinking. Yes, she'd had violent urges, and they disturbed her. But she hadn't acted on them; no. Bemused, she heard Deryth Mangentes say, "I think Goral's wrong. The colony could survive Malden's death; what it may not survive is the turn his leadership's been taking."

"Kill him, then, why not?" Shrugging, Houk said it.

Her face showing grief, Mangentes said, "Because I can't."

Then, turning to Lisele, "*You'd* better be ready to do that, though. Because—"

"Because what?"

"Because afterward, in the next room cleaning my blood off me, I could hear him muttering to himself. That he'd get you. That you'd tricked him, but next time he'd have tricks you've never heard of. And that compared to what he'd do to you, then, what he'd done to me was *nothing*."

"I see." Rearranging her thoughts, her feelings built on all her life's experience: "I see," said Liesel Selene Moray. *Or do I?* Frightened and angry, she fell silent.

As they neared the scoutship, Lisele saw that the four colony women were sitting outside the dining tent, shaded by its front canopy. Further, they seemed to have their visiting-kits packed. "Oh, damn everything!" said Mangentes. "I forgot."

Her hand on the woman's elbow, Lisele said, "Forgot what?"

"After Mr. Houk, here, has his final session in the tent today, I'm supposed to take this batch home. Four more come out tomorrow."

"But what—?" Then Lisele realized. Cochrane! She and Deryth could keep their mouths shut, but four women who knew nothing about the danger and might not understand it?

Houk was ahead of her. "A story, quickly, tell them. To stay this night, they must."

"But the commodore—?"

Lisele's hand squeezed the elbow. "You'll have to take some blame, there. Tell him you misunderstood. I know it's—"

Mangentes nodded. "So do I. More than you can imagine. But you're both right. It's my only out."

This time, "I'm sorry" was all Lisele could find to say.

Houk did better. "Tired, I am, and needing rest. Not until after sundown will I be ready. It should justify. My fault, not yours, the night's delay."

Reluctantly leaving the woman to face her situation, then following Houk up the scout's ramp, Lisele said, "Chief? I think that's two I owe you."

Pausing, he looked around to her. "And to collect, how many does it take?"

On the face of it his words were offensive. But somehow, his tone wasn't.

First, after minimal greetings to everyone who was in or near Control, Lisele had a shower. Then, hungry, she went to the dining alcove, expecting to cook something for herself.

But there Arlen met her. "Sit down and relax. I've been waiting for you, and our dinner's almost ready."

"Well—hey, thanks." She sat. "I appreciate it."

In only a few minutes, the two were eating. When they were finished and drinking coffee, Anders Kobolak joined them. His presence stopped the halting confidences Arlen wished to impart, so those would have to wait. The scout captain said, "Lisele? The Chief told me some of what happened at the ship. Let's hear your version."

As accurately as she could, trying to leave her feelings out of the account, she told it. Including what she'd learned on the walk back, but not how much the future prospects frightened her. Looking deadly serious, Kobolak nodded. "That's it, then, I can't let you go back there. It's too dangerous."

He was probably right, but she couldn't bring herself to say so. "I *have* to go! Who else is there?"

"That's a problem," he said. "Until today I'd have thought we could substitute anyone. But now it seems to boil down to you and to me. So I guess it's me."

Of all the objections that came to mind, only one could be stated first. What came out was, "You're *captain*." And not much good with a needle gun, and two men would be off the scout at one time, and the tent and watch skeds would be messed up even worse than now, and who could he leave in charge, and—!"

But surely Anders knew all those things, so she shut up and listened, as he said, "I've let this mess keep me off balance! Haven't done some perfectly sensible things I very well might have." He gestured toward Limmer. "We've got navigation sims on here, including lifts and landings. You should have been practicing those and it's my fault that you haven't. I—"

Lisele reached to clasp his wrist. "Anders. Quit blaming yourself. You've had lots to worry about."

He shook free, then looked apologetic. "But—guns, though. No reason we couldn't have trained more people on needlers."

Thinking about the idea, Lisele said, "Like who?"

"Naomi Gray. Molyneux, maybe. Alina—?" He shook his head. "No. Guns scare her. Always have. And—"

"And using any of the men," she said, "would leave us with more of you off here than we decided was a good idea."

He frowned. "Yes. You're right, of course. But that leaves us nowhere. What should we do?"

The answer was easy. "Just send one more person along with us. And do it the way you did before. With Brower."

XXVII

Kobolak's brow wrinkled. "I don't understand."

"Sure you do," said Arlen Limmer. "First time we went groundside to meet those people. Chief Brower doesn't know guns, so you told him, shoot if it comes to that, but make sure not to hit any of *us*."

Lisele nodded. "That's what I meant, yes. Naomi Gray—she's steady enough."

Frowning again, Anders shook his head. "I need her here, to keep tabs on the Drive when Brower's groundside. How about Molyneux?"

Now it was Lisele who frowned. "How about if you use her here? In a pinch I'd rather have Gray."

Shrugging, Kobolak said, "So would I. Okay if I think it over first?"

No point in arguing. "Sure. Tomorrow's soon enough, to decide." And what was she doing, questioning the scout captain's decisions? Well, after all it was her butt on the line, not his. And according to Mangentes, quite literally.

Now, as Kobolak went back over to Control, Lisele said, "If you want to talk, Arlen, maybe the cubby's free."

It was. Inside, with the Occupied sign turned on, the two sat. She said, "Anything bothering you? Especially?"

"Not so much, now. Ardissa and I, we've talked. And we're in the same kind of problem. I felt guilty about you, and she's troubled about some fellow named Arnet Kern. So—"

Kern! She had to tell this. "Arlen—something you need to know." He wanted to talk but she shushed him. "He was going to challenge you. This Submissuals thing they have here. To the death. So I—" Trying to save Arlen's pride but knowing she couldn't really do that, she told of her combat with the other man. "So you see, now he thinks that since *I* beat him, you'd have his leg down his throat to the knee-joint."

She laughed, hoping he'd join in, but he didn't. Instead, "You had to fight my battle for me. You won, and I wouldn't have, most likely. I don't—"

She reached to hug him; for moments he tried to pull away, then with a groaning breath he returned the hug. "Lisele—"

"Don't feel bad, Arlen! It's just the training, you don't have. When there's time—Anders is good, they tell me."

And why had scarfaced Derek Limmer allowed his oldest son to grow up with no such skills? Maybe it was his memories of the Slaughterhouse, UET's sadistic Space Academy where Derek's face had been marred for life, that forced him to ignore the need.

Well, no way of knowing, and right now it was Arlen who needed help. Lisele said, "You're finished, are you, with Ardissa?"

"What? Oh. Yes. Tomorrow there'll be somebody else."

"But not tonight."

"No." Her hand slipped inside his shirt. "Lisele?"

"These colonists don't *own* you, Arlen."

Not much later, Lisele found herself wishing she could talk with Ardissa. The colony woman certainly was a good teacher!

Lying quietly, with Lisele's head resting on his shoulder, Arlen said, "I feel ashamed."

"No, Arlen! I *told* you—"

"Not the combat thing. You're right; I can't expect to know what I've never been taught. But me, just now—worrying so much about my own peacetwisting pride when you're the one in real danger and I can't help. Lisele—"

Not hard, she put fingers to his lips until he quieted. "Arlen. Things happen the way they happen. If I—" She thought back; what *had* dictated the course of her life? She nodded. "Do you know why I was on Tregare's scoutship, so that after the Tsa mind-attack crashed us we all spent years walking back to Sassden, one step at a time?"

"No. You hadn't told me."

"I didn't think they'd let me go to Shtegel with them if I asked, so I sort of stowed away. Waited until Rissa and

Tregare were up in Control, then boarded and went to a bunk and strapped in. The others there—Hagen Trent and Jenise Rorvik—thought I had permission; I figured they would."

He laughed. "That's funny! But I don't see your point."

"Simple. If I hadn't done that one silly childish thing, I'd have been on *Inconnu Deux* when my uncle Ivan took it up through the Tsa blockade. Instead of walking nearly a quarter of the distance around Shaarbant, I'd have been in freeze all that time, the same as you were." From the start he gave, then, her caress might have been too abrupt; she said, "If things had gone that way, Arlen, right now I'd be about ten years old, bio. So we wouldn't be here like this."

"Yes. I see." Under the prompting of her hand, he wiggled. But then sat up. "Do you suppose we could have a snack first?"

Pretending to give the idea careful thought, eventually she nodded. "Why not? We can come back here later."

When they did, they had to wait until Anders and Alina, due to go on watch, vacated the cubby. But eventually, settling back for sleep, Lisele decided that the waiting might even have helped.

After eating, early next morning, Lisele sat in for half a watch while the new quartet of ship's women arrived. Escorted, she noticed, by Goral Craig. Without much curiosity, on an aux screen she watched the choosing ritual; Kobolak's pick was tall, but the other three looked to be much of a sort: medium in size and build, bio-ages in the twenties. One redhead, chosen by Eduin Brower.

When, except for Houk, the men came aboard, Lisele beckoned to Kobolak. At his gesture, Molyneux relieved her; she joined him and Arlen in the dining nook and accepted Arlen's pouring of a glass of native berry juice. "They brought some more today. It's a little different from the last batch."

"Oh?" About to sip, Lisele paused. "You've tried it, then?" He nodded, and she thought, either she was too paranoid or he was too trusting. But, gifts from Cray Malden—! Still, nobody had turned blue. Then, silently she laughed at herself. *Who do you think you are? Muriel Morbid, Girl Victim?*

The byplay wasn't getting any questions answered, so she said, "Anders? Who goes with Houk and me, to the *Patton?*"

Not looking especially happy, he said, "Oh, you're right, Moray. Molyneux isn't up to it. You get Gray; I've told her."

"Aren't you both forgetting something?" said Arlen Limmer. "So far, the commodore doesn't suspect that Gray even exists. Or Molyneux, either."

Anders began to frown, but before he could speak, Lisele said, "That could be a good reason to take her along." The two men didn't seem to understand, so she added, "Show Malden there's something he didn't know, about us. Make him wonder what *else* he doesn't know."

Kobolak looked dubious, but Arlen's face lit with comprehension. "She has something there. Put the peacewaster off balance."

Anders nodded. "Good enough. Gray it is."

Not much later the three went groundside. Craig must have been watching from the dining tent, because he was outside and waiting before the group reached the ramp's end. "Ready?" he said, though obviously they were. The man was sweating, and now Lisele noticed that Sitdown's heat was still increasing.

Leading off, Craig motioned Lisele to come walk beside him, leaving Houk and Gray to follow. After a few moments he said, "Who's that woman? There's only supposed to be six of you."

"Supposed? Who says so?"

"Why, the commodore told us—"

"Yes. He assumed that's all we have here. First meeting, it didn't seem polite to correct him."

"And since then?"

Lisele shrugged. "Slipped our minds, I guess."

After a pause, he said, "How many more?"

She thought about it. "You'd have to ask the captain. Our scout captain, I mean."

"You're not allowed to tell?"

"Nobody's said that. But I'd rather leave it up to him."

His face cleared. "Yes, I see. The whole system works that way. If you're going to make a mistake, let it be on the side of caution." He said nothing more, but every now and then, as they walked, he gave her a sidelong glance.

*   *   *

He wants to talk. What about? Well, it was his move;
she kept silence until he said, "I'm not blaming you; I want
you to know that."

She could have said "For what?" But why pretend she
didn't understand? "Thanks. Of course I couldn't know he'd
do things like that. But even if I had—"

"You'd protect yourself. Sure. Who wouldn't?" He made
a sour grimace. "If they could, that is."

She thought of several replies, mostly to the effect that
Deryth could protect herself if Craig would *let* her, but finally
decided against using any of them. The man looked over to
her and said, "How do you do it, a kid like you?"

"Do what?"

"Cochrane's tough; she's vicious. One move and you took
her out. Then stuck your needler in the commodore's ear and
chased him off his own ship!" Shaking his head, "It beats *me*."

No point in correcting his version of what had happened.
Lisele said, "Training," and let it go at that.

When they reached the colony area, Sprague and Arnet
came out of the large building to meet them. In lieu of
handshakes or other semblance of formality, Craig waved a
hand at his erstwhile charges and said, "You'll want to get to
work, I expect. Call in when it's time for food, or for anything
else you need." Not once, Lisele noticed, had the man
spoken to Naomi Gray. *Utie!*

"Fine; thanks," said Houk, and began walking toward
the ship.

"Just a minute," Lisele said. "Yesterday's lunch wasn't up
to standard."

"Oh?" Craig looked puzzled. "I can't imagine—"

"The commodore can. If he wants good work, he sends
good food."

"I can't tell him that!"

"Then don't. Just tell whoever dishes up the meal. If that
doesn't work, we won't be back."

Looking a bit shocked, Craig went into the building. To
Lisele, Houk said, "Best move, you think that is?"

Before Lisele could answer, Naomi Gray spoke. "I'm not
sure what all this is about. But from what I've heard, taking
any dreck from Commodore Malden is a certain way to get
more of it."

Lisele gave the woman a grateful look. No doubt about it, she'd picked the right person!

The two ship's people had brought the tools needed for groundside work. As they all neared the ramp, Houk said, "Near done we are, testing." And went on to say that he felt this last part would go faster if remaining readings were taken without interruption; when those were done, he'd come down for the plug removals and relocations. "And also, upship I have work, needs doing." So as Sprague and Kern checked their instruments, he led the way up the ramp.

When they reached the Control area, he instructed Gray in what had been Lisele's job: how to specify which facet plug to read next, then enter that reading in the proper space on his chart. After she'd done these things for several units without error, he nodded. "Fine, you are," and gave her shoulder a pat.

He turned to Lisele. "Main airlock, now, we test. And the ramp, will it raise? Procedure, from the lock I call in to you."

"All right." The Control-to-airlock link was one they'd checked out on their first visit; personal communicators, with their capacity to work through bulkheads by inductive "hitchhiking" on signal-cable circuits, wouldn't be needed.

Before the Chief went downship, he said, "You two. At all times, stay together. Each other's protection, you are."

Then he left, and soon Lisele's intercom station chimed. When she answered, he directed her to try the circuits moving the inner and outer airlock hatches. "A nudge each; no more." She did so, and understood why Houk wanted only momentary activations: the intercom brought metallic squeaks and groans loud enough to alert the whole colony! But so brief that no one would have time to identify them. Mumbling something about idiots, and fifty years without lubrication, the Chief told Lisele to wait until he called her again.

Agreeing, she cut her Send switch and looked over to Naomi Gray. "How's everything coming along?"

Marking down the latest reading, then pausing, Gray said, "All right. Except that I'm getting thirsty."

Checking her chrono, Lisele said, "Time for a break, anyway. Sprague and Kern could use one too, I expect." So Gray told the two, groundside, to take ten. Lisele stood.

"Come on down to captain's digs with me. There's some chilled juice."

"Shouldn't one of us stay here?"

Lisele grinned. "You heard the Chief. Come on."

They went downship, procured the cold liquid, and returned. As they walked together, Naomi said, "I didn't get the details, of your difficulties on here. If it's all right—"

So, omitting the specifics of Malden's "revenge," Lisele explained the problem. "And remember—all you'd have to do is what Anders said: don't shoot that energy gun unless I say so, and be totally peacekeeping sure you don't hit any of *us*."

"Yes. I can do that. You're safe with me. And so's Houk."

The woman's expression puzzled Lisele. "You and the Chief—you have problems?"

A shrug. "Not really. For a time we were lovers. Then, after the radiation sickness and the treatment, maybe too soon, we tried and he couldn't. So then he'd have nothing to do with me. Couldn't face the possibility of failure, I guess."

But that would be when he was asking me. I wonder— Before Lisele could speak, the other said, "Yes, it hurt. But I'm over it now; we were never more than casual and friendly. Still, though—"

"I know. Nobody likes to lose a friend."

They were at the doors to Control. Entering, Lisele nodded toward the latrine. "Before we get to work again, might be a good time." Gray didn't look convinced so Lisele went toward the facility. "Never pass up a chance, my father used to say. You might regret it." So she and then Gray followed Tregare's advice.

The intercom was sounding when Lisele approached it, but from Houk's tone of voice he hadn't been calling for long. Still, "We took a little break, Chief. Okay?"

"Of course, yes. Now, though—" His instructions, now, were to close and open first the inner hatch and next the outer. Each functioned perfectly. "So," he said. "The interlock, activate. And both hatches test." Groundside, often both would be open at the same time; in space, of course, only one could be. Outside vacuum operated the interlock automatically; only a deliberate override signal could open either hatch, and never the two at once. But for testing in atmosphere a manual control was provided. Lisele ran the procedures through, and the system passed inspection.

Noting an offship channel trunk light blinking on or off with each move she made, Lisele had a disturbing thought. "Chief?" He answered, and she said, "I'm getting a bad idea here." Explaining what she'd seen, she went on. "This looks like a monitor setup. To report for another set of controls. But where would those be?"

Houk sighed. "For the commodore, I think, someplace handy."

"I don't understand."

"So? Next then, the ramp, try. Again, a nudge only."

"Toward raising it, you mean. But not enough that anybody might see it move, really."

"Correct, you have it. Movement, though, I think not."

And Houk was right. The circuit drew power, more and more of it, but the position-meter showed no change at all, until with a crash of circuit breakers the power reading dropped to zerch.

"Chief—?"

"As expected. Some welding here, I see. And to cut it free, no use. Because fused solid, I believe, the mechanism."

Yes, it figured. Outside lines to override the airlock hatch controls, and a ramp that wouldn't lift. Someone— Orval Sprague or Bull Cochrane or even Cray Malden—had made sure that no one could ever lock him out of his own ship.

XXVIII

Chief Houk went groundside; with nothing else to do, Lisele spelled Gray for the rest of the morning. The testing was so nearly finished that they delayed lunch in order to complete it. When Lisele's call to the colony raised no answer, Arnet Kern volunteered to go fetch food and drink. In turn, Houk invited him and Sprague to have lunch upship with the rest of them.

The Chief came up first, though—on the excuse that

while climbing the ramp, Kern might need Sprague's help
with the trays. "Real reason, though," he said when he
reached Control, "before they get here, to talk."

Unusually, for him, he lit a drugstick; both women
declined his offer of sticks for themselves. Lisele didn't know
about Gray, but she herself—though she had come to like the
things in moderation—wanted no euphoria in enemy territory. She said, "Talk, sure. What about?"

He gestured, and she was relieved to see that after only
two draws on the stick, he butted it dead. *A little nervous,
maybe, but not bad.* As he said, "Intercom channel out?"

Headshake. "The lights show good. No one's answering,
is all." He said nothing. "Oh, it's just the commodore being
petty again. If this work was for him instead for us, then
given one centum, maybe two, I'd walk off this ship and stay
off."

Before he had time to answer, Sprague and Kern could
be heard approaching; Houk's recess for talk certainly hadn't
lasted long enough to be productive. "Later," he said. And
with the colonists present, during the meal all talk concerned
the business at hand.

Pettiness or no, this time the food was up to previous
standards.

After coffee—well, the colony's not-coffee for Kern and
Sprague—those two and the Chief went groundside, to remove malfunctioning facet plugs and relocate good ones.
Gray took over the business of plotting relocations on deWayne
Houk's chart. Lisele would have liked to wander around the
ship, do a little aimless exploration and possibly learn something. But Houk had said for the two women to stay together.
Lisele saw no possible danger now—surely if the commodore
or anyone else boarded the ship, Houk himself could call and
warn her. But still—if due to some fluke she got in trouble by
disobeying instructions, she really wouldn't want to face the
Chief.

So, bored, she stayed put. At the main comm panel, not
for any particular reason, she tried the offship call again. Still
no answer. Irked, this time she didn't terminate the call;
instead she left the channel open, so that at the far end the
calling signal would keep blaring away. *See how you like it!*

Sure enough, after about ten minutes an irritated voice answered. "What do *you* want, anyway?"

This was more like it! "Why, to make sure you're not all dead, there."

"Dead? I—"

"An hour ago I couldn't get any answer at all. This time it took you 'til half-past forever. Are you having problems? Do you need any help?"

"Of course not! The commodore—"

"Yes. While we have the connection I'd like to speak with Commodore Malden." No "please," just the statement.

Come to think of it, though, she had no idea what she intended to say.

A time passed, and then, "Malden here. Who's calling?"

"Moray, sir. For the scoutship."

"But I thought you were aboard *my* ship."

"I am, commodore. Here, and working."

"Working? Sounds to me like you're wasting my time, instead. What is it you want, Moray?"

"Our meals delivered."

"But you just *had* your lunch. One of our people, working with you there, came and got it for you."

"That's what I mean. It wasn't delivered, because when I tried to call in about it, nobody answered. Sir."

Familiarity didn't improve the man's laugh. "Mistakes happen; surely you realize that."

"Of course, sir. Do you?" She waited, giving him time to think over what she'd said. Then, cutting into his first word before he had time to finish it, she said, "Mistakes can be distracting. I hope we won't have any more of them. Sir."

He paused first, then said, "From now on, Moray, I intend to make no mistakes whatsoever."

The circuit went dead.

"Whew!" said Naomi Gray. "Was that wise, do you think?"

Lisele shrugged. "You said, yourself, taking crap from Malden was a bad idea. So—"

"Shouldn't you have checked with the Chief first?"

"He's busy." As if to prove her point, Houk called up more relocation data for Gray to mark on the chart. When that was done, Lisele said, "Maybe I should have. But the whole thing just happened, spur of the moment. I think it came out okay."

"Well, I hope so."

More than an hour before the afternoon work shift was due to end, Houk called a halt. "Down here, finished we are. Help carry defective plugs upship, will you both, now?"

So Lisele and Naomi went groundside, and all five made several trips. This time the test instruments, but not those for removal and installation of plugs, were brought aboard. Then after treating Sprague and Kern, along with his own people, to a glass of wine each, Houk dismissed the colonists. "Tomorrow, some installations we do. But today, the rest of it, some free time to enjoy."

When the two were gone, he said, "Main airlock hatch, the outer, now we can close." When Lisele had done that, and patched a circuit to ring alarms if the thing were opened, the Chief said, "Facet plugs, now you help me with. Until dinner."

So in the Drive room the two women lifted plugs onto Houk's test bench and wrestled them down again, held instrument leads to various points as he directed, handed him tools and took them back as he desired. At one point he smiled. "With this extra help, faster the work goes."

They took only one mid-afternoon break, but when dinner time came, nearly a dozen plugs remained for testing.

Up in Control again, after Lisele had called to ask that their meal be delivered, she cut the alarm circuit and reopened the hatch, then went to the airlock. She didn't recognize the two young men who brought the trays, but since they were unarmed and she herself couldn't carry both trays in one load, she told them to make delivery at captain's quarters. "I'll wait here, to see you offship as my orders provide." *Orders: works every time.*

When they were gone, Lisele made a detour to Control: hatch closed, alarms back in operation. Then she joined Houk and Gray.

During the meal, which for the first time featured some kind of poultry, the Chief's silence put a lid on small talk. Then, while they had coffee, Houk took no wine; instead he lit a drugstick. "Tomorrow," he said. "Not morning, but shortly on return here, from scout. Good as can be done, this Drive will be." From the stick's smoke, he showed no effect.

"And then what?" said Lisele.

"That, to discuss now. Your thinkings, too, I need."

Naomi Gray frowned. "How can I give you any input? I don't know enough about the problem. What do you want to do, and what limitations are involved?"

The trouble was that a person's own expertise on a subject can make explanations difficult. Time and again Houk lost his listeners by overestimating their knowledge. So, painstakingly, he tried to rephrase.

After several repetitions, Lisele thought she understood. "Let me tell it back to you, now—see if I have it straight. Naomi, if I put one over your head, call me on it." Two nods. "All right. Chief, you're saying that by the law of averages you have enough repairable plugs in the batch you haven't worked on, to balance off the three nodes." He agreed. "And that with a little rebalancing of the power feeds, refining what you did earlier, this ship could lift." Again, yes. "But you can't lift full fuel tanks and still make low orbit."

"Right, you have it, Moray." Looking now at Gray, "Understand, do you?"

"Yes, deWayne. You're saying that if we could get rid of a lot of fuel—two-thirds of it, maybe?—the low orbit option would be feasible." Houk didn't contradict her; she said, "Then for that scenario, the problem is how to dump some fuel?"

"Yes." He scowled. "For this, no provision is."

Ships are refueled, primarily, from groundside pumps. At the input coupling there is an aux pump to ease the load—but it pumps *in*, not out. Even if the motor leads were gimmicked to reverse the flow, the rotors are shaped for max efficiency in the designed direction; the other way would work very poorly. And of course the pumps are above the tanks; without some kind of rather complicated priming, a reversed pump could suck only air.

Or at least that was how Lisele understood it; when she said as much, Chief Houk merely shrugged. She thought about the problem. "The tanks have no drains, then? Uh-huh. Could we flange one up, and move the pump down to push it?"

He told her the hitch to that idea; given Malden's full cooperation, they could. Without his knowledge, no chance.

Desperation gave her one more idea. "What if, just as the *Patton* lifted, we blew a hole—a *small* hole—near the bottom of the main tank? Let some fuel spew out? Once *March Hare*'s fixed, in shape to land, one way or another we could refuel locally."

This idea, she learned, had some serious problems. While the fuel was heat-stable—well, *enough* heat could burn it, especially in atmosphere, but the process wouldn't be self-sustaining—ionization by the Drive nodes could set off the entire spill. "And likely, those nodes in turn, destroy."

"Then low orbit's out? Totally?"

Surprising her, Houk shook his head and almost smiled. "No. Choice, if enough power from the Drive, one other."

"Well, tell it!" said Naomi Gray.

"To manage, two days at least. Or rather, at night do the work, on side away from the colony."

"To do what?" said Gray.

"One-third from bottom of tank, cut hull with torch. A circle, half-meter diameter perhaps, and not to perforate but only weaken. Apply shaped explosive charge to that circle, detonation to be from Control or Drive room." He almost smiled. "Poof! Instant drain."

Puzzled, Lisele said, "But what about the thing you said before? The nodes flaming the escaped fuel?"

Now Houk did smile. "Past atmosphere, lift. Cut Drive, coast. *Then* the fuel, dump." He shrugged. "When Drive again fires, fuel in space spread out thin and no air to help, ignition too diffused to harm. And with remainder of fuel, then, low orbit should achieve."

Sipping coffee, putting the cup down when she realized she'd let it sit until stone-cold, Lisele thought about the idea. "We'd still need one more of us aboard, to make it work. That means landing the scout on the cargo hatch."

Houk nodded, as Naomi Gray said, "That hatch won't close, I seem to remember. Which means, when the balloon goes up, everybody on this ship needs to be in spacesuits. And the scout only carries two. So we'd better—"

The Chief grinned. "Time to check this ship's suits, we will have. Thirty-six, issued would be, at start. And of power suits, one. Fully workable, though, not to expect."

"If the power suit worked at all," Lisele said, "we could use it to help dismount the Cube."

"After fifty years, still to operate? Miracles, you ask."

"And why not?" Lisele said. While thinking, *the more this man gets in charge of things, the less he talks like most people*. Well, maybe he'd grown up speaking German. Or, like one oldtime friend of Tregare's, on a backwoods planet with its own dialect.

After dinner, as Lisele had expected, they returned to Drive and tested the remaining plugs. Houk's prediction proved out; this day's haul had a good proportion of repairable units. Marking his chart, now a bit rumpled and coffee-stained, he nodded. "Enough, when installed again, for proper lift. Within limits already agreed. A few more units, tonight I repair; tomorrow the rest, and then the power flows and thrust indicators to balance."

For sleep the time was still a little early, but Lisele felt tired. Maybe her period was due to start; with these thirty-hour days, she'd lost track. "Will you need me here now, Chief? If not, I think I'd like to go to bed."

He paused, then turned to Gray and said, "You also?"

She shook her head. "I'm good for all evening, if that's what it takes."

Houk nodded. "Good. One helper, enough."

"Fine," said Lisele. "Thanks, Naomi." She was going to say, "Try not to make too much noise when you come in," then realized that although physically the huge bed had plenty of room for three, maybe for this particular three it didn't.

She waited for someone else to raise any objection that might exist, but no one did. "Okay, then. See you."

Down in captain's digs she showered and went to bed, positioning herself well to the edge of "her" side as defined by previous visits. She wasn't fully asleep when Houk and Gray came in, but pretended to be, while various plumbing fixtures made noises that didn't quite tell her what was happening. Eventually, sounds and movements told her that one and then another person were sharing the bed.

All right. Again she relaxed, and had fallen into a light doze when she felt the fleeting touch of fingers on her thigh. Instantly alert, she still feigned sleep, giving what she hoped was a natural-sounding sigh and making a jerky, sleeplike turnover to lie on one side, facing the bed's edge.

She heard a giggle, then a whisper: "Almost woke her. Sorry, deWayne. Now then—"

Even toneless, the whispered answer managed a sound of protest. Lisele couldn't hear the words, but the import was clear, for Gray breathed, "Sure you can. You were still sick, before; that's all. And haven't you been doing just fine with the Utie women? Here; let me—"

Houk's whisper, half-growled, nonetheless held a note of acquiescence; Lisele heard and felt movement, someone sliding toward the bed's foot. For a time came other, moister noises. Then there was a scurry of someone moving up again, and rhythm of both sound and motion, until Gray gave a thin, stifled cry.

More movement then; momentarily, warm flesh bumped against Lisele's back. Whispers, soft sounds of kissing.

Then nothing more. Except that before Lisele slept, she heard someone snoring.

In the morning, neither Houk nor Gray gave any sign that the incident had occurred. So neither did Liesel Selene Moray.

XXIX

After an early breakfast of scout's rations the three went to the Control room, where Chief Houk directed Lisele to punch up the ship's structural plans from the computer, for viewing on an aux screen. At first she had trouble with the indexing system, but in less than twenty minutes she found the portion they needed: a cross-section of the main fuel tank, showing its placement with regard to other identifiable features.

Standing, Houk pointed to a bulge, where the top of a landing leg met the hull. "There. Not exact optimum level. But close enough, will be." For the fuel spill, Lisele knew he meant, as the man went on to explain that the leg's bulk would help dissipate the outrush, deflecting it away from the Drive nodes.

Looking well satisfied, he nodded. "Had thought necessary, rope ladder to climb down, from one side of cargo hatch. Easier, this." Musing that of course the ladder would be plastic, not rope, Lisele took a time to understand his meaning. Then remembered that the outward-facing surfaces of landing legs were formed to constitute ladders in their own right.

Elseth Sprague's voice on the intercom announced her arrival, and Arnet Kern's. Leaving Lisele to shut down the computer research before joining the others in Drive, Houk and Gray went to meet the colonists.

As Lisele had guessed, first order of business was carrying the rehabbed facet plugs downship. Groundside, the Chief made a point of demonstrating the exact procedures for correct installation of a plug. Obviously Sprague had seen him do that chore a number of times, but only after he'd installed two and then supervised while Sprague and Kern did three more, did he nod approval. "Good, so. The rest, by yourselves tend to. Gray, from Control will assign positions," and Lisele realized he'd placed these five from memory, his chart pictured in his mind. "Moray, you with further repairs will help."

So the three went upship, and for the rest of the morning, with one break, Lisele worked in aid of the Chief.

No problems, this day, with lunch delivery. Sprague and Kern stayed groundside to eat; Gray and Lisele joined the Chief in captain's digs. Afterward, for all, the same work resumed, and shortly before break-time Houk announced to Lisele that all the plugs he could fix with materials at hand, were now in working order. So after that break the repaired units were taken groundside and installed.

Estimating, rather than taking an accurate count, Lisele decided that the plug positions were almost two-thirds filled. And as near as she could tell, evenly distributed between the nodes.

Again the two colonists were released early. Houk's next move was to send Lisele to Control while he and Gray went into the Drive room. "Low-power excitation of nodes, Mo-

ray," he said. "As before, power loading and thrust indications
to balance—but now to the finest possible, tuned."

So, much the same as she had done when the Chief
made his first crude approximation of balance, Lisele called
readings down to him, then made the adjustments he specified. Taking a long time at it, seeming to reverse previous
changes as often as not, eventually he said, "Good, I think, as
can be. At cargo hatch, meet us now."

She grimaced; as she cut the circuit she muttered, "Oh,
you're quite welcome, Chief." Her irritation didn't last, though,
because suddenly she guessed why he'd made so many
back-and-forth changes. Some of the adjustments weren't
continuous; they had to be moved a notch at a time. So for
balance, he might have to trade one notch in outer, higher-
leverage positions for two at a point farther in.

When she joined Houk and Gray on the open hatch she
stated her guess. The Chief smiled. "That, yourself you
figured? Good, Moray. Because the method, only today I
invented."

So, waiting to hear what he wanted done next, Lisele felt
more than a little self-satisfaction.

Standing at the right of the hull's opening, looking past
the edge of the massive hatch, Houk pointed downward.
About two meters off to the side and at not much greater
vertical distance below, the upper bulge of a landing leg
protruded. "This one," he said, "we use."

Gray spoke. "Because it can't be seen from the colony?"

Houk nodded. "That, one other leg also would do. Here,
though—spotted from groundside, up and inside I could
climb."

"Sure," said Lisele. "The rope ladder idea." She visual-
ized how to make it work: swing the plastic gadget over
where Houk could catch it and loose-tie it to the leg. Then if
a roaming colonist saw him, he wouldn't be treed. Get onto
the ladder, untie it to swing free, clamber to safety and pull
the thing up after him! "You're not apt to need it," she said,
"but it's like what my father used to say: Just-in-case is what
wins arguments." Suddenly she grinned. "I don't suppose
you've ever met Bran Tregare?"

"That pleasure I have not. The reason you ask?"

"After a while, I think you might get to like each other."

*   *   *

There was nothing more, the Chief said, that needed doing here today. If this were a night for staying aboard, they could, well into the wee hours, begin scoring the hull. But that would have to wait until the next visit.

So Lisele called to arrange the formality of an escort back to the scoutship. By the time the three reached the large colony building, that escort was there to meet them: the young woman named Ardissa, who had been Arlen Limmer's first breeding assignment in the tents.

Lisele wondered if this woman knew she'd been the inadvertent cause of a demonstration combat. Might be interesting to find out, so Lisele moved forward to walk beside her. Ardissa didn't seem to be the talkative type. As they walked the first hundred or so meters, with the exercise and unshielded sun bringing copious sweat, Lisele considered several possible openings and then decided to jump in with both feet. She said, "How long before you know if Arlen got you pregnant?"

"Huh? Oh, ten days, I guess."

While Lisele took a few seconds to realize that those ten days were thirty hours each, she saw that Ardissa was turning to look at her. "You're the Moray one, aren't you? Arlen's woman."

"That's my name. And we're paired, yes. Why?"

"Arnet told me about you." Not wanting to ask the obvious question, Lisele waited, until the other said, "That he was going to do something really stupid, and you convinced him not to."

"I suppose that's one way to put it. Kern isn't stupid, though; he lacked a few facts, was all."

Another sidelong look, and Ardissa said, "I like Arnet. A lot. Things were different, I'd be with nobody else." A pause. "Your man's nice, too, Moray. Didn't know much, though."

What to say? "Hadn't had much time to learn. We're pretty new together—and our firsts, each." Trying to think how to make sense, to this poor Utie sex-serf, of the way free people managed these things . . .

"Firsts, huh?" Ardissa snorted. "*Both* of you? Your captain must be awful lazy. Or maybe past it?"

There had to be some way to make her understand. Lisele said, "Your colony's breeding program—that's not how it is, other places. With a limited gene pool, your people needed to make some changes. So—"

From Ardissa's expression, Lisele knew the explanation wasn't getting anywhere. Shaking her head, she said only, "Where I come from, we don't have new-adult initiations. Or shifting women around, to one man and then another. We just pair. When we want to, that is."

They were nearing the scout now, and Lisele was glad of that fact. Because she'd run out of conversation.

Inside the scout, first Lisele showered and changed clothes; then she went to Control, where Chief Houk was telling Anders Kobolak and Eduin Brower about the fuel-spill option for achieving low orbit. The idea aroused some discussion. Alina, sitting Comm, listened but said little. Gray hadn't joined the group and Molyneux was probably off somewhere, sulking. *As usual, lately*. And Arlen was resting.

"If you could manage the whole thing tomorrow night," said Anders, "scoring the hull and planting the shaped charges, we could bring the scout over, transfer personnel and lift the *Patton*, the very next day."

Houk shook his head. "Could, maybe. But not to count on." He frowned. "Happens we do manage, call you, I will."

"We don't have scramble," said Alina. "The colony can overhear."

Brower made a snort. "Let 'em! If you do have things ready, just say you've got the goddamn job wrapped up. Maybe some cover-talk crap about final checking, and then having to tote all those bloody test instruments back here in the heat." He shrugged. "Sound a little pooped, even irritated."

Lisele looked at the unkempt man. "That's good. And if we're not ready—"

"Use your brain, kid. You ain't ready, you fuck-aye don't call in the first place."

"That's exactly what *I* was going to say!" Well, almost . . .

Soft-voiced, Alina spoke. "Tomorrow night, then, I'll take the midnight-to-dawn watch." She grimaced. "I think Molyneux's scheduled for it. And we need someone who will stay awake."

"That's it, then," said Anders. "Set up to fire off this info when the comm window opens next." Alina, Lisele saw, had been taping the entire briefing and exchange of views; now she fed the recording into wide-burst input and arranged for its automatic sending, when the time came, to *March Hare*.

"By the way," Lisele said, "what's the latest from Captain Delarov?"

"Damn' net-tending squaw! Too softhearted." But Brower's tone of voice didn't match the harsh words.

"What the Chief means," said Kobolak, "is that he thinks Delarov is too concerned about casualties, especially among the colonists." He spread his hands. "Maybe so, maybe not. But it's true that if our people were in suits, raising the *Patton* to low orbit would be faster and safer, for all concerned, than transferring its Nielson Cube to the scout with both craft still groundside. Less time, less chance for people to get shot."

"So," said Lisele, "what's wrong with that?"

"The *Patton*," Brower growled. "No offense, Chief Houk—but *maybe* that shitcan makes orbit. And maybe it don't."

Showing no resentment, Houk stood. "What you say, I agree. Although best I could, have done. Decision, though, still the captain's. Especially, when our newest plan she has. Now, however—for me, tent duty. And before that, food. But first, to shower." With a nod to everyone in general, he left the area.

As the group began to scatter away, Lisele looked over and saw Naomi Gray at the cooking niche, stirring a pot that steamed. Approaching, she said, "Smells good. Is there plenty of it?"

"Enough for several. You and me and the Chief, at least. Maybe even a couple of moochers." She smiled. "Sprague brought me some meat this afternoon." As Lisele's brows raised, Gray said, "Oh, it's all wholesome. I dumped the native vegetation, though. When we crossed the stream, coming back here."

"I don't like that stuff too much, either."

As they sat to sample from the bowls Gray filled, first Houk joined them and then Arlen Limmer. For a time, no talk. Then the Chief, after eating rapidly and washing his utensils, left. And soon Gray, accepting thanks from her fellow-diners, followed suit. Watching a silent Arlen, Lisele waited.

Finally he said, "I'll be glad when we're out of here."

"Who won't be?" Then, "Your new assignment giving you problems?"

Reddening, he said, "Sort of. She's—she wants to get

away. Keeps asking me to take her with me when we leave. Well, I can't, of course. No room. But she won't believe that."

"If you could take her along, would you?"

"Sure! In a minute." What her face showed, Lisele couldn't know, but Arlen said, "Hey—not for *me*! I just meant—she, and Ardissa, and that fellow of hers, for that matter—some of these colonists are good people, and if I could get them out, I would."

"Sure, Arlen." She reached to pat his hand. "So would I. Well, if we do get *March Hare* working, and find our way back to someplace decent, I expect there'll be a ship sent here to straighten things out." One of the big ones, maybe, that she'd heard about but never seen—one that could carry a thousand people in freeze? And to evacuate the colony, or to reinforce and—well, "civilize" it? *Don't count your chickens....*

"But right now, Arlen, we don't have time to worry about that sort of thing."

"I suppose not." He looked at his chrono. "Are you doing anything particular, next? We might—"

She looked over to Control, where Gray sat watch. "Naomi's worked harder than me, today. I thought I'd take maybe the first half of her shift, now." He looked disappointed, so she said, "Arlen, this isn't the right time. I can't really put my mind to anything but the *Patton*—that peaceforsaken Nielson Cube. And aren't you supposed to be saving yourself for tent duty?"

"The other night, you didn't say that. You—"

"Night before last, you mean." She shook her head. "I know, Arlen. But some way it's different now. I'm sorry."

His grin, then, looked forced, but he said, "Sure, Lisele. Once we lift off this mudball—!"

They shared a warm kiss, and then he left.

Ships' Regs now being observed largely in the breach, Lisele carried a cup of coffee when she joined Naomi Gray at the comm panel. "Hi. If you'd like a four-hour break, take a nap or something, I'll sit in for you."

Gray looked surprised. "Why, yes; I would. Thanks."

"It's all right; I'm not tired yet." The woman didn't leave, though, and her face held a questioning look.

She wants to talk. Lisele waited, until Naomi said, "You heard us, last night?"

"Some. Does it matter?"

"Not to me, except that maybe it wasn't very polite of us, doing things while you were there. It might bother deWayne, though, having someone else know he needed help."

"Could happen to anybody." *I hope that's all of it.*

But Gray said, "We'd been lovers; friends, too. Then, after the radiation sickness, he said he couldn't. Even after he was going to the tents, groundside, he stayed away from me. Here on the scout, there was never any way to talk with him. So, aboard the *Patton*, you see—I had to make my chance."

"All right; I'm glad you did, and I won't say anything to the Chief. But look! Our main problem is fixing *March Hare* and getting out of here. For now, can't we all just work on that job, and put a lot of other things on hold?"

Gray stood. As she turned to leave, she said, "You're right, of course. I only wish it were as easy as it sounds."

Four hours later, after the woman returned to take the rest of her watch, Lisele found that sleep came easily.

She rose early; in nearby bunks, Houk and Gray still slept. Not dawdling, Lisele soon went above and began making her own breakfast. As she sat to eat it, over in the Control area she saw Chief Brower relieving Alina Rostadt from watch duty. After making an intercom call, Alina came over to say hello and begin some cooking of her own. When, a few minutes later, Anders Kobolak joined the group, Lisele knew what the call was about.

Finding that the coffee urn yielded him only half a cup, Anders put a new batch going. Then he sat down. "Alina? Anything from the skipper yet?"

Before Rostadt could answer, Alys Molyneux came in. "Anything to eat, here? I'm hungry."

Anders began a gesture; from his expression, Lisele was certain he was going to say, "Make free." But Alina caught his hand, and said, "There's plenty to eat, Alys. When you cook it." Thinking back, Lisele realized that Molyneux did tend to hitch free rides on other folks' work; before, she hadn't really noticed.

But not wanting her morning spoiled by dissension, she said, "I made more than I need. Not enough extra for a full meal, I'm afraid, but it's in the pan if you'd like to have it." And then Alina, not quite shrugging but giving that impression, offered Molyneux some of her own surplus.

With a grunt that might have meant thanks, the woman

dished up and sat to eat. As she did so, on her scalp the light showed a few golden glints. Lisele leaned forward. "Alys? Come here; let me see. I think your hair's starting to grow."

Surprising her, Molyneux drew back. "By now, I don't care. By now—" Saying no more, she sat to eat.

"Well, you will. I sure did." Getting no answer, she turned to Alina Rostadt. "The captain, I was asking about."

The fresh coffee was ready; Anders offered refills, poured when indicated, and filled his own cup. Alina said, "She likes Houk's new idea. Well, all along she's preferred the low-orbit option over having to transship the Patton's Cube here groundside, but until the Chief came up with a way to spill the excess fuel into space—"

Anders spread his hands. "Well, that's it; now there's a real chance to do it all in relatively peaceful style."

"Except for burning that big hall," Lisele said. "They would have to build it inside the safety perimeter."

Kobolak waved the comment aside. "We can't let ourselves be stopped by their poor judgment. Now," he said, "the skipper wants to be advised, right away, as soon as decisions are made. Such as, whether the Chief can have the fuel-spill requirements set up tonight, and lift that ship tomorrow, or need to wait two more days. And most especially, if the whole plan goes splat and we have to transship the Cube onto this scout under fire, when that would happen." He scowled. "Brings up another matter. Even without having to report to Captain Delarov, we've got a problem. How to get info here, for fast action, past the colony and in clear text."

XXX

Lisele knew the answer, but Alina's expression showed understanding, so she kept quiet and let the older woman talk. "Why, I'd think it would be much like what Chief Brower said, earlier. A few prearranged code phrases should do it."

So they set it up, keeping Brower's suggestion that "The

job's done" meant things could move the next day; lack of
such a statement indicated the two-day wait. "It's really
getting hot" was to mean "Bring the scout, right now," while
"It's getting hotter," combined with an apparently unconnect-
ed reference to any given time, pinpointed a later rendezvous. "Hotter than the hinges of hell" would tell Anders that
the fuel-spill scheme was off. "So in that case," Alina said,
"we'd have to move the scout fast, pull the Cube, and
transship it right there. Now, are there any other possibilities?"

Anders smiled. "Oh, lots, I suppose, but we can't rig
codes for all of them." Shrugging, "If something comes up
that we haven't planned for, we'll just have to say it out loud
and hope the commodore's people aren't too fast on the
uptake."

Naomi Gray and Chief Houk arrived, wanting breakfast;
after morning greetings the group dispersed. Molyneux went
below; Anders and Alina moved to talk with Brower at the
comm position.

Trying to decide what she needed to do next, Lisele
stood for a moment, then saw Arlen enter the area. He was
carrying the cage that held the small native animal, which at
present showed only as a small, inert bundle of grey-brown
fur. "Arlen?" Lisele said. "It didn't die, did it?"

He grinned. "Oh, no. But he's not very active lately,
Extra Sensory isn't. The main things, though, are that I don't
have time to gather enough fodder for him, and we'll be
leaving pretty soon anyway. So to be sure I don't forget, when
I go down to the tents today I'll set him free."

"Him? How do you know?"

"Hey, I don't even know that 'he' or 'she' *apply* to
animals like Extra Sensory. But I have to call him something."

"Sure." She looked at the little creature; slowly but
steadily, its sides pulsed with breathing. "I wish we'd had
more chance to study—uh, him." With a finger through the
cage wires she stroked the end she thought might be the
head; sure enough, three ears raised, exposing the tiny eyes
they lidded. And thinking of a gerbil she'd once owned—
hardly an exciting pet but inoffensive, pleasant to have around—
she felt sadness that she'd never be able to *learn* about these
creatures.

Because if ever she got off this particular mudball, she
definitely wasn't coming back!

*   *   *

Arlen began making his breakfast; Lisele, walking over and nodding to Eduin Brower who was sitting watch, took an aux position. Using a headset, she listened in full to Captain Delarov's latest message.

It was much the same as the summary already reported; still, it sounded better in the captain's own words. Until at the end, when she said, "My best to you all. I do hope to see you soon. I've never thought I minded solitude, but—" Her laugh sounded a little shaky. "—I know the eight of you, down there, aren't having an easy time of it. Still, right now I'd trade with any one of you." Her voice went soft. "Here in orbit, the ship hardly even creaks. Aside from when your tapes come in, almost the only sounds I hear are my own."

Her sigh was audible. "Katmai Delarov, Captain, out."

Putting the headset aside, Lisele turned to Brower. "You think she'll be all right?"

Looking puzzled, he blinked. "Who? Oh—you were hearing Katmai's tape, from yesterday? Hell, yeah; sure." Around the cigar stub at the corner of his mouth, he grinned. "I called her back, right away. Told her—well, what, exactly, is none of your damn business. But mainly, get off her fat squaw butt and set some nets out." *Delarov wasn't fat!* "And sometime this here gahdam week, she could catch herself a lousy ol' renegade, if she worked at it."

Despite herself, Lisele had to laugh. "Did she answer?"

"Damn well didn't have to." He butted the cigar out, the dying fumes smelling worse than the live coal. "Moray? You gonna relieve me here a while, or ain't you?"

She looked at him. About time to show the man that his language didn't abash her. "Fuckin'-aye, Chief," she said.

With a nod, he stood and left.

A bit later, on an aux screen Lisele saw Chief Houk go groundside. Tent duty, yes. For a time, then, not much happened. The main thing that didn't, was that when Houk came aboard again and Arlen debarked, no one came to relieve Lisele of the watch. Considering the wholly-amorphous state of watch-skeds, she wasn't certain who was derelict, but she suspected Alys Molyneux. When, a half hour past her relief time, she flagged Anders Kobolak over to Control, he confirmed her guess. "We'll straighten it out later," he said.

"You and Houk and Gray are due to leave for the *Patton* in a few minutes. Go get ready; for the time being, I'll sit in here."

"Thanks, Anders." So Lisele went below, collected her gear, and met the other two at the airlock.

"Ready?" she said.

"As can be," said Houk. Gray nodded.

"Then let's go."

Groundside, armed and waiting, stood Thela Cochrane.

Common sense curbed Lisele's natural urge to speak a greeting. She nodded; barely, grudgingly, the woman returned the gesture. If Naomi Gray made any acknowledgment, Lisele didn't see it. Houk, though, said, "Better, the foot now?"

"It walks." With only a slight limp, Cochrane turned and moved away, toward the ship. Side by side, none of them showing any inclination to catch up, the three followed.

With the hostile Utie in earshot, Lisele found little that needed saying. Once, pointing to a stand of spiral-branched bushes, she noted that the increasing heat seemed to be fading the foliage. In turn, Chief Houk spotted a scurrying group of small animals that could have been relatives of Extra Sensory: two that were roughly the size of that creature, and several smaller ones. So, Lisele told the Chief, maybe they did have two sexes, after all. "How nice for them," said Naomi Gray. Cochrane looked back and glowered, but made no comment.

When they reached the slight dip in the trail, hidden from the colony's view, where three days ago Cochrane had been left to wait, that woman stopped and turned to face the others. Pointing to Lisele she said, "All right. You're so good, unarmed, are you? Whipped one of us, I heard hints." She unbuckled her weapon and let it drop. *She has guts; I'll give her that much.* "Drop your piece; out here, no chance for tricks, like with that door, we'll see how good you are. To the death?" Cochrane sneered. "Or just 'til I make you beg to live?"

There's no time for this kind of idiocy. Still, though, taking one deep breath, Lisele said, "The hints you mention. Did they say I could have crippled the man for life, but didn't?"

Cochrane shrugged. "Didn't say all that much, and it

don't matter." She moved forward. "What matters is, yellow-belly, get rid of that gun and fight like you mean it!"

Oh, the hell with this. Ridding herself of gun and harness, shucking her jacket to wrap around those items, she bent to lay the bundle gently on the ground. And wasn't at all surprised—was expecting, in fact—to see in peripheral vision that Thela Cochrane launched her attack while Lisele wasn't looking.

Or so the woman must have assumed.

Standing up would have pitted Lisele's slighter weight and zero velocity against Cochrane's bulk and momentum. Instead, she hunkered down to dodge the impact. Then, like a spring uncoiling as Cochrane's leap brought the woman directly overhead, Lisele straightened and thrust. The jar hurt her neck and shoulders, but she stood to see Cochrane windmilling, landing hard, face first on the rocky soil.

She wouldn't stay down, though. Coming to her knees, wiping blood and gravel from her face, Cochrane grunted. "Tricky bitch, ain'tcha? Well, try *this*!" Not leaping now, but staying in a half-crouch with arms widespread and flailing, she charged.

From no source she recognized, Lisele's move came. Without thought she saw her right leg thrust like a spear, the foot pointed squarely between Cochrane's eyes, just under the heavy ridge of brow. But time stretched; she had long moments to realize that in light shoes this was a certain way to break some toes, and still without volition her shin muscles pulled the foot up, no longer pointing. So that her sole slammed into Thela Cochrane's forehead, and the heel smashed the woman's nose.

Force of impact threw Lisele back and away; off balance, twisting sidewise, she caught herself with one arm flung backward to the ground and again came upright. On shaky legs—and what with adrenalin and muscle strain, her hands shook, too. So that her sudden fragility wouldn't be seen, she put both hands to her hips. Briefly she wondered why she felt no fear, then remembered her mother's words: "If you're lucky, you'll find there isn't time for it."

Wiping gouts of blood off with her forearm, trying to snarl curses through more blood bubbling from the ruined nose, Thela Cochrane still came forward.

Enough of this! And keeping her foot pointed forward

now, Lisele kicked the woman directly in the solar plexus. With that blow, Cochrane went down and stayed there.

Time came back to normal, and after a few moments the shakes were gone. Stepping forward, Lisele locked fingers in what there was of Cochrane's greasy hair and pulled upward, to look at the woman face-to-face. "Do you quit?" she said. "Or do I have to kill you? Say it fast; there's no seconds on this." After enough time for Lisele to take three long breaths, the woman nodded. Since she made no other move, Lisele took the gesture to mean surrender. "All right." She stepped back. "Naomi? You think you can plug that nosebleed?"

"I can try." Gray knelt, tearing swatches of cloth from her first-aid kit to stuff into rapidly swelling nostrils.

Lisele felt an arm around her, and Houk said, "All right, you are? What you did, shouldn't have."

"Had to, Chief. No other way." A shudder racked her. "All right? Yes, I am. Well, give it a minute; I will be." His arm squeezed once, then he moved away.

When Cochrane could stand again, and walk, the four moved over the next rise and approached the colony.

To Lisele's surprise, no one seemed to pay the group much attention. As they passed the large hall, Houk told Cochrane, "From here to the ship, not needed, you are. Some rest, get." With a sullen nod, the woman left them.

"She'll go straight to the commodore," Lisele said. When neither of her companions seemed to know what she meant, she added, "If we have to deal with that man, let's be on the ship first." So all three stepped up their pace, and made their way upship without encounter.

Before they could discuss anything, Houk called the colony switchboard to say that the services of Elseth Sprague and Arnet Kern would not, this day, be required. Lisele didn't find his explanation especially coherent, but deduced he was saying he'd be working on the remaining facet plugs, trying to fix some with parts from others. Cannibalizing, that was called; yes.

"Well, then," she said when he was done talking and had cut the circuit, "should we get to it?"

Houk grinned. "All done, that part. Yesterday. For today, our want from those people, only privacy."

"Then what *are* we going to do?"

"For tonight's work, necessities gather, the successive steps plan. And of less urgency, yet helpful, other matters." He gestured. "Between Control and Drive, more flexibility of operation I would like. Some additional channels then, to restore, perhaps."

Lisele shrugged. "Fine by me. Where do we start?"

They began by working on the inship communications, but shortly it became evident that most of the dead channels had been sabotaged beyond the group's ability to repair. In the probable time available, at any rate.

So, giving up on that plan, the three went down to Stores and located a flexible plastic ladder of sufficient length, a cutting torch, a limited-field working light, a packet of small, adhesive, shaped charges with connecting wires to engroup them, a remote-controlled detonator, and the requisite firing device to be plugged into a Control panel. Plus a few other items Houk gathered, for which Lisele could see no particular use. By the time they'd carried all those things up, and stashed them in a cubby near the cargo hatch, it was time for their lunch break. And the way they'd been hurrying upship and down, Lisele could certainly use the breather!

Still, she went to the ramp's top to take delivery of food, and was surprised to see two persons carrying trays. She didn't know either of them, but they weren't armed so she escorted them to captain's digs and then back to the airlock. When she rejoined Houk and Gray, the latter was chuckling. "Somebody got their wires crossed. Sent lunch for our usual five, not just three. I put the extras in the fridge, just in case."

While eating, no one had much to say. Except the Chief. "Next," he said, "the ship's spacesuits, we inspect."

XXXI

After the meal's leavings were cleared away, it was time to head downship. From Tregare's original *Inconnu* Lisele remembered the general layout as Houk led them, past the deck that held part of Ship's Stores, to the training area.

What awaited, there, was disappointment. The power suit, the mechanism that gave its wearer an extra magnitude of strength, lay a shambles. She touched the burn-sliced remnant of an armored sleeve. "Happened in the mutiny, I'd expect."

Of the three dozen non-powered suits the ship could be expected to carry, only eight remained. Four were clearly hopeless, with too many vital parts either missing or damaged beyond repair. The others? Clucking to himself, Houk nodded. "To exchange some components now. How many of these fit for use, we will learn."

Slow and tedious, that work, but by break time the Chief had two suits refurbished well enough to approve them. Those, he and Lisele carried up to Control and placed out of sight behind a row of equipment racks. Then, downship again after coffee, an hour later he pronounced one more suit usable.

The fourth, though, took longer. He tried parts from one or another disabled unit, and finally put down his tools. "This," he said, "not guaranteed. *Perhaps* safe. But only at last extreme, to be risked."

Still, along with the third good suit, that one was taken to the Drive room and placed in an inconspicuous location.

The afternoon had been long and tiring. Leaving Houk still puttering with the Drive, as he refined some adjustments for at least the third time, Lisele and Naomi went up to captain's quarters and showered, then sat sipping some native wine, chilled from the fridge. When the Chief arrived and began undressing for his own shower, Lisele asked, "Should I order dinner now? You'll be ready before it gets here." He nodded, so she made the call.

When it seemed to Lisele that food delivery should be imminent, Gray was lying down and had dozed off, so she herself went to the main airlock. Her timing was close; ascending the ramp, carrying three trays stacked, came Deryth

Mangentes. Nearing the top, the woman smiled. "This time they got the numbers right."

In a way, Lisele wished there were an extra tray. For some reason she felt empathy toward this woman who twice had sat unprotesting while red iron seared her face, who suffered Malden's painful whims without acceptance but with little complaint. Since there were several hours before secrecy would be needed, Lisele might have invited her to join them at dinner.

As she thought it, Mangentes said, "I've eaten, but could I stay and talk with you folks for a few minutes? There are some questions...."

"Can't see why not. C'mon."

At captain's digs, the Chief was dressed and Gray awake again. Both looked surprised to see the colony woman; Lisele said, "You know Second Officer Mangentes. She'd like to get some information, if it's all right." Gray made no sign; after a moment, Houk nodded.

As they prepared to sit around the table, Naomi bringing out wine to pour, Deryth set down her shoulder bag. "Save that for a while; I brought along some of our beer." She shrugged. "It's not very good; tastes stronger than I like. And not chilled. But—" Undoing complex fastenings, she opened a bottle and filled the four glasses, then raised hers. "Here's to the restoration of the *Patton*."

Momentarily, after the ritual touching of glasses, Lisele paused. *Poison?* Because who could know what insane plot Malden might hatch? But the woman led off with three hearty swallows, made a minor face and a hearty belch, and seemed healthy enough. So Lisele, more cautiously, sampled the stuff.

Strong-tasting, yes, but not bad. Not bad at all. It was like—what was she trying to remember?—oh, yes. The leaf-bulb wine, concocted by Hagen Trent back on Shaarbant. The time they were all stuck in the box canyon bivouac for over a year, because of the mysterious illness of the two Shrakken. And one morning Tregare had said to Hagen, "I've got a name for that booze of yours. 'Old Head-Splitter.'"

She must have smiled then, because Mangentes looked puzzled. Bringing her thoughts to the present, Lisele said only, "You needn't downgrade your product here. I've had worse."

Before anyone else could speak, Houk turned to Mangentes. "Information, you wish? In particular, what?"

As the colonist asked and Chief Houk answered, context
was roughly what Lisele expected. And the Chief, making no
slips, stayed with the agreed-on fictions. Was it decided
whether the *Tamurlaine* would come here and land? It would,
yes. When? Not precisely determined, that decision. Soon,
though? Yes. "Well, then," said Mangentes, "shouldn't we get
on with putting the galley and quarters back into shape,
stocking food and supplies as best we can? Things like that?"

The Chief looked stumped for answer; Lisele thought
fast, and said, "Start *gathering* food and all that; sure. But it's
going to take our experts, when they get here, a lot of time to
put everything to rights. And they can't do their work with a
lot of people running around the ship, trying to find storage
space that isn't ready yet." *Why am I so good at lying when I
don't like it?* Especially to this woman . . .

But her story did its job. Nodding in agreement, Mangentes
stood. "Well, I think I have most of what the commodore
wanted to know, and thanks. So I'll leave now; it's near dark
and I have work to do before sleep."

Curious, Lisele said, "What with our watch skeds, I
don't think any of us have settled accounts with this thirty-
hour day of yours. What are *your* normal sleeping hours? In
general, I mean—not personally."

Deryth's brow wrinkled. "Hours. Earth has twenty-four;
right? Well, we sleep, average, about a third of our day, too.
And usually rise about dawn." Standing then, the woman left.

Looking after her, Lisele thought. About five hours after
sunset, it should be safe to get to work.

Actually the delay was longer. Up in Control, with an
aux monitor set for night vision, Houk insisted on waiting
until the visible part of the colony showed no persons moving. Then, hanging dark goggles and a cutting torch and
worklight alongside the canteen on his equipment belt, and
adding the straps that allowed it to double as a safety harness,
he went groundside. Behind him Lisele closed the airlock,
setting an alarm to ring if the lock were opened by Malden's
remote-control channel. Then she and Gray went to the cargo
hatch, secured the plastic ladder to its edge, and allowed the

ladder to dangle below. As they had estimated, it hung well
past the bulge where Houk would stand.

Then, since at least one of them should be getting some
sleep, Naomi Gray left the area.

Sooner than Lisele expected, the Chief reached the top
of the landing leg, stood on its bulge, and secured his safety
harness. Not speaking, he waved a hand upward. Lisele set
the ladder to swinging back and forth, first gently and then
increasing the amplitude of the swing, until Houk caught it
and could fasten it to hull-cleats. From her vertical view the
sidewise slant looked severe, but considering the distance
involved she knew it was relatively mild.

For a few minutes, as the Chief marked his half-meter
circle, the worklight shone. Then, dousing it, he activated his
torch. Much brighter than Lisele had expected, the cutting
tool was also disturbingly noisy; for a moment she had to
reassure herself that a fair distance, plus the bulk of the ship
itself, stood between torch and colony. Then, relaxing, she
waited.

The job seemed to take forever; occasionally Lisele found
herself nodding off. Although the torch was one of the earlier
catalytic-combustion models and lacked the fierce actinic
glare of an electric arc, she couldn't look at it except in
fleeting glimpses. Even then, her retinas burned with color-
reversed after-images. So only now and then, and using
peripheral vision, did she glance down to see what Houk was
doing. Not that she could gauge his progress, anyway, from
up here!

Occasionally the torch dimmed for a time, while perhaps
the Chief drank from his canteen. Or, though Lisele hadn't
seen any sign of food in his gear, had a snack? At one pause
she heard the faint sound of liquid splattering on the ground
far below; looking at her chrono and seeing that more than
five hours had passed, suddenly she felt the demands of her
own bladder, and made a brief inship visit.

Hurrying back, she saw that once again the torch was
working at full glare. But less than an hour later its light died
and did not resume. The worklight came on, and swaying of
the ladder combined with sounds of movement below, to
indicate that Chief Houk was done, down there, and climbing
to enter the ship.

*   *   *

His breathing seemed labored, so when she saw him nearing the top she reached to take his hand, helping pull him up onto the hatch. Grunting, he turned to lie on his back. After a time he sat up. "Slower, this thing, than believable."

"The torch, you mean?" He seemed to want to get up, so she gave him a hand and he managed it.

He nodded. "Two hours, I'd thought. Six, though, isn't it, more likely?"

"Roughly. Did you finish?"

"Cutting, yes."

"How about applying the explosive charges?" She checked her chrono. "There's still some time before dawn."

He made a snort. "But who to use it? No youngling, me. To go again down there, that work to do, beyond my strength is."

Lisele felt shame. He'd done *all* the real work, while she merely stood by. "I'm sorry, Chief. If I knew how, I'd do it myself. But peace take me, I don't!"

He was shaky on his legs, so going inside she ventured a little support; he didn't protest. Once into captain's digs he stripped only to undershorts and went directly to bed.

Hoping the hot water would relax her for sleep, Lisele showered first. It didn't help much.

The next morning, beginning her sixteenth day on Sitdown, wasn't one of Lisele's best. Tired and tense, lacking both time and privacy for alpha-state relaxation, she found equal annoyance in Gray's rested vigor and Houk's taciturn grumpiness. After breakfast from rations, she said, "Do we go back to the scout now, or what?" Then, rethinking the matter, "No. We don't break pattern; right? So for the colony's benefit we have to fake some work on here, most of the day, and go back at our regular time."

"I'll do the faking," said Gray, "while you two catch up on some sleep."

Well, yes—she and the Chief, Lisele realized, had each been up and awake for nearly thirty hours. But, "Fake it how, Naomi?"

Sounding exasperated but not looking it, Houk said, "Kern and Sprague, to supervise. Facet plugs, at your direction they shift. You—"

Lisele protested. "But you have the nodes balanced *now*!"

Headshake. "*Mine*, the charting. No difference, the moves will make. The Uties to keep busy, is all."

"Whatever you say, Chief." After cleaning her own dishes, Lisele went back to bed.

From the intercom Gray's voice woke her. "I'm ordering lunch. Just in case, you two should probably be up to eat it."

"Right." DeWayne Houk was also coming awake; when Gray arrived with the food, the two were dressed and presentable.

Rested, the Chief was about as cheerful as he ever got. When Gray asked about his plans for the afternoon, he went so far as to smile. "Coordination, Drive and Control, Moray and I practice." Sure—because what with the sabotaged channels, some operations normally handled directly from Control would have to be done on voice command, in Drive.

One thing, though. "But isn't it Anders you should be practicing with?"

"If could be done, yes. Time for that, though, we'll not have. The scout to *March Hare*, Kobolak must take. You, with Limmer to help, low orbit will achieve."

"But I can't—"

"The hell you can't," said Naomi Gray. "This isn't like matching an orbit from space. All you need to do is get your speed up enough to hold altitude."

Well, yes. Even if the orbit-matching function of the ship's computer wasn't working—and here, groundside, Lisele had no way to check it out—the radar altimeter would do the job. She knew that gadget was operating; she'd taken a reading on the big mountain and the results jibed with optical triangulation.

So she nodded. "All right. If I have to, I'll do it."

At first the coordination exercises seemed cumbersome, but when break-time came, Lisele had the feel of it. Houk seemed to agree; when they'd finished coffee he announced readiness to return to the scout. So after a few minutes' delay, groundside, their escort joined them for the walk.

"Ready?" said First Officer Goral Craig. "Then let's go."

Craig and Houk walked ahead, of course. Following, alongside Naomi Gray, Lisele listened to the men's talk and was surprised to hear the Chief announce that next day he expected to test the *Patton*'s Drive with power close to redline max, and enough thrust so that "outside of safety perimeter, all should stay." Because certainly such a test would kick up enough dust and heat to endanger anyone who came too close.

And why was he making such a move? Finally Lisele figured out the motive: to keep the area free of Uties, except when they were specifically invited. *Not bad, Chief!*

Aboard the scout, the three learned that a new group of colony women had arrived for breeding, and that all but Houk's had been duly bedded. "You wasn't here for the picking," said Eduin Brower, "so you're stuck with what's left."

Houk shrugged. "No difference, it makes. Today and tomorrow, the two times only. Because the day after, this world we all of us leave."

Well, it was about time the discussion got down to business! "I see," said Anders Kobolak. "Tomorrow you go back, and fake work again through the afternoon, then finish your preparations during the night. And at dawn I bring the scout."

Definitely, that was about the size of it. Now Alina told of Delarov's latest message. "It's pretty long; you can all hear it if you want, but here's the gist." Basically, the captain had become worried about both her own stability and that of the Nielson Cube, so she'd roused the Chief Engineer. On both counts, Darwin Pope had reassured her.

"Even a tough squaw can need some hugging," Brower said. "And if there was more, be damned if I grudge her!"

For dinner, Arlen and Lisele shared the small table. Obviously he also wanted to share the cubby, later. But she said, "Arlen, I'm too tensed-up. Let's wait for low orbit."

XXXII

Next morning Lisele felt good; definitely, she'd caught up on the missed sleep. At breakfast, first across the table from sullen Molyneux (*what* is *the matter with her?*) and then from Anders Kobolak and Arlen, she had good appetite. Talking with Anders, rechecking any code phrases that might still be needed, now that most of the alternatives were settled, Lisele felt that finally the situation was coming to a head. "By this time tomorrow, the lot of us should be free of here!"

Agreeing, Anders left to relieve Chief Brower at Control. Certainly that wasn't the way the watch order had been set up, but by now, the whole thing must be totally catch-as-catch-can.

Arlen, now, was looking a bit pouty himself. Lisele said, "Hey, look. About last night, I'm sorry. But I couldn't. My whole mind—I can't think about *anything* but getting us off this mudball." Reaching, she gave his hand a squeeze. "I wouldn't have been with you at all. Don't you see?"

His smile was slow to come, but eventually it got there. "Yes. I guess so. Maybe the difference is, you're in the middle of all of it, and I'm not. Though I'd like to be . . ."

"Sure you would. And pretty soon, we all will."

Sooner than usual, Chief Houk returned from tent duty; he didn't look like a man who wanted to answer questions, so Lisele asked none. Not much later the two of them, plus Gray, were groundside, ready for the now-familiar walk to the *Patton*.

Their escort was the tall woman with large, sagging breasts, the one who had been the Chief's first breeding assignment. In all the long walk, only a few words were said. First, Houk: "To know, I suppose, more time is needed."

"If it took? Yes. I hope it did."

"Then also do I."

When they reached the large building, with only a hand-sign of goodbye the woman left them.

Aboard ship, Houk and Gray went to the Drive room while Lisele climbed to Control. Coordinating, she and the Chief brought the ship's Drive power drain up to idle and a little better, then practiced powering up and down, first as a whole and then—simulating course changes—changing power to each node differently but simultaneously. When Houk was satisfied he called a halt; he and Gray came up to join Lisele. "The commodore, now tell. Thrust, we next test. This area, his people for their own safety to clear."

So she called, and eventually Malden's peevish voice came over the channel. When Lisele was done explaining, the man said, "We can't evacuate the whole safety perimeter; you know that. I *told* Orval he shouldn't build this hall so near the ship, but he wouldn't listen. You'll have to—"

"We understand, sir. We'll hold the thrust tests down enough to keep the building safe." She paused. "Of course, once the *Tamurlaine* arrives, if we're able to get the *Patton* spaceworthy again, the structure can't be saved. So—" Hey! Good idea! "So you might want to start evacuating equipment and valuables, right away. Salvage everything you can, before you lift your ship."

"You're right! I hadn't thought of that!"

"Until now, sir, neither had we."

"I see. Well, thank you—Moray, is it?"

"Yes, sir. How much time, do you think, will you need to clear the danger area?"

"Uh—half an hour should do it. Or better—I'll have someone call and advise you when we're ready."

"Yes, sir; that's best. Moray out." Cutting the circuit, she turned to Houk and Gray. "Well. Now we have something to keep that peacewaster busy for a while!"

Malden wouldn't be calling back immediately; there was plenty of time for a midmorning break. In captain's digs the three had coffee and, from rations, a snack. While they were cleaning up afterward, Houk said, "The thrust tests. As with testing just completed, both overall adjustments and differentials between nodes, we must practice."

Lisele nodded. "Sure." There was no reason for Houk and Gray to climb to Control and then go back downship, so they went directly to the Drive room. Upship, Lisele waited for word from the colony. After a few minutes a voice she didn't recognize told her that the testing could proceed, so she called the Chief. "We have the go-ahead. So crank up thrust and twist its tail!"

She wasn't certain that he laughed, but he might have.

*   *   *

At half power and ten percent thrust the ship didn't even vibrate, let alone show sign of any effort to lift. Aux screens monitoring groundside showed soil disrupted, flying upward as dust and pebbles, in a circular area that included the feet of the ship's landing legs but fell just short of the bottom of the boarding ramp. About what Lisele had expected.

In increments, sometimes the same for all three nodes and sometimes not, she and Houk upped both thrust and power. At nearly redline-max for the latter and forty-percent thrust, its three nodes equalized, the *Patton* began to quiver. Still far short of lifting, but showing signs of wanting to. "Chief? If the curve holds all the way, we can *do* it!"

She missed his answer, because from an offship channel Malden began shouting. "What the miserable fuck do you think you're doing? Dirt, hot mud, splattering all over us here!"

She checked the screen. The commodore wasn't making it up; the circle of disruption had expanded to within less than fifty meters from the great hall, and wind was carrying upflung debris across the colony. *Oh, peace take it!* "Chief? Crank down a whole lot, and fast! We're spraying crud all across the colony, and Malden's chewing nails!"

Even as he acknowledged she saw the groundside tumult begin to wane. On the panel before her, indicators showed power drain dropping to ten percent of redline max, and thrust to a bare idling minimum. On the offship channel she said, "All right; we've cut it. Is that better, sir?" Malden's profane thanks conveyed more anger than gratitude, but so what?

She called Houk again. "Too bad we have to stop testing."

But he said, "All we need, we know now," and went on to say that he was leaving all units fired up, minimum, so that when the scout came, no warmup period would be necessary. "Also, a process called burning-in. The entire assembly to stabilize."

"Right." She didn't understand it, but it sounded good. So when Gray and the Chief came up to Control, Lisele asked if she should get word to Kobolak that this part of the plan had been completed.

He shook his head. "Not until all is."

"You mean tonight. After the explosive charges are set."

"Yes. Paraphrasing, coding, for partial information only, too risky is."

She really would have liked to announce some progress, but caution was probably best. Lisele looked at her chrono. "It's a little early for lunch. I guess I'll punch up some liftoff sims from their Tinhead, and practice. Using reduced thrust and power, to see just how little we can get by with and still get out of atmo for the fuel spill."

Houk nodded, so she began. Setting her parameters at barely short of redline-max power for the number of facet plugs in place, postulating fuel tanks so near to full as made no difference, she wanted to determine the necessary minimum thrust percentage for initial liftoff, and then the speed and altitude that could be attained before spilling fuel. After the spill, of course, there'd be plenty of margin to reach low orbit.

The routine was familiar enough; during waits while Houk, below, moved facet plugs around, Lisele had run the calculations using purely arbitrary figures. Just for practice.

Now, with real data, she found that for a safe lift the partially-equipped nodes didn't give much leeway. Frowning, she extrapolated with power drains both greater and less than her initial values.

The answers weren't encouraging. Best procedure, to avoid overstressing the nodes too long in the slow-speed stage, came from putting power all the way to redline-max and thrust at over sixty percent of capability. For a fragile, flanged-up Drive, that was pushing it. Ten percent was the least safety factor she'd ever heard recommended; the best Lisele could get was a little over two.

Well, you can't argue with facts. Looking over to where Gray and the Chief were discussing other data as they watched it on an aux terminal, she announced her results.

To her surprise, Houk made a kind of grin. "Good, that. Safety factor, any at all, very pleasant surprise is."

Once again Lisele adjusted her opinion of the man. Yes, he and Tregare *would* get along. After a time, of course.

By now, it wasn't too early to order lunch. But as Lisele moved to call the colony switchboard, the offship channel rang first. Flipping the switch, she said, "Yes? Something?"

No picture, but the voice of Anders Kobolak, sounding urgent. "Moray? Houk? Gray? You there, any of you?"

"Moray, Captain. The others are here, too. Go ahead, sir."

She heard him clear his throat. "A matter you should know. Er—" He was certainly having trouble, figuring out how to say it. "We've discovered that a component is missing. One of eight, that we brought along. It's—uh—it's the A. M. unit."

A. M.? One of eight? *Alys Molyneux!* Lisele tried to think fast. "Where's the last place anybody saw it? And when?"

"Early this morning, I think. In—in the area above the upper supply hold." The sleeping dorm, that would be. "I—"

With UET probably listening, what to say? Well, *try*. "I understand your concern, sir. The unit's been operating erratically, so of course you want it repaired as soon as possible." Hmmm. "Any idea where it might have been mislaid?"

She missed his answer because on the aux screen, the one that monitored groundside at the ramp's foot, she saw movement. She turned to get a better look.

"Captain, I've located the component. It's groundside here." For below, approaching the ship and all too near it, came nearly forty colonists. And alongside the commodore, who was leading, the bald head of Alys Molyneux couldn't be mistaken.

No time for games, for subtlety. Closing the channel momentarily, Lisele yelled to Houk and Gray. "Downship! To the Drive room, and lock it from inside. Emergency!"

"No! Fight, we have to."

"We can't fight all those, Chief." Quickly Lisele punched for airlock closure; nothing happened. Damn all; the commodore's groundside override channel! Improvising, she tried to plug it off. No luck, so against all Regs she crosspatched it to the high-level side of the board and saw the indicators blow.

But still the hatch didn't close. *He has a backup that doesn't show on the board!* No use staying here; she couldn't do anything. "Operator! Keep this relay channel open. Your ship's safety is at stake." Silence. "Acknowledge!"

Hesitantly the voice came. "Yes. Orders acknowledged."

"Good." Cutting Send again, she said, "Peace take you, Chief, we *have* to secure Drive. I'll come down with you, far

enough to cover the lock while you get past that deck. Then
I'll get back up here fast, and seal *this* place."

"And then, to do what?"

"I don't know yet. But until we have ourselves some
safety, we can't do *anything*. So move it."

Abruptly, then, he did. And Gray also.

As Lisele followed, running for the deck's landing and
starting downship, she reviewed what she'd done. Anders
would stay on the channel, yes. And what she'd told the
operator—well, it was true enough. Just not quite the way
the operator thought it was.

Tregare would have liked that touch. She only hoped
that someday she'd get the chance to tell him.

But when they reached the airlock level, those chances
didn't look good.

The commodore had got there first.

At least nobody was shooting yet. Lisele didn't remember pulling out her needler but now it moved, almost without
her volition, back and forth across the dozen or so Uties who
stood near the lock's inner hatch. She gave Molyneux a glare
that by rights should have peeled skin, then ignored the
woman. "Commodore? What's this all about?"

"Don't try to lie, you mutinous bitch!" His voice went
shrill. "Trying to steal the guts out of *my ship!* Said you were
fixing it for *me*, and all along—"

Fighting shock, Lisele tried to make her mind function.
The only thought that came was a saying of Tregare's, that
sometimes it pays to break all the rules and tell the *truth*. So
she said, "In a way we *are* doing it for you. Without the Cube
we can't land the *Tamurlaine* here, or go get help for the
colony. So—"

Sneering, Malden shook his head. "You think I believe
that? I know better. What she said—"

Grating, Houk's voice overrode. "Molyneux! Turncoat
slut! Told, you did!"

His words weren't helping the situation, but Lisele said
only, "Alys! *Why?*"

For the first time, Molyneux's face showed expression. "I
didn't plan to. Just to get away, join the colony. But it struck
me, once you take the Cube—*what* colony?"

"But we were—" Lisele stopped. No point in trying to

explain that they hoped to leave the scout's Cube to power the colony; Malden wouldn't believe that, either. All she found to say was, "Alys? Why did you desert in the first place?"

Baring teeth, the woman's mouth squared. "Because your plans, they're no good. You keep changing them, they're still no good. If I follow you and Kobolak, what happens is you get us all killed." It looked as if she tried to spit, but nothing came out. "So go to hell, you; I'm saving *me*. And making a good place for myself, too." Her arm went around Malden's waist. "Commodore's woman!"

"Commodore's whore! Traitor!" Peripherally, as the Chief shouted, Lisele saw movement; a hard shove caught her from behind, and she fell forward. Rolling to one side she saw Naomi Gray also on the deck; then, between them, deWayne Houk landed prone, in full firing position.

"*No*, Chief!"

Too late: his needler snarled; bright red spurts made a slanting pattern from below Molyneux's right breast to above her left. As the woman fell, something stung Lisele's forehead; she brushed at her eyes, trying to see through the sudden gush of blood, but caught only a brief glimpse of Malden, scuttling for shelter.

As guns beyond her counting began to flare.

Sideflash from an energy beam seared her right shoulder; instinct sent her eeling behind a stanchion. With one torn sleeve she wiped blood from her forehead; then, by squinting, she could see again.

Not all Malden's people had been grouped with him; now shots came from either flank. His troops weren't trained very well, Lisele found herself thinking; in the glare and confusion, some were being shot by their own side.

With her mind now gone ice-cold, no room for fear or worry, all that existed for Lisele was a deck-landing full of Uties, and the problem of shooting them without herself being shot. Wait—there was something more she should be noticing; what was it? Oh, yes: where were Gray and Houk? She wouldn't want to shoot *them*.

They weren't in sight, and now the near-miss of an energy gun, close enough that she smelled her own hair burning, brought her out of daze. Stretching flat, bracing her gun hand with the other, from her shelter she raked needles across every visible part of the deck. Until no return fire came.

After a moment of quiet, she saw Naomi Gray pull Chief Houk up from a shelter much like Lisele's own. Gray's jaw carried an angry burn and the Chief was bleeding; from where Lisele lay, no way to tell how bad it was. She waved. "Get down to Drive! Do you want cover?"

With a headshake, Naomi held up an energy gun. Lisele nodded. "Then move!" Once they'd left, Lisele stood. There were still Uties aboard; she'd seen glare-limned shapes fleeing the area. But where they were now, she had no idea.

So ordinarily, the only sensible thing would be to go looking.

Except that she couldn't. It was more important to get back to Control.

XXXIII

As she turned toward the exit to other decks, suddenly Lisele *saw* the sprawled bodies, burned or bleeding or both. Until this moment, the carnage had been only background to the situation she desperately needed to evaluate. Now, though—

She didn't count them; she couldn't afford to look that closely. Her stomach clenched, not in nausea but in prelude to a wash of grief and horror. But she had no time for it!

There was a man, hands still opening and closing though half his head was burned away. A woman, mercifully no longer moving, with a bloody pit for a face. And something an energy gun had rendered unidentifiable, besides cutting it nearly in half at the waist. At least the thing wasn't one of *her* kills!

And of all these, how many were? Houk and Gray had done their own shooting. And she still thought that in the confusion, some of the Uties killed each other. Well, however it had gone, she couldn't let it matter. *Just keep thinking that!*

Several who lay there were not yet done with breath and movement. Tregare, she knew, would have finished them— whether out of mercy or to leave no living enemy behind him. But for good or bad, she couldn't do it. Deliberately, Lisele made her attention focus on what she needed to do next, and nothing else. Nothing else at all.

The blood, still seeping down through and past her eyebrows, bothered her. Stepping over another dead Utie— female, this one was—Lisele found herself looking down at the corpse of Alys Molyneux. Around the woman's neck was a gauzy scarf. Lisele undid it, shook it out, and tied it to bandage her own forehead. Good enough; no more dripping.

Starting to turn away, she paused to look again at Molyneux. And felt nothing: no grief, no personal regrets. *Well, after all, I didn't kill her!* But if the Chief hadn't, maybe they'd still be talking instead of shooting, and a lot of people wouldn't be lying dead. Still, as Tregare's father—Hawkman Moray, Lisele's youthful-looking, very tall grandfather—used to say, "'Perhaps' applies only to the future, never to the past."

Sounds roused Lisele from reverie. Danger? About time she began paying attention! Most of what she heard came from safe distance. But what she had to do now, she reminded herself, was get back up to Control. Such as about five minutes ago.

Sudden fatigue caught Lisele by surprise. Climbing upship she heard sounds at one landing and another but was simply too tired to investigate. Then, reaching the lower level of ratings' quarters, along a corridor she saw a man and a woman approach.

Too late to avoid them; Lisele shouted, "Go back! If you do, I won't shoot." But already, seeing their guns rise to aim, she was dropping flat. The energy hiss went over her head— too close! By reflex, her needler spat. Return fire spanged needles against the deck alongside her. Then, abruptly, the trajectory raised; the last few needles took out two overhead corridor lights. *Got one? Must've.*

She heard retreating footsteps, irregular but hurried, and brought herself upright. In the dimness she couldn't see which Utie she'd dropped, but whoever, it wasn't moving. There was neither time nor reason to go look. And since she heard no sign of the survivor, might as well forget that one, too. So again, after putting a fresh magazine into the needler, she began to move upship.

Ahead, though—above, rather—came noises of someone

preceding her in the climb. A new problem? Pausing first for
a few deep breaths, Lisele put all effort to moving faster, in
the best silence she could manage.

At the level of the darkened galley, still several steps
below that deck but looking across it, her pursuit reached
its end. His gun in hand but not quite aimed, Cray Malden
awaited.

She knew she should be frightened horribly, but couldn't
muster the energy for it. Against all reason she tried to shout
past his cursing—to say something, *anything*—when she saw
his trigger finger tighten. With the amount of practice he
probably managed, he *had* to be a lousy shot—but her
reflexes didn't agree. Before he could bring his needle gun to
bear, Lisele's own needler fired. Whether she actually hit his
weapon or he simply threw up his arm by instinct and lost
grasp, the gun flew skidding across the deck.

Forcing leaden muscles, she clambered up to face the
man. With one hand dripping blood he moved toward her,
and suddenly kicked her own weapon free. "Now then," he
panted. "Now then!"

And turned to retrieve his gun.

But hers was closer. Veering, he vacillated between the
two goals.

With no hesitation at all, Liesel Selene Moray charged.
Keeping low, she caught him just above the knees, kept her
legs churning, and lifted.

When they hit the landing rail, he went over and she
didn't. Judging by his screams, as he clanged and thudded
from one railing to another, it was a long way down.

She found no need or inclination to look and see for
herself.

Shuddering as she retrieved her needler, checking Malden's
for good measure but finding its magazine so nearly empty
that the piece wasn't worth carrying, again Lisele climbed. As
she reached the deck just below Control, behind her she
heard footsteps. With a sprint that left her breathless, she
reached her objective and tugged the heavy doors shut, then
slammed the crude lockbars into their slots. Rust deposits
stopped them from seating cleanly, but she didn't have time
to be picky.

She ran to the comm panel and hit the intercom to Drive. "Chief! Are you there? Are you all right?"

After a pause that frightened her, she heard Naomi Gray's voice. "Just a minute. I'm nearly done with the bandages."

"How bad is it?"

"Needler. Nasty gash across the ribs, and one of those is either bruised or cracked. Not dangerous, though."

"Thank peace! I thought—but hurry!"

"You want, in such hurry, what action?" More angry than hurt, the Chief sounded.

"We need to fire up the Drive! Power close to redline, and thrust at ten percent, to chase any groundsiders away."

"For what, this power? Already aboard, they are, those that you would repel. Why, then—"

"Peace take you, Houk—*do it!*"

No answer, but the Drive hum rose and she felt the ship begin to vibrate. On the groundside monitor she saw Uties running for cover and was surprised to see how many there were: another contingent must have followed Malden's group. But thrust hadn't built fast enough to interdict the ramp; nearly half of those who fled were heading *up* it.

It was past time to call Anders Kobolak, so now she reported, talking as calm-voiced as if her guts weren't churning with what she'd seen. Only part of her mind paid heed to what she was saying; the rest was chewing on the question: "*Now* what do we do?"

From the huge doors came a creaking sound; she looked and saw that they had been pulled open a couple of centimeters. Momentarily at least, the loosely-seated bars held, but then began to slip again. She couldn't let this happen!

Running to the doors she hammered at the locking bars, first one and then the other, with both hands. They wouldn't move, and soon she saw why: between the doors protruded the barrel of an energy gun. It was pointed off at an angle, away from her, but as she watched, it began to pivot. Keeping away from its field of fire she ran back to the comm panel, where she'd set her needler down, then approached the doors again. Aiming her gun at the crack, "Pull that thing out of there or lose a hand!"

"One shot, and we destroy the control panel! *Then* what can you do?" And she saw that two guns, not one, now showed at the opening. Far enough apart, vertically, that she

couldn't be sure of disabling both gun-holding hands before
one of them could shoot. And it would have to be the hands,
because a needler wouldn't destroy a blaster's capability of
firing.

Stalemate. Swiftly, again avoiding her enemies' target
area, she ran to the comm panel. On intercom, "Chief—
apply thrust! Enough to lift us!"

"The plan, this is not. Under blaster attack, our doors
are. I—"

"*Lift*, you peacetwisting weasel! And right now!" Her
breath came out in a sob. "Damn you, it's our only chance!"
If there were still any chance at all . . .

For moments she couldn't breathe. Then she felt the
ship's vibrations build; the Drive's hum grew to something
near a roar. Indicators showed thrust rising very slowly;
below, the downside monitor pictured the Drive-node disruption area still short of making the ramp's lower end unsafe.
Maybe this damned can couldn't get off groundside, after all!

But even so—! If the ship were cleared of Uties, then
the scout could still come here. She put the intercom to
all-ship broadcast. "All you groundsiders! If you want to keep
breathing, get off this ship right now! Because we're lifting
out of atmosphere, and the cargo hatch won't close." What
else? "Once you're down, run like hell, out past the safety
perimeter." *If you can*.

In a language she'd never heard before, she could hear
Houk cursing; his tone of voice said it all. "Thanks, Chief.
Sorry I had to call you names!" And now what? If the *Patton*
lifted before she could seal Control—! Moving quickly, Lisele
wrenched the helmet and oxygen tank free of one of the
spacesuits; she tore two fingernails, but bleeding or not,
they'd have to wait.

Staying well to one side, she approached the door again.
Still two gun muzzles showing. "Didn't you hear me? Get off
here, or you'll die. If you blow the panels now, you'll just kill
yourselves along with the rest of us. Because no matter what
you do, this ship's lifting!" And the way the vessel shuddered
now, liftoff began to seem more likely.

"Moray? You don't understand!" Distorted, still the voice
seemed familiar. "We're not trying to stop you. This is Deryth
Mangentes; Goral's here with me. Go ahead and lift. But this
is our ship, too; we want to come with you. So *please* let us
in!"

* * *

Trust Uties? Lisele shook her head. There wasn't *time* for
this—not when she still had no idea what to do next, if the
ship did lift.

The *Patton* tilted, straightened. She couldn't just stand
here! Frantic, uncertain whether she was doing the right
thing, Lisele pulled the lockbars free and shoved at the
doors. Facing Craig and Mangentes she set her needler aside.
"Forget guns. Get in here and help me seal this place!"

When she'd confirmed that the air-circulating system
was closed off, and Drive's also, Lisele took the chief pilot's
seat and put her hands to the controls. Her fingers trembled;
her breath came fast. She could have used a moment to try
her relaxation techniques, but once again there was no *time*.

As the *Patton* shuddered, vibrating all around her, she
came near to panic. Could she get this crippled clunker up
safely? Could *anybody*? Though she felt no pain, the taste of
blood told her she was biting her lip; annoyed at the distraction, she unclenched her jaw and licked the wound.

*When there isn't any other chance, you go with what you
have!*

Then, as the deck and seat pushed *up*, everything—
except the task before her—ceased to exist.

Afterward, Lisele was never clear on the details of how
she managed liftoff. Mangentes, whether or not she understood the computer's attitudinal readouts, nonetheless relayed them to Chief Houk. Craig monitored the power balance between nodes, and in a soft, carrying voice, kept Lisele
informed. While she herself, on the primary board, fought
the bucking, listing, hesitating ship into something that resembled a straight lift.

When on the main screen the sky blackened to show
points of light, the *Patton*'s erratic jerkings began to smooth
out. Not Lisele's thoughts, though. Once liftoff was past, part
of her mind kept asking "What do we do *now*?" It didn't help
that over the offship channel, which she couldn't help hearing
but tried to ignore, Anders Kobolak was harping on that same
question.

Out of atmo now, in line-of-sight with the scout, relay
through the colony switchboard was no longer necessary.

Still, Lisele waited a few moments before switching to direct contact. Because she didn't know what to say.

And then, suddenly, she did.

"Anders? Moray here. I guess you saw us lift. We're now above atmosphere."

"—can't make orbit, you know that. So why—?"

Peace take the man! "We had no choice, captain; they boarded us in force. Now listen—"

When he did, she said, "I'm not trying orbit, just moving the ship: The way Bull Cochrane did; remember?"

"But what—?"

"Wait a mo." To Houk she said, "Tilt us to the south; ease thrust. I'll check the angle later. Let me know when we stop rising." Then back to Anders. "A couple of hundred kilos south, probably. Maybe a little more, depending on where the next flat ground is. Far enough, though, that when you bring the scout we'll have plenty of time to transship the Nielson Cube before any Uties could reach us. Even if they knew where we were."

The funny part, she thought while she waited for Kobolak's answer, was that when she ordered liftoff she had no idea what to do with it. *Tregare would've. But I'm not Tregare.*

Why south, Kobolak wanted to know. "Past the equator," she said. "Where the heat won't be so bad. To make the work easier."

She didn't have time to answer his next question, because the Chief said, "Topped rise, we have. Now start sinking, will."

"All right. Let me reverse the tilt from here. And then you run thrust the same way we came up, but backward." Easy at first, she meant, then heavier—the mirror image of their rise curve. "What I mean, Chief, is—"

"Meaning, clear is. With starting velocity—zero—to reach groundside."

"You've got it, Chief." The ship was dropping; if she wanted to talk more with Kobolak she'd better get to it. "Anders?"

"Yes?" His voice sounded strained.

"You might as well raise the scout as soon as you can. With luck, maybe you can be high enough to *see* where we land, instead of having to zero in on signal." *If we land, instead of crashing.* But even if the ship tipped over, anyone who was strapped-in had a good chance of survival. Unless the Drive blew...

"There's something you don't know, Lisele," said Anders Kobolak. "I tried to tell you, but you must have been too busy to listen." A long pause; then he said, "We can't lift the scout."

"Why not? Something gone wrong? What could? I thought you had it in top shape."

"It's not that." In his voice she heard something like agony. "It's the Uties. They—"

"They *what*?"

"They've tied Arlen Limmer to one of our landing legs. If we lift, we'll fry him. We can't get to him, because they have snipers covering our airlock hatch. And they're demanding our surrender, or *they'll* kill Arlen."

XXXIV

Panic struck, then grief. Her hands shook; she fought back tears by shouting words she'd heard only once: the time Eduin Brower spilled the coffeepot in his lap. Peace take all of it! Everything they'd done—their work, and now the fighting, the killing—was it all for nothing? Maybe if she'd listened to Anders earlier, she could have thought of something else to do. But then or now, what other way *was* there?

Try as she would to keep it from her consciousness, grim certainty came. "Kobolak?"

"Yes, Moray?" His voice betrayed no feeling.

"There's no choice. Lift the scout." The hardest thing she'd ever said in her life—but now that she'd said it, she had to back it up. "If you can't save Arlen, then you can't. But if you give in to those peacefuckers, likely they'll kill him anyway, and the rest of you, too." *And when we run out of rations packets here*—but no point in bothering Anders with that part. More important: "Katmai Delarov is sitting in *March Hare*, waiting for a Nielson Cube! If she doesn't get it, *they're* all dead."

"But I can't—"

"You have to! *It's for the ship!*"

In the pause she could hear him breathe. Then, "Moray, you're a demon. There's no heart in you."

Furious at the unfairness of him, she shouted, "So kill me later! But right now, *raise* that bucket."

"It's your own husband, you're asking me to murder!"

Flat-voiced herself, hoping her inner tremors couldn't be heard, she said, "Is that what you call it? For the *ship*? If I were tied down there myself, I'd have to say the same thing."

Because there was only one possible way out of this mess. And even for that one, the odds didn't look too good.

Slow and sullen, finally his assent came. "But there's one more thing we want to try first. I'll get back to you."

"You won't have time." Still drifting horizontally, the *Patton* had begun its slow acceleration downward; Lisele felt the jar as Houk built counteracting thrust. "In a few minutes we'll be below your horizon." She overrode his attempt at answer. "*Listen.* We're headed almost due south. I can't give you the distance but you'll be able to spot us." A shudder took her; then, sounding calmer than she felt, she said, "We have maybe half a chance of landing this thing straight up. If it tips over, we still might live through it. But either way, unless the Drive blows, you get that Cube up to Delarov!"

"And if the Drive does blow?"

"Then take the scout back to *March Hare*. And the captain will decide, between whatever options she still has."

Anders kept talking. Since nothing he might say could make any possible difference, she rid herself of the distraction by cutting the circuit. She'd done all she could; either he would bring the scoutship—and the consequences of that move made her gut wrench!—or he wouldn't, and *everything* was down the spout. Well, once she'd heard Tregare say that Anders Kobolak was a good officer "—but I'm not sure he has the command-type mind. Or ever will." *I guess this is where we find out.*

But now the *Patton* needed her attention. As the ship dropped, its fall neither smooth nor straight, once again Goral Craig reported power imbalances to Lisele, who used Tinhead to incorporate those data into overall attitude readings, which Deryth Mangentes called down to the Chief.

At one pause, while the ship unexpectedly stayed firm

on path and decel, Houk said, "Moray? The other voice, is who?"

So it took him this long to notice! "We knew I couldn't handle this end by myself, didn't we? So I recruited some help. It's all right; I'll explain later." Maybe that wasn't exactly how it really happened, but it's the way it worked out!

Again the *Patton* bucked and tilted; no time for talk or even thought, as the impromptu team fought the ship dreadfully nearer to groundside. Coordination was far short of perfect; toward the end, Houk had to run thrust up past redline max, and the ship's long axis was wobbling.

When the landing legs struck ground, impact caught Lisele unprepared. The ship tilted, a long way and very slowly; for moments she thought they were going over, but after an excruciating period of hesitation, wobbling on two legs with the other not touching ground, the *Patton* settled back again and stood nearly vertical. Further oscillations came—but now, she knew, they were down *safe*.

Like a machine, feeling nothing—or perhaps not *allowing* herself to feel—she called downship. "Chief Houk? Shutdown checklist. Are you ready?"

"Ready, am." So first one and then the other read off the necessary steps in proper order. The procedure seemed to take a long time, but finally it ended. "Clear, is Drive," said Houk.

"Control's clear, also. Moray out." She turned to Craig and Mangentes. "So much for that. And to both of you, thanks."

So this part was done with. Unbuckling, Lisele tried to control the shaking of her legs, and stand.

She couldn't. Suddenly, without warning, her body doubled over in deathly cramp. As she writhed, gasping, it seemed a very long time before the first hoarse, racking sobs came. She felt as though she were being torn in half, but dimly realized: *now it's all letting loose!*

"Those who kill and do not grieve, will rot and die of it." Who had said that? As firm arms restrained the violence of her paroxyms, now ebbing, a detached part of Lisele's mind searched in memory. Rissa, yes, quoting her own father, and then saying, "Even for your enemies, child, you would find that you must. I have never understood the need, but it is there."

And now she knew the truth of her mother's saying. For it was not only Arlen who caused her grief, though that reminder convulsed her once again. It was all of them: the dead Uties, faceless to her now, since she couldn't know which kills were hers. Even Cray Malden—perhaps *especially* the commodore, because that killing had been face to face. Although with Malden there had been no choice, none at all. . . .

Around her, the arms relaxed. "Are you all right?" Blinking away the residue of tears, Lisele looked to see Goral Craig disengaging his hold and standing, while Deryth Mangentes, who had asked, still kept a light embrace.

"Yes. I think so. Well, mostly. And thanks!"

His frown looking puzzled, not angry, Craig spoke. "That thing you kept saying, when you could make words at all. About needing to grieve for killing, or you rot and die. Where did you get that? Do you think it's true?"

"For me it seems to be. And for my mother. It's—she told it as a saying from my grandfather. Before that, I don't know."

Whatever Craig might have said next, it was interrupted. At the doors came a hammering. "These things, open!" shouted deWayne Houk. As, from outside, came the hiss of an energy gun.

"Peace take it!" At first still shaky on her legs, then moving more surely, Lisele ran to the doors. "Hold it, Chief! Everything's all right in here." The gun-hiss ceased. "We'll open the doors. But—" He'd been trigger-happy earlier, Houk had. Now, he *mustn't* be. What could she say? "Nobody is holding a gun. So put yours away, too. All right?"

"That which you say, I believe *how?*"

What?—there was something—oh, yes! The agreed password, to let someone onto the scout in dubious circumstances. Now if he only remembered—. "I assure you, Chief. *I assure you.*"

A pause, and then, "Can believe, yes. Gun put away, is."

So with Craig's help, Lisele raised and deployed the lockbars. Still looking skeptical but with his hand well away from his gun, slowly Houk entered. To Craig and Mangentes he nodded, before saying, "Moray? These are here, why?"

"I *told* you." Because damned if she'd bother repeating the whole thing; it didn't matter. Instead, "They're on our side now. They helped us fly this ship, didn't they?" No answer, so she continued. "Now let's go eat some rations and have coffee. I don't know how many hours we're overdue for lunch, but it's a lot." And until she said it, she hadn't realized how her body craved nutriment.

Houk shook his head. "Food, yes. But first, to clean this ship. Many dead Uties to remove."

Shit oh dear! He was right, of course, but still—! "Yes, you do that. I'll go fix something to eat."

"If you don't mind, Houk," said Craig, "I'll help you."

The Chief grunted, and the two left Control.

On the way to captain's digs, Lisele and Mangentes met Naomi Gray. "Lisele! What's going on?"

Headshake. "Too long to tell. Later. I'm starving."

"We're almost out of rations," Gray said.

"Wait a minute!" said Mangentes. From her belt she unshipped a small dittybag and held it out. "Here. Malden had no idea the ship could lift, so he planned this boarding as a possible siege operation; we all carried subsistence rations. Damn all! I'll have to go catch Goral and Houk before they dump the food off with the corpses!" Before Lisele could find answer, the woman was gone.

In no hurry, Gray and Lisele went to captain's quarters. On the way, Lisele tried to explain their situation and how it had come about. "Everything happened so fast," she concluded. "I don't know if I did right, or not. But the way it went, there never seemed to be any choice." Inside herself she felt barely alive, and not at all sure the living was worth it.

Entering the rooms, Gray closed the door behind them. "You're too tired and hungry to track straight. Sit down; have a glass of wine while I fix up a meal."

Sitting, nonetheless Lisele protested. "Why shouldn't I help? What makes me any worse off than you are?"

Busy at the cooking module, Gray looked back over her shoulder. "After that first quick shootout, all I had to do was stay safely in the Drive room and help the Chief. While you were fighting your way upship and then *flying* this piece of junk."

Lisele felt her face contort. *If only that were all of it!* But all she said, after downing the glass of wine and standing to pour herself another, was, "Very well; cook away. You have my gratitude." And exchanged smiles with the other woman.

Almost relaxing now, Lisele sniffed the aroma coming from the stewpot; the contribution from Mangentes made a considerable improvement over unaided standard rations. She was nursing her second glass of wine; the first, taken so fast on an empty stomach, had her slightly dizzy.

There was something she wanted to say, but before she could put words together the door opened; all seeming to talk at once, the other three, each heavily laden, came in.

Houk was complaining; Goral Craig seemed to be placating him. Deryth Mangentes said, "Oh, go get yourselves a drink! And one for me, if you would, Goral." She plonked herself down in the chair next to Lisele's. "Your Drive tech didn't want to rob food from the dead; he and Goral had quite an argument." Accepting a glass from Craig, she shrugged. "We salvaged most of it. Now whether you have fridge and freezer space, is something else." Looking more closely at Lisele, the woman frowned. "Right now you don't give hell about any of that, do you?"

Silence must have been answer enough; Mangentes said, "What *do* you care about?"

Voice sounding wooden, from a throat that felt the same way, Lisele said, "Overall, what are the casualty figures?"

Mangentes made a gasp of indrawn breath. "I might have known. You, from outside, you're not used to killing. We've had to live with it, I guess you know. All right; we kept track of the figures. Goral?"

So the big man came to tell her.

"Groundside we can't know; not many, likely. The fight inside the main airlock, thirteen dead. That includes your own traitor. Around the ship—" He shrugged. "Twenty-three died without air. There may be more. We haven't checked every room where someone might have taken last-minute refuge. And we found the commodore himself; no way of knowing how he splattered himself flat, at the bottom of the main stairwell." No way to know? But Lisele wasn't ready to talk about *that*.

Then the man's face went grim. "There's one I hate to have to tell of. You recall Arnet Kern?"

"Yes, I do. More than not, I liked him. You mean—?"

"He must have tried to leave the ship but waited too long, until liftoff was under way. He made it to the main airlock and used the local manual controls to close both hatches. But during the firefight the inner hatch was breached by gun blasts. So—"

She waited, until he said, "He tried to plug the holes with his clothing. It didn't work; he ran out of air."

She had no energy left for feelings; she said, "I'm sorry." And then, "Chief Houk? We need to decide what to do now."

"For the scout, wait?"

"If it were coming, it'd be here by now. Or damn well soon. No—what I mean is, we could still go for low orbit."

Forestalling his protest, she said, "First you get some rest. Then go out and plant those charges. And tomorrow—if the scout doesn't come, and I don't expect it will—we *lift*. And spill the fuel, as we'd planned, and wait for *March Hare*."

"One problem," said Naomi Gray. "This ship and that one don't have any direct comm channels."

Buddha in a basket! Gray had it right. But still—she shook her head and tried to think.

There had to be a way. But unless somebody told it, there wouldn't be. Not exactly listening, Lisele heard herself say, "Delarov hasn't had contact for a time. She'll be watching. We lift when this mudball is turned so she can see us do it."

"See us? From way out *there*?"

"Detect our Drive emissions, I mean. We know she has instruments monitoring in this direction." And Gray nodded.

Lisele stood; her head didn't seem to like the idea. Watching the room begin to spin, she said, "There must be somewhere—a place to sleep? I need—"

If anyone answered, she didn't hear it. She felt herself falling, then nothing more.

The ship was lifting; she heard the Drive's throb. But Houk must have done a lot of work on it; she felt no vibration. And she couldn't see anything; where was she? Maybe in the topside airlock; up that far, the sound would be muffled like this.

Suddenly alarmed, she tried to move, but something restrained her. *Who had put her in here? And why?*

The commodore! But he was dead, wasn't he? Or was he? Yes! So who—? Craig and Mangentes—they'd only pretended to change sides, and now they were going to space her!

As she tried to fight loose from whatever held her, she saw dim light, and a hand clasped her shoulder.

No! You can't *kill me now!*

XXXV

"Hold still, won't you? Let me get those covers free. What's the matter, anyway?"

The voice was Naomi Gray's. Able to sit up now, Lisele looked around. She was in captain's digs, in the big bed, not the topside airlock at all. She said, "The ship's lifting; I heard it. But there's no accel. What's happening? I—"

"What you heard was the scout landing." The scout? *Arlen's dead.* But she had no time to feel reaction, for Gray said, "There's someone here to see you." She gestured, and behind her Lisele saw a man standing. A spectral figure at first; then she saw that the face was masked with bandages.

"Anders? What *happened* to you?"

"Not Anders," the man said. "Arlen. Arlen Limmer."

She tried to move, to speak or think; nothing worked. The dream had been so *real*; was this another? Then without conscious volition she was on her feet and across the room; hard hands embraced her nakedness.

"Arlen?" The bandages didn't give her much opportunity, but her tongue thrust at an opening and she tasted blood on his lips. "But Anders said—!" Then she remembered, and drew away. "Oh, you must hate me now!"

He reached to pull her close again, but she resisted. "Hate you, Lisele? Why should I?"

Her tears welled. "I told Anders to kill you, didn't I? To lift the scout, even though I knew it meant your death? I don't see how you could ever forgive that, and I don't expect you to."

His snort, almost a laugh, startled her. "Forgive you? For what? You broke the deadlock, is all."

"Deadlock?"

"Between Kobolak and me. I *told* him he had to lift, but
he wouldn't. When you came on the line—and I could hear
you, barely, on my comm-unit—you tipped the scale, was all.
Forgive, hell! I *thank* you."

As she tried to absorb what Arlen said, again Lisele met
the welcome of his arms. Then, "But how did they get you
loose, and inside the scout?"

"They didn't."

"But—"

Haltingly, he told her what little he knew.

The plan was Eduin Brower's. He was the only one free
to implement it, and the way things were, he goddamn well
had to do it *right now*. The insulating sheets, he said: the
ones they'd brought along to wrap the Nielson Cube and
keep it from warming and going sour. The layered composites
were fucking-aye heatproof, too, weren't they? And good for
shielding against bloody-damn ionization?

Well, yes; Anders agreed. So the two men hauled out
one of those sheets, unfolded it and made it into a loose roll
that the Chief could carry over one shoulder, along with three
tie-lines of sufficient length.

Brower was no kind of shot and never would be. Alina
Rostadt feared guns so much that she'd never even tried. But
now, as Kobolak warmed the scout's Drive to just above
idling, short of thrust mode but not far from it, Brower threw
the hatch open and sprayed energy-gun blast at the Utie
sniper-positions. Then as he went down the ramp's steps
three at a time, Alina moved forward and swung her own
blaster across those same positions. Back and forth, trying to
make the hidden snipers keep their heads down.

For a time it worked. Brower reached groundside and
ran to the landing leg where Arlen was tied. For a moment
he paused, fired once, then turned to augment Rostadt's
firing. After that, not listening to Arlen's bewildered questions, he flung the insulating sheet around Limmer, landing
leg and all, and secured it with three ties: one above his
head, one at the waist, and the third around the ankles.

But the temporary lack of Brower's firepower gave the
Uties a better chance to shoot back. Unable to see, Arlen
heard the frying hiss when a Utie beam licked at his own
protection. Worse, the indrawn breath and startled curse
from Brower, carrying the sound of sudden pain. Then

the man's irregular retreating footsteps, splattering gravel.

More noise came: hissing of energy guns, the splat of needles—he felt stunning impact as some of those struck his sheltering wrap. The scrape of something along the ground; it had to be the foot of the scout's ramp moving, beginning to raise. A war scream that might have been Alina's. The clang of a closing hatch.

And then the scout lifted.

There was so *much* to ask, but she could feel that Arlen was wobbly. "Here. On the bed. Sit down. Or lie down." He sat, and at random she chose her first question. "How did you breathe? Did Brower bring down a tank and helmet?"

"Kobolak didn't take us that high. There was a time I blanked out, I think, but it couldn't have been for long."

She reached to touch the bandages that covered nearly all his face. Heartsick, she said, "The insulation wasn't good enough, was it? How—how bad are the Drive burns?"

"Where the wrap blew loose? Well, I won't want to walk on my left foot much, for a while, and the shin's going to need some synthetic derma, once we get back to *March Hare,* but—"

"I mean your *face,* Arlen!"

Stiffly, against the bandages he shook his head. "The Drive didn't do that. A Utie did, while I was tied there. A brute bitch who called herself Thela Cochrane."

She had whipped him, beaten him with wooden sticks and metal rods, keeping his comm-unit open to the scout so that those aboard could hear his moans of pain. Trying to force their surrender as the only way to stop his torture. But his clothing protected him from all but bruises, so she changed her tactics and assaulted his head and face. When he still kept silence, or mostly, she went away and came back with a bucket of coals.

And a knife.

Some of that, he withstood. When she made threats against his eyes, he shouted into the comm-channel she'd kept open. To tell Anders Kobolak to lift the scout, because it would be the greatest favor Kobolak could do him.

Baffled, Thela Cochrane drew back, taking a pause to think things out. But before she could manage that chore, Eduin Brower came charging down the ramp. When he

turned toward the place where Arlen was tied, Brower's first
energy blast cut Cochrane's head in two. Straight across, just
below the nose.

Arlen Limmer couldn't quite manage a laugh, but to
Lisele it sounded like a good try. "You know my dad."

"Yes, of course." Derek Limmer, whose face carried
monstrous scars from the Slaughterhouse, UET's sadistic
Space Academy. Aside from those mutilations, Arlen greatly
resembled his father.

"Some people," said Arlen, his voice held carefully even,
"called him a gargoyle."

"I've heard that, yes. But *I* never thought of 'uncle'
Derek that way. He and your mother, they're so nice."

This time his attempted laugh almost made it. "Good old
Felcie! Six questions in a row, and never waits for an answer."

"Yes. I remember." But what did he need to *say*?

It came. "She's a bit of all right, mom is. And my father,
too, of course. But, Lisele—"

"Yes, Arlen?"

"When these bandages come off, then between Derek
and me, he's going to be the good-looking one."

She didn't say, "Oh, Arlen!" or "I'm sorry," or "Don't
worry; it won't be that bad." All she did was tug at his
garments and say, "How can I get these off if you don't help "

"Like this? All right. I can smell me, though. And I stink
like wasted hopes!"

Too right! But, "I don't care. If you can, now, let's!"

It wasn't easy for him; she could tell that. But he did,
and she also. Lying quiet then, she said, "Arlen?"

"Yes, Lisele?"

"For the ship, you put your life on the line."

She felt his shrug. "It was already there, wasn't it?"

"But you didn't pull back, you didn't ask Anders to give
in, to save your neck. You—"

"Lisele! Don't give me that much credit. As long as there
was a chance to negotiate, I tried. But then I couldn't."

Hearing his deep sigh, Lisele said, "Yes. That's the
point, Arlen."

"What point?"

"When you couldn't help yourself without risking everybody else, you spoke for *the ship's* good."

Another shrug. "What else was there to do?"

Driven to vigor, Lisele leaned and dug stiff fingers into his shoulders. "Don't you see? That's *it*, Arlen."

Gentler now with her hands, she leaned back and away. "I liked you before, even loved you. But the one part I didn't like was that you couldn't ever see past the end of your own weenie." She waited but he didn't answer. So she said, "You always were a nice kid, Arlen. But now I think you're a grownup man."

Wrapped in her own concerns and Arlen's—*no matter how bad his face is, it'll still be him, behind it*—for the moment Lisele had no thought of anyone else.

After a time she felt hunger; Arlen confessed to the same craving. Getting up, she checked and found enough stew left, from the meal she'd last shared, for the two of them. When she'd heated it and dished it up, and was putting the pot to soak, suddenly she was reminded of Eduin Brower's cursing when he tried to clean charred debris from a similar pot.

Feeling sudden guilt at her own self-absorption, she gasped. "Arlen! Chief Brower—he was hurt, you said. How badly?"

His voice carried pain. "The first hit, when I heard him yell—nothing serious, just a nasty burn. But just as he reached the top of the ramp, a step away from safety, naturally he was blocking Alina's field of fire. And some Utie got him bad."

The pot was full of water; putting it down, Lisele came to sit across from Arlen. "How bad?"

"Because we're here, several days away from getting to *March Hare* and its medical facilities, the leg had to come off."

"Oh, peace take it!" But the crippling wouldn't estrange Katmai Delarov; to his "spear-fishing squaw," Brower would always be a whole man. And to Lisele, also. "Arlen? We mustn't forget, ever, how much we owe that foul-mouthed saint!"

XXXVI

"So the *Patton* isn't going anywhere, after all."

"I'm afraid not, Deryth," Lisele said. "Not right away, at

least." They sat in a corner of the ship's galley, now jury-rigged to feed more people than captain's quarters could handle. "Later, a salvage ship may come and fix the Drive." STL ships, crewed by groups of families, still had limited use on freight runs. "But *March Hare* doesn't carry the parts to do it."

Mangentes shook her head. "*March Hare*, not the *Tamurlaine*. It's still hard to believe that UET lost its power over Earth, decades ago. And that now you have faster-than-light travel."

"You do see why we couldn't tell you."

"Yes. Of course. The commodore . . ."

"And some others." She paused. "You and Craig—you're certain you want to come with us?"

The woman looked troubled. "There's nothing here for us. Goral's always been worried—that even if he survived the commodore, which was never a certain bet—he isn't the one to command the colony." A shrug. "He's not the Bull again, no. If he was, I couldn't love him. But he'll be a good officer."

"The colony, though. Who *will* take charge?"

"Of what's left? You might be surprised. The commodore's excesses—there's been a lot of resentment building. Almost toward a new Women's Rebellion. And with Malden dead—" Her smile was tentative. "If Elseth Sprague's still alive, I've always felt that everyone underestimated her."

Disdaining pain pills, Eduin Brower insisted that alcohol was best for his condition. And that he'd set his own dosages, thank you a whole goddamn lot! Never quite drunk but seldom far from it, he seemed more aggrieved at running short of cigars than at losing the leg.

Patting his bandaged stump, ending short of where the knee had been, he said, "Moray, I was never much for running, so a shitass prosthesis should do me fine."

"Not for a while, Chief. On the *Hare* there's no way to build one." She checked her chrono; time to leave the scout. "One thing, though, I need to say. What you did—"

His face darkened. "Don't the fuck say it!" Across the room he threw his soggy cigar stub. "The time come, somebody got to move. If'n I *hadn't* gone out there, Katmai she'd of spaced everything I own. And been right."

"Whatever you say, Chief." And without regard for cigar

stench, she gave Eduin Brower the best kiss she could muster.

Climbing out of the scout's dormitory area, Lisele saw Alina Rostadt sitting watch. And asked, "How's progress coming?"

Anders hadn't tried to land on the cargo hatch, and until the second day after moving the *Patton*, Lisele didn't feel up to it, either. When she did, the tricky maneuver went like clockwork. Now the Cube was pulled and wrapped, ready to be manhandled out to the hatch, hoisted, and fastened securely to the scout. Then there would be only the waiting, to get the best liftoff vector from Sitdown's rotational velocity.

Alina said, "They're still moving the Cube up to the hatch deck. It's too bad the power suit couldn't be used."

Lisele nodded. "Chief Houk says we don't really need it."

"I hope he's right. Lisele?"

Peace take me, she *wants to talk*. "Yes?"

"You mustn't think too hard of Anders."

"I don't. Why should I?"

"Well—" Alina paused, then said, "He did his best. I wish I could feel the same way about myself."

"You? What should you have done, that you didn't?"

"I—I dream. The killing. Every night, it happens all over again." She looked thinner now, but in no healthy way; below her eyes the skin was dark and pasty.

What could be said? "Alina? Would it be better if you had to dream of Arlen's death, and your husband's? Or if a *Utie* dreamed—about having killed the lot of you?"

No answer. "See you," Lisele said, and left the scout.

At the bottom of the ramp, stepping down to the *Patton*'s cargo hatch, she paused. Her landing had left barely enough room for people to bring the Cube out and haul it up. Good thing she hadn't cut things closer; having to lift the scout and drop it on the hatch again, for a matter of decimeters, wasn't her idea of fun. She went inside, to the nearest stairs, and began climbing.

Upship Lisele found no one; everybody else was out doing some sort of useful work. And she should be helping.

But somehow—she wasn't sure why—she couldn't face any more work, or talk, or people.

For no reason she could define, it was all just too peacefucking *much*.

Hungry, but with no taste for food, she went to captain's digs, lay down and tried to sleep.

It didn't work. Halfway dozing, still her mind raced, filling vision with pictures she wanted to forget.

At the airlock landing, all that bloody shambles. The commodore: she hadn't looked down to see, but imagination showed only ghastliness, probably worse than the truth of it. Teeth gritted, she shook her head and sobbed. *I only did what I had to!* She could rationalize the killings she'd grieved for—but still, from a shattered face, Cray Malden keened of death.

And lucky outcome or not—no credit to herself!—she *had* passed sentence of death on her husband.

There has to be a way out of this! Sitting up, Lisele slapped her own face until she knew she was awake. And then, no longer gasping in horror, breathed a susurrus of relief.

Shaken, she faced herself. What was *real*? The ships were. And *March Hare*, now, would live.

She didn't dare think of the damage she'd done the colony. Maybe it would survive, maybe not. In that group there'd been good people as well as bad. Of both kinds, many were dead. And either way, nothing she could do about it.

I've done things I can't forgive myself.

But when had there been any choice? She took a deep breath.

Peace take me, I saved the ship!

After a time, she slept.

From her pilot's seat, a monitor showed the Cube lashed firmly to the scout. Some of the lines they'd had to secure inside the airlock; now its outer hatch couldn't be closed. But once docked in *March Hare*'s scout bay, and that bay sealed, there would be no difficulty.

It was time, now, to lift the scout. Slaunchwise, because of the unbalanced load. Well, Tregare had done as much, and she'd read his logs and run the simulations. For that reason, among others, she now sat pilot.

But somehow her hands didn't want to move. Until, from the Comm seat, Brower growled, "Get your head straight, Moray. Time to lift this shitpot."

Yes. There was work to do; her doubts would have to wait. Lisele opened comm to *March Hare,* to Katmai Delarov.

"Captain? Moray here." Lisele's breath came hard. "Calling at fifteen hundred hours. We're on our way." The signal needed an hour to get there, so . . .

"You have seventy-two hours to ready up some chow."

As the cargo hatch wobbled under thrust, she lifted the scoutship free.

Someday, maybe, she'd figure it all out.

ABOUT THE AUTHOR

F. M. BUSBY's published science fiction novels include the three volumes of *Rissa Kerguelen*, the related *Zelde M'tana* and *The Alien Debt* plus the early life of Bran Tregare as told in *Star Rebel* and *Rebel's Quest*. In different timestreams exist *All These Earths* and the now-combined volume *The Demu Trilogy* (*Cage a Man*, *The Proud Enemy*, and *End of the Line*.) Numerous shorter works, ranging from short-shorts to novella length, have appeared in various SF magazines and in both original and reprint anthologies, including *Best of Year* collections edited by Terry Carr, by Lester Del Rey, and by Donald A. Wollheim. Some of his works have been published in England and (in translation) Germany, France, Holland and Japan.

Rebel's Seed completes the eight-volume exploration of Rissa Kerguelen's universe; the writer is grateful for readers who urged him into going two books farther than he originally intended, but now feels it's time to move on.

Buz grew up in eastern Washington and holds degrees in physics and electrical engineering. He worked at "the obligatory list of incongruous jobs" before his initial career as communications engineer, from which he is now happily retired in favor of writing. He is married—with a daughter finishing medical school and due to enter residency, plus a grandson who roots for the Chicago Bears!—and lives in Seattle with his wife Elinor and their cat *Ms*, who obviously runs the whole place but is relatively tactful about it.

During Army service and afterward, Buz spent considerable time in Alaska and the Aleutians. His interests include aerospace, unusual cars or guns or other gadgets, dogs, cats, and people, not necessarily in that order. His upcoming novel requires its own brand-new universe, and will introduce you to varieties of persons you couldn't possibly be expected to recognize, because as of this writing they exist only as bytes on floppy diskettes.